PERSONAL EFFECTS

By Rex Reed

Fiction

PERSONAL EFFECTS

Nonfiction

TRAVOLTA TO KEATON
VALENTINES & VITRIOL
PEOPLE ARE CRAZY HERE
BIG SCREEN, LITTLE SCREEN
CONVERSATIONS IN THE RAW
DO YOU SLEEP IN THE NUDE?

REX REED

PERSONAL EFFECTS

A NOVEL

 *ARBOR HOUSE* *New York*

Manufactured in the United States of America

10 9 8 7 6 5 4 3 2 1

Library of Congress Cataloging in Publication Data
Reed, Rex.
 Personal effects.
 I. Title.
PS3568.E3694P47   1986   813'.54   85-22928
ISBN: 0-87795-685-5

The author gratefully acknowledges permission to quote from "Like a Rolling Stone" by Bob Dylan © 1965 Warner Bros. Inc.

ACKNOWLEDGMENTS

The author gratefully acknowledges the creative support of George Coleman for his early and continuing encouragement of the ideas in this book, H. B. Gilmour for her expert assistance in organizing them, Deborah Chiel for editorial services above and beyond the call of duty, and Marcia Coburn for being there when I needed her.

*"Pearls don't break.
They hold together
and bring you bad luck."*

—*Greta Garbo*
in Grand Hotel

PERSONAL EFFECTS

PROLOGUE

G ilda would have hated it.

    Billy Buck stepped out of the black limo into the blinding sunlight at Forest Lawn. He felt as if he were walking into the spotlights at the opening of a movie. The same crowd hovered nervously, like extras in *The Day of the Locust,* this time amid carefully manicured lawns the color of lime Jello and scrubbed, white statuary instead of concrete sidewalks under a flashing marquee, so high on the smell of murder you could almost taste their excitement.

    It was a glorious morning. On a day when the world should have been shrouded in gray despair, the smog had lifted over Glendale to let the sun blast through the San Fernando Valley all the way to Hollywood, as hot and yellow as an exploding lemon.

    Gilda would have preferred a rainy funeral. Like Ava Gardner's in *The Barefoot Contessa,* with stricken mourners weeping under black umbrellas. She had always envied James Mason's funeral scene in *A*

1

Star Is Born, with all those demented fans clutching violently at Judy Garland, her pinched face drained and corpselike in the mob of dripping raincoats. "George Cukor knew what he was doing giving Judy the best funeral scene of all," she had told Billy on more than one occasion. "When I go, baby, make sure it's pouring."

Billy elbowed his way through the mass of people straining on both sides of the path to the chapel, imagining how Gilda would have taken it all in. He could picture her flinging back her thick, auburn hair and raising her face to the sky—that rapturous kisser with its cat's cheekbones that no amount of Max Factor could make ordinary. He could just see her gray-green eyes, like the water in Mykonos, tapering to a wide, canary-swallowing grin, lifted in three-strip Technicolor to curse the white-hot sun that was denying her a proper Hollywood send-off. Chewing on her blessed pearls. If anyone could curse the sun to flight, Gilda Greenway could.

Picturing her that way, his throat caught.

Billy Buck had always been a little bit in love with Gilda. Through his teens he'd worshiped her, watching her from the center of the seventh row in the close-bodied warmth and darkness of whichever movie house was playing *Night Anthem* or *Young Daisy Ashley* or *Only the Damned.* Pep rallies, sock hops, homecoming games—he'd sacrificed them all to spend countless Saturdays with his favorite star. He wouldn't have thought it possible that one day the same goddess, the Aphrodite of his nocturnal fantasies, would reach out and stroke his cheek. She'd owned him from that moment on.

He felt, he supposed, as if she'd taken his cherry that afternoon at the Screenwriter's Club. It was 1965, he was the hot new columnist from New York, the new terror in town, the Group A mascot on the Beverly Hills social scene, and although Gilda Greenway was above and beyond anything as tacky as status, she was still curious. "How old are you, Billy Buck?" she asked him, a minute after they were introduced by Garson Kanin. He told her. She was three vodkas ahead of him, and her shimmering Aegean eyes were all squinty.

"Twenty-seven?" she repeated. "Why, you're just a baby." She'd reached out and brushed her fingers across the skin of his face. "By the time I was twenty-seven, Ted Kearny had already broken my heart. He broke my cherry when I was seventeen." She laughed off the line, but

Billy never forgot it. He mentioned Gilda and Big Ted Kearny in a column and was flooded with calls from the studio where Gilda was working, demanding a retraction, and from his friends, questioning his sanity. It was true—everyone knew the big Irishman had brought Gilda west in 1940, orchestrated her career at MGM in its golden era. She'd been his mistress for several years.

"This is Hollywood, Billy," she chided him later, goosing his ignorance. "Why print the truth when you can create the legend?"

Now the legend was gone.

Shot to death on Christmas Eve.

"Who's *that?*"

"He must be *somebody*. You practically need a blood test to get in here."

"I got Victoria Principal."

"Forget it. King Godwin's the big draw today."

Billy walked up the path to the chapel, trying to tune out the voices of the craning, gaping autograph hounds, the matrons clutching linen handkerchiefs and wearing pearl necklaces, old men in golf sweaters, young gays clinging to each other, the sensation seekers all jazzed up to a neurotic pitch by the *Los Angeles Times* headline screaming "PEARLS GIRL SHOT DEAD IN BEVERLY HILLS ESTATE—KING GODWIN QUESTIONED BY POLICE."

He wondered if he was the only member of the Hollywood community who had shown up today *without* a Pinkerton bodyguard or a Mace gun. They should be frisking us at the door, he thought, remembering the panic after the Manson murders. The stars had come out for Gilda, but they were nervous. As murders go, hers had not been spectacularly brutal. But the images moving across the landscape of everyone's mind as they sipped their Christmas morning coffee—a legendary star with a bleeding gunshot wound, eerily lit by the festive glow of Christmas tree lights while a younger but equally legendary star stood nearby, staring at her body in a state of shock—didn't exactly inspire complacency in a town where almost everyone lived one foot ahead of the sheriff already. And the police weren't doing much talking.

Billy's Givenchy sunglasses hid his puffy eyelids and the dark circles that erupted whenever he didn't sleep. He'd scarcely slept at all since the night Gilda was killed. He still couldn't accept the fact that she was dead. He'd been stroked—as the old Metro slogan put it—by more stars than there are in Heaven. But he'd never fallen for anyone the way he had for Gilda—rendered stupid and weak in the knees and flushed by her touch.

"Take me to dinner at Chasen's," she'd insisted, changing their original plan to attend Inez Godwin's Christmas Eve party in Holmby Hills. "I'm not in the mood for cheap melodrama and I sure as hell don't want to stay home." Her housekeeper, Mrs. Denby, had the week off, and Gilda seemed suddenly very aware of how empty the big estate was without the grim reaper who guarded her as jealously as if she were her own daughter.

Maybe it was the lonely holiday season. Maybe it was grief for times gone by. But Gilda had been nostalgic that night. Chasen's was dead except for a loud party thrown by the Aaron Spellings, and Gilda didn't know a soul present. "Those are the people running this town today. It's all television. And the stars have no faces. Gable, Cooper, George Brent, Cary . . . those were the men I knew. What have we got now? I wouldn't kick Clint Eastwood out of bed on a snowy night, but the rest of them look like hamburgers. If Spencer Tracy came back from the grave, bless his soul, he probably couldn't get a job playing Santa Claus in the Paramount parking lot."

They were toasting the good old, dead old days, when Hollywood still had style and definition, with their second bottle of Cristal when the maitre d' appeared and said, "I'm sorry to disturb you, Miss Greenway, but there's a phone call for you. The lady insists she *must* speak with you urgently and refuses to give her name."

"Shit," Gilda sighed, and took the call. When she returned to the table, she said, "Sorry, Billy. Hate to break up this cozy party, but I have something very boring to attend to. Stay. Finish the champagne. It's silly to spoil both our evenings."

Characteristically refusing his offer of a lift—"A taxi's already on the way, baby"—she fled in a crackle of hunter-green taffeta.

Billy finished his turkey hash and shared an after-dinner Courvoisier with Roddy McDowall, who told him the most amusing story about what the Reagans served Queen Elizabeth on her visit to their ranch. He was home in time to catch the last hour of *Waterloo Bridge*.

His last thought, before he fell asleep, was wait till Gilda hears what the Queen, up to her knees in mud, thought about burritos.

He never got the chance.

The cops roused him at 7:00 A.M. on Christmas Day, pumping him for information. After the tenth call from curious gossips offering condolences before diplomatically asking which suspect did what to whom, Billy had taken the phone off the hook, closed the drapes, and snuggled up to a bottle of Chivas, watching videocassettes of Gilda's old films, and staring at color photos of the Pearls in an old *Architectural Digest.*

An aggressive reporter in heavy pancake stuck a mike in Billy's face, trotting beside him to the open doors of Wee Kirk o' the Heather, her spike heels clacking against the slate tiles like the unclipped nails of a high-strung poodle. In front of them, a man with a minicam on his shoulder backed up, catching them on film. The reporter brushed a strand of hair from her ceaselessly moving red mouth, and addressed the camera, never looking at her subject: "Billy Buck, how are you going to remember Gilda?"

"In private, with my mouth shut," he replied.

Billy remembered the first time he had been in this strange, ironic place. He was covering Jeanette MacDonald's funeral in 1965. The same hysterical fans were gathered that cold, brittle day in January. Could they be from Central Casting? The Wee Kirk o' the Heather had been filled with real live birds chirping away like spastic parrots, and they played Jeanette's recordings of "Indian Love Call" and "Ah, Sweet Mystery of Life" in stereo. The MGM survivors were there in 1965, but where were they now? Gilda had outlived them all.

Billy spotted Victoria Principal, Robert Evans, Mike and Binnie Frankovich, Allan Carr—but what had any of them to do with Gilda? And where were they when she needed industry support in her declining years? Wasn't it true that the people who never return your calls always show up when you're dead, especially if the *National Enquirer* is taking pictures?

The only Hollywood face Billy recognized from Gilda's reign was Bess Flowers, queen of the extras, who had appeared, at the star's insistence, in each of her forty-five pictures as a superstitious good-luck charm. There she was, faithful to the end, in a pink satin Helen Rose gown on loan from studio wardrobe, serenely beatific ("Extras never act, they *react,*" Gilda had warned her back in 1945)—an ironic angel of death from a thousand movie funeral scenes, playing it for real at last.

Just inside the chapel, a slight, bald man greeted Billy, pointing a big unlit cigar at him. "So?" he demanded.

"Hello, Sam," Billy said to Sam Durand, a retired exec from the studio. "Good to see you."

"Good? You fuckin' believe this? Gilda Greenway murdered." He shook his head. "Christ, she was just a kid when we signed her at Metro. Gorgeous like you wouldn't believe. That picture you dug up for your column didn't begin to do her justice. *Oy,* what a life that lady had. From the first day Larry Malnish saw her picture in the window of a photographer's shop in Tulsa, she was star material. That's the picture you should have used in your column. Not that other one. The Fourflushers? The Four something."

"The Four Fans," snapped Billy.

Ed Sullivan had run the photo in the *Daily News* with the caption, "The Pearls Girl With Her Four Fans." It was impossible to think how long ago that picture had been taken. Impossible not to say goodbye to Gilda without it. Billy had found an extra copy among Devon's memorabilia late one night a lifetime ago.

The Four Fans: Devon, King, Inez, and May. How innocent and hopeful they'd looked that winter day in 1956.

"Any of them here yet?" Billy asked.

"From that crazy photograph?" Sam Durand made a face like a baby with gas. "Yeah, King's wife. Inez."

"Ex-wife," Billy corrected.

"She's with a kid. Looks like hell. Great tits, though. How many kids did she and King have?"

"Just one son. Hollis."

"That's what I thought," said Sam. "A woman like that, sitting with a boy her son's age. In my day, women didn't go around with kids. Not in a church."

"New game, new rules."

"New don't mean better," the old man snapped. He motioned

with his cigar. "May Fischoff's sitting next to her. I thought she'd sit with Hollis, since he's her live-in business partner and all." He winked at Billy. "But he's over there next to King."

"I guess Inez needed an old friend by her side today and she goes back a long way with May. Besides, she and King are barely talking now that they're divorced."

"Well, that May sure turned out to be one smart cookie. Hell of an agent. And one of the first people who discovered the power behind agency packaging in this town. Try to make a deal with her for just about anybody in the business today and you think you're talking to Howard Hughes. A real survivor, that broad. That leaves only Devon Barnes, who hasn't shown up yet. What the hell happened to her? Stunning girl. Good little actress. And a *body, oy vey.* We thought we had a real winner when Gilda teamed up with her and King in that *Cobras* picture a couple of years ago. But it was too arty. Hell, nobody goes to pictures anymore except kids and they get so bored they punch holes in the screen with slingshots if you don't have three gang rapes and fourteen car crashes in the first reel. You don't hear a word about Devon Barnes anymore."

Billy nodded. "See you later, Sam."

Inching his way toward the side of the chapel, he was stopped again by a husky voice wafting in his ear. "Standing room only. God bless her, she's still packing them in." He turned to greet Bud Dahlripple. "Hello, Billy. What're you doing back here with the hired help?"

Dahlripple had been Sydney Guilaroff's assistant at MGM when Guilaroff was Hollywood's king of coiffure. Bud had set Ava and Lana and Rita and Gilda. Guilaroff styled them and combed them out. Then he'd let Bud laquer them.

"She was the best. You wrote her a lovely send-off, Billy. And that picture—I couldn't believe it. Leave it to you to dig it up. She really did discover all four of them, didn't she? Amazing. God, what a woman she was. Remember that famous scene in *Night Anthem?* Peter Lorre says, 'He's just a soldier. He's got nothing.' And Gilda tosses that rope of pearls over her shoulder and says, 'He's got *me!*' What a scene."

That line—and those pearls—gave her career wings. Three little words and every woman in America had wanted a pearl necklace for

Christmas. Pearls became Gilda Greenway's trademark. How many photographs had Billy seen through the years of Gilda, holding a fabled pearl necklace in her teeth?

Several years later, when Patrick Wainwright moved into Gilda's life, he presented her with a seven-strand necklace that became her trademark for the rest of her life. Mr. Box Office himself, all bowlegged, six-foot-two, eyes of blue. In fact, Patrick had taken most of those photos; he wanted to be a director. He knew just how to set her up, how to light the red highlights in her auburn hair, how to make her stick out her tongue and drag thousands of dollars worth of perfect pearls over it, sucking them just for him. Gilda had always teased him that being America's favorite macho star was ruining his directorial career. It was true.

Billy remembered when he first learned about Gilda and Patrick, one of Hollywood's favorite secrets. The day after he met Gilda, a friend told him she and Patrick had been lovers for years. *Holy shit,* he'd thought, *Patrick Wainwright!* The stuntman turned cowboy star. The cowboy star turned Broadway lothario in 1956. One of the greats. Married to a devout Catholic who had been a bedridden asparagus ever since the car crash that killed their only child. Patrick Upright, who would never divorce her. East of Palm Springs, he belonged to his wife, mom, and apple-pie America. But west of it, he was all Gilda's. It suited her fine. She was lousy at marriage, she'd told Billy—she'd tried it three times. The only thing she *was* good at, she'd said, was being bad. And she had the vocabulary to back her bravado.

"Like it?" Billy turned to face Byron Kerr, a vicious but ineffectual rival columnist for a Chicago syndicate, who was stroking the lapel of his wrinkled white linen suit. "Picked it up at a celebrity auction."

"Sydney Greenstreet," Billy guessed.

"Tom Wolfe," said Byron indignantly.

"Nice," Billy said icily. "You wouldn't want to look too downbeat at a funeral."

"Gilda was a class act—she'll forgive me. I hope she'll be as kind to Sam. I overheard. Puh-leeze. If MGM discovered Gilda Greenway in a Tulsa camera shop, then I discovered clean living. And speaking of dirt—I notice only three of the Four Fans showed."

"So far."

"Billy, you always were soft on Devon Barnes. You think she'll come out of exile to pay homage to her murdered mentor? I hear the cops are very eager to have a chat with that one. Let's ask Lieutenant Biggs."

"Good morning, gentlemen."

Billy didn't even have to turn around. The Chicago accent, like Mayor Richard Daley's, the assault of Aramis, the sudden scented bulk behind him exuding perspiration, were all he needed to identify the dick. Detective/Second Grade Lionel Biggs of the West LAPD was wearing civvies—white-on-white collar open at the neck, American flag pin in the lapel of his plaid Robert Hall sports jacket, miniature gold bullets for cufflinks. He wore two chains—a thin one that disappeared in his white chest hair and a short thick one that rode the shaving line around his neck like a gold-plated noose.

Billy had met Biggs on a movie set. One of King's movies, a Technicolor remake of a Fritz Lang film *noir.* King was playing the Mitchum role, a seedy but honest cop trying to nail the Everett Sloane character without implicating Gloria Grahame. Lionel Biggs had been moonlighting as a technical advisor on police procedure. He'd wound up in the film—blink-of-an-eye scene written just for him—because he'd covered King's ass, when he'd found it uncovered, humping the producer's lady.

King had gotten the screenwriter to add a gag for Lionel. He cajoled the director to go along with it, and even persuaded his agent, May Fischoff, to rep Biggs.

"Sorry to have gotten you up so early yesterday," Biggs said.

"Don't sweat it, Biggs."

"Please, Billy. Call me Lionel. You know I was a great fan of Miss Greenway.Not one of the *Four* Fans . . ."

"Spare me, Biggs. I'm beginning to regret I ever ran that picture. It's old news, but suddenly everyone's talking about the four of *them,* instead of Gilda."

"Seen the morning paper yet?"

Billy shook his head. "I wasn't in the mood for any more stunning revelations."

"Well, you missed a good one. We were trying to keep it a secret, but some idiot in the department talked, so you might as well know what the rest of La La Land already knows. We found a copy of that picture crumpled up in Miss Greenway's hand."

"The picture of the Four Fans? Maybe she was just feeling sentimental and going through old photographs."

Biggs raised one eyebrow. "Right. And you just struck a deal to share your exclusives with Byron Kerr here. Let's talk this afternoon," he said, walking away. "I got to work the crowd."

"Ashes to ashes, dust to dust . . . "

"What's a sweater without a bust?"

"For God's sake," May Fischoff admonished Inez Hollister-Godwin. Despite the air-conditioned chill in the chapel, Inez's pallid face was slick with sweat. The makeup she'd painstakingly applied in her four-way Joan Crawford bathroom mirror was dissolving. Her nostrils had returned to their more or less permanently inflamed state. To the untrained eye, Inez would appear to be properly distressed. But May knew the truth. She had seen the same Susan Hayward movies.

Unfortunately, the chapel was crowded with trained eyes, and ears. There probably wasn't a soul present who didn't know Inez had a drug problem. (Perhaps there was *one*, May amended: Inez herself.)

"Look, here comes Mrs. Danvers," Inez pointed, using the nickname she'd bestowed upon Mrs. Denby, Gilda's housekeeper, years ago when Gilda had first invited her to California to stay at The Pearls. "That ghoul—her sour picklepuss doesn't decompose no matter what happens. Every time I see her, I think it's Halloween."

"Didn't those nuns back in Brooklyn teach you it's not polite to point? Pull in your talons, honey," May admonished her.

"Go fuck yourself, sweetie," Inez hissed, sucking on a Valium. That May had had her nerve, pretending to care about her. Just like Gilda, who'd pulled her prima donna act and skipped out on Inez's Christmas Eve party, robbing her of one last chance to make the society columns in this town of bloodsucking social vampires. Well, her days of taking care of Miss Gilda-Fucking-Greenway were over. Inez had no regrets. Survival, she had learned, meant never having to say you're sorry.

May was another betraying bitch. She'd seen her outside her own home, practically fucking Mitch, Inez's live-in boyfriend, standing up against May's white Corniche. Wouldn't Hollis just love to hear about that? But Inez didn't want to break her son's heart. Unless, of course, she had to. Besides, now she had a better story to tell. She looked around and saw Billy Buck at the back of the chapel. I'll call him this afternoon, she thought. Tell him he has to help me write *From Hilltop to Hollywood: The Gilda Greenway Story.* By someone who knew her when . . .

The drugs and the drama made her suddenly shake inside. Tears were streaming down her face as some invisible thermometer sent rushes of florid heat through her pores. "Got a Kleenex, May?" she mumbled, poking her friend's arm.

The woman can actually still feel something underneath all that coke and whatever else she's flushed through her system, thought May. Inez had been so stoned out of her Princess Borghese volcanic-mud-rinsed head on Christmas Eve that May had feared for her sanity, especially when King had walked through his ex-wife's front door. Lord knows how she somehow managed to drive herself over to Gilda's mansion without an accident. Fortunately, she sighed with relief, Inez had been too wasted to recognize *her* there, too, hiding in the shadows behind the wheel of her Corniche.

May's heart ached with grief and remorse. She looked at the alabaster urn on the wrought-iron stand directly in front of the stained-glass window. It seemed to glow in the sunlight with a titty-pink aura, vaguely translucent. She found herself wondering if the urn was warm inside, where Gilda's ashes were, imagining the tiny shards of bone settling in like bread crumbs.

"You're gonna have it all, baby," Gilda had promised her when she was five years old. "Brains, beauty, success, and love. Listen to the old gypsy fortune-teller here. And then you're gonna come stand right in front of me and look me in the eye and say, 'Gilda, you were right.' "

Well, Gilda *was* right. Gilda had predicted it all.

King had become a comet in the Hollywood sky, but he walked through his career like a zombie, sleeping his way from location to location, staying away from home as often as possible to avoid a marriage that had never worked. Inez was the one with ambition, yet her writing career had been doomed from the start. When she finally gave up on herself she tried to achieve fame by association with a celebrated husband, but that didn't work either. Devon's beauty and sensitivity had worked in her favor, but she had treated her own film career as an irritating stopgap between bigger priorities. That left May. May, the one who never had any drive, ambition, looks, career motives, or talent. The long shot who came in first.

May.

The most successful of them all.

Ten of Hollywood's leading money-makers were her clients. Three $40-million picture deals were sitting on her desk waiting for signatures. Headwaiters genuflected when she entered the Bistro. She had her own table phone at the Polo Lounge. Her new house was going to make the cover of *Interior Design*. *The Ladies' Home Journal* had named her one of the Ten Most Admired Women in America. She had power, wealth, and influence. She also had Hollis—her 21-year-old godson, and the only person in her life whose love was as full, as perfect and as unconditional as her father's had been for her mother. But unlike her father's love, Hollis's adoration didn't shut anyone out.

In the two years since Hollis had moved into her bed, her life had changed. She taught him the agency business, he brought in the rock stars she knew nothing about, and now they shared an office as well as a bed. Gilda had disapproved from the beginning. They had quarreled violently. May's happiness and renewed sense of purpose made her immune to generation-gap logic. Still, there were days, when, despite the fact that she'd lost eighty-six pounds in the past two years and finally made the transition from tents to size tens, she still feld old and ugly and fat. She had almost worried herself into a case of shingles wondering why Hollis would want to spend the rest of his life with a woman his own mother's age.

She looked over at him, seated across the aisle, next to King. He was taller than his famous father now, and for May's money, twice as handsome. His sun-kissed hair was only a slightly darker contrast to King's wheat-yellow streaks, flecked with gray, his face a preppie version of his mother's once-beautiful features. But his lapis blue eyes, ringed with thick dark lashes, were King's. Genetic algebra, May thought. King's eyes, cloned to an infinite power.

King glanced up, saw her drinking in Hollis like spring wine, and managed a tired smile. For once he wore a dark blue Cerutti suit instead of the T-shirt, brown leather jacket, and faded Levi's that were universally regarded as his standard uniform. His tinted Dick Tracy Ray-Ban glasses hid his eyes, the brilliant sailboat-blue aggies that had made him a fortune and plunged him into two nasty, well-publicized paternity suits.

He felt utterly exhausted. Hadn't slept since the night the cops showed up at The Pearls and found him next to Gilda's blood-spattered body. The scene had been a rewrite from a B-movie he never wanted to be in. He'd been released early Christmas morning after they questioned him. Now he was waiting for the forensics lab reports to clear him for good. But he knew that most of Tongue City was still holding its Binaca-drenched breath, waiting to hear that he'd been charged with first-degree murder. Well, he wasn't going anywhere. He was tired of running. He'd spent his life running away and now he had nowhere left to go.

"Who *is* that guy, May?" Inez was asking. "The preacher. He looks so goddam familiar."

"Oh, God," May murmured, recognizing him. "An *actor.*"

She couldn't remember his name, but he'd been a client of her father's in the early days, when ethnics and character actors and cabaret acts made up 50 percent of the agency, and Gilda Greenway made up the rest. It was an odd name. He'd chiefly played squealers, rats and Gestapo agents, and once, quite brilliantly, a psychotic young killer stalking John Garfield.

Samson Pope, May finally remembered. The only priest who'd walked Gilda the last mile to the electric chair in *Only the Damned.* ("Aw, father, I don't wanna fry," Gilda had begged him while all of America wept. "I'm innocent. I don't wanna burn.") Now here was old Samson, ironically reading over her ashes in his best Orson Welles baritone. *What a town,* thought May, *ironies to the end.*

May looked at King again to see if he was registering any emotions, but he seemed distracted. As he raked his fingers through his already disheveled blond hair, he involuntarily glanced toward the open door of the chapel and the freedom that lay beyond. He caught a glimpse of a tall woman in black, trying to fight her way through the crowd that blocked the entrance.

I miss her so much that now I'm imagining her, he thought, rubbing his eyes under the shades. Then, in the next instant, he realized it was Devon—suddenly, magically reappearing after vanishing just as quickly, two years before. "No, Dad, don't," said Hollis, trying to stop him as King unthinkingly stepped into the aisle.

"It's *her*," May heard someone gasp. There was a commotion. May saw her too: black hat, black net veil, black Chanel suit. Not new, but like the old Adrians Gilda had saved from MGM, always fashionable. All black. Except the pearls.

From the far side of the chapel, two men moved authoritatively through the frenzied crowd that gathered around Devon Barnes. One of them was Biggs, the other was Billy Buck. Flashbulbs were popping. The video crew that stalked the funeral like vultures rushed through the open doors to get a closeup. "This way, Devon," they shouted. The TV reporter plunged her mike hand through the fracas, inadvertently knocking into Devon in her greedy determination to get the first exclusive.

There was a cracking noise, like a burst of buckshot, broadcast through the solemn chapel over the mike in the reporter's hand, as Gilda Greenway's fabled pearl necklace was yanked from Devon's neck. Pearls as big as grapes clattered to the floor, rolling through the aisles. The crowd dove for them, under the carved wooden benches and between each other's Guccis.

Someone yanked the hat off Devon's head. Raven hair cascaded over her shoulders. Her eyes, a mirror of terror and desperation, met May's. As King had done, May reached out a hand to help. But it was Billy Buck's arms that Devon found. "Billy, get me out of here," she cried.

"That's what I'm here for, beauty." He shielded her with his body, wrapped her in his embrace, and kicked open the side exit of the chapel, roughly maneuvering a path through the screaming magpies waiting in the blinding sunlight. "Two years of exile and this is what you came back to? Great timing, Devon."

"Oh, Billy," she said as they dashed through the crowd to his XKE. "Tell me none of this is happening."

Inside, they locked the doors and Billy started the car. The paparazzi were climbing on the hood, snapping away. Reporters were banging their microphones on the car windows. Everyone was screaming.

Billy gunned the accelerator. "Jesus, what a homecoming. And it's going to get worse."

Inside the Wee Kirk o' the Heather, Inez Godwin's face was like an unbaked muffin now, beaded with sweat. Her parched lips were open, her tongue felt like a used eraser. Her hands were chalky, too. They clutched Mitch Misyak's muscled arm, her tapered pomegranate-red nails gripping him like the claws of an eagle. "Get me out of here," she managed to croak. "I can't breathe. Mitch, get me the fuck out of here before I scream."

May Fischoff sat down heavily. King had left, like Inez, aching with nausea and anguish. Devon was gone, on the arm of Billy Buck. The pounds May had shed seemed suddenly to be resting on her heart. She was 39 years old, she reminded herself, too young to feel this tired. Too young to be filled with this much remorse—not just for Gilda, who still glowed from the alabaster urn in front of the slowly-emptying chapel, but for all of them.

The famous Four Fans. Gilda had chosen them, adopted them, nurtured them, cursed them, and led them to this cursed place, far from home. Now she was gone. She couldn't pull them out of this one. If there was a way back, they'd have to find it on their own.

PART 1

ONE

F or nearly eight years, the Westbridge School had been May Fischoff's home. She'd seen the ivy creep from the first-floor dorm, where she'd roomed when she was a frightened eight-year-old newcomer, up the gothic brick facade of Hinton Hall, nearly to the dormered windows of the senior girls' rooms on the third floor. She'd watched the scrawniest tree in the quad bloom and grow tall enough to obstruct her view of the library and chapel across the way. Even today, in the dead of winter, the young maple was stretching. Its barren arms implored the overcast sky to be fair, to be kind, inviting the sun, because it was a very special day.

It was May Fischoff's sixteenth birthday.

It was supposed to be her *sweet* sixteen, but leave it to her three roommates to wreck the day practically before it had begun. It was bad enough that Harriet had picked yesterday morning to run off with Ezra "Ten Inch" Tennich.

Now Inez Hollister had decided to pitch a fit.

"I hate her, hate her, *hate* her!" Inez pounded the pillow Harriet had left behind.

Most of May's birthday morning had been spent with Inez and Devon in the Dean's Office convincing the wary dowager that none of them had any idea what Harriet had been planning. They'd been as stunned as she to find their roommate gone and the note about Mr. Tennich, the English teacher, pinned to her pillow—the pillow Inez was now pulverizing.

"What's with you, Inez?" May could not make sense of the sudden hysteria that had seized her friend. "It's not as if she did anything to *you.*"

"She knew I was in love with him!" Inez shrieked. "He was *my* English teacher. Harriet didn't even have him this term."

Devon Barnes came out of the bathroom with a dripping wash-cloth in her hand. "Oh, for cryin' out loud, Inez. He's been crazy about Harriet all year. You know that."

May loved Devon's Texas accent. *Eye-neyuz,* she said, and *You know they-at.*

"You even saw them making out, remember? Hell, Inez, you're the one who named him Ten Inch." Devon held out the wet cloth. "Here, wipe your face and get your clothes on. We've got less than an hour to catch the train."

"Yeah, hurry up," said May, surprising herself. She never ordered Inez around. Inez was a scholarship student from Brooklyn, New York, and the angriest girl May had ever met. She'd say things that could make your cheeks burn with shame. Her family were shits, she said, illiterate low-life losers. Her mother was a doormat who let her father get away with murder. Her father was a real wacko. Not just a drunk, but the kind who'd cry and slobber all over you one minute, then start beating the hell out of you the next. Either way, his hands would wind up where they shouldn't be.

May had never met anyone who hated her own parents. But then again, she'd never met a father who'd feel up his own daughter. She didn't even want to think about it. But Inez was a poet, and poets were supposed to have tragic, sacrificial childhoods. Try to look at the bright side of life, May's mother always said. Inez wouldn't have won the

Margaret Hannah Scholarship to Westbridge if she hadn't been such a terrific writer. And she probably wouldn't have been such a terrific writer if her father hadn't been so disgusting. If you looked at it that way, he'd done her a favor. Sort of.

May had thought Inez was exaggerating, at first. But one night, she had overheard Inez and Harriet talking in the dark.

"Your own father? He really *touched* you . . . down *there?*" Harriet hadn't sounded stunned or disgusted. She'd had this sort of amused chuckle in her voice. Harriet and Inez had a lot in common —they were smart, they both had forty-carat vocabularies, and their parents *never* came to Connecticut to visit.

The two of them were smoking in the dark, sitting together on Harriet's bed. May could see the red tip of the Pall Mall moving between them, glowing more brightly when either of them inhaled.

Inez sounded amused herself. "Down there and . . . ohmygod, yeah, right there. Yeah, like that. And up here, too."

"Mmmm," Harriet said. "Well, I can understand that. You have got the most fantastic bust."

"Mmmm," Inez said. "Oh, God, Harriet."

"Mmmm," Harriet said, and chuckled her deep-throated chuckle. "Fan. Tas. Tic."

There was some more mmmming while the cigarette, now motionless, maintained a steady glow. Then Harriet, May supposed, picked it up again and took a drag, because it was Inez who sighed and said, "Do you think I'm too big? I mean, I don't want to be tucking them into my socks when I'm thirty."

"I think," said Harriet, pausing to exhale, whooshing out a great sigh of smoke. "I think your father was a creep and a pervert, but a fan*tas*tic connoisseur of tits."

What May didn't understand, though, was where Inez's mother fit in. Didn't she care about what was going on? Didn't she know? May's mother would never let anyone do *that* to her. Not that anyone would. Fat chance someone would want to feel *her* up. Least of all her father, who never even looked at other women.

Everyone knew that Frankie and Norma Fischoff had eyes only for each other. Every anniversary, birthday, Christmas, and New Year's Eve, as far back as May could remember, Frankie had gotten a famous singer or bandleader or orchestra to serenade Norma with "I Only Have Eyes For You."

She'd hated it as a child, but now whenever she heard "I Only Have Eyes For You," she'd think about what Gilda had told her, how she'd leaned over once, in themiddle of that song, and said to May, "You're going to have it all, baby."

It was New Year's Eve, May thought, long ago, in her parents' big apartment on West End Avenue. It must have been midnight because she remembered her father kissing her mother. Had she tried to join them? Had she wanted a kiss, too? To this day she couldn't remember why she'd been crying. She only remembered the salty tears rolling down. And Gilda's milky white hand lifting her face, wiping the tears with a handkerchief scented with White Shoulders. May blowing her nose on cloudy Porthault.

It had been about a year since she'd seen her famous godmother. But Gilda was in New York this week. Her boyfriend, Patrick Wainwright, was starring in a Broadway play. It was strange to think of Patrick Wainwright, the cowboy movie star, standing on a stage right in front of you, saying lines to something besides his horse. When her mother first told her of the birthday treat her father had planned, May had thought the play would be like the rodeo at Madison Square Garden. She'd imagined horses trotting in circles and Patrick in a spotlight, waving his cowboy hat and doing rope tricks. But, no, her mother had said. This was a serious play by one of America's foremost dramatists, Avery Calder. May was eager to see it, though she couldn't imagine Pat Wainwright without a saddle. She'd never met him. No one was supposed to know he was Gilda's boyfriend.

It would be wonderful to see Gilda again. May's excitement gave her courage.

"Come on, Inez, get dressed. It's my birthday. And anyway, don't you want to meet Gilda? God, wouldn't you rather have lunch with a real movie star than sit around moping about some horny old lech!"

"He was mine! That bitch!" Inez cried fiercely and hurled Harriet's pillow at May.

"Hey!" Devon said. "That's not fair." She tossed her wet washcloth at Inez's scowling face. Then, convulsed with laughter, she ran, ducking and weaving, to hide behind May's dresser.

Inez pulled the washcloth off her head and stood abruptly. Her hands balled up into fists at her side. "Damn you, Devon Barnes," she hissed. "You think you're so cute. Well, he may be just a horny old lech to you, but he was *my* horny old lech!" Her hand flew up to her mouth. "I don't believe it," she said. "Did I say that? Did I really just say—"

" 'He may be just a horny old lech to you,' " May dared.

" 'But he's *my* horny old lech,' " Inez, Devon, and May completed the sentence together.

"Yes, ma'am," said Devon. "That's what you said."

"You did, Inez," said May, emboldened and happy, basking in her best friends' sunny laughter.

Suddenly, Inez was scowling again. "I can't go. Even if I didn't feel so awful, I look a mess. Look at me—" She examined her face in the mirror over Harriet's dresser, patting her swollen eyes with the washcloth. "Anyway, I don't have anything to wear." She turned and tossed the washcloth onto Harriet's bed and, looking nearly as wrung-out, sank down beside it.

"Come on, Inez," May said gently. "Anything you have will be okay. Honest, you don't have to dress up. It's just lunch."

"Just lunch with Gilda Greenway at '21,' that's all." She looked at May, whose waist was easily twice as thick as her own; and then at Devon, boyishly slender with no bust to speak of. "Damn Harriet for deserting me," she said. "At least she could have loaned me something decent to wear."

Devon Barnes brightened. "Like what?" she asked, flinging open the door to Harriet's closet. It was jammed, a rainbow of skirts and blouses carelessly crushed between hanging quilted storage bags. Shoes cluttered the floor, and cashmere, Irish woolens, and angora sweaters piled high on the shelf like a Seventh Avenue showroom. On the back of the door hung a cascade of ribbons, belts, scarves, and school ties.

Devon tugged loose a navy blue cashmere sweater and tossed it to Inez. "Something dark, I think. Sophisticated but not, you know—"

"Somber," Inez offered, grinning. She leaped from the bed and opened the top drawer of Harriet's dresser. Tossing socks, panties, and slips over her shoulder, she finally found the pale blue garter belt she was looking for.

"Oh, God," she crooned, crushing the satiny fabric against her cheek. "How could she leave something so gorgeous and sexy behind? What a dumb cluck. Ten Inch isn't going to buy her lingerie like this. Not on his measly salary. And he *loves* to see her walking around in garter belts and fancy bras."

"He does?" said May.

"You know he does. I told you all about it."

Devon was wrestling inside the basic black sheath her mother had sent her from Neiman-Marcus last Christmas. She tugged and pulled the shapeless dress down over her head and smoothed it over her slender body. Thank God she hadn't outgrown it. On the other hand, she thought, seeing Inez change into one of Harriet's lacy bras, when would she ever fill out enough for the dress to fit? "Harriet knew you were watching, right?" she prompted Inez.

"Shhhh," May said crossly. "Let her tell it." She was sitting in her slip, barefoot, the bobby pins still in her hair.

"You'd better get dressed, too," Devon said, "or we'll miss the train into the city."

May shook out one of the stockings lying beside her on the bed and carelessly slipped her foot into it. Her attention remained riveted on Inez. "Go on," she begged, "after Harriet took off her skirt, then what happened?"

Inez pretended to be bored. As she yawned, her breasts heaved in the tight lace bra, which was too small for her. With her thick dark hair, delicate nose, and full sensual lips, and especially in that bra, May thought, she looked like Jane Russell in *The Outlaw.*

"God, you've heard all this before. Aren't you sick of it yet?" she asked.

"No," May shouted shamelessly. "Quit teasing, Inez. Just tell the story, okay?"

"I never saw anything so big and red in my life," said Inez. "I mean, he opened his buttons and pulled back the slit of his shorts and the thing just jumped out, fat as your arm. Just shot out, like a Nazi salute."

May got up from the bed and hurried to the mirror pulling bobby pins from her hair as she went. "Come on, we'll be late," she said breathlessly.

"That's not the part she wants to hear," said Devon.

"No, really, it's just that we've got to catch a train. You even said so, and there's not that much time . . . "

"And you can't stand the thought of Harriet putting this thing in her mouth, right?"

May whirled around. "Yes. Right. Okay? Are you satisfied now? I think it's completely revolting. I don't understand how anyone can put something in their mouth that people pee out of."

"Tell you the truth," said Devon, "I don't understand it, either. But what I find *really* weird is how he could kiss her, you know, down there."

"I don't even believe that part," May challenged.

Inez shrugged. "Can I borrow your lipstick, May?" She was very pleased with the way she looked in Harriet's soft sweater and beautiful skirt with the Saks Fifth Avenue label inside the waistband. Too pleased to meet May's challenge or explain the facts of life to Devon. She knew all about what women did for men. Hell, when she was seven or eight, she and her best friend, Bianca Ferra, had found a couple of tiny comic books in Bianca's father's sock drawer. And there was Olive Oyl with Popeye's great big zucchini stuck in her mouth. And there was a picture of Pluto or maybe it was Goofy, Inez couldn't remember, but Minnie Mouse was doing the same damn thing to one of *them*. For chrissake, even Little Lulu did it.

Inez inhaled, put her hands on her waist, and pressed in hard. Her waist looked tiny in Harriet's full skirt. She wondered if she could get her fingertips to touch. She did, and whirled happily before the mirror. The skirt flared beautifully, displaying, beneath it, the same powder-blue satin garter belt she'd watched Ezra Tennich grasp. She had seen him go down on his knees before Harriet, like she was Rita Hayworth in *Miss Sadie Thompson.* His big hands had grasped her thighs, his thumbs slid under the satin ribbons that hid the stocking hooks.

She'd seen Harriet lean back on the leather sofa and close her eyes until Tennich put her thighs over his shoulders and bent his head between them. Then Harriet had arched her back so fiercely Inez had expected to hear it crack in two like a wishbone. Her chin pointed at the ceiling, her arms were outstretched, her hands clutched the worn leather sofa pillows in a crucifixion of ecstasy.

Inez shuddered suddenly. *They're sharing something and shutting me out!* That's what she'd thought when she was little and sleeping in the same basement room as her brothers and their parents. She'd felt frightened and lonely in her narrow bed against the wall. Her brothers said she was the lucky one. They had to share a bed nearly as small as hers, two of them sleeping head to feet. But Inez's bed was against the wall, where only a thin coating of paint and plaster covered the cavelike cold cellar stones. Things were always scratching, trapped inside that wall. And the floor under her bed, under her feet when she dared to walk on it at night, was a cheap, thin layer of oilcloth over packed earth.

The only human sounds in the night were the noises from her parents' bed. Her mother would laugh or whimper, crying the names of saints as her father panted, hoarsely, like the sound of a saw. She'd strain through the darkness to watch their shadows undulating like swooping ghosts. And she'd think that it wasn't fair for them to have each other and for her to be alone. Then, one night when she was seven and her mother was in the hospital with pneumonia, he'd let her sleep with him in the big bed.

"God, Inez, come here, quick. Devon, look at him." May was at the window, looking to see if their cab to the depot had arrived. What she saw instead was a motorcycle pulling up to the gates and, on it, a blond got in a black leather jacket.

Inez looked down through the tall barren branches to the front gate. "Jesus, he's cute. Who is he?"

The boy had hooked one leg over the top of his bike and was sitting out there waiting for something. Or someone. He raked a hand through his long saffron hair, which had been blown around like dandelion fuzz. Hunched over against the cold, he blew into his hands. Then he looked up.

Devon took a step back from the window. She felt as if she'd looked into the face of the sun. The boy on the motorcycle wasn't much older than they, but his face was rugged, broad-boned, hungry. Only his eyes were young. They were clear and blue and, it seemed to Devon, full of hope.

When he grinned she thought, No, not hope. Certainty. His dark weathered face lit with sudden pleasure. Mussing his hair again, he got off the motorcycle and came through the gates toward Hinton Hall.

Devon could hear his footsteps with stunning clarity; the sound matched the pounding of her heart. Finally he reached their window and looked up, grinning.

"Hey," he called, "is Harriet Brinkley up there? Tell her it's King —Kingston Godwin."

He kept wanting to look at her, the willowy girl in black—black coat, black dress, thick black eyelashes, and bold violet eyes.

Devon Barnes, she'd said her name was.

Dehvun Bawnes. It made him smile inside the way she'd said it, drawing it out like Aunt Jemima. A thin slip of a girl with her pale face and tangle of winter-thick hair that had a mind of its own.

Devon Barnes.

She was beautiful. The face. The body. He was getting a hard-on just thinking about her.

He was sitting on his Harley-Davidson just outside the school gates, where they told him to wait.

"Where're you from?" King asked her, taking care to keep that *y'all* out of his question. He'd been practicing his best actor's diction —the all-purpose Rock Hudson I-could-be-from-anywhere accent that would get him into the Actor's Workshop someday. He just about had it licked.

"Texas," she said, shrugging, like it wasn't her fault.

She looked at her friends. She looked at her feet. Two spots of color rose on her cheeks, like strawberries in a bowl of cream. She had soft skin stretched tautly over delicate cheekbones. Then she looked at him again, grinned, and turned away. What she wanted, King realized, was a place for her eyes to rest, where his eyes couldn't claim her.

Yes, definitely. Devon Barnes. He wanted her. He was making her nervous, and the other two were jabbering at him like mynahs about the defecting Harriet.

"I'm really sorry," the fat girl said. "I mean, you must be disappointed—"

"Well, wouldn't you be?" interrupted the sweater girl, not taking her eyes off him. "Coming all the way up here on a motorcycle to find out your girl ran off with another guy."

"She wasn't my girl," King said, already bored, knowing it was what the busy tomato was waiting to hear, but wanting the Texan to know. "I met her at the White Horse Tavern in the Village a couple of weeks ago. She invited me up here. Hey, it's a nice day. I didn't have anything better to do."

"Well, that figures," the fat one said, irritated. "Leave it to Harriet to make a date on my birthday."

The Texas belle laughed. "And then run off with old Ten Inch." She had a big laugh for such a skinny kid. Big laugh. Great body.

"Devon, honestly!" Inez, the sweater girl, was shocked. Actually blushing. She didn't look like the blushing tea rose type. More like the thorns. It was 40 degrees out and she was standing there breathing smoke, with her coat over her arm so no one would miss that incredible figure she had wrapped in cashmere and wool. Tits that made Marilyn Monroe look flat-chested, tiny waist, and show girl legs that extended into next week, like Cyd Charisse. There was no doubt about it. Of the three, the one named Inez was the looker.

He'd be crazy not to take her up on the offer she was making every time she batted her eyes, or shrugged until her breasts heaved, or stretched so they rose, or bent over to adjust the seams of her stockings so he could follow her hand up the awesome length of her legs. So he could see her ass high and tight, tilting toward him. Imagine her opening to him. Bending that way, she could just about back up to him. Back right on to him. He'd hardly have to move at all.

He'd have to be crazy not to accept, considering the torturous hard-on in his jeans.

"It's May's sweet sixteen today," the Texan told him.

"Happy birthday," he said. Sixteen maybe, maybe not. Harriet had said she was eighteen. He'd believed her. She hadn't believed that he was twenty; he looked at least twenty-five, she said. Thanks a helluva lot, Harriet. He told her he didn't lie. She hadn't believed that either.

"Thank you," said the birthday girl, "but we've got to go. Sorry about Harriet. Boy, I don't even know what I'm going to tell my parents. She was supposed to come with us."

"We're going to '21' for lunch," Inez purred. Her breasts danced for him again.

"We're going to have lunch with Gilda Greenway," said Devon. "She is my absolute idol."

He figured she was lying about the lunch, but he sure could understand that Greenway was her idol. If someone had asked him which movie star the Texan reminded him of, he'd have said Gilda Greenway. Although she wasn't nearly as sexy as Greenway.

He wanted to look at her now but knew she'd start blushing and look away again. Not sexy? Who was he trying to kid? The boner he was sitting on jumped every time he glanced at her. Even her laughter got to him. She looked classy and clean, this Texas beanpole. She'd smell like soap, he bet, not an unmade bed.

"She's practically family, right, May?" Inez said.

"Gilda Greenway?" He still didn't know whether to believe the girls. "That must be nice." He turned to May, trying to see the resemblance. Scrape off twenty-five, thirty pounds, you still wouldn't find Gilda in there, he thought. Not behind that Pinocchio nose. Strangely, though, it was . . . *interesting.* The kid had nice eyes, a pert mouth, straight teeth. The nose gave her face character.

"Sincerely," he said to May Fischoff, "I mean, being related to a movie star. That is sincerely nice." He looked down at the gravel road and said, "I'm studying acting myself."

He wanted Devon Barnes to know who he was so she'd know what she was getting into. He believed in that. He was twenty, but he'd been hard-scrabbling on his own for a while. Five years that might as well have been fifty. He'd seen things she wouldn't believe; done things he wouldn't have believed he was capable of. Maybe he'd tell her about them some day. Not to shock her. Just so she could never say he hadn't told her the truth right from the start.

Most people didn't understand about acting, he thought. That it was about telling the truth, not making believe. He wondered if Gilda Greenway felt that way about it. She'd have to, he decided, because she was good. She wasn't what he'd call a *great* actress, but then movie stars didn't get much chance to act.

"I admire her," he told May.

"We're not really related. She's my godmother. Devon's going to be an actress, too. Aren't you?"

Devon Barnes grinned. " 'Actor' is more like it. The only parts I've gotten so far are playing men, right, Inez?"

The sweater girl ignored her. "May," she said pointedly, "didn't you hear what he said? He's studying acting in New York. I bet he'd *love* to meet Gilda."

May was annoyed. "I was going to ask him, Inez. *God.* Listen, um, my parents are giving me a party. Sort of," she added shyly, realizing she was already in over her head. "For my sweet sixteen. It's just lunch, really. Would you like to . . . join us? I mean, you could take Harriet's place. She was supposed to come." Her ears were on fire with embarrassment. Suddenly more aware than ever of her weight, she kneaded her elbows as if they were mounds of dough, praying they would disappear.

King looked at Devon.

"I hear she's real nice," Devon said. "I mean, you always read about how she likes to help young people. Isn't that right, May?"

The pink spots were back in her cheeks. She was having trouble returning his gaze. "Sounds cool," he said, hesitantly, doing James Dean. "Maybe I could give one of you a ride to the city—"

"Fantastic," said Inez. "I'll get my scarf. Be right down." She tossed her coat to him and hurried across the quad toward Hinton Hall.

I'll get my scarf? Shit! Why did *she* have to butt in? Talk about a goddam thorn!

King tried to catch Devon's eye, but she wouldn't look at him. May grabbed her hand. "Come on, Devon. The cab's here. It's Fifty-second between Fifth and Sixth," she called over her shoulder to King. "Be good. And if you can't be good," May giggled, "be *careful.*"

TWO

11:00 A.M., DECEMBER 26, 1979

A fter Gilda Greenway's funeral, homicide Detective/ Second Grade Lionel Biggs went back to the West LAPD's headquarters on Butler Avenue. He took the elevator up to the second floor and walked into his cluttered office. Shoving some reports off his chair, he loosened his tie and thought, Some Christmas.

Since Harry Monahan, the West LAPD's supervising homicide detective, was still at Cedars of Lebanon recovering from a shot in the groin he got during the course of an investigation the previous week, Biggs had been handed the Greenway case. It was a case any homicide cop would give his right ball for.

On Christmas Eve, just before midnight, he'd been called to Greenway's mansion. A patrol car, responding to an anonymous phone call, had arrived and found Gilda Greenway DOA. Iced in her own living room. Right by the fucking Christmas tree. And King Godwin, one of Hollywood's superstar bad boys, was found standing right over her.

The press was hungry, and this was front-page chow.

The medical examiner had already officially pronounced her dead, and they were loading her into an ambulance when Biggs arrived. The Crime Unit photographer was taking shots of the scene.

Biggs had never met Gilda Greenway, though he'd seen her a few times at the occasional Hollywood parties he'd been invited to, thanks to playing occasional bit roles in cop movies. But over the last few years, Greenway had become, it was said, a virtual recluse.

He had known King Godwin, though. In fact, he'd once saved Godwin's ass in an embarrassing situation. The last thing Biggs had ever expected was to be questioning the famous star about a murder. But that's exactly what he'd done in the wee hours of the morning on Christmas Day.

"And when did you first get to The Pearls?" Biggs had asked. They were sitting in his office at headquarters. It was one o'clock in the morning, less than ninety minutes since the discovery of Gilda's body. Outside Biggs's office, several officers kept walking by, trying to get a glimpse of the famous movie star.

King Godwin hadn't even wanted to call his lawyer. He seemed in a daze.

"I guess it was just after eleven-thirty. The news on my car stereo had just come on."

"What were you doing up there? It's Christmas Eve." He glanced at his watch. "Well, Christmas Day, now."

"My ex-wife had thrown a Christmas Eve party. Gilda didn't show up. I called a couple of times, but there was no answer. I got concerned and decided to go see her. I thought maybe she just couldn't hear the phone."

King wondered whether he should mention the other reason he'd gone to The Pearls. No, he decided. Why complicate things?

"And what did you find upon arriving at Miss Greenway's residence?"

"Well, the place was dark. Very dark. And silent. Except for the dogs barking in the kennels. When I drove up, the gate opened automatically. And when I got to the top of the drive, the front door was open. I should have known something was wrong. Gilda was very security conscious, obsessive about privacy. She'd had a lot of overly attentive fans, you know."

"And then what?"

"Then I parked my car and walked in. I called out her name. The only answer I got was more dogs barking out back. I glanced into the living room and noticed the lights from the Christmas tree on. It was very strange . . . the only light in the room was this horrible blinking . . . red and green. Stop and go. It was eerie. And then . . . "

Biggs noticed King Godwin's eyes misting up. The movie star glanced uncomfortably at the ceiling, then down at the floor. The movie tough guy was biting his lip, blocking emotion. He cracked his knuckles.

"Please, go on."

"Then I saw her. She was lying on her chaise longue, by the tree. Not really lying, but sprawled back, like she'd been knocked back. Forcibly, I guess, now that I think about it. But when I first saw her, I thought, 'Oh, God, she's been drinking again.' If I remember correctly, she was holding something in her hand. And she—she seemed to be smiling. It was like the smile she'd taught us to imitate a long time ago."

"Us?" Biggs lit an unfiltered Camel, blowing a cloud of smoke up toward the ceiling.

"Yeah," he said softly. "The Four Fans. Me, my ex-wife Inez, May Fischoff, and Devon Barnes. We were known a long time ago, back in New York, as 'the Pearls Girl's Four Fans' because of a picture we had taken with her the day we all met. She'd been our idol and helped us get started."

Biggs nodded. That would explain the picture, he thought.

King Godwin sighed and ran his hand through his famous sun-bleached blond hair. Then he massaged his insured-by-Lloyd's of London blue eyes and the bridge of his nose.

"Anyway," he continued, "I said her name again and she didn't answer. She didn't stir, didn't even seem to be breathing. I went up to her very quietly, thinking, Oh, God, she's just asleep, that's all. Just asleep.

"Then I saw the chaise she was lying on. It was splattered with blood. And her eyes. They were wide open. I think I must have gone into shock, or something. I felt very faint. Like I've never felt before. I realized then that she was dead. I was just about to close her eyes when a cop walked in and said, 'Freeze! Police! Hold it right there.' I turned around and there was this fucking gun pointed at me. It was like the second reel of a bad movie. Then the cop said, 'Shit, you're King Godwin, aren't you?' and I said, 'Yeah, and this is Gilda Greenway.' "

"And what did you do with the gun?"

"What gun?"

"Come on, King, you and I go back a long time. Don't fuck around with me. Lady takes a slug, you don't ask, 'What gun?' You say, 'Oh, *that* gun.' "

King Godwin sat upright. "Listen, Lionel, I don't know what you're talking about. I never saw a gun. I didn't even hear a shot. All I know is what I've just told you."

"And you're tellin' me you don't know nothin' 'bout a gun? That you didn't hear a shot, that you didn't see anyone leave the estate?"

"Right."

Biggs humphed. After another ten minutes of questioning, King was released.

"Just don't plan any holiday trips," he told King as the star got into the elevator.

Back in his office, he reviewed the notes he'd made during the questioning. He knew King Godwin, but only peripherally. And he liked him. The one thing a cop can use to his advantage, in fact the only thing that can often crack a case, is his gut instinct. Intangible, undefinable, but always there, like a smell.

And Lionel Biggs's gut instinct told him something very definite about King Godwin.

Seven hours later, without any sleep, Biggs went over to the L. A. County Forensic Science Center on Mission Street to view the body for himself.

What a way to start your Christmas Day. But, hey, was he complaining?

No way. The trip wasn't really necessary, but this was his case and he was going to do things his way. After all, it wasn't every day somebody rubbed out a Hollywood legend. It was the kind of case every homicide dick waits for, sometimes for a lifetime. If Biggs cracked it, there could be a promotion. Maybe to supervisor, like that bastard Monahan. Maybe a book. Maybe a movie. Hey, maybe a new career like Joseph Wambaugh. He shrugged his shoulders. The L.A. coroner had gotten "Quincy." Who was to say what he could get?

He went down to the security and service floor, on the level above the sub-basement. There were three rooms located on that floor: Room A, the main autopsy room; Room B, known on the inside as the "VIP Room" since it was reserved for cases of special medical difficulties or significance; and Room C, which was larger than the other two and reserved for cases of infectious diseases or bodies in advanced stages of decomposition.

Gilda Greenway was in Room A.

She would have resented the fact that she wasn't in Room B, Biggs thought. The VIP Room. Movie stars were all the same.

The night before, Gilda's body had first been taken to the large staging room before going to Room A. Here, she was placed on a gurney and weighed on a huge scale.

She probably would have hated that, too, Biggs thought. What woman wants her true weight revealed? Especially a movie star.

At the same time, a personal-effects inventory was taken by the M.E. who'd been at The Pearls, and he'd turned in a receipt for her personal property. The responding LAPD patrolman who had walked in on King Godwin that night was also required to sign the receipt.

Biggs glanced over it in the staging room:

1. One photograph. Old. Victim pictured w/4 youths—3 female, 1 male
2. One Piaget gold watch (ladies)
3. One diamond solitaire ring, approximately 6 carats in gold setting, surrounded by 8 rubies, approximately .5 carats each
4. One set of diamond earrings, approximately 1 carat each
5. One slim bracelet with 25.5 carat diamonds and one solid gold clasp

Well, it sure as hell wasn't robbery.

The Crime Unit boys had also removed several slugs from the chaise longue where she was found, and placed them in a plastic baggie marked "EVIDENCE—WARNING!! POLICE SEAL. DO NOT REMOVE." Ballistics would run a make on it, Biggs noted mentally, and that would be in the autopsy report.

The M.E.'s staff photographer took pictures, first of the body fully clothed, and then continuing as layer after layer of clothing was removed.

Fingerprints were taken.

Then they put Gilda Greenway on a huge metal table and locked up her personal effects.

Biggs remembered that even under the harsh, stark light of Room A, Gilda Greenway looked beautiful. Not as stunningly so as she had in her younger years, perhaps, but there was still something special that separated her from the ordinary actress. Something that made her *look* like a movie star. Those perfectly chiseled cheekbones, beautiful cat eyes, and the almost-pouty lips.

A few minutes later the infamous L.A. County coroner himself walked in, snapping on a pair of rubber gloves. They exchanged greetings and then the coroner, in a brisk, cold fashion, took an initial, quick once-over of the body.

"Gilda Greenway had one bullet entry wound," he said. "It appears to have been fired from a relatively close range and entering, as you can see, the upper left breast. Exiting," he said, raising Gilda up like a rag doll, "through her back, in the left shoulder blade. And what an exit. Looks like she was hit by a hollow-point slug."

He pointed to the dispersion of skin tissue.

"We'll run some tissue more thoroughly under an SEM. That's a Scanning Electron Microscope. It's a great piece of equipment. It tells us a lot about the changes in surface tissue, especially the precise route a particular bullet traveled through a body."

"The Crime Unit boys recovered a couple of slugs," Biggs said.

"I know," the coroner said crisply. "You'll get a preliminary report tomorrow morning. Hopefully before lunch. Maybe just after."

"Why tomorrow?"

"Because today is Christmas Day. I'm working with a skeleton crew. We'll also run the blood tomorrow and you'll get that tomorrow afternoon. Okay?"

Biggs knew the coroner wanted him out. As he walked away he heard the sound of an electric saw starting up.

Biggs looked at his Timex. It was 11:15. Gilda Greenway's funeral had ended just a little while ago. Jesus, what a mob scene. All those weeping fans. Half were in the business, the other half were queers. Of course, that didn't mean they weren't interchangeable. Biggs hadn't seen a turnout like that since Marilyn's death. Reporters all over the goddamn place and more melodrama than that soap opera his wife watched every day with the phone off the hook. What was it called? "As The World Turns." Biggs called it "As The Dinner Burns."

He sat up and leaned on his desk, his elbows on the blotter and his hands folded in front of him. A passerby might have thought he was praying. In fact, that was just about what he felt like doing. He had a murder to solve. One of the biggest in years. Certainly the biggest in his career. And very little time.

Every investigator knows the first twenty-four hours of a murder investigation are the most crucial. Well, he'd been working from the moment they'd shoved Gilda Greenway into the ambulance. He'd questioned King. Then, before going over to the morgue, he'd roused Billy Buck, the journalist, out of a Christmas morning sleep.

And yet, he felt he hadn't really begun. Someone had blown this dame apart and there was very little time to find out who.

He got up, put on his coat, and walked out. His hernia was killing him, but this was not the time to hang around the house on sick leave.

It was time to take another look at The Pearls.

THREE

FEBRUARY 12, 1956

O n the train to New York, May and Devon sat opposite each other, resting their feet on the seats. The car was nearly _____ empty, except for a man across the aisle reading *Variety*.

May watched the winter weeds shivering along the tracks against a blur of bare trees and evergreens, fallow fields and backyards cluttered with rusting pickups and cars on cinder blocks. But Devon, lost in daydreams, saw nothing.

Devon Barnes, sixteen years old, was in love. It was awful.

She'd done everything wrong. She'd laughed too loudly. Her grandmother, Maybelle Barnes from Mullin, Texas, was right: she laughed like a braying jackass. She'd stared at King Godwin, too, with her mouth wide open. She had gaped at him; then turned beet red and looked away feeling a tingling, a warmth *down there* she didn't understand, but knew felt wonderful. Very attractive, Devon Barnes told herself, very cool.

She wanted to tell May how she felt. But May would think she was ridiculous. Perhaps. How could she be in love with a boy she had known for fifteen minutes? But he *was* dreamy. He rode a motorcycle. She'd never *known* anyone who rode a motorcycle. He had the bluest eyes she'd ever *seen.* He was bold *and* shy.

And he had chosen Inez Hollister.

Lulled by the rhythmic clack of the train, Devon closed her eyes against the sting of tears and sighed, thinking about her good friend Inez Hollister. Inez, on the back of his motorcycle, gripping King with her thighs, leaning her cheek against his leather jacket and hanging on tight. Tighter than she needed to, Devon was sure. Holding him with her thighs, shoving her big boobs into his back. Rubbing up against him. And she was wearing Harriet Brinkley's powder-blue garter belt.

She felt the tingling again.

Down there.

Wonderful.

"May," she said suddenly, "do I have sex appeal? I know I'm not built like Inez. I mean, I'm not *stacked.* But do you think I've got it? Even a little?"

May stared at her. "You're serious," she said finally.

Devon nodded forlornly.

"Oh, I don't know," she said, pretending to be blasé. "Not much, I guess. Like you're only *perfect,* is all."

But Devon was gone again, sailing out the train window, soaring through the gray sky, looking for a blond Adonis on a motorcycle.

Picturing King and Inez together, her heart broke as they saddled the wind, becoming small as circus pinwheels in a rearview mirror— a handsome, laughing boy and a beautiful girl soaring off on a great adventure. Just the two of them alone.

Without her.

How many times had she felt that way before?

"You are just like them, Devon Barnes," she could hear her Grandmother Maybelle say. "A wild dreamer same as your daddy. More pig guts than horse sense. And just as willful and stubborn as that mama of yours."

Devon's grandmother was very rich. So were her four sons, who had parlayed the land their Texas ancestors had deeded them into vast wool and mohair ranches until they owned "everything in Mills County the squirrels didn't want or the cows didn't drink."

Devon had grown up in Mullin, a bump in the road between Goldthwaite and Brownwood that looked just like the dried-up hick town in *The Last Picture Show.* There was no picture show in Mullin, but years later, when Devon saw the movie on TV, she would swear Peter Bogdanovich had filmed it in her backyard.

Devon's father was the youngest of Maybelle's boys, the one who caused her the most pain. Tom and Bridges and Rodney spent their lives riding horses and driving tractors. They went to Texas A&M, married Dallas girls, and helped nail the sign over the Mullin bus station that warned black passengers passing through: "Nigger, don't let the sun set on you in Mills County!"

Harris Barnes was different. His three brown-eyed brothers were weathered as old Stetsons, sported moustaches, and looked like Marlboro ads. Harris was fair and freckled, with a shock of black hair and eyes blue as gumdrops. He looked young and vulnerable, like Robert Walker, and spent his four years at Baylor writing passionate editorials for the campus paper blaming the state legislature for spending too much money on the football team instead of a new library and student symphony.

Once, during a student rodeo, Harris was burned in effigy by the entire agriculture department; and his brothers, who were sitting in the bleachers, didn't even let out a rebel yell in protest. "Damn fool made the whole Barnes family look like a bunch of dumb-ass mules," they complained to Maybelle, who calmly tried to salve their wounded macho egos, without much success, by saying, "Now boys, your brother's just twenty years ahead of his time, that's all."

Nobody crossed Maybelle, but the Barnes boys always considered Harris the black sheep of the family. They hadn't seen anything yet.

Too weak to attend his senior class commencement exercises because he was in the middle of a particularly debilitating case of hepatitis ("One of them Yankee Communist diseases," snorted Tom), Harris tried to join the army. He had an early premonition of things to come as news filtered home about the storm clouds gathering over Europe, and he wanted to be ready for the action. But the army rejected him from service duty because of a hole in his heart the size of a watermelon seed. At last, thought Maybelle, the chance we've been waiting for. Now Harris will manage his share of the interests in the ranch business and amount to something.

Harris had other ideas. He came home from college and started a newspaper in the old deserted Mullin drugstore. Clearing tumbleweeds from the pile of dead mesquite that blew down Main Street and emptied into Feeney's boarded-up drugstore where the windows had long been punched out by Saturday night rednecks, he installed a printing press and surrendered what was left of his frail health to "enlightening the dead consciences of the flea-brained hillbillies still dumb enough to live in Mills County."

The venture gnawed away his capital like a hungry alligator. The peanut farmers from Rising Star and Priddy who milled around in their Justin boots and Roy Rogers shirts playing dominoes and sipping Dr. Peppers outside the *Mullin Weekly Call* were not interested in stories about a madman named Hitler or the Nazi invasion of Czechoslovakia. They were interested in the price of pork rinds and who was screwing Millie Daws, the waitress at the Howdy Neighbor Truck Stop Café on Highway 84. The paper had twenty-five paid subscribers and was $50,000 in debt when Maybelle closed it down. Harris never forgave her and they were at war from that day forward.

Devon's father moved to Shreveport at the urging of some Jewish friends who wanted him to organize a union among the cotton pickers and cane cutters in northern Louisiana. They worked out of basement room in the only synagogue in Shreveport. For all Harris knew, it was the only one in the South.

Harris knew nothing about Jews. "There are only two Jews in Texas," Maybelle had told him once, "Mr. Neiman and Mr. Marcus."

But these Jews were poor and dedicated to helping oppressed minorities, and that's all Harris cared about. "You know the difference between karate and judo?" he asked them once, trying to win them over. "Karate is used for self-defense and judo is used to make bagels." The joke went over like a dead sparkplug. Once he left a ham and cheese sandwich in the office fridge near the mimeograph machine and they had to call in a rabbi to bless the refrigerator.

But they loved him in the field. Harris stood on the red clay, his Yankee loafers sinking in mud, and handed out leaflets to bewildered cane cutters. He made speeches in sugar cane fields, informing people with faces like parchment paper of their rights. He was insulted, threatened, and mocked. The tires on his Ford were slashed and once, on his way to a meeting of cotton gin wholesalers in Alexandria, the Klan fired shotgun blasts at his car and broke his windshield before speeding on down the Dixie Highway.

"If the damn fool gets his head shot off, it'll serve him right," said his brother Tom, after hearing about his escapades at the Howdy Neighbor Truck Stop Café. Maybelle suffered every indignity in a silent rage.

One day, on the banks of the Cane River in Natchitoches, Harris was talking up the advantages of a cotton picker's union with his customary Baptist Sunday-go-to-meetin' zeal, when he spotted a skinny little gal in a gunnysack dress with her arm raised above a head of hair the color of an orange creamsicle. "This union," she said in a voice half-moonshine, half-giggle, "will it keep these guys from bailing me up with the rest of the cotton?"

Harris was in love.

Her name, she told him over a cherry Coke at the Boll Weevil Cafe, was Mavis Toomey. She worked for a sewing factory where they took raw cotton and spun it into yarn, weaving and dying it into vertical patterns for nylon-blend pants suits and elastic-band circus-stripe stretch tops for a sportswear manufacturer in Baltimore.

Mavis made half a cent per seam and an extra four cents for each buttonhole. She had saved $100 in four years, which she reckoned made her just about the richest gal in Natchitoches.

"You don't have a Chinaman's chance of startin' a union here, boy," she told Harris. "Never has been one, never will be. These coonasses are wise to you and if you don't go back to Texas they'll serve you for red-eye gravy and send you home in a jar."

Harris had never met a girl with so much spunk. She taught him how to peel the tails off crawfish and make gumbo and dirty rice. On the days she played hooky from the mill they'd lie under the loblolly pines drinking Jax beer and talking about the future. Harris confided how he wanted to make the world a better place and Mavis said she reckoned all it would take to make her happy was a new Nash with real sideboards you could stand on. Harris promised to buy her one if she went home to Texas with him.

They were married the following Thursday.

But life didn't work out like a Lana Turner movie. Maybelle hated her new daughter-in-law on sight and cut Harris off without a penny. They lived in a trailer house on farm road 183, eight miles from Mullin, where Devon was born in 1940. She was named for a place in England Harris had seen in a "Bundles for Britain" poster at the post office— a place of rolling meadows and fertile valleys that stood out in peaceful contrast to the grim reminders of approaching war.

Four years later, it was ironically the same place that bore the final postmark from Harris's brother Rodney, who was killed in a London air raid while serving with the 9th Infantry Division. The name served as a nasty reminder to the Barnes family of something gone wrong in paradise. Even when the war was over and Maybelle had forgotten what it was, she remembered only that there was something about the name she didn't like. The word *Devon* stuck in her craw like a chicken bone. She grudgingly called the girl "D" for short, when she called her at all.

With two brothers stationed in faraway places like Dunkirk and Guam, Tom, the eldest, managed the wool business at home while Harris, the baby, disgraced the family further by organizing demonstrations to protest segregated training camps in Texas. Then he devoted himself to the humanitarian task of voluntarily organizing and shipping blankets, medical supplies, and mobile canteens to the Allied forces overseas, canvasing door-to-door for cash contributions.

After the war, dreams of prosperity turned into further nightmares for Mavis and her daughter. Harris was out of the state most of the time, squandering the portion of his dead brother Rodney's inheritance that fell to his trust by Texas law. He invested in get-rich schemes that always failed. To make ends meet, Mavis worked at the A & W Root Beer Stand, making chiliburgers, while Devon got farmed out during the day to whichever aunt would take her in. On rare occasions, Maybelle would pick her up in front of the trailer on Saturday mornings in her red Cadillac and floorboard it down the highway before Mavis could say good morning.

At home, she lived on peanut butter and Cheezits; at Maybelle's ranch there was always chicken and biscuits and homemade ice cream. This is where her grandmother, whose eyes were fierce and huge as the bull's-eyes on a target board, disdainfully relayed the latest news of her father's whereabouts.

Harris's first disaster was a slice of property in Florida in the middle of what turned out to be an uninhabitable swamp. The U.S. Environmental Board condemned the water and declared the sale illegal. Harris only got a nickel back on each dollar of his investment.

Then he got involved in a scheme to move an amusement park to a town in Arizona, only to discover he couldn't interest any businessmen in the deal. Harris was stuck with ten thousand bumper stickers.

Next came a dry cleaning establishment in the middle of the Panhandle where the humidity was so high it took the crease out of your pants the minute you got out of the door. Even Maybelle could've told him you don't landscape a golf course in Fargo, North Dakota, where it snows seven months a year.

Harris invested his last dime in a resort near the Mojave Desert in California. After signing the deal, he discovered there was no way to pump water to the property, so nobody built on it. Harris was undaunted. Instead of moving into the center cities like everybody else, he was hell-bent on moving people back to the land. Who knew there would be a fuel crisis? Who knew economic necessity would force postwar veterans to migrate toward urban renewal?

Years later, when she was old enough to read and understand the follies of economics, Devon was shown a book by her grandmother. Some writer had compiled a list of the six biggest real estate frauds and land defaults in American history. Harris Barnes was involved in five of them.

As a child growing up in the dust and deprivation of postward Texas, all Devon knew or cared about was the fact that her father was never around to love. When she saw him, he was a hail fellow well met, grinning ear to ear with a smile wide as the Pecos River. He took her to see her first picture show in Austin when she was seven. It was *Rich Girls Don't Cry* with Gilda Greenway.

On the way home her beloved daddy bought her a Gilda Greenway paper doll book at Woolworth's. She kept them in a shoe box under her bed in the trailer and on blue days she dressed her favorite movie star in bathing suits, mink coats, and evening gowns and pretended they were both visiting her father in California, where his last letter was postmarked.

The last she heard he had followed the fruit pickers to a place called Bakersfield, somewhere in the San Joaquin Valley, where he died of a fever. She never forgave him for that, and neither did Mavis. If Devon knew the pang of loneliness, her mother ate it night and day. Even in a hick town like Mullin, Mavis's awkwardness stuck out. Her speech was rough and lumpy as the rock clay of northern Louisiana, her clothes ill-fitting as potato sacks. Unprepared for the responsibilities of motherhood, she neglected Devon, leaving her to Harris's relatives to feed and clothe while she worked long hours at the root beer stand and baked pecan pies at night for the Mullin Bakery.

After Harris died, when it finally hit her that she'd never see a penny of the Barnes fortune, Mavis started selling Stanley home products. With arms full of cleaning fluids, mops, and brushes, she spent her days driving up and down the dusty dirt roads of Mills County in her Nash, ringing doorbells, drinking coffee with farmers' wives, and selling her wares. She started as a dealer, but by 1950, when Devon was ten, she had hired five other women and was drawing a percentage from their sales. She sold the trailer, moved to a motel with a swimming pool in Austin, and worked her way up to the position of branch manager. Maybelle had a hissy fit. "No granddaughter of mine is gonna be livin' in no motel," she hollered at Mavis. "The child's gonna grow up as ignorant as you are."

Devon was certain her mother would explode. "Well, what have you got to say?" Maybelle roared.

"Don't let the door hit you on your way out," was her reply. Maybelle left, all right, and dragged her granddaughter with her. From that day on, Devon lived on the big ranch like an unwanted visitor. Her days were alike: school, chores, rules, obedience, and discipline.

Once a month Maybelle put on her pre-creased white Brisa panama with a six-inch crown to keep her head cool and her gingham shirt with white pearl snap buttons, stuffed her Levi's into her custom-made Tony Lama boots from El Paso, threw a mink coat over her shoulders, and drove to San Angelo in her red Cadillac to order seeds and supplies from M. L. Leddy and Sons. On these rare occasions, Devon would tag along and wait in one of the air-cooled movie houses.

"Those damned places gonna give you polio," her grandmother said with a scowl. But she was secretly relieved to have the girl off her hands. In the darkness, fortified by a bag of chewy Mary Janes, Devon went to war with Van Johnson, attended board meetings with Rosalind Russell, cried her eyes out with Margaret O'Brien, and fell in love with Gilda Greenway. The movies were the only place where the child had a life of her own.

Devon had a cheerful disposition and an open face brightened by a broad grin. Her violet eyes were a dramatic variation on her father's smiling baby blues. By the time she was thirteen, though, her expression had grown guarded and solemn, her full mouth pulled into a thin, unsmiling line. The father she worshiped could never protect her now, could never take her away on the trains that passed through Texas in the middle of the night on their way to palm trees and movie stars, and her mother rarely paid any attention to her at all.

Sometimes Mavis would stop by the ranch on her way to a sales meeting long enough to drum into her head one of the Stanley slogans. "The speed of the leader is the speed of the gang," her mother would say. She heard it so often it became a rule to live by.

But Devon knew she would never be a leader. She was a follower, a dreamer like her dashing, romantic daddy. So she lost herself in the movies, sent away for autographed photos, collected them on Dixie Cups. In her dreams, she swam with Esther Williams, skated with Sonja Henie, danced with Betty Grable, and suffered with Gilda Greenway.

Gilda was her favorite. She never forgot that day after *Rich Girls Don't Cry* when her father told her she was just as pretty as Gilda, that when she grew up she'd be just like her. Rich girls didn't cry, but poor girls did.

Maybelle didn't approve of movies, or much of anything else. Watching her granddaughter slip farther from her influence, she made the decision to send Devon to the Westbridge School—an eastern boarding facility with nothing to recommend it but the fact that K. C. Carstairs, the biggest tycoon in Brownwood, had sent his daughter Vicki there for two years and Vicki had come home engaged to the richest man Mills County had ever seen.

Maybelle gave Devon one of her old purses to take away to school.

In a zipper pocket inside the purse, speckled with cigarette tobacco and lint, was a letter her father had sent from California a month before he died. It told about the vineyards, the bruised peaches he lived on, the dreams that had never died in his heart. And it told how happy he was that Devon had nourishing food and a good home where people loved her.

But most of all—and this was the true part—it said, "True happiness comes from living a useful, productive life and not screwing everyone to the wall to do it." So Devon took the letter east with her, packed carefully next to the Gilda Greenway paper dolls he had given her when she was seven, soiled with the stains of a thousand chiliburgers. And she left home, holding her father's definition of happiness close to her heart. So she wasn't June Allyson, but was June Allyson happy?

FOUR

FEBRUARY 12, 1956

B
etween a dry Manhattan and a gold cigarette case from Cartier, a cigarette with lipstick traces still smoldered in the "21" ashtray.

Gilda Greenway was missing from the table when May and her guests arrived. Inez and King were waiting in the entrance, by a crackling fire hissing with the sound of maple logs. King was scowling. The maitre d' had forced him to don one of the restaurant's boring compulsory ties and everyone was eyeing him suspiciously. "They're not this stuffy at Downey's," he groused, submitting to the dress code with reluctance.

Jack Kriendler and Jerry Burns, two of the owners, brightened considerably when they saw May Fischoff, and ushered them to Frankie Fischoff's table personally. They were reserved in the "21" club room near the bar. ("Where the A tables are," whispered May to Inez, who was trying to fake indifference.) The lighting was flattering at "21," one of the reasons Gilda preferred it, and the noise from the bar was friendly and full of laughter. Inez thought it odd that the tablecloths were red-and-white checks, just like the pizzerias in Brooklyn, but when she saw the gleaming china, so clean and white she could almost see her reflection, she knew she was a long way from Fulton Street.

"My God," Inez gasped. "There's Faye Emerson!"

"And Arthur Godfrey," added Devon under her voice and through her fingers, trying not to look conspicuous.

"And he's looking right at *me!*" gushed Inez, patting her hair.

King stared at the king of broadcasting's Hawaiian shirt. "They didn't force *him* to wear a used tie."

"They're on a lunch break. CBS is right down the street." May pretended to be nonplussed. "*All* the executives and television people eat here."

Frankie stood to hug his daughter, after some prompting from his wife, and even managed to wish May a happy birthday. Then he exchanged a quick glance with Devon as King was introduced. May saw it, but stumbled on.

"He's a friend of Harriet's, Daddy," she tried gamely to explain, biting off what remained of her last fingernail. "King is, um, an actor, Daddy. Or at least he's going to be, isn't he, Devon? Maybe you can be his agent when he's famous. Um, this is my daddy. I mean, my father—"

"Hi, Mr. Fischoff," Devon said quickly, trying to rescue her sputtering roommate, kissing Frankie's tanned cheek.

May was always as nervous as Victor Moore around her parents, especially her father. "He likes you better," she'd once complained to Devon. "Don't worry about it, though. He likes *everyone* better than me." Devon had tried to assure May it wasn't true. But even now, the look of impatience on his face dissolved as he turned to smile warmly at Devon, then Inez.

"Well, aren't you pretty?" he said, flirting with Inez. "Look at her, Norma. A beauty, no? This one takes care of herself." He glanced significantly at May. "And are you an aspiring actress, young lady?"

"Oh, no, Mr. Fischoff, I'm going to be a writer."

"Don't you remember, Daddy? Devon's the actress—"

Devon shot her a desperate look.

"Did you hear that, Norma? A writer. What the world needs now, no? Another Dorothy Parker to drive us all crazy. Sit down, sit down everyone."

"Where's Gilda?" May asked.

"She wanted a doggie bag for Tallulah, so she actually talked Kriendler into letting her invade the kitchen for a piece of porterhouse steak."

Tallulah was the surrogate child Gilda took with her wherever she went. A mixed-breed—part cocker spaniel, part dachsund—named Tallulah because her growl was so deep, like Bankhead's. While Gilda dined, Tallulah would wait in the limo with the chauffeur, thumping her tail impatiently. "She may be just a hooked rug that barks, but she's a helluva lot more loyal than most of my so-called friends," was Gilda's standard response when anyone complained about the dog, who occasionally forgot she was housebroken.

May took a breadstick, smeared butter over it, and finished it in three bites. She'd consumed three Hershey bars with almonds before she even left Grand Central, but she was still starving. "May, if you can lay off the starch for a couple of minutes, I'd like to propose a toast to you and your beautiful mother."

May was pierced with humiliation, but her mother began to stroke her unruly hair, and soon she was practically purring under Norma's tender attention.

Frankie began twisting the cork on the Moet & Chandon chilling in the silver ice bucket next to his chair. "But darling, it's not *my* birthday," Norma Fischoff said gently, as he poured a glass for each of the guests. "Besides, shouldn't we wait for Gilda?"

Frankie put down his glass, took his wife's hand away from May's hair, then cupped her face in his own hands, kissing her nose. "Sixteen years ago today, sweetheart. I almost lost you that day, and there isn't enough champagne in France to celebrate how I feel about you."

Devon loved watching them. They were always like this—at school when they visited May; at their Christmas party in New York. Watching them was like watching a movie with William Powell and Myrna Loy. Although sometimes she found herself wishing, for May's sake, that they'd behave like *real* parents. Not that she knew how real parents behaved, but this got a little yucky.

Anyway, Norma was more beautiful than the mothers in lux ads. She was slim and tall, with blonde hair that did not come out of a bottle, as Frankie proudly pointed out to everyone. Frankie also liked the fact that she was taller than he, even in the low-heeled shoes she often wore. Devon pegged her for Dorothy McGuire. And Frankie, with his thick wavy hair, perpetual tan, and those big brown eyes May had inherited from him, looked like a Jewish Glenn Ford, gooey and grinning with love. They were the perfect couple, Frankie and Norma Fischoff. May even had the newspaper clippings to prove it.

King Godwin shifted beside Devon. As he stretched his arm along the back of the banquette, Devon suddenly found herself sitting very nearly in his embrace. "Are they really married?" he whispered.

She couldn't look at him. That he should even whisper the word *married* to her, that she could feel his breath on her cheek, nearly paralyzed her with pleasure. She wanted to turn her head, take King Godwin's face in her hands, and kiss him as tenderly as Frankie had kissed Norma.

"How do you do it, kiddo?" Frankie was saying to Norma. "Hey, you get more beautiful every year. You know," he addressed them all, "this girl could have been a bigger star than Gilda—if she hadn't been nuts and married me."

"Oh, Frankie, stop. I never had the talent. One lucky break—"

"I'll tell you what was a lucky break. That you even looked twice at me, was the luckiest break in my life—"

"Sonuvabitch," a voice boomed suddenly. "Bring me a bucket of cold water, the Fischoffs are at it again!"

"Gilda!" May shouted and leapt up to greet her godmother, knocking over Norma's glass of champagne on her brand new silk Dior.

Devon saw it all in an instant: Norma gasped. Frankie stood red-faced with anger. Inez giggled nervously. King Godwin murmured, "Oh, shit." May cringed. And Gilda Greenway, arms outstretched to receive her godchild, smiled radiantly.

Devon had expected to be disappointed. She knew Gilda Greenway would look different in real life. She wouldn't be in costume or wearing movie makeup. Her hair wouldn't be coiffed and lacquered each time she moved, the way it was in VistaVision. She wouldn't be ten feet tall. Devon had prepared herself for disappointment, but Gilda was breathtaking.

Standing there, arms outstretched, hands gloved in creamy kid, diamond bracelet glittering from her slender wrist, fitted silk draping her spectacular figure, she was impossibly beautiful. Devon knew the dress. Helen Rose had designed it for *Fools Rush In*.

Her eyes, the gray-green cat's eyes that had swept seductively over Gable's brawn, reduced Cary Grant to a comical stutter, and insolently met Patrick Wainwright's clear gaze, now devoured chubby May with love. Devon couldn't believe her flaming hair, the coppery tresses that thousands of GIs who pined over her "pinups" knew as well as her famous pearl necklace.

It was the sight of those fabled pearls, that long strand of creamy, priceless, perfect pearls that nearly unhinged Devon. She couldn't tear her eyes away from her heroine. Gilda's long, dark lashes swept suddenly in Devon's direction. Seeing the pale, startled child staring at her, she winked.

If May hadn't run into Gilda's arms just then, blocking the goddess from view, hiding the dazzling, hypnotic pearls, Devon would have died on the spot, incinerated by excitement. Sitting beside King Godwin, staring at Gilda Greenway, Devon Barnes would have died, gladly, in a banquette at "21."

"Happy birthday, baby." Gilda cheerfully ignored the fact that May was close to tears. "Why, you look so grown-up," she cooed, stroking May's back soothingly. "She looks fabulous, doesn't she, Norma? Doesn't she, Frankie? Just fabulous, baby. It's so goddamn *good* to see you."

"Yes, she looks wonderful," said Norma. "Frankie, please, I'm fine. The dress is fine. It was only champagne."

"Champagne? What were you trying to do, baby, launch the SS *Normandie?*" Gilda laughed and May smiled, at last. Even Frankie Fischoff chuckled.

The waiter brought a new bottle of Moet to the table, "compliments of Mr. Kriendler," and uncorked it carefully. May squeezed into the banquette beside her glamorous godmother, introducing her friends.

"Gilda, this is Kingston Godwin," she said.

"He's auditioning for the Actor's Workshop soon," blurted Inez. "He's going to be a movie star."

King Godwin coughed. "An actor," he corrected, "not a movie star. Anyway, I'm just thinking about it—"

"Enough to know the difference, I guess." Smiling, Gilda saluted him with her Manhattan, then took a sip.

He reddened. "What I meant was—"

"Forget it. I know what you meant," she said kindly. Then she laughed. "It's a shame, though. With those eyes."

"He's already been in two movies," Inez announced proudly.

King winced. "Hey, come on now."

Frankie Fischoff shot Gilda a quizzical look, but she was studying King, peering at him silently over the rim of her Manhattan. She liked his looks. The boy was sexy as hell. If she were only a bit younger . . .

"Devon wants to be a movie star, too," said loyal May. "Don't you, Devon?"

Devon shut her eyes and thought, Oh, God. How could May do this to me? But when she opened them again, May was staring at her with such dewy-eyed affection and pride that she acquiesced.

"Well, sure," she said. "I mean, who wouldn't want to be? Why you'd have to crazy—"

"Oh, man," King mumbled disdainfully, and slumped down in his seat.

"I wouldn't," Inez volunteered, arrogantly.

"Inez is a writer," May told Gilda. "She writes the best poems. She even won a scholarship to Westbridge on account of her writing."

"Why, that's swell." Gilda beamed. "I'm wild for writers. When I first hit Hollywood, it was writers who saved my ass. Scruffiest bunch of alcoholics you ever saw."

King's arm brushed the back of Devon's neck. His hand fell casually over her shoulder, fingers extending toward and casting a warm shadow over the upper reaches of her chest.

She stiffened, more afraid he'd felt her heart thudding than he'd touch her breast. She took a deep breath and said, conversationally, "So, uh, was that the truth? I mean, have you really acted in two motion pictures?"

"Yeah, I was in two pictures, but I wouldn't call what I did 'acting.'" He straightened abruptly. "What do you mean, 'Is that the truth?' " he demanded, suddenly aware that she might be challenging his honesty.

"Well—"

"Truth is all there is," King told her. "If you knew anything about acting, if you knew anything about *life,* you'd know that."

"If I hurt your feelings, I'm sorry." She could barely breathe.

"Hey, listen," he said sullenly, "if you knew anything about acting, maybe I'd be upset."

She felt as though he'd slapped her. "Thanks a lot," she gulped, turning away from him.

Gilda was talking to the others. "Hey, this is a party—not Madison Square Garden. I've been monopolizing it long enough. It's May's birthday," she concluded. "And I don't think we should wait another minute for the menu."

"I don't know what to order," said Devon, trying to disguise her drawl.

"Neither did I, honey, the first time I came here," Gilda said, ignoring the waiter who had suddenly appeared. "I was fresh out of the hills of Oklahoma and I came to New York with my sister Vy. MGM paid for us, and this talent scout took us to the Stork Club and I ordered a glass of chocolate milk." The laugh started in her midriff and worked its way up to her throat. "I didn't take long to catch on, though. After that I just ate whatever they brought out—as long as it was expensive and on fire!"

May had been to "21" before. Her mother had also taken her to places like the Colony and Quo Vadis. But Devon and Inez had never been anywhere fancier than Walgreen's. Half of the menu might as well have been written in Sanskrit.

"I think I'll have the *beignets de cervelle sauce tomate,*" announced Inez, knowing only that it had something to do with tomatoes.

"What's that?" Devon asked.

Gilda laughed and leaned forward, wrinkling her nose. "Cow brain fritters with ketchup." Everyone roared while Inez turned green. "Don't worry, doll, the first time I came to '21' I tried to eat an entire artichoke with a knife and fork. Why don't you try the spaghetti?"

When their orders were taken (Devon asked politely for chicken hash, King settled for a hamburger), Gilda demanded they bring on the graft. "Not another minute, Frankie, I want to see how the kid cleaned up!"

"Not another minute," Norma agreed, picking up the tempo. "Frankie, darling." She drew a Bergdorf-Goodman shopping bag from under the table and passed it to her husband. "Will you do the honors?"

"For you, my beauty, anything." He winked at her, then covered his eyes and made a show of reaching blindly into the bag. "Well, what have we here?" he asked, slowly drawing out a small pale blue box tied with a white ribbon. "Let's see. Is this Norma's present?" He turned the box this way and that. "No, I don't think it's for Norma. Well, then, it must be for—"

"Me!" May shouted.

"Gilda!" Frankie laughed.

"You bastard," Gilda said.

"A bauble. A nothing. For you, my darling star. To celebrate the most rewarding sixteen-year relationship—"

Gilda snatched the little box out of Frankie's hand, and resolutely tucked it into her purse. "Sweetheart," she growled, blowing him a kiss.

Bewildered, he turned to Norma. "She's not even going to open it?"

"Frankie, darling," his wife said, "it's *May's* birthday."

"You think I forgot?" Frankie reached into the bag and brought out a smaller blue box, extending it across the table to May. "Happy birthday. You believe this? Your mother and your gorgeous but sometimes a little cuckoo godmother thought I forgot your birthday? In sixteen years, have I ever forgotten such a thing?" He looked at May. "What's the matter with you? You look like you're going to cry. What is going on here, has everyone gone bananas on me?"

"I'm just happy, Daddy. Honest."

"So open it, already."

Sniffling, May tugged at the delicate white ribbon. "Oh, look, it's from Tiffany's. Isn't that great? Oh, Daddy, Mama, thank you." She opened the box and carefully drew out a gold charm—a circle of gold around a tiny gold birthday cake with a candle flanked by the numbers 1 and 6. The candle was lit with a diamond.

"I know a diamond isn't your birthstone, darling, but I wanted you to have it. It came from your grandma Alyce's wedding ring."

Frankie was stunned. "Norma, you took a stone from your mother's ring? What made you do such a thing?" He turned back to May. "Well, I hope you appreciate it."

"Oh, I do, I love it."

Gilda stood to let May slide out of the black booth and rush to Norma, to kiss her mother's cheek.

"Don't forget Daddy," Norma whispered. "He picked out the charm."

"Oh, you picked it out," May squealed, hurrying to Frankie, who offered his cheek. With a kiss, she threw her arms around him. "It's the greatest, Daddy. I love it. I—"

"For God's sake, May, do you have to make a scene? I'm glad you like it. Just say thank you and go sit down." He straightened his tie and smoothed back his wavy hair.

"I'm sorry," May said miserably.

"Frankie," Norma began, but his eyes were downcast. "He's just cross because he needs another boilermaker. Right, darling? Go on, honey," she said to May, "sit down and let's order another round before the food arrives." Norma started to signal for a waiter.

Suddenly, Inez shrieked. "My God, it's Humphrey Bogart! And he's heading this way! I think I'm going to die."

"Bogey!" cried Gilda.

"How's it goin', gorgeous?" Humphrey Bogart and Gilda Greenway were embracing, right in the middle of "21." The Four Fans could not believe their eyes. Even Frankie was impressed. Introductions were made. Inez stared at her hand, which Humphrey Bogart had just shaken. She felt faint.

"What are you doing in town?" Gilda asked.

"Doin' time, doin' time. Earl Wilson's over in the corner pumping me for some hot news about my health."

"How are you?" asked Gilda, touching his arm with concern.

"Fine, fine," he coughed. "Starting a new picture next month for Harry Cohn. A John P. Marquand story. Betty needs a new pair of shoes."

"Give her my love. And good luck."

Humphrey Bogart said he was glad to meet them. Inez knew in her heart he was looking directly at her when he said it. "I will never wash this hand again."

"He isn't looking at all well," Gilda said to Frankie. "He's lost a lot of weight. I've heard rumors."

"I thought he looked super," said Inez, flushed with the glamor of it all. "But who's Betty?"

Gilda laughed. "Baby, that's Lauren Bacall's real name—Betty."

"Okay, okay," Frankie said, trying to restore the table to order. "There's one more piece of business here."

From the shopping bag, he took a final gift. A Tiffany box slightly larger than the ones bearing Gilda's and May's gifts. He presented the last box to Norma. "Sixteen years ago today, I almost lost you," he told her solemnly. "I would not have wanted to live if, God forbid, you hadn't. She almost died for you, kid," he told May.

"Yes, Daddy, I know," May whispered, flushing with shame. "I'm sorry, Mama."

"Don't be silly," Norma began, but Frankie silenced her.

"This is my thank you, to you and to God, Norma."

May stood behind her mother, head lowered, tears streaming down her cheeks.

Opening the box, Norma took out a solid gold compact, round and delicate, slightly larger than a man's pocketwatch.

"Open it up," Frankie urged her. "Go on, darling."

She lifted the lid and out of the gold case wafted the clean, sweet scent of her favorite Schiaparelli face powder and the distinctive strains of "I Only Have Eyes For You."

May sobbed.

"If we're finished with the Fischoff gifts," Gilda said, "please allow a lowly godmother to present a small token."

"Not too small," Frankie cracked.

"May, I have two tickets, front row center, baby, to the hottest opening on Broadway. Will you be my date tonight?"

May shook her head. What was the point of even trying? It was time she faced facts.

"Please," said Gilda. "You remember my friend Avery Calder, don't you?"

"The Way Back Home?" King shouted. "You've got tickets to Calder's new play? Oh, man, that's fantastic! Incredible!"

"It's Avery's best play in years," Gilda told May. "Starring none other than Patrick Wainwright, in his triumphant return to Broadway."

"I can't, Gilda," May whispered. "I don't feel well. Thank you, really."

Frankie shook his head. "What the hell's the matter now? It's your birthday. We're throwing a lunch for you at '21'. Gilda's here, all the way from California. All your friends are here. And you're bawling like a baby. What does it take to make you happy, May?"

"No kidding, May," King said, "you really ought to go. I mean, Avery Calder . . . he's God, man. The best playwright in America. Maybe in the world. And, hell, Patrick Wainright is about the biggest star in Hollywood—"

"He's just Gilda's boyfriend," May blurted out. She gasped, covering her mouth. "Gosh, I'm sorry Gilda," she blubbered. "Honest, I didn't mean it." With a terrified look at Frankie, she fled.

Devon followed her to the powder room.

"Don't be silly, May," she urged. "Gilda's not mad at you. No one's mad at you."

"He hates me, he hates me," May shouted hysterically. "Why, Devon? I never did anything to hurt him. He's my father. And you know what the worst thing of all is? He won't let me near my own mother! He can't stand it if she looks at anybody but him, even her own daughter. It's like he's crazy about her, Devon. It's not just a saying. He's really, truly *crazy* about her. And don't tell me I'm imagining things!"

A hundred soothing lies came to mind as Devon cradled May in her arms. And then she heard King Godwin's strong sullen voice: *Truth is all there is. If you knew anything about life, you'd know that.*

"No, you're not imagining it, May."

To her relief and amazement, May's sobbing began to subside.

"Do you think it's because she almost died when I was born?" she asked, hiccuping back the last of her tears. "I think he thinks it was my fault. It's not fair. I didn't even *know* her. He acts like I'm to blame for everything. For every single thing that goes wrong, like I'm a murderer or something. And if you wanna know, that's how I *feel* when I'm around him."

"Is that why you're always spilling stuff and breaking things and acting like such a *ninny* whenever you're around your parents?"

May shrugged forlornly. "I can't help it. You think I'm a crazy neurotic, don't you?"

"Not a chance."

"I just wanted to know. Gosh, I hope Gilda's not mad at me."

"Never," said Devon. "Now *that's* crazy."

Of course Gilda wasn't angry. In fact, when they returned to the table, they discovered that Gilda had confessed to the star-struck King and Inez that, indeed, Mr. Wainwright was the man she loved, but as everyone knew he was married, and so their love had to remain . . . a devoted friendship only.

Inez sighed. "That's beautiful. I'll never tell a soul."

"You're not mad at me?" May knelt to kiss Gilda's cheek.

"Never."

"That's exactly what Devon said."

"Then she's bright as well as beautiful." Gilda smiled gratefully at Devon, then turned back to May. "About the play this evening—"

"Why don't you take King with you?"

Gilda began to protest, but when she saw the girl's determined jaw, she patted her hand reassuringly. "Mr. Godwin," she turned to King, "if you're not otherwise engaged, how would you like to see a movie star bring Broadway to its knees tonight?"

"Oh, wow." King raked his blond hair with his hand. "You really mean it?"

Gilda nodded.

"I'm your man."

Gilda winked. "That's exactly what the *Daily News* will think."

"I didn't know you were in town, Gilda. What brings you to New York?"

"Speak of the devil," Gilda said, as Ed Sullivan suddenly appeared, his long, gloomy face looming above her. "Hello, Irish. I hope you're here to be nice. But if you're digging for dirt, give me a break. I've got enough trouble with Kilgallen already."

Devon couldn't believe her ears. Ed Sullivan? *The* Ed Sullivan?

She'd been devouring his column in the *Daily News* ever since she'd come east and she never missed his Sunday night "Toast of the Town" on TV. He seemed to know everything about everyone. And here was Gilda, suddenly turned sour, talking to him as if she'd known him all her life.

"Mind if I send my photographer over for a picture? My hunch is you're here for the opening of Avery Calder's new play. Rumor has it you're a great admirer of the male lead."

Gilda didn't skip a beat. "Sure, Ed, anything for your readers. We'd love to have a picture, wouldn't we, kids?"

The photographer dropped to one knee in front of Gilda like a courtier paying homage to a queen.

"This way, Miss Greenway. Girls and boys, let's squeeze in together, okay? Big smiles all around?" He signaled for Devon and Inez to move closer to King.

Inez lifted King's arm and snuggled in beside him. Devon moved toward him cautiously. Without warning, King put his arm around her and clamped her tightly to him. Dazed, she glanced up at his face and was rewarded with a stunning, sheepish smile.

"That's it, that's nice," said the photographer. The flashbulb caught May with her mouth open.

"Oh, no," she said, "that was awful. I wasn't ready."

"Let's do it again," Gilda told the photographer. "All right, babies, watch me now."

Devon watched. She saw Gilda lick her lips and smile brightly. "Tongue behind your top teeth, like this. Do you see? Okay, try it."

Devon licked her lips and smiled and put her tongue behind her top teeth. She felt silly. She caught May's eye and May began to giggle. Inez glared at her. "Don't," she whispered. Then she, too, began to laugh. Devon looked at King. He was smiling now.

"That's it," Gilda said, looking right at Devon. "You've got it. Fabulous. Fabulous fucking face on the kid, Frankie. Did you see her? Okay, babies, big smiles at the count of three. The secret is to look directly into the center of the camera. Come on, Norma, let's show them how."

"No, no, my dress is a mess. Not me, darling."

Frankie tucked a fiver into the photographer's pocket. "Leave us out of this one, okay?"

"One, two, three," said Gilda.

The flash went off again. "Great. Thanks, Miss Greenway."

"So who have we here?" Sullivan asked, taking out a small spiral-bound notebook.

"Ed, meet four of my friends—"

"And fans?" Sullivan said with his characteristically toothy grin.

"Absolutely," Inez said.

"Oh, definitely," May and Devon announced in unison.

"Me, too, Mr. Sullivan," pronounced King in his best Actor's Workshop audition voice.

"The Pearls Girl and her Four Fans. . . . I like it," Sullivan said.

"Let's see how it plays in the morning edition," said Gilda.

"You've always played well, Gilda," Sullivan said.

"So I have, Irish, so I have . . . "

FIVE

1940

O n a snowy winter day, Big Ted Kearny, the Wall Street
tycoon, brought Gilda to the Fischoff-Donovan Agency for
the first time. She dressed carefully for the occasion in a navy
blue dress with white polka dots, carried a big square purse, and tried
her best to appear as composed as Ginger Rogers in *Fifth Avenue Girl*.

The agency shared the fourth floor of a building overlooking
Times Square on Forty-sixth and Broadway with a costume rental
house and a magician's equipment outlet. Fischoff-Donovan's outer
office was decorated with framed head shots of their clients. While Ted
Kearny conferred privately with Frankie Fischoff, Gilda gazed nervously at the photographs of heavies, ethnics, juveniles, and peroxided
tomatoes—the character actors who were the agency's bread and butter. She looked at the headshot of a freckled boy with an upturned Irish
nose. The kid was wearing a professionally engaging grin and a baseball
cap, peak turned to the side.

There was no name on the picture, but Gilda thought she recognized him from one of the two low-budget programmers she'd done bits in—*Babes in the Woods* and *Judy Falls in Love.* She'd played a woodland sprite in the first one, and a waitress in the second. She thought the Irish boy had been in one of the movies. His name was Danny or Donny or something.

Then she remembered. She'd danced with him in the jitterbug number at the malt shop. Between takes, he'd told her he was a regular, he'd done three Andy Hardy pictures on the Coast and was "in tight" with Mickey and Judy.

He was the first kid in the cast who'd tried to make friends with her. In fact, he was the only person on the set, except for the director, who'd spoken to her at all.

She liked him. He was friendly and treated her like a regular person. Then at the end of the day's shooting he saw her walking over to Kearny's big white convertible where the driver in his white chauffeur's uniform was holding the door for her. He watched her climb into the back seat where Ted Kearny was waiting. And she guessed he'd seen the kiss that followed.

The next day, when they had to do the jitterbug number again, he felt her up. And, just kidding around about it, just to tease Big Ted, she told him. Fairy dust. The boy disappeared.

A couple of days later, Kearny said, "Stay away from the guys on the set. They're kids. You get them all worked up. They don't know how to handle it."

She had been all of seventeen when they'd made that picture. The boy was nineteen. But Kearny was right. He was a kid and she wasn't. Hell, she'd already been through one abortion. She could have had a screaming brat on her hands, Ted reminded her, if Larry Malnish hadn't talked her into getting rid of it.

It was Ted Kearny's baby. She wished she hadn't let Malnish take her to the creepy doctor in Washington Heights. She had been so frightened she almost passed out on the dirty examining table. She kept her eyes closed tight, but she felt it all—the banging of her heart, the cold hands opening her, entering her, and the pain, like a hundred darning needles—until he said, "Okay, little girl, try to stay out of trouble next time."

But it had hurt so much. He had given her only one aspirin to chew.

Three hours later, while Gilda's sister Vy, who'd come up from Oklahoma with her as a companion, was brewing her some tea, she started bleeding. Terrified, she made Vy phone Larry Malnish.

"I'll be right over, Vy," he said. "Tell her not to move and not to worry."

The next thing she knew she was waking up in a nice clean bed at Lenox Hill Hospital and Larry Malnish was grinning like a sonuvabitch.

"It's all set, Gilda," he said. "Soon as you get out of here and get a little color back in that fantastic face of yours, we got a date with a screen test—for Sam Durand at Metro!"

Now here was Big Ted, walking out of Frankie's office with his arm around the agent, like Mutt and Jeff. He seemed to dwarf Frankie, but he had that effect on most people. Few men were as big as Ted Kearny.

"Mr. Fischoff's just been telling me he saw both your movies, honey," said Ted.

"You're a natural, Gilda, and you're also twice as gorgeous in person as you are on the screen. I wish I could stick around and talk to you for a while, but I gotta rush over to the hospital."

Without giving Gilda a chance to thank Mr. Fischoff for his compliments, Big Ted started helping her into her mink coat.

"Listen, Frankie, why don't we give you a lift over there? My driver's waiting for us downstairs. Frankie's wife just had a baby, Gilda."

Fischoff frowned. "It was touch and go for a while. My Norma almost died. I'd never have allowed her to go through this if I'd known, but the damn doctors promise me she's gonna be all right. I mean, kids are great and all that, but my Norma—well, we got something very special and—" Frankie's voice broke.

"C'mon, we better get going. Your girls are waiting for you," Kearny said heartily. "Hey, Gilda, I bet you'd like to take a peek at Frankie's daughter, wouldn't you? Gilda loves babies," he said as they closed the door to the office behind them. "I do, too. Yeah, this is a great day, Fischoff. You got yourself a brand-new daughter and a brand-new star."

When they got to the hospital, Frankie hurried off to see his wife, leaving Gilda and Ted at the nursery window.

"Which one do you think is his?" Gilda asked, staring at the infants wrapped in pink and blue swaddling blankets.

She looked up to find him gazing intently at the babies displayed in the window. A chill ran down her spine. Gilda thought of what Vy always said when she shivered like that: "Someone just walked on your grave."

The doctor at Lenox Hill had told her she could forget about any more babies.

"How can he know that?" she'd screamed at Larry Malnish. "He's wrong, I don't believe it!"

She'd gone crazy. She cursed the doctor, then the abortionist, with every vile obscenity she'd ever heard behind the barn in Oklahoma. When Larry had tried to calm her down, she cursed him too, and pounded his arms with all the strength of her hysterical fury.

Larry grabbed her wrists. "Hey, hold on, kid," he'd said. "Whatcha blaming me for? I woulda married you if it was mine. You want to beat someone up? Go beat up Big Ted."

Now, looking at Ted Kearny's face reflected in the nursery window, Gilda heard herself whispering, "God help me."

"Oh, Teddy, if only—" She began to sob. "Don't you wish—" She broke down completely and pressed her face into the warm fur collar of his coat.

"No," Kearny said, pulling a clean handkerchief out of his breast pocket to wipe away her tears, "don't be silly. I don't wish anything. Gilda, honey, I've got everything a man could ask for right now. I've got the most beautiful girl in the world in my arms. That's enough for me."

"Do you swear? Teddy, do you mean that?"

"Shhhhush," he said, patting her back.

Gilda looked through the nursery window again, wondering whether her baby had been a boy or a girl. She closed her eyes and thought, The first baby I see when I open my eyes will be mine.

She opened her eyes, and there was May Fischoff.

A nurse was gently cradling in her arms a sleeping infant. On the baby's wrist was a tiny bracelet of alphabet beads spelling out the name Fischoff. Someone must have informed the nurse that the child's father had come to see her because she held up the infant's wrist and gestured to Kearny.

Later, Frankie Fischoff joined them at the nursery window, but he didn't look in. "Let's go," he said to Kearny. "Norma's asleep. They'll call me as soon as she wakes up."

"Your daughter's beautiful," Gilda said as they walked out of the hospital.

"Terrible," Frankie said, almost chalky. "You should have seen her. My sweet, wonderful Norma." He looked pale, the sickly color of asbestos. "She almost died, the doctor said." He sighed and shook his head. "That I put her through such agony. Never again. God as my witness, she will never suffer like that again."

The same day Frankie Fischoff became Gilda's agent, Gilda became May's godmother. Gilda presented May with a gold locket and a silver spoon from Tiffany's, and Frankie presented Gilda with her first speaking part in a picture. She spoke one line of dialogue to Norma Shearer, but the public paid attention. And then, after a few more bits, came the picture—and the line—that launched her.

The picture was a wartime romance called *Night Anthem*. As the publicity posters proclaimed, it was "The Story of the Girls They Left Behind." Gilda played a virtuous chorus girl (in a lineup that included two other comely starlets, Janet Blair and Marilyn Maxwell). Peter Lorre was the Nazi-sympathizing nightclub owner who was trying to seduce her, while the faithful Gilda's boyfriend was overseas. In her big scene, Lorre grabbed her as she was coming offstage and forced her back against the wall.

"I'll give you everything," he rasped. "He's not coming back. And he's got nothing . . . *nothing.*"

Gilda tore free of the sweaty little villain, turned abruptly, and tossed over her shoulder the long strand of pearls she wore with her skimpy nightclub costume.

"He's got *me,*" she told the camera.

Men in the audience, particularly servicemen, went wild. Women loved her, too. Gilda spoke for them to the rich seducers, the draft dodgers, and the Nazi sympathizers. What did the brave GIs have that no amount of money could buy? Their love and fidelity.

"He's got *me,*" became a catchphrase, a song lyric, a line written in lipstick on powder room mirrors.

A strand of pearls became the goodbye gift most requested by fiancées of departing GIs. Two weeks before Christmas, Harry Winston reported a depleted inventory of every pearl necklace in the store. Newsreels showed women at Macy's battling over a bin of pearl necklaces.

The movie still of the moment showed the sultry young Gilda staring over her shoulder, pearls dripping down her nearly bare back, pearls and that amazing fiery auburn hair. Stills and posters were stolen from the fronts of countless movie theaters that fall.

Frankie ordered and distributed hundreds of copies of the shot. He had two girls working full-time, signing Gilda's name to glossy 8 × 10 photographs under the legend "You've got *me.*" Metro sent out thousands more.

Gilda became their "Pearls Girl." *Movietone News* showed her serving donuts at the Hollywood Stagedoor Canteen and autographing pictures of herself for a mob of servicemen at the USO in Times Square.

She was loved.

She was launched.

She was seen at parties, premieres, and bond rallies. She was interviewed on Bob Hope's radio program, and on *Hollywood Calling.* Louella Parsons broadcast an "exclusive" between Lustre-Creme commercials. She was photographed holding hands with every young stud in the studio stable and hiking up her skirt alongside Lana, and Ava, and Rita. *Photoplay* snapped her on a hayride with Peter Lawford. Sidney Skolsky described her as the girl most likely to land Hollywood's sly young millionaire bachelor, Howard Hughes. *Modern Screen* invited along its readers "The Day Van Johnson Fell for the Pearls Girl."

Anonymous, powerful, and ever-watchful, Ted Kearny choreographed his child-mistress's metamorphosis into a movie star. He hired a press agent to keep his name *out* of the gossip columns, and Gilda's *in*. With slick finesse, she was even linked with other men, younger men.

He had Larry Malnish supply the bodies—good-looking, fun-loving guys who needed publicity and rent money more than romance. He hired private detectives to make sure Gilda's companions observed the rules of the game. His goons reminded the amorous ones they had a lot to lose if they tried to link more than their names to Gilda.

Ted Kearny phoned Gilda daily from New York. He flew out to Hollywood to be with her at least once a month and to check on the progress of the estate he was building for her in Beverly Hills. The mansion was going to be as grand as San Simeon, as smart as Pickfair.

On Gilda's twentieth birthday, the studio threw a party for her on the set of *Gone Wrong*, the movie she'd recently finished filming. She was photographed feeding birthday cake to Herman Gehrig, a soccer player from Norway who had a bit part in the movie.

The picture ran in the *New York Daily Mirror*. Gilda braced herself for a jealous tirade. Instead, Kearny cabled to say they made a terrific-looking couple. "Were you thinking of marrying the guy?" he asked when he called that evening.

"Oh, no, Teddy," Gilda replied, horrified. "I'm in love with *you.*"

"Marry the kid. Do it for me."

"It was just a dumb crush, Teddy. Don't be mad." Gilda swore never to see the boy again, but Kearny was suddenly serious about marrying her off.

"Just for a little while," he told her. "Just to confuse the columnists, give them something new to think about. They'd eat it up. The Pearls Girl and the soccer star." And he could use a break from Gilda, he confided to Malnish.

He told Gilda that a big splashy wedding right after the premiere of *Gone Wrong* would give her career a fantastic boost. She played an easy girl who'd been around. A nice, white wedding would counteract the tough image, Kearny said. Sam Durand told her the same thing. So did her hairdresser and the studio publicist. Even Larry Malnish agreed.

Only Frankie thought she ought to wait and think about it. "Marriage is sacred," the agent advised solemnly. "It's not just a role you play until a director yells, 'Cut.' "

She didn't dare tell him that Kearny was pressing her to get married. She didn't dare admit, even to herself, that this was his way of punishing her for the innocent crush she'd had on Gehrig.

Gilda's marriage to the handsome young soccer player was front-page news. The night of her honeymoon, she phoned Ted Kearny. "What am I supposed to do now?" she asked the man she loved and trusted most in the world. "What is my next move, Teddy, you bastard?" she wept, drunkenly. "Am I supposed to tell him I got it shot off in the war?"

Kearny roared with laughter. "I love you, doll," he said. "Have a good time. Think of him as my birthday gift to you."

The marriage broke up a week before *Photoplay* was to run a four-play spread entitled "Hollywood's Dream Couple—Gilda and Gehrig." Instead, the studio promised *Photoplay* an exclusive on Gilda's broken heart. *Photoplay* gave the breakup two pages and was able to salvage some of the photographs from the ill-fated dream couple story.

Gehrig, they explained to their readers, was a Norwegian patriot forced to return to his war-torn land. Much as Gilda loved him, she was shattered by the revelation that theirs could be a marriage in name only until Norway was liberated. It was a marriage born of love, destroyed by war.

Herman Gehrig never bothered to read the studio's version of "The Truth About Gilda and Gehrig." He took the long way home, through Latin America. Living in style on Kearny's payoff, he was the star of the sports crowd and café society until VE Day.

Not wanting to alienate *Photoplay*'s rival, Metro offered *Modern Screen* an exclusive on "The Man Who Launched a Star." The story of how Larry Malnish discovered Gilda gave hope to scores of young, aspiring actresses and set cash registers ringing in neighborhood photography shops from Montana to Maine.

It was Larry Malnish who'd come up with the Norwegian patriot angle for *Photoplay*. As a reward, he was promoted from Kearny's pimp to a genuine studio talent scout. And it was Malnish who tried to warn Gilda about Kearny. He felt he owed her one, a big one, for having taken her to the abortionist in Washington Heights. Once in the studio commissary, when he brought up the subject of the abortion and tried to apologize, Gilda had stood up from the table where they were lunching. "Don't ever mention it to me again, you prick," she'd said, and turned abruptly and left the restaurant. The next day, she greeted him cheerfully, as if the incident had never occurred.

"If you're so nuts about Ted, marry him," Malnish would say.

"Don't be an ass, Larry," Gilda invariably responded, smiling her sad, dimpled smile. She was stewed half the time now. Herman Gehrig had introduced her to Aquavit, a potent Scandinavian liquor, and Gilda had taken to swigging it back to back with beer. A Norwegian boiler-maker, she called it.

"You know what would happen to me if I married a guy older than my father?" She narrowed her gray-green cat's eyes at him one night at Ciro's and smiled her flawless, joyless smile. "Mayer would drop me like a hot potato. The fans would, too. They'd fucking crucify me. Overnight I'd go from being somebody special to a has-been. I'm in love with Ted but I'm not crazy, baby."

"You have a contract," Larry reminded her. "They can't just cancel it because you get married. Did Frankie Fischoff say the studio would dump you?"

"No, but Sam Durand hinted at it. He said a girl who'd tarnish her image getting hitched to someone the public thought was unsuita-ble, someone too young or too old, you know, the studio could use the morals clause to break her contract."

Malnish knew that Metro was playing the same game they played with Hedy and Lana and the others. Durand was Kearny's pal and business partner. If Big Ted had really wanted to marry Gilda, Sam would walk her down the aisle whistling "Here Comes the Bride." But Gilda didn't want to listen to reality.

"Forget it," Gilda said, dismissing the problem with a wave of her hand. "It'll work out." Tossing back yet another hit of Aquavit, and topping it with a sip of beer, she'd kick off her shoes at Chasen's or The Derby, at The Screenwriters Club or her favorite, Mocambo. "Let's just have some fun," she'd say. "Dance with me."

Ted Kearny encouraged her to befriend and date the studio screenwriters. They were bright and cynical, but neither rich nor pow-erful enough to be threatening. Kearny also believed all writers to be sexually docile.

They were all wild about Gilda, her sexy voice and quick laughter, her Oklahoma candor, her Irish temper. They adored the generosity of her smile and spirit, and confided in her their secret loves and their deepest doubts. When she began matching them drink for drink, they shared hangover remedies.

One of her favorites was a young playwright, Avery Calder. He was slim and fey, and in the California sun his ghostly anemia made him look like a visitor from outer space. Like Gilda, he was foul-mouthed and vulnerably southern and half-bagged on booze a good deal of the time. The studio had brought him west to write a screenplay for Margaret O'Brien, a trick of fate that made him wallow in frustration and misery. Although he was almost a decade older than Gilda, he was new to Hollywood and naive.

Bored, he would wander over to her set and collapse while he watched her work. Sometimes she'd walk over to the Thalberg building, where he was ensconced in a small office with a rocking chair and a portable typewriter. He would most often be found staring at a page of blank white paper, and he could always be relied upon to produce a bottle from the desk drawer. Avery was Gilda's first real friend in the land of coconuts and gauze.

Late one balmy afternoon in 1943, they drove down to the beach in his new green Ford convertible and whiled away the dying daylight listening to pop songs by Jo Stafford and the Andrews Sisters on the car radio and drinking Norwegian boilermakers.

"The kid's picture is canceled," sighed Avery. "In twelve weeks all I produced was a scene where they threw Margaret O'Brien's ashes off the *Queen Mary* in the middle of a rhumba contest. I told them, 'I cain't write dialogue for nobody in pigtails moonin' over her lost skate key. I'm much better with whores.' So they gave me a whore."

Gilda had read the new script for *Murder in Manhattan.* Every contract player on the lot was itching to play Margo, a prostitute who killed a big-deal mobster to avenge her kid sister's death, then went into hiding and turned state's evidence to send the whole mob to Sing Sing. In the final shot, a heroine without a friend, she killed herself in a steaming flophouse bathtub.

"The studio wants to use Mayer's new Pasadena blonde to play Margo," Avery sighed. "She's too cold, too controlled, a statute of vanilla ice cream. My Margo is absolutely wild, held back by just the slimmest, silkiest thread of sanity. You'd be a perfect Margo."

"Ah, the Pasadena blonde," said Gilda. "The new toy in town. She must be hotter than she looks. I hear she's got herself a stockholding sponsor."

"Captain of industry," Avery corrected.

"No kidding? You know who it is? I've been dying to find out, but no one's talking."

"Honey," said Avery archly, "everyone's talkin'. It's Ted Kearny, the priapic pirate of Wall Street."

He passed her the flask.

"What's wrong, Gilda? You look sick."

She closed her eyes and took a slug of Aquavit. "What's that mean, *priapic?*"

"Oh, just that he's a horny beast, dahlin'. You know him?"

"Avery," she said, sucking the last gulp of liquor from the flask and hurling it with all her might over the front of the car toward the ocean, "I think you're absolutely right. I'm the perfect Margo."

She and Avery Calder became best friends, but he never knew how she managed to talk Sam Durand into giving her the part of Margo. He saw her through Kearny's affair with the ice queen. He took her to the Coconut Grove and made her laugh, but he never heard about the scene in Durand's office—one of Gilda's greatest performances—when she threatened to kill herself and/or phone the wire services with a few facts that did not appear in any studio bio if she didn't get the role. When the Pasadena blonde left Kearny for a married movie star, Avery celebrated with Gilda, then stepped aside when Big Ted came knocking on her door.

Gilda had been living in a two-bedroom apartment on Comstock, but after the crisis passed, she moved into The Pearls—the sumptuous mansion Kearny had built for her as an elaborate token of undying love and eternal reconciliation. She posed there daily for the studio publicity mill: Gilda in halter and shorts, slicing watermelon for Alan Ladd and Roddy McDowall; Gilda in the grotto playroom with its indoor waterfall, entertaining "best pal" Esther Williams in the naturalistic, heated pool; Gilda in the screening room, in trousers and tailored blouse, showing *Murder in Manhattan* to a star-studded preview audience; Gilda feeding apples to the horses stabled behind the house; Gilda and Jane Powell licking cake batter from a wooden spoon in the enormous country kitchen; Gilda in different fashion ensembles in the guest rooms decorated in the motifs of her various pictures—from the rustic tree-limb chairs of *Babes in the Woods* to the leather and leopard skins of *Dark Safari.*

A handsome blond Adonis stood behind her, his hands clasping her waist, as she posed for a wedding portrait in a pale beige suit at the ornate railing of the balcony. They were both so young, so beautiful, their Pepsodent smiles radiant with joy. They were unmistakably in love.

"Now throw the orange blossoms, Gilda," the photographer called. "And Chunk, give her a great big hug. She's all yours, kid. And you can't wait to grab her, right?"

The boy was an actor friend of Avery Calder's. An hour after the photographer from the publicity department left, the boy did, too. He showed up dutifully for premieres, parties, and photo sessions, and he came along with Avery whenever the writer visited The Pearls. But he was a relentless kid. The studio had spent a lot of money hushing up a scandal he'd been involved in at the Fantasy Club. They wanted him to spend more time under Gilda's thumb and less time on the streets of downtown Hollywood.

But their marriage of convenience was not mutually convenient. In the public spotlight, they were dream kids, fawned over by bobby-soxers, patted and primped by studio stooges. In private, they had nothing to say to each other.

Gilda paced her bedroom like a caged cheetah, while Chunk ran old movies in the projection room and jerked off in his silk pajamas. Avery dumped him. The studio ignored him, throwing all of the parts he wanted to Robert Walker or Van Johnson. He was a nice boy. Gilda tried to help, but the studio considered the file on Chunk Williams paid in full.

One night, Gilda was awakened by a crash. She threw on a robe and made her way cautiously to the garden. The gardener, a Mexican who always crossed himself before he buried even the smallest nasturtium seed, met her in the moonlight, covered with blood. "Go back to the house, Miss Gilda. There's been an accident. Get police quick." The man was crossing himself, praying to the saints, and wiping blood on his white cotton pajamas all at the same time.

Gilda was never sure what happened next. She remembered phoning Avery. "It's Chunk. I think he's dead. You got me into this fucking mess, now get your ass over here and get me out of it." She was hysterical, half asleep from the pills she had taken before bed, and completely confused.

Sam Durand sent a limo over and had her driven to the Palm Springs home of a director at Metro. She pieced together some of the details from the newspapers.

Chunk had swallowed lye and weed killer, then stuffed dry bread down his throat to keep from throwing up the poison. When the pain began to chew and then shred his insides, he had thrown himself through a glass window in the greenhouse. His body was ripped in 127 different places, and two arteries had been severed. The actor's wife, famous movie goddess Gilda Greenway, was out of town at the time and unavailable for comment.

Ted Kearny and Avery Calder supervised the funeral arrangements, and with nobody to dispense further information, the press moved on to other stories. It was a nasty scandal, but Gilda was spared. In public, she always said, "My second husband was a charming, romantic boy who became an early Hollywood casualty. I miss him very much and will always regard him with the utmost affection."

Personally, the experience shook her badly. She had recurring nightmares of bodies floating in the swimming pool, falling out of her endless wardrobe closets, sprawled across the marble-floored entrance hall. She relied more than ever on sleeping potions and barbiturates, and cursed herself for being such a damned, gullible fool. She did not return to work for six months. Then she made one film after another, back to back, sometimes working on two films simultaneously.

Kearny begged her to slow down. "You have everything any woman could possibly want," he told her one evening when she was so exhausted she could hardly eat her favorite Chasen's chili. "You got the most beautiful home in Hollywood, a golden career, and me to make sure nobody and nothing ever harms you. Now, how about a six-month vacation in Acapulco?"

But Gilda shook her head, fanning herself with the menu. "Take me home, Teddy," she said. "Not even a year in Acapulco is going to cure what ails me. And I have a seven o'clock date with the makeup man."

SIX

1944

B y 1944, Gilda had made ten pictures, not counting cameos in such star-studded musicals as *A Song for the Boys* and *Victory Canteen,* for which Louis B. Mayer loaned her out for ten times her contractual salary. In one such deal, Gilda found herself at Fox working with Betty Grable and her bandleader husband, Harry James. Gilda jitterbugged briefly at a USO dance. She was tossed, pitched, twirled, and spun from soldier to soldier while Harry James played the trumpet and his orchestra rose from a revolving stage in the bottom of the floor.

One of her partners in the jitterbug sequence was a former stunt-man named Patrick Wainwright. Gilda had never met the rugged movie idol, although she'd seen him play a cowboy, a prizefighter, and a rangy private eye. His Broadway background and his years of training as a hoofer came as a total surprise. In recent years, he had become quite a box-office champ in boots and Stetsons, and his guest appearance in the Grable picture was one of 1944's major screen surprises. She knew he looked virile in a saddle, but in his starched army uniform he looked even better.

When the tall, rangy star with the ease and swagger of the great outdoors took her in his arms, she was startled and disturbed by her reaction. She missed her cues. She stumbled and fell. She twirled past him, and only his flawless timing and long, strong arms kept her from crashing into the camera.

Patrick Wainwright caught her and pulled her toward him. And just before he lifted her to bounce her on his hips, he gave her a great, big, open-mouthed crusher of a kiss.

It took every ounce of her concentration to keep from hollering "ouch." She managed to finish the dance sequence on automatic pilot. When the take was over, she touched her lips and glared at Wainwright. "What'd you do that for?"

"Don't take it personally, sweetheart." He winked at her. "Just wanted to see if you were still boozing. Throws your timing off."

"You prick," she said, and started to stalk away.

Wainwright reached out and caught her arm, pulling her back, holding her close to him. He gripped her for a moment, pinned against him, her chin caught against his collarbone, her head forced back, her body arched against his groin. "I didn't say I didn't enjoy it," he said, smiling.

When Kearny called her from New York that night, Gilda said, "Teddy, let's get married."

"Gilda, we've gone over this a hundred times. Is it the run-in you had with Wainwright? Is that what's bothering you?"

"Jesus, that was three hours ago. How do you know about it? He practically called me a juicer. I wanted to kill him. I'm so damned depressed, Teddy. I feel so lonely."

"You're not drinking again, are you?"

"Up yours! If you already know everything, what are you asking me that for? No, I'm not drinking again. Why? Are you fucking around again?"

Kearny laughed. "I love you," he said.

Later, as she paced in front of the bar, clenching her knuckles to keep from chugging down a bottle of Aquavit, she realized that he hadn't answered her question.

The day before Gilda's twenty-second birthday, Avery saw Ted Kearny leaving Sam Durand's office with a pretty kid who looked like she was on her way to Vacation Bible School. Avery thought the girl, who couldn't have been much more than fourteen, might be Kearny's granddaughter, the fruit of some long-forgotten love affair. She was a button-nosed little thing with eyes like big black olives and precocious high cheekbones, dimpled like Gilda's.

When Avery telephoned Gilda the next day to wish her a happy birthday he mentioned that he'd seen Big Ted leaving Durand's office. Undoubtedly, he joked, he'd been negotiating some fabulous birthday present for her. He didn't mention the little girl. Still, Gilda was shocked. She didn't know Kearny was in town. His secretary had phoned to say he might be late, but that he was doing everything in his power to get to Los Angeles in time for their birthday dinner at Mocambo.

"Shit," said Avery, "he's probably goin' to surprise you, and here I've gone and tipped you off that he's lurkin' in the area. Sorry, darlin'. Don't say I told you. Act surprised."

Avery showed up at Mocambo later that evening, after making the rounds with a couple of friends. Gilda was at her usual table at the back of the restaurant, where the press would be less likely to spot her dining with Kearny.

Seated around her were Big Ted, Frankie Fischoff and his handsome wife, Norma, and Larry Malnish, flanked by a pair of smiling starlets. As Avery made his way through the glittering crowd, moving slowly lest anyone of interest or importance hear—as he was hearing —the sound of I. W. Harper sloshing in his hollow body, he spotted Kearny's kid.

He had reached for the back of a chair to steady himself and found her giggling up at him. She was a charmer, a slip of a girl all down and dewy and ready to sprout, in a cute little gown that clung to her cute little curves. On a whim, Avery bent his head and kissed her cheek.

He straightened up, pleased with himself. His impulsive gesture would goose his image a bit, confuse the local trash who dismissed him as a pansy. The little girl hadn't screamed or winced. She merely looked across the room, laughed and shrugged as if to say, "My heart belongs to Daddy."

Following her eyes, Avery saw that it was Grandpa Teddy to

whom the little girl was miming her excuses. And with the clarity of instant sobriety, he realized that the girl, the kid, was Kearny's lover.

Big Ted stood up and pulled out a chair for him. Avery turned his back on Kearny and, bending to kiss Gilda, showed the bastard his ass.

"Christ, Avery," said Gilda, "you ought to be bottled and bonded." Then she kissed him again, smack on the lips. "That's as close as I'll come to getting stinko tonight."

"You're quite the ladies' man this evening," Kearny said, laughing.

"Or vice versa, big fella," said Avery.

Norma Fischoff held out her arms to him. "Hello, sweetheart," she said. "Come breathe on me. I'd prefer the bourbon from your breath to all the Dom Perignon in town."

Kearny shook his head. "I must be doing something wrong."

Avery smiled coldly at him. "Give me news, not history," he said.

Three months later, Frankie Fischoff telephoned Larry Malnish in Los Angeles. It was 8:00 A.M. in New York, five o'clock in the morning on the West Coast.

"We got big trouble," Frankie said, when Malnish answered the phone with a sleepy hello.

"Goddamn right," said Malnish. "I only got to sleep three hours ago, and there's a hot tomato lying next to me needs her beauty sleep, too. This better be important."

"I just picked up the *New York Times*, Larry, and read about the wedding of Morgan Edward Kearny."

"Fischoff, what the fuck are you calling me in the middle of the night to talk to me about wedding announcements?"

"Malnish, Big Ted Kearny got married."

"Holy shit! To Gilda?"

"No, you idiot—to some deb who's been making the café society circuit lately. Brenda McCormack."

"A regular grown-up?" said Malnish. "I don't believe it."

"Positively geriatric. A world-weary eighteen-year-old. Malnish, I'm catching a plane to L.A. at ten o'clock, but you and Avery Calder better be at The Pearls before Gilda wakes up. The shit's going to hit the fan and you better be the ones to break the news to her before anyone else does."

"What about Rita?

"Rita who?"

"The kid Durand signed for the horse movie. Ted was fucking her too."

"Let *her* agent look out for her. Gilda's the one I'm worried about. I'm calling Dr. Habib. He'll prescribe a sedative. Then I want you to give her a nice cup of tea. By the time this whole thing sinks in, I'll be there, God willing."

They were too late. When they rang the doorbell at The Pearls at 7:30, they were greeted by a frightened maid whose fingernails were chewed to the quick. "Thank goodness, it's you," she said to Avery. "I was getting ready to call the police, but I knew I shouldn't, the scandal and all."

"Where's Miss Gilda?"

"Dear Lord," the young girl said, "I wish I knew. Some nosy reporter called her up from New York last night and said, did you know Mr. Kearny had got married? So of course she didn't believe him, but he said, well, read about it in the *New York Times* tomorrow morning. So then, poor soul, she asked me would I mind calling Mr. Kearny's home because she was too nervous to talk to the operator and all. And Jesus help us, they said, no, Mr. Kearny wasn't home because he was on his honeymoon."

"Do you know where she might have gone?" asked Malnish.

The maid was weeping so hard she could barely manage the information that Gilda had thrown on a fur coat over her pajamas and driven away. "She made me promise not to call anyone—not even you, Mr. Calder. She told me not to wait up for her."

Larry telephoned Sam Durand, who was already at the studio. "What is this, an epidemic?" the little man stormed. "I got Rita Marshall missing, too. They're trying to shoot around her. I got maybe a million dollars worth of talent sitting around playing pinochle on the set because two spoiled brats get dumped by their boyfriend and decide to take a holiday."

Durand instantly agreed that the police were absolutely not to be informed of any disappearances until the studio could figure out what to do. "That fucking Kearny," Durand fumed. "How could he do this to me? Gilda's in the middle of a dynamite picture! Let me know if you hear anything."

By the time Frankie arrived that evening, Larry and Avery had visited all of Gilda's favorite bars and haunts. They alerted her hairdresser and a couple of her other drinking buddies. They were considering phoning the hospitals when, on a hunch, Larry tracked down the mother of Rita Marshall, the sweet young starlet whom Kearny had discovered.

"Yes," she said, "Gilda Greenway came by last evening and picked up Rita. Rita called me just a little while ago from San Diego, just to check in and say she wasn't sure when she'd be back."

Malnish and Avery took turns calling every hotel and motel in the navy town. By now Frankie wasn't capable of much more than slowly shaking his head from time to time, sipping Alka-Seltzer, and moaning, "God in heaven, I'll never forgive the bastard." Finally, a desk clerk at the Sunburst said, "Yeah, a redhead and a cute brunette checked in last night. Their bar bill ain't to be believed, and, buddy, they got so many sailors stripped down to their skivvies that their room's beginning to look like the draft board."

Larry and Avery drove down to San Diego, arriving in the middle of the night. The desk clerk traded the room key for two $50 bills.

"I meant to ask you," he said, rubbing his eyes sleepily. "I told the redhead she looked like Gilda Greenway, the movie star. And she says, yeah, like she won a lookalike contest. But what would a girl beautiful enough to win a lookalike contest for Gilda be doing shacked up at the Sunburst? So I figured she was full of shit. Am I right or am I right?"

Avery's heart pounded as he unlocked the door. In the bathroom light, he could see Gilda, lying across the double bed stark naked. Rita was curled up against her, one leg thrown over Gilda's thigh, her long chestnut-brown hair covering Gilda's breast. On the floor, at the foot of the bed, a boy in undershorts was snoring.

Avery bent down over the boy and cupped his hands together to form a megaphone. "Ship to shore, cutie," he said. "The marines have landed."

Gilda moaned and turned over to look at Avery and Malnish standing at the side of the bed. "Who the hell invited you to this party?" Then she put her hands over her face and began to sob.

"Avery," she cried, "did you hear what that cocksucker did?"

"Yeah, sweetie, I did," said Avery, cradling her in his arms. "But guess what, honey? I hear she's got the clap."

Rita Marshall returned to the set of *Kentucky Yearling*, playing an all-American farm girl whose unshaken belief in a nag bound for the glue factory led them both to win the Derby. And, fueled by pep pills and 100-proof gin, Gilda finished filming her first domestic comedy, ironically called *Nice Girl*.

She was depressed and bleary most of the time, but Avery and Larry took turns baby-sitting for her. Frankie checked in nightly at nine, to make sure she had made it to the set that day and eaten something solid. One night an unfamiliar, crisp voice answered Frankie's call.

"Greenway residence," the woman announced starchily.

"Tell Gilda it's Frankie," he said.

"Miss Greenway is not available to take any calls at the moment."

"The hell she's not!" roared Fischoff, in a rare display of temper. "Tell her it's her goddamn *agent.*"

Gilda was laughing when she picked up the extension in her bedroom. "Blame Larry," she said. "You've met Mrs. Denby, my new live-in housekeeper and baby-sitter. Larry found her taming wild dogs up in the Hollywood Hills. He figured if she had a way with wild animals, she'd be perfect for this place, considering the tarantulas, monkeys, dogs, my goddamn zebra, and *me!*"

When Ted Kearny returned from his Bermuda honeymoon, he phoned Gilda to apologize, assuring her he had signed The Pearls over to her "lock, stock, and zoo" and had even deposited enough money in her bank account to make her a rich woman. He believed she'd understand and be happy for him when he told her that Brenda was pregnant. Brenda was young and strong enough to give him what he now wanted most in the world—a child.

Gilda called Larry Malnish. She'd obviously been drinking, but she spoke very clearly and slowly.

"Larry," said Gilda, "I want the address of that bastard butcher abortionist."

"For chrissake, Gilda, what the hell for? If you have a friend in trouble, there are better people right here in Los Angeles. Besides, for all I know, he was arrested the day after we walked out of that snake pit."

He called back the next day, after waking up at 3:00 A.M. to wonder whether the impossible had happened, whether Gilda had become pregnant. But if she were, she couldn't possibly be thinking about an abortion, he told himself.

Mrs. Denby answered the phone. "She's not here. She had urgent business in New York."

Malnish called Frankie Fischoff immediately.

"Gilda's in New York," he said. "It's a long story, but she's probably wandering around Washington Heights looking for a Dr. Lawrence. You gotta find her, Frankie. I think she's gone a little wacko this time."

Gilda gave Frankie Fischoff's name as "next of kin" when she was checked into Bellevue by the cops who'd found her wandering down Ft. Washington Avenue.

When Frankie went to Bellevue to bail her out, the intern said, "I know she's who she says she is, but I'm charting it as delusional. She's in terrible shape. Get her a doctor out there. Keep her away from babies for a while. If she behaves promiscuously, try to be understanding. She's trying to fill her womb."

Frankie knew nothing of the abortion. He didn't understand what the young doctor was talking about—womb, shwomb. But clearly the intern was a bright boy, because, sure enough, the next couple of years were a nightmare of drunken promiscuity. Not even the intimidating Mrs. Denby could keep her at home and sober. Every other week, Larry Malnish or Avery Calder would be summoned by a phone call from Gilda's housekeeper.

"She's wrecked her car in Laurel Canyon."

"She's all right, but one of the four boys she was with had a concussion."

"She just called from Arizona. She was having a couple of drinks with a cowboy and sobered up standing in front of a Justice of the Peace."

During a trip to New York City, she lost her shoes at Eddie Condon's jazz club and spent the rest of the night—and on into the morning—being carried from club to club by a drummer with a reputation as a ladykiller and a junkie. Another time, she crawled out of a ladies' room window to escape a boring date and found herself on a ledge nine stories above downtown Chicago. She thanked two of the firemen who rescued her by entertaining them in her hotel room for the next two days.

Why Gilda's womb didn't balloon with babies was an utter mystery to Frankie. It was a miracle of birth control. "God must be looking out for her," Frankie told Norma, "because no one as drunk as Gilda could remember to look after herself. I was even relieved when I found her with two girls in her bed. At least from girls she can't get pregnant."

Work saved Gilda's life. It took all of Frankie's skill and patience to get her off suspension and onto the set again, but she came through for him. If she drank on the job, it didn't show and no one ever caught her at it. She was the first person on the daily call sheet to arrive for makeup. She knew her lines. She was a pussycat with her directors and costars. Between takes, she'd play gin rummy with the grips in her trailer.

She told Sheilah Graham in an interview, "The secret of my success is that I always cuddle my crews. It's nice if you get along with Gable, Gable's a great guy. But it's the light man who makes you look good for posterity. Win over the grips, the electricians, the sound man, and the go-fers, and you got it made."

At lunchtime, she usually avoided the commissary, where the Gilda Greenway fruit salad was a popular item, and dined on a Miltown sandwich in her trailer. She neglected to tell Sheilah Graham about that.

Louis B. Mayer couldn't stand her. She was never invited to his birthday parties where Kay Thompson and Roger Edens directed the other MGM stars in private skits and songs for the old man's delight. Lena Horne, who knew what it was like to get by on beauty and talent without the benefit of social acceptance, befriended her. Judy Garland, who pulled her own weight at the studio despite her own run-ins with the old man, sometimes appeared at the end of a day's work in Gilda's dressing room to say, "C'mon, girl, let's get fried."

Gilda had her drinking buddies, but she remained a loner, a mystery girl in an industry where there were no secrets. Even Hedda and Louella, the twin titans of terror, protected her. Every Christmas when the vans pulled up at their homes loaded with graft, payola, and shut-up bribes, Gilda's elaborate gifts took up most of the space. Once, when Hedda Hopper declared war on Mary Astor, the veteran actress who had played Gilda's mother in two films called for advice.

"How do you handle the old rattlesnake?" asked Mary.

"I sent her a statue of Veronese marble for her swimming pool and installed a new sauna in her pool house last Christmas," was Gilda's answer.

"Well, that explains everything," said Mary. "All I gave her was an Irene hat."

If Gilda was a hit with the press, her fans adored her even more. She made fifteen more pictures for MGM between 1945 and 1950, and except for the occasional turkey like *Daughter of the Nile* and *The Pumpkin Coach*, they all made money. Gilda, the studio discovered at the silent box office, was no capricious Egyptian princess and no starry-eyed Cinderella. In 1946, the studio gave Gilda the old Greta Garbo dressing-room suite, dormant and dusty since the silent Swede stalked out into permanent exile five years earlier. They didn't even have to change the GG on the silver-and-tortoiseshell hairbrush.

Mayer was queer for gloves and hats, for ladies who could keep their shoes on and their legs crossed. With Greer Garson, he beamed. With Gilda, he scowled all the way to the bank. The studio grapevine buzzed when the old man imported Deborah Kerr from England to share top billing with the Pearls Girl in a 1947 postwar soap opera, but it was Gilda who got the fan mail. In furious retaliation, Mayer instructed Sam Durand to loan her out to Paramount for three comedies in a row for a record-breaking fee.

Gilda stopped sleeping around when she married crooner Artie Bender. But it was a rotten tradeoff.

Bender was a hot-tempered, devoutly macho lush who expected women to worship him, and punched them out when they didn't. Before the war, as a kid singing in clubs in Brooklyn and Hoboken, he'd gotten used to, as he put it, "blow jobs before the show and box lunches after." During the war, he'd studied bullfighting in Mexico, where he'd strut around the ring in Mexico City with one arm raised to the adoring crowd.

He liked to boast that while the smell of blood was still on him, the movie stars and bullfight fans would line up to gnaw on his bone.

Gilda liked to say she'd rather gnaw on Rin Tin Tin's bone than Artie's. It was bound to have more meat on it, for starters. One night in Tahoe, after a drunken, two-hour fist fight, she married him.

"She'd be better off, pardon me," Frankie told Norma, *"shtupping* the 82nd Airborne than getting knocked around by that low-class *shicker,* Artie Bender."

"He's working for her," Malnish told Avery Calder. "She doesn't have to beat herself up anymore, she's got that asshole to do it for her."

In 1950, Gilda was paired with Hollywood's number-one leading man, Patrick Wainwright, in a wacky war comedy called *O'Connor's Wife.* She played a navy nurse named O'Connor. He played the gruff, wounded commander who falls in love with her. They want to marry but, thanks to red tape and navy snafus, their papers list the nurse as bridegroom and the commander as bride.

In the six years since the Grable picture at Fox, they had each survived a heartbreaking loss. Patrick's wife, Marie, had been paralyzed in a car crash that killed their only child. Wainwright had been driving and escaped without a scratch. For Gilda, the loss of Kearny had awakened her to a deeper, more wrenching loss—a life without children.

The two of them were older and wiser now, battle-scarred and warier of life. But from the very first day of shooting, the scent of excitement and sexual electricity permeated the set. It didn't help that the first scene they were supposed to shoot was a squabble.

The script called for them to argue, then the nurse was to turn on her heels and walk away from the bedridden commander. He had to grab at and accidentally tear her skirt. She whirled to scold him, and he was out of bed and kissing her before she knew what was happening.

"Wainwright, if you grab me like a hunk of hamburger again, I'm going to turn you into a bald soprano," Gilda stormed.

"Lady, if you'd act like a woman instead of a slab of dead meat, we could find better things to do with my nuts."

"Cut!"

"You're a sleep man, Commander Morrison. You need your sick." Gilda slapped her forehead. "Shit, I blew it!"

"Blow this," said Wainwright, grabbing his pajama crotch. "What's that, Eddy, take four thousand one?"

"Cut!'"

"You're a sick man, Commander Morrison. You need your rest.''

"Sleep. The line is 'you need your *sleep'!*''

"The line is 'You're a sick man'! I got that right, didn't I? Type-fucking-casting, too!''

"Cut! Five minutes. Let's take a break, kids.''

During the second week of shooting, Wainwright smelled liquor on Gilda's breath. At the first break, he grabbed her arm and pulled her away from the girl who was touching up her cheek blush.

"Hey!'' she protested.

"Ditch the bottle,'' he growled through clenched teeth. His jaw actually rippled with anger.

She looked everywhere but at his eyes. "What the fuck are you talking about?''

He didn't say anything. He just held her arm tightly, until, finally, she looked at him. She saw what he wanted her to see. He was not kidding around. This one was nonnegotiable.

Gilda nodded. "Okay,'' she whispered. "Let go.''

He did. But later in the day, when she stumbled during a take, Wainwright grabbed her arm again, and spun her to face him. "Jesus, ain't life hard enough for you, lady?'' he shouted at her in front of the entire crew.

Gilda tore free of him and ran off the set. "Shit!'' roared Wainwright, following her.

By the time Pat Wainwright got to the Garbo suite her gin rummy buddies were taking up a pool. The technicians put their money on Gilda making mincemeat of Pat. The creative crew said Wainwright would cream her.

"What are you bawling for? Didn't I tell you booze would fuck up your timing?'' he hollered. She was on her knees, rummaging through a wastebasket under her dressing room mirror. "What're you doing down there, on your hands and knees?''

"Yeah, you did. And I ran out crying that day, too, I remember. I wasn't even drinking then. I was on the wagon, you dumb bastard. Here!'' she yelled triumphantly, brandishing the whiskey bottle she'd thrown out earlier. "I threw it out, see! You told me to ditch it and I did! Here!'' She stood up. "I'll ditch it again!'' She hurled the bottle past his head.

Wainwright ducked as the glass shattered. He lunged for Gilda, and knocked her back against the wall, away from the flying shards of glass. "Dumb bitch, are you crazy?" he said, touching the side of his face that the bottle had grazed.

"Me? I remember that crusher you planted on me. You remember that?"

"Yeah." He smiled. "I do." He put his arms around her and leaned forward.

She reached down and grabbed his balls. "It's a draw, Commander."

He tilted her face up to his. "You're better looking now than you were then," he said, parting her lips with his thumb. "Your face has thinned out. And look at those lips," he said, rubbing his thumb slowly across her lips. "I remember these lips," he said, sliding his thumb into her mouth and out.

She closed her hand around his groin and felt him moving, growing in her grasp. She laughed at his nerve.

Pat laughed, too. Then he pulled her face up to his and bent his head. "I've thought about you a lot," he said, lightly biting her lip. Then he kissed her, softly at first, with his lips, and then, as he had the first time, with his lips and teeth and tongue.

His balls were shifting in her hand, his cock thickening. Gilda tightened her hold and he pressed his mouth against hers, harder. He caught her bottom lip in his teeth and laughed.

But she could feel his heart pumping as wildly as her own. She loved how heavy and hard he was growing in her hand. She wanted him to touch her, to feel how much she wanted him.

There was a knock at the door. "Gilda, uh, Miss Greenway, are you okay in there?" It was one of the grips, one of her card-playing buddies.

Wainwright released her. She slid weakly to the floor. "I'm okay, George. I'll be right out."

Wainwright was standing astride her, smiling down at her, shaking his head, laughing quietly. His hospital pajamas were bulging, tented at the groin. He offered her his hand. Reaching up, she caressed him with both hands, drawing her palms along the full length of his hardness.

"So long, Commander," she whispered.

He caught her hand on his groin and held it there. "George," he called, "tell them to fold it. It's nearly four. We have to work through this scene."

"Uh, sure, Mr. Wainwright," the man said tentatively. There was a whisper. Then, more voices saying, "Go on, George, you ask."

"What is it, George?" Gilda called, staring up at the grinning Patrick Wainwright. She rubbed her cheek against his leg.

"We want to know who won!" someone shouted. And there was laughter outside the bungalow.

"It's a draw," Pat Wainwright called. "I've met my match."

They drove to Azuma Beach that night and walked along the water's edge, arms around each other, until he spread his mohair sweater on the sand and pulled her down beside him.

They sat silently, holding hands, taking in the ocean and the stars and the full moon.

"I'm married, Gilda," Patrick said after a few moments. "I'm not going to divorce her, not ever."

"I figured."

"She's away most of the time. She's either at the clinic or up at the ranch, but I want you to know the way it is. What about you and Bender?"

"That asshole? We're finished. I threw him out ages ago. He's on his way to Spain, I think."

"I wasn't kidding this afternoon when I said I'd thought about you a lot. I even got a print of that godawful film, so I could see myself kissing you."

"No one's ever kissed me like that," said Gilda huskily.

"Like this?" Patrick wrapped his arms around her and gently but insistently worked his tongue deep inside her mouth. They fell back together onto the sand, eyes closed, still kissing.

Gilda drew away first.

"I'm in big trouble, Gilda."

"Tell me about it, baby."

He undid the buttons of her silk shirt and the hook of her bra. As Gilda moved to pry open the big branding-iron buckle on his cowboy belt, he pushed her full skirt up to her waist so the moon shone like a spotlight on her white lace lingerie.

"It's been a while since I've made love on anything but silk sheets," moaned Gilda.

"That's what you get for taking up with a saddle tramp," Patrick said, pulling off his leather boots and Levi's.

He bent his mouth to her breasts, teasing first her right nipple, then her left, with his teeth and lips and tongue.

Tiny cool grains of sand rubbing against the back of her legs fell away as she lifted herself to capture Patrick.

"Got a spare room for me up at The Pearls?" Patrick said, pinning her inside him.

"No problem, cowboy," she said, looking up at him and thinking, I *love* this man.

Then the night and the beach disappeared and all Gilda knew was that Patrick was probing the depths of her need with a fire that matched her own.

SEVEN

FEBRUARY 12, 1956

K ing walked a few blocks from his apartment in Hell's Kitchen to the Morosco Theater for Patrick Wainwright's opening night. He might just as well have been crossing the English Channel to another world.

He couldn't believe it. One minute sitting in "21" for the first time in his life, with Devon Barnes on one side, and Gilda Greenway, the biggest, most beautiful star in the world on the other . . . and now, now he was escorting *Gilda* to a Broadway opening! Who *would* believe it?

Gilda had offered to send a car, but he told her not to bother. He lived practically around the corner, in the same three-room cold-water walkup he'd lucked into five years ago when he first arrived in New York.

He had drifted past the theaters in the Times Square district nearly every day for three years before he'd ever set foot inside one. An old lady who lived in his building, an usher at the Helen Hayes, offered to sneak him in one night after the curtain went up. From then on, he saw practically every show on Broadway from the second act on. Now he knew most of the ushers, many of the stagehands, some of the stage managers, and even a couple of gypsies, as the chorus kids called themselves.

They looked like gypsies, too, King thought. When there was an open audition, or "cattle call," they'd line up at the stage entrance, stretching, reading, gossiping, in brightly colored sweaters, tight pants or flaring skirts, and stockings, socks, and leg warmers of every hue and texture. The girls would tie their hair up in bright Ukrainian scarves or black bandanas. The boys imitated their idols: some were Jimmy Dean, smiling mysteriously behind turned-up collars; others wore dark glasses, sideburns, and slicked-back shee-bop cuts like Brando. Some were collegiate types with the somber, boyish beauty of Montgomery Clift.

Week after week, King would pass the same kids lined up for a chance to read or sing and dance. They'd ask him to go for coffee, and sometimes he would. He liked their gossip and great expectations. But he didn't like the way they had to stand outside in the suffocating heat or freezing cold and rain, waiting for someone with a clipboard and a whistle to call their names.

One of them stuck out: a tall Negro vet of the Korean War who dressed in combat fatigues and a silk bomber jacket, with a rugged jaw, serious eyes, and a grin worth waiting for. The girls flocked around him, batted their lashes at him, laughed too loudly in his presence. His name was Deauville Tolin. He was studying acting at The Workshop, and Uncle Sam was paying his way through school. He paid his own rent doing carpentry and odd jobs in the Village, waiting on tables wherever, whenever he could.

He was the first Negro King had ever met who talked like a white man. What he talked about was acting, truth, The Workshop, and getting laid. But his first words to King were, "Hey, kid, get me a coffee, will you?"

Now Deauville scarcely blinked when he heard Gilda Greenway had invited King to the opening of Avery Calder's new play. He handed over his white dinner jacket and black pants, saying, "Listen, Cinderella, just get the suit back to me by four tomorrow, okay? Or else it'll turn back into a waiter's uniform. Before you know it your arm'll be up in the air like you're holding a tray and you'll find yourself in the middle of Sardi's hollering, 'Who's got the medium rare?' "

Seated between Gilda Greenway and Avery Calder at Sardi's after the show, King grinned, remembering Deauville's words. People had stood and cheered when they entered Sardi's, and Vincent Sardi had personally escorted them to their table. Gilda had squeezed his arm as Avery and Patrick basked in the adulation. They bowed, smiled charmingly, and held up each other's hands like victorious prizefighters.

Gilda was every inch the big thrill from Hollywood, shimmering in midnight-blue Ceil Chapman chiffon with diamonds big as doorknobs. Patrick Wainwright, the man of the hour, was busy autographing the neck brace of a woman in a floor-length Maximilian sable. And Avery Calder, who had survived many nights like this and lived to tell about it, just got drunker.

Calder was immensely tall and cadaverous, with a stormy, unkept, hideous face, and eloquent sad eyes that seemed always to be changing color in their deep sockets. If a swamp possum could talk, it would probably sound like Avery Calder. His tongue seemed coated with rum and molasses as it darted in and out of his mouth, licking at his moustache like a pink lizard.

His voice wavered shakily like old gray cigar smoke in a room with no ceiling fan, rising to a mad cackle like a wounded macaw, settling finally in a cross between Tallulah Bankhead and Everett Dirksen. His delicate hands fluttered like dying birds, and tragic flamboyance masked tortured sensitivity. At forty-four, the world's most famous playwright sat precariously on the edge of vulnerability. One more double bourbon and King was afraid he just might jump.

"A penny for your clearly amusin' thoughts," he said, playing with his oyster fork.

King shrugged. "Are you kidding? Look at us. Look at *this.*" People were admiring them from every corner of the restaurant.

The word was out on Broadway. *The Way Back Home* was a smash. It was Avery Calder's most profound play. It was Patrick Wainwright's long-awaited triumphant return to Broadway, where he'd begun as a "hoofer," a chorus boy, a gypsy, decades before.

Those were the days when fortune—or lack of it—had sent Patrick Wainwright out west to try his luck in movies. But hoofers were a dime a baker's dozen, and in Busby Berkeley's symmetrical Hollywood there was no place for a chorus boy who stood head and shoulders above Astaire's top hat. When everyone tapped in unison, no one wanted a dancer whose knees ended where the other hoofers' thighs began. So Wainwright had done stunt work. Patrick had tried his hand and busted his ass at gags none but the desperate would attempt.

And it paid off.

The studio began to get mail about the big, handsome cowboy who rolled under the horse or swung over the precipice or whisked the little gal out of the raging stream. They erased New York from his bio and launched him as U.S. Grade-A Wyoming prime, selling him in *Modern Screen* as the kind of hero who thought tap dancing was how you hurried to the can after too much tequilla. But the Broadway faithful knew better. They knew where Pat Wainwright had come from, and they were on their feet welcoming him home tonight. Godlike, he walked among them, his handsome smile inviting them to "come on in." He was the same movie star who had dived from rafts and swum across rivers in countless outdoor sagas, but now he was accessible, languid, and open.

Women sighed and reached out to touch Patrick when he passed their tables, blowing kisses and offering him cocktail napkins on which their phone numbers were scrawled.

"Pure music, *paisano*," said Ezio Pinza, a big hit that year in *Fanny*, "pure music."

Burl Ives slapped him on the back.

"Sayyy, buster," said Ruth Gordon, with one hand on her hip, coming toward him in a pillbox hat and Mary Jane shoes and walking like an anchovy, "you were *grr-ayyt!*"

The parade of well-wishers was long and astonishing. A lot of Patrick's Hollywood chums, who had made the perilous but rewarding trip to Broadway ahead of him, lavished him with welcome.

"Thumbs up, big guy," said Edward G. Robinson who was the toast of the town himself in *Middle of the Night.*

Shelley Winters recommended a good shrink while she helped herself to something on Patrick's plate. In the crowd of celebrities,

King spotted Gwen Verdon, Ben Gazzara, and the jumbo patty-cake knockers of Jayne Mansfield.

And tonight Gilda remained in his shadow, regal and adoring. Patrick sat there, smoking the pipe she had bought him at Dunhill, and King could tell he adored her, too.

Gilda put her arm around King and said in a warm, boozy whisper, "Isn't my lover beautiful?"

"Gilda," Avery remonstrated, "shame on you. You've got the boy blushin'."

"Yes," said Gilda, tossing back her head and lifting slender arms to stretch like a cat. "Shame on me. Shame on me, and I wear it so well."

Patrick grabbed her chin, pulling her face toward him. Gilda arched her neck and closed her eyes, her mouth parting for his. Instead, he lifted the long strand of pearls Gilda wore and placed it on her lips. When her mouth was filled with pearls, he kissed her.

It was like a movie, King thought, sitting under a caricature of Carol Channing.

And Kingston Godwin was in it.

Why else was he there? What in hell was the son of a white-trash Bayou trucker doing in Sardi's with three of the most famous people in the entire fucking universe?

King could still remember the two-room shack on Bayou Lafour-che where his family had lived until his mama threw his daddy out for drinking rotgut out of a Mason jar. Then, remorseful that he might die out in the swamp with nothing but a jug for company, she had packed up King's two shirts and the rag quilt she'd made him and sent him north to Kenner to take care of his papa. Barely twenty-eight years old, she had six other children to feed.

"Yes, ma'am. I'll look after him," he said, and he had tried. He'd stuck to that gentle man like glue. Hungry and half asleep, he'd sit up on a strawberry crate in the front of his daddy's rig and ride with him through the dead of night. One night was just like another. He was always tired. He was always hungry. They were always hauling bootleg whiskey between Covington and Kenner.

King was keeping his promise to his mama that night: he was keeping his daddy company. His belly was empty and aching. All he cared about when they stopped at the shut-down filling station to siphon some gas were the stale candy bars in the machine padlocked to the side of the outhouse. He was staring at those Baby Ruths while his daddy jimmied the pumps, cussing the dark night, and hunted for his old trusty Zippo to see by.

King started messing with the candy machine like his brother Denzil had showed him. When he first heard the explosion, he thought it was God punishing him for trying to steal a Baby Ruth bar. Scared and guilty, he looked over his shoulder. Bright red sheets of snapping flames were shooting up into the night sky.

King thought he saw his daddy, flying through the air like a barbecued scarecrow. He thought he saw a million sparkling stars carrying his daddy to Heaven, as the hot fist-hard air slammed into him, nailing him like a crucified child against the splintered glass of the candy machine.

Before he heard the sirens racing toward the filling station, King thought of his mother. She couldn't afford another mouth to feed. He had failed her. Alone in the dark, he stood as still as a jackrabbit caught in a blaze of headlights. Then he started running.

He thumbed his way to New Orleans on the Airline Highway. The people who gave him a lift didn't even know they were hauling jail bait. He was well-developed for his age, and a wise, cocky self-assurance hid his inner fears.

When he was nine, he had fallen off his daddy's truck and sliced open his knee on a rusty license plate. The doctors said nothing was left holding his knee together but skin, so they had to transplant muscle tissue from his calf. The process of coming to terms with his physical limitations was traumatic. He was determined to prove the doctors wrong. One day he was jumped at school by a gang of Cajuns and left with broken ribs and a broken jaw. Confronting the problem head-on, he persuaded the gym teacher to let him fight the bullies one-on-one in the boxing ring. He won. All of a sudden he was tough, and then *everybody* wanted to fight him.

His coach enrolled King in a martial-arts class, where his aptitude and passion to prove he wasn't a sickly sissy turned him into a first-class athlete. Football, track, diving—he was good in all of them. But each time he got to a certain point with a sport, he lost interest. Years later he told an interviewer from the *New York Times*, "All my life I've been looking for something that would keep me challenged till the day I die. Sports didn't do it. I wanted spiritual as well as physical fulfillment." As a towhead on his way to New Orleans with muscular thighs and arms big as fence posts, he knew nothing about either.

He found out in the French Quarter.

Dixieland jazz poured forth from the open bars of Bourbon Street like a merry bubble of hedonistic pleasure. King bought a pink drink called a Hurricane. It was midnight and the Hurricane worked. He wandered down to Decatur Street, crossed the railroad tracks, and fell asleep on a bench on the levee of the Mississippi near the Jax brewery. A riverboat blazing with carnival lights was discharging its nightly haul of tourists, laughing drunkenly and singing like high-pitched sailors. King had never felt so completely alone, so achingly homesick for the cracked linoleum of his mama's kitchen.

When he woke, a man was sitting on the bench beside him, rubbing his neck. The bench was cold under the frosty moon, and the man's hand was warm.

"Does this embarrass you?" the man asked in a voice soft as dandelion fuzz. "No, sir," answered King.

The hand moved lower and touched his thigh. King was positively amazed that he felt so little revulsion in the gesture. He remembered something his daddy told him once: "Son, ain't nothin' wrong with nothin' long as it smells good, tastes good, or feels good." The warm thickening in his groin felt good.

The man, whose name was Michael Browning, took King to the Café du Monde in the old French Market for hot "N'Awlins" coffee, thick and bitter with chicory, and hot swollen beignets, freshly deep-fried and drowning in powdered sugar. Browning lived in a carriage house on Elysian Fields, near the edge of the Quarter. The walls were lined with books and French doors opened to reveal a cobblestone courtyard below, lush with pots of bougainvillea.

King liked it there. And he knew when he unveiled the source of his secret power, the man would want him to stay. He was right, as usual.

"How old are you, son?"

"Eighteen," King lied.

But when he unzipped his jeans, the man believed him. Or didn't care. There before his question-mark eyes was the thing his daddy called "the biggest tallywhacker in the Delta." King had been ashamed of its humongous size when he was a child. When he was bad, his mama threatened to cut it off and feed it to the chickens. Later, when his brothers charged their friends a nickel each to look at it, King realized being over-endowed could be profitable. He was growing hair on his balls at nine, and by the age of ten he was jerking off behind the gym while his classmates watched. By then, the price had increased to a dime, and King was in business.

During the winter that followed, there was never the slightest discussion of guilt, remorse, or—better yet—school. Somewhere a truant officer was probably looking for him, but King didn't care. He did worry about his mama, wondered how she survived his daddy's death, thought about her red-raw hands scaling fish and changing diapers. But they were too poor to own a telephone, and King would never *ever* return to Bayou Lafourche.

Browning treated him like a son. A sportswriter for the *Times-Picayune,* he covered wrestling matches but abhorred violence. He was a Buddhist and a homosexual. He was gentle as a newborn colt in bed yet capable of great bursts of demonic rage whenever King came home late from the bars on Bourbon Street. The man had a cocker spaniel named Daisy and during the day King would walk the dog in Jackson Square. In the afternoons he'd eat po-boys and play the pinball machine on Rampart Street. Some nights the man would take him to the fights or to the movies.

On rainy days, King would lie in Michael Browning's big brass bed reading books by Hemingway, Faulkner, and Fitzgerald—listening to the monotonous rain that dripped off the crepe myrtles and clattered down the drainpipes into the gutters below. On days like these, he was happy to be alone, lost in a world of make-believe. The cocker would snuggle up next to him in bed and snore stupidly, twitching and dreaming of some long-lost tabby cat victim in Pirate's Alley.

King felt as if he belonged to something. He wasn't sure what, and he wasn't sure he would like it if he knew, but he felt more purposeful, more content than ever before. All his benefactor asked in return was the privilege of licking that big ol' tallywhacker till it shot right up to his armpit. It was a fair exchange. And he didn't have anyplace else to go.

Through his job Browning got King a pass to a local gym. He worked with the punching bag, lifted weights, pumped his biceps until the sweat ran down his spine. He was growing into a hunk, and when he sauntered down Royal Street on Saturday afternoons—sandy hair bobbing in the winter sun, muscles rippling under his white T-shirt, eyes like swimming pools of clear-eyed ecstasy—everyone wanted him. A woman in a mink coat offered him $50 if he'd spend the night with her at the Pontchartrain Hotel. He just stared at her blankly. "Well, you *are* a hustler, aren't you?" He turned away, red-faced with tears. The woman had called him a name that didn't fit.

Sometimes he'd sit with the queers on bar stools at a place called Tony Bacino's, watching an outrageous drag queen called Kitty Litter squirt seltzer on a wall poster of a naked muscle-builder. Everybody called him Baby Buns. But he didn't identify. He hated labels, especially since none of them were accurate.

He knew he was special. Everybody kept telling him so. But how, he wondered, could a person be special and still not fit into any category, not feel anything at all?

One night he went home to the carriage house on Elysian Fields to find his friend in a highly charged emotional condition not brought on by alcohol. Browning had a confession to make. He had a wife. The wife lived in another town, but she wanted money. She found out he had a lover young enough to be his own son. She planned to make trouble. It could cost him his job at the paper.

King was bewildered. *Lover* was as odd a word as *hustler.* He pretended to fall asleep, exhausted, the cocker nibbling at his feet. He heard the man sobbing as he kneeled over King's motionless body and said, "I love you." He was terrified for the first time since he watched his father roasted like a marshmallow. He liked the man, but he didn't love him.

He didn't love *anybody.*

In the middle of the night, while the moon lit the room like a hazy flashlight, he slid silently out of bed, climbed into sneakers, jeans, and a red windbreaker, and stuffed his clothes into an overnight gym bag. Then he took $200 from the man's wallet. Okay, maybe he *was* a hustler. The cocker spaniel moaned a low, anguished sigh as he closed the door behind him. He felt a tug at his heart, a small pain rising toward his throat. He *felt* something. Okay, maybe he was queer, too. He hated himself for even thinking it. Then he walked all the way to the Greyhound depot on Canal Street and climbed aboard the next bus going north.

New York City was melting in a 100-degree heat wave, but the movie houses were cool as ice. He watched *Treasure Island* eighteen times and was reciting aloud Bobby Driscoll's entire role when someone complained and had him thrown out by the manager.

He came blinking into the boiling sun of Times Square. The news on the street was about Americans heading for the big fight in a place called Korea. King had never heard of Korea. But it was hot in New York, and he knew soldiers got paid. He hurried across the street to the recruiting center and promptly offered himself in the service of his country.

They turned him down. The year was 1951. King Godwin was fifteen years old.

Avery Calder asked King if he'd like another drink. He nodded, losing count. The playwright ordered another round, then pushed himself away from the table. "I'm goin' to the Johnny Carson," he announced, standing unsteadily. "Godwin, will you come with me?"

"I think you better," Gilda said kindly. "Avery's stinko. He'll crack his head on the tiles if someone isn't there to hold him up. That is, if he can make it across the room."

King stood and caught the swaying man. Navigating the room with or without the playwright in tow would be a chore. He was looped himself. "Shit," he said, as they moved cautiously between the tables. It came out "Shee-yit."

"Young man," said Avery, drawing himself up suddenly, striving for dignity, "young, beautiful, blue-eyed Adonis. I am in no condition to damage you or your reputation. We are talkin' here about simple necessity and survival."

"Mr. Calder, suh," King heard himself say, heard the Spanish moss swamping his words, "I'm honored to accompany you. I admire you, suh."

Avery Calder blinked at him. "Did you say somethin'?" he asked.

King shook his head and laughed.

Avery Calder laughed, too.

As they passed, King heard "bravos" and "darlings." Also, "He's smashed again. . . . Still on Ritalin. . . . Nervous breakdown . . . Aging queen."

It made him mad. "Fuck 'em."

"What?" Avery asked.

"I'm honored, Mr. Calder. Honored," he enunciated clearly.

Avery Calder nodded, reaching up to stroke King's face in front of everyone. "As am I," he said. "As am I."

At the door of the men's room, a woman with a Toni home permanent in a seasick-green pants suit the color of a Greyhound bus interior tackled Avery, gushing and banging his chest with an autograph book. "Please sign, Mr. Calder. Charlie, it's Avery Calder, the playwright!"

Charlie, her husband, was less impressed. "Oh, yeah? Well, autograph my dick!" Weaving close enough for Avery to detect the smell of fermenting bourbon on his sour breath, Charlie unzipped his pants and grabbed his balls, displaying the contents while his wife gasped.

Before King could rush to his friend's defense, Avery pulled himself to his full height, snorted with disgust as though he had just swallowed a fly, stared into the drunk's nostrils, and delivered one of the lines that made him famous.

"I'm sorry, sir, but I'm afraid that would be quite impossible." Pause. "Perhaps I could *initial* it for you, though."

The men's room attendant knew Avery and rushed to his aid. "That's all right, sir," he told King, "I've got him. How you doing, Mr. Calder? I hear you got a real hit on your hands." He gave King a cold towel, settling him into a chrome and cracked leather chair, while he tended to Avery.

King closed his eyes and the room spun. Opening them again, he carefully made his way to the sink. His reflection in the mirror surprised him.

King had expected some raggedy-assed little redneck to be staring back at him, but what he saw was a handsome young man in a white dinner jacket, white shirt and black tie. His hair was slicked back, his face so flushed it looked like he had a California tan.

He looked like a movie star. Honest to God, he looked about as handsome as old Pat Wainwright. He looked like he could be Gilda Greenway's boyfriend. Like the kind of guy a sophisticated playwright would have a drink with.

He wished that girl Devon could see him now. Why the hell did she have to ask him if he'd really been in two movies? Why the hell had he ever mentioned the goddamn movies in the first place? He'd wanted to shock Inez Hollister, that's all. She'd been acting so superior, he'd wanted to let her know he'd been around. He wasn't just some cracker from the bayou. He'd done two movies.

King groaned, splashing cold water on his face, then stumbled back to the chair. Someday he'd have to tell that girl about those goddamn pictures. He'd call her tomorrow, maybe. Devon Barnes. He liked her name. He loved the way she laughed. When he finally got around to telling her what *kind* of pictures he'd been in, he'd try to make her see the humor of it.

And if he could pull that one off, he wouldn't need to get into the fucking Workshop. He'd be the best actor in the world already. He covered his face with the towel, stuck his feet up on the chrome ashtray stand and waited for Avery.

"Dahling, remind me to phone Vincent Sardi tomorrow and suggest some new rules for this august monument to mediocrity. The cognoscenti should be protected from people who reside in trailer parks."

"Yes, yes, darling. First thing." Standing in front of Sardi's, Gilda clutched the collar of her mink coat against the biting cold. The wind lashed her hair.

"Would you mind seeing Mr. Calder home? Pat and I've got to get back to the Sherry-Netherland. Poor Tallulah, she'll be having a fit."

Avery Calder leaned against Pat Wainwright as if the big man was merely a handy lamppost.

Would King mind doing anything Gilda Greenway asked him to do? Hell, no! "Ma'am," King said, "I'd be glad to."

Amused, she swept her swirling hair back and repeated, "Ma'am"?

King grinned sheepishly, happy to be her fool. "Miss Greenway." He tried to bow, but Gilda gripped his shoulder and, laughing, hauled him to a standing position.

She kissed him while Wainwright dumped Avery into the back seat of a cab. She'd meant to kiss his cheek, but King moved his head and caught her lips. He knew she was smiling, even while he kissed her. God, he was getting hard.

Pat Wainwright tapped his shoulder. "For the cab," he said, stuffing a fistful of dollars into King's hand and turning him toward the taxi.

"Oh, no, that's okay."

"Go on, kid. Could be the best investment I ever make, getting you away from her."

King fell into the cab, feeling higher than air, his hard-on killing him.

"Look after him, honey, won't you?" Gilda called, as the cab pulled away from the curb.

Avery gave the driver his address, then fell asleep against King's shoulder.

They woke at the same time, as the taxi stopped in front of the Fifth Avenue apartment building where Calder lived.

"Ah, Duke," the playwright said, as King yawned and stretched beside him. "What good deed have I done to earn the pleasure of your company?"

"It's King," King reminded him. "Miss Greenway asked me to see you home."

"Well, come on then," said Avery, stumbling out of the cab. "Takin' me home is like unemployment—it's a dirty job, but someone's got to do it. King. Now I remember. Kingston Godwin, isn't it? Southerner, right? Alabama?"

"Louisiana," King said, following the weaving playwright into the lobby.

"N'Awluns," Avery sighed reverently.

"Bayou Lafourche."

Avery rolled his eyes. "You were probably very young," he said. "I forgive you."

In the elevator, Calder patted his pockets. King thought he was looking for his keys. Instead, he pulled out his pill case again and rummaged through it with his finger. Finally, he chose a capsule and stuck it in his mouth.

"You feeling sick?"

Calder shook his head and swallowed the capsule. "I never feel sick. I never feel well, either. Except when I write. I try to feel as little as possible." He glanced sidelong at King. "Well, every line can't be a pearl, now can it? I suppose you're straight?"

"Well, sure," King said. Then he reconsidered. "I don't know. I think what I may be is jes' a little bit high." He grinned at Avery, feeling a sudden affection for the sweet, screwed-up writer.

Calder rolled his eyes. "Come on in."

He threw open the door to his apartment. Sherry-brown walls and cream-colored moldings attested to former elegance, but any claim to chic was now camouflaged by a steady stream of clutter. Ties and jockey shorts were tossed on the arms of chintz club chairs. Scuffed shoes peered in unmatched pairs from beneath Queen Anne wingbacks. An antique harvest table groaned under the weight of manila folders, yellowed news clippings, and a red Smith-Corona portable typewriter that appeared to have been used as an ashtray.

King had never seen so many books. Massive mahogany bookcases had long ago reached their limits. Now the overflow littered the Oriental carpets and lined the edges of the living room floor in mad literary profusion—and no particular order. Carson McCullers rested uncomfortably next to Sigmund Freud, Hawthorne held up a Bible with a broken spine, Plato shared a shoe box with Mickey Spillane.

"Excuse the disarray. I can't stand maids. They all want theater tickets and they don't do windows. I just fluff up the pillows once a week and pray. Relax. I'm too tired to corrupt anyone tonight, I just want a drink. Would you get me a drink, please? Bourbon, neat."

He tore off his bow tie. "I've got to get out of this monkey suit. Please, help yourself to a drink." He did a Loretta Young twirl toward the corridor leading to his bedroom. His knees buckled and he went down hard.

King hurried to him.

"Crap," the playwright muttered, touching his face gingerly to feel for blood. "Midnight the swan turns back into a turkey." He took

King's hand, trying to haul himself up. His ankle gave way. "Oh, shit. Help me up, dear heart."

He held out his arms and King leaned down to scoop him up, lifting him as if he were a child. The playwright held onto King's neck, letting himself be carried into the bedroom.

"Come in, sucker. Come in, sucker."

King was startled.

"Pay no attention, baby," said Avery, gesturing to a white wicker bird cage containing an overfed cockatoo with ruffled feathers. "Part of Gilda's traveling menagerie. They wouldn't let it in at the Sherry-Netherland, so she parked it with me. That's the only thing it says, but it's got lousy timing."

"Come in, sucker," said the bird, looking fried.

"You're very kind," said Avery, as King set him down gently on the bed.

The bedroom was slightly less cluttered, only because it was smaller. More reading material lay discarded and abandoned on every available surface. A wicker chaise with faded pink cushions looked like a set piece from *Baby Doll*. Stereo equipment and phonograph records crowded the shelves of an ancient armoire. The room had a wicked medicinal smell—a combination of stale whiskey and dead cabbage roses—and on the nightstand next to Avery Calder's unmade bed was a kitchen saucepan filled with a profusion of pharmaceutical boxes, prescription drugs, cough remedies, nose drops, and laxatives.

A serving cart had been set up as a makeshift bar near Calder's dressing room. "You want that drink?" King asked, glancing down at the man on the bed, who was limp as a teddy bear and feeling no pain.

"Terribly, terribly kind," the playwright murmured.

"Not always," King said. "You know, I've read your stuff. Your plays. You know how I know they're good? I want to do them. When I read your stuff, I want to be all the characters. Know what I mean?"

He opened the bourbon, righted a Baccarat highball glass, and began to pour Calder's drink. "They're so, I don't know . . . full, I guess." He carried the drink to the bed where Calder was snoring softly. "You probably think I'm nuts, right?" He shook his head.

He downed the bourbon, then poured himself another, and collapsed in an overstuffed armchair at the foot of the bed, sipping it slowly. The wind howled outside, rattling the panes of the French doors leading to the penthouse terrace. It reminded him of the French Quarter. Another time, another situation, not altogether dissimilar.

He liked listening to it from the luxurious, almost maternal depth of the pumpkin-colored armchair. He liked the warm pastel colors and soft lights of Calder's bedroom, the rich patterns of the dhurrie rug, and the deep wood grains of the lacquered floor and paneled walls.

Kicking off his shoes, he put his feet up on the foot of Avery Calder's bed. He thought about Devon Barnes again. He'd have a lot to tell her when he called her tomorrow. About those movies, maybe. About tonight, for sure. About the play and Sardi's and how he'd helped Avery Calder home and guarded him like a sentinel through the night because Gilda Greenway asked him to.

"Look after him, honey," she'd said. And King had promised her he would. Just like he'd promised his mama, long ago. Only this time, he was going to keep his promise.

No matter how tired he was.

He took one last sip of bourbon, rested the Baccarat crystal, and closed his eyes. There was a draft from the French doors. He folded his arms across his chest and let his head drop. He wished it was warmer in Avery Calder's apartment.

He thought of the heat wave he'd stepped into his first week in New York City.

He was fifteen years old and the sergeant told him to scram.

Just outside the recruiting center, a man with dark glasses and a black bristly crew cut grinned at him. "Don't be glum, kid," he said, "this is your lucky day."

It wasn't a friendly grin. It was the kind you'd see on a fella getting set to spit and lay down a challenge. "What part of Louisiana you say you're from?"

Glare from the man's glasses cut into King's sight, made him wince. "Didn't say," he answered, shielding his eyes. "Who wants to know?"

Sure enough, the man spat. "You some bad judge of people," he said. "I heard you talking to that army sarge. I was just trying to help you out." He pronounced it *hep*. "Just tryin' to hep."

King tensed, half expecting the guy to take a poke at him. Instead, he shrugged, stuffed his big hands into his pants pockets, and sauntered away.

Heat rose in sheets from the street. Red-faced men mopped their necks with handkerchiefs; women fanned themselves with their hats. There wasn't even a hint of a breeze. A nickel Coke bottle and a crumpled pack of Camels lay side by side in the gutter, sinking into the melting asphalt.

King looked longingly at the movie theater across the street. A blue sign, decorated with white icicles and a penguin, hung from the marquee: AIR CONDITIONED.

"Hey, wait up." King scurried after the man in dark glasses. "I'm from Bayou Lafourche and up around Kenner. Where you from?"

The man was only a boy himself, barely twenty-one years old. His name was Alvin Beamer, but folks called him Lucky, he told King. He had a three-room railroad flat over on West Forty-sixth Street, and a dog, also named Lucky, who did tricks for money.

Beamer had come up to New York from Bogalusa, Louisiana, about two years back to get into show business. He thought maybe he'd like to be a movie star, but so far his dog was making out better than he was.

He'd been surprised to find out King was only fifteen years old. He'd figured him closer to eighteen. But then, he said, boys from down home grew up fast.

Beamer had just enlisted in the marines; that's what he meant when he said it was King's lucky day. The boy needed a place to stay. Lucky needed someone to take care of his apartment and his rent-paying dog while he was off fighting in a place called Panmunjom. He wasn't sure exactly when he'd be called up, but the recruiting sergeant told him he'd be heading for boot camp pretty soon.

Beamer's apartment was smaller and his dog a lot bigger than King had imagined. Part collie, part shepherd, he was ferociously handsome and surprisingly gentle, though King was still wary. The apartment was a fourth-floor walkup, three little boxcar rooms with an airless toilet and a bathtub in the kitchen.

Beamer slept in the bedroom, overlooking Tenth Avenue. In the center room, where two bare windows faced a brick airshaft, King curled up uncomfortably on a military cot recruited from the Salvation

Army. The dog whimpered and sighed against the cool zinc of the kitchen tub until daybreak.

Three times in the month before he left for boot camp, Beamer was called to the hall phone and came back grinning sheepishly. "That was Mr. Opportunity on the line," he'd say, leashing his dog and leading him out. Twice he came back with a pocket full of cash. The last time, he came back fuming.

"Check is in the mail?" he grumbled. "You believe they're telling me that shit? Yeah, I told 'em, so's my dog's dingaling. And you get to see it again when that check is cashed and the green is in my palm. You know the three biggest lies in the English language, boy? 'I won't come in your mouth,' 'I love you,' and 'The check is in the mail.' "

Beamer left King $25 for September's rent, the telephone numbers of three people who owed him money, and a month's supply of Kam dog food. "Make sure you get cash in advance from anyone who wants to use Lucky in a moving picture," he told King, "especially if it's the Hungarian woman."

But none of the people who owed Beamer money knew who King was. In fact, they told him, they'd never heard of anyone named Beamer. Soon King had finished every drop of food in the apartment. He was trying to decide whether to share the Kam when the Hungarian woman called.

"Okay, okay, you bring me Lucky Stiff. I give you twenty-five bucks, okay?"

King dug out Lucky's fancy leash and winked in the mirror. "Showtime, boy," he said.

The address was a four-story firetrap on Forty-second Street, as close to the Hudson as a building could be without getting wet. The windows facing the elevated West Side Highway were boarded up with tin. Instead of the Hungarian woman, a burly, cigar-smoking man called to him from the top of the stairs. "Who the hell are you? Where's the redneck? How'd you get ahold of that dog?"

A door opened behind the man. In the white light that poured into the stinking hallway, a woman in a thin kimono appeared. "I thought she said the redneck was bringing the dog. What is this—a setup?" the burly man asked her. "Who sent this kid?"

She was pale and very blonde, and the light behind her made her kimono look as if it were constructed of cellophane.

After staring at him for a moment, she whispered something to the fat man, who laughed loudly. Then, cocking her head coquettishly, she drew aside her kimono, resting a hand on her hip. The thick bush of pubic hair was darker than the platinum curls framing her face. Her breasts were bare and full. As she leaned forward, they swung heavily toward him.

King gulped. The big dog whimpered, backing away from the stairs.

"Listen here, now," King addressed the burly man. "I had a call to bring this dog by. Said there'd be twenty-five dollars in it. Cash in advance."

"She meant ten," the man said. Without taking his eyes off King, he elbowed the pale girl. She sighed. Then, staring up at the ceiling, she spread her legs.

He wanted to stop her, to shield her from humiliation. To run up the stairs and knock that smoking turd out of the fat man's face. Instead, he said, "Go to hell, mister," and turned to leave the building.

"Jesus, George," the pale blonde spoke at last. "Give him the fuckin' twenty-five bucks, clean the dog's dick, and let's make a movie, okay?"

King followed Lucky and the platinum blonde into a brightly lit loft that looked as if it hadn't been cleaned in a very long time. A big mattress covered with a dingy white sheet took up most of one corner. King noticed a pile of whips and chains just within reach of the mattress.

"You sit over there," the man told him, pointing to a folding chair stuck in a shadowy corner. "You can be the producer." Beamer's Mr. Opportunity, whose name was George Oppotachevsky, seemed to find himself very clever and funny.

"Aw, George, leave the kid alone," said the girl, as she took off the kimono and fastened her net stockings with a black garter belt. "I bet you ain't never seen nothing like this before."

She was right. King watched with a mixture of revulsion and excitement as the girl, whose name was Margie, lay down on her back in the middle of the mattress, propped herself up on her elbows, and said, "Okay, Lucky, come here, good doggie."

She held a dog biscuit in her right hand.

Lucky barked and trotted over to her.

Margie let him sniff the biscuit, and then spread her legs wide open, and said, "Okay, Mr. De Mille, roll 'em."

As George moved in close with his camera, she smiled at Lucky and slowly inserted the dog biscuit between her legs so that King could just barely see it sticking out beyond the tangle of her pubic hair.

"Find the biscuit, Lucky," she said.

The dog barked and sniffed her stomach and thighs.

"Raise your legs, Marge, he's going for your asshole today," George said.

"No kiddin', George. Good thing you got a high school diploma."

But she obediently lifted both legs, until her face was hidden and all King could see was Lucky's long pink tongue roughly licking Margie's small pink rosebud. Then she slowly lowered herself down to the mattress, again spreading her legs as far apart as she could.

She looked over at King, who was hardly breathing, winked, and slowly began to fondle her breasts, stroking and pinching her dark pink nipples.

"Find the pussy, Lucky," she whispered to the dog, who was nibbling and licking her belly. With one hand, she carefully guided his head until he found what he wanted and buried his face deeper and deeper inside her. Margie thrust herself forward against the dog, pulsing rapidly until he suddenly withdrew from between her legs, licked happily at the wet fur around his mouth, and wagged his tail.

"Okay, doggie, time to get hard," Margie said. "Think of Lassie." Lucky mounted her from behind.

King came before the dog did.

The fourth time King was summoned to the makeshift movie studio on Forty-second Street he met Hannah Rugoff, the Hungarian woman. Margie was waiting in the doorway, as usual—kimono open, hands on her bare hips, breasts a fleshy canopy above him—as King climbed the stairs. He couldn't help brushing against her breasts, which were so pale he could see blue veins running under the skin, running right down to her nipples, which mashed back against his arm as he passed. "Excuse me, ma'am," he murmured.

There was booming laughter from within the room. "Her name

is Margie. And I am Hannah." King recognized the laughing woman's voice. She was the one who had phoned him.

Hannah Rugoff was the most extraordinary-looking woman King had ever seen. Her coal-black hair was short as a boy's crew cut. Her eyes, huge and oval as black olives, were the only gentle feature in a face of severe angles and angry planes. She wore khaki pants, a Hathaway shirt, and a string bow tie, and smoked a skinny black cigar. But she laughed a lot and when she did, she was almost beautiful. Hannah was Margie's roommate—and, obviously, a great deal more.

When Margie took her place on the mattress with Lucky, Hannah crossed the loft and stood next to King, leaning against the wall with her arms crossed rigidly in front of her.

"She likes you," Hannah said unexpectedly.

King gulped nervously. "You think so?"

She laughed her bawdy laugh and clapped him on the shoulder. "That's why I am here. I want to see you. She been saying maybe she gonna fuck you. I tell her wait till I see this beautiful fella, okay?" Hannah winked. "Now I see you. I say, okay."

"Naw," he said again, shaking his head. "Come on, now. What're you saying?" He was embarrassed and thrilled.

And utterly unprepared for what happened next.

Hannah began to strip. Standing beside him, she tugged off her bow tie and opened her shirt. She stood there for a moment in an undershirt and rough cotton boxer shorts. King was fifteen years old, thought he had seen it all, but now he could meet God smiling.

Hannah took him by the hand and led him to the mattress where Lucky and Margie were paying the rent. Sweat-soaked and trembling, King felt like a kid waiting in front of the principal's desk. His erection suddenly disappeared.

"Shoo," Hannah shouted and clapped her hands. Lucky disengaged himself with a whimper, and Margie looked up, a smile lighting her face.

"Oh, Hannah, now we're going to have us a *good* time."

"What's the big idea here?" George yelled. "We're making a picture."

"I am telling you to shut your face, Mr. Cecil B. De Mille," said Hannah. "Go, give the dog a drink of water. And when you come back, we going to make a real good movie. Yes, boy?" she said to King.

He was too astonished to do more than nod.

Hannah was kissing Margie gently and hungrily, like a lover, King realized. Like a boy would kiss a girl. It stunned him. He had never seen anything so strange and stimulating. He was watching two naked people making out in bed, and they were both women.

King didn't notice George returning. George was just there suddenly, behind the camera. When he caught King's eye, he winked and made a sign with his fingers, a circle that said everything was A-okay. And when King looked back at the bed, Hannah was lying on her belly with her head between Margie's open legs. Margie moaned as Hannah's tongue licked and caressed her. She pulled the dark-haired woman forward until Hannah's generous breasts hung just above her lips, so she could raise her head and slowly kiss first one nipple, then the other.

King ached to rip off his pants and release the ol' tallywhacker, straining against his zipper, to push his way deep inside of Hannah, then thrust himself into Margie's open mouth, to have her lips close around him. He wanted to grab Hannah's large, pear-shaped breasts and bury his face between them, biting and bruising her nipples, just as Margie was doing now. He groaned, longing to feel both women against his naked skin.

Hannah sat up on her knees.

"You don't want some fun, boy?" She slowly shoved two fingers farther and farther inside herself, then just as slowly withdrew them, dripping with her sticky juice, and pushed them gently into Margie's straining mouth.

"First I work you over, boy; then Margie's turn, yes?" The woman's big hands, strong as a lumberjack's, pulled his clothes from his body.

In the stillness of the room, a dark head moved slowly along the length of his huge and very hard cock. Hands fondled and stroked him. The dog joined in. Everything became a blur of mouths and thighs and eager, throbbing orifices, with the camera rolling.

A dark head was moving in his lap. A stranger's mouth held him. But suddenly he realized it wasn't Hannah or Margie. He wasn't kneeling against a dirty mattress. He was sitting in a chair in Avery Calder's bedroom and it was Avery Calder's mouth that was embracing him with such tenderness and skill. The most famous playwright on Broadway was giving him a blow job.

King turned his head. The wind was rattling the panes of the French doors leading to the terrace. He saw the moon outside the penthouse windows, a pale full moon big and yellow as a lemon pie, watching coldly behind discreet clouds. Under that same moon, Devon Barnes was warm in her bed. He closed his eyes and gave himself to her. And when he came, it was her hair tangled in his fingers.

In the morning, he woke alone in Calder's room. The bed was empty and unmade. He was still stretched out in the chair. There was a baby blue quilt thrown over him and a downy pillow behind his head. The draft from the French doors chilled him. He wrapped himself in the quilt and went into the bathroom.

Avery heard the shower running and came into the bedroom. He was wearing a dressing gown from Sulka, gray flannel slacks, and embroidered velvet slippers. When King emerged, dressed and toweling his wet hair, Avery was pacing nervously.

Last night, with the cheek blush and the collagen, the playwright had looked almost like a contemporary of Gilda Greenway's, not much older than her extraordinarily youthful thirty-four. This morning he looked closer to Wainwright's forty-seven, and not nearly as fit. He had aged a decade overnight.

Avoiding King's eyes, he handed the boy a glass of orange juice from the breakfast tray.

"Thank you," King said softly.

Calder gave a crisp nod and resumed pacing.

"Mmmm, good," King said with false enthusiasm, setting down the empty juice class noisily. "Just what I needed."

Avery Calder sighed. "A shot of gin would help. I'd like to—"

King threw the towel he was holding over his shoulder. "Listen here, Mr. Calder," he began.

The older man held up his hand. "Let me finish, please. Let me apologize for what—"

King felt a crimson flush. "No, don't," he said so forcefully he silenced Calder. "Just listen to me, okay?" He didn't know what he was going to say, only that he had to talk fast. He didn't want to humiliate

Avery Calder. He didn't want to see the great man's anguish. He couldn't bear to be the cause of it.

"You know I was awake," he finally blurted out. "I only pretended I wasn't. But I was trying to tell you something last night, before you fell asleep. I was getting you a drink, remember? And I was telling you about reading your plays. So, I just want you to listen now. What I was saying was that I think you're great. Maybe the most brilliant writer alive, okay?"

Avery Calder sat on the edge of the bed. He put his face in his hands. His sagging shoulders trembled as he broke into sobs.

King turned his back. "Okay, I'm going. I'm sorry, okay?"

"But it's cold out and you haven't had breakfast," Calder said from behind his hands. Then he took a deep breath and shook his head, and he was laughing.

For the first time that morning, he looked directly at King. "My God, I sound like your mother."

"Not to me," King said, reaching for a slab of toast from the tray and slathering it with jelly. "Sounded more like my daddy, when he was sober enough to notice."

EIGHT

FEBRUARY 13, 1956

N ursing a slight hangover, King walked south on Fifth Avenue, hair tousled, still wearing his rumpled dinner jacket as he thought about the events of the night before. This was New York, he told himself, quickening his steps, where a person's whole life could change in twenty-four hours. Turning west at Rockefeller Center, he stopped at the NBC drugstore across from Radio City Music Hall, bought the morning papers, and called Devon Barnes in Connecticut from a pay phone.

The girl who answered the phone said to hold on, she'd go see if Devon was in her room. Waiting in the drugstore phone booth, King flipped through the *Daily News*. He wondered if there'd be a review of Avery's play or maybe a shot of Pat Wainwright. The girl came back on the line just as he spotted the picture in Ed Sullivan's column.

"Devon's not in," she said.

But it was Devon he was looking at. King couldn't believe it.

There she was. And there *he* was. And Gilda. And the birthday girl. And the other one, who was smiling at him instead of the camera. Inez.

"Is Inez there?" he asked the girl.

He couldn't believe how fantastic Devon looked. Better than he remembered. Then he zoom-lensed in on Gilda Greenway's voice, saying something about Devon, just before the picture was taken. "Fabulous face." She'd said it to the agent, to the birthday girl's old man. Fabulous fucking face. Had any of them seen the papers yet? If Inez wasn't there, maybe May was. He had to let them know, had to tell one of them to get the *News*. "The Pearls Girl With Her Four Fans" read the caption beneath the photograph.

"There's nobody in the room." The girl sounded annoyed. "Everyone's at chapel but me and I've got a hundred and one fever and I'm supposed to be in the infirmary but the nurse said I could stay in the dorm as long as I didn't get out of bed."

"Sorry, kid," King said. "But this is very important. Would you tell her King Godwin called? Just take my number and ask her to call me back, would you? Please. It's *very* important."

He held on while she went to find a pencil. Then he gave her the number of the pay phone in his hallway and went home to wait for the call.

He went from room to room in the railroad flat on West Forty-sixth Street, pacing the three narrow cubicles the size of boxcars. He tapped a window, writing his name with his finger in the mist on the pane, idly at first, then with a flourish, the way Gilda had signed *Playbills* and autograph books the night before.

Then he marched back into the bedroom where the newspapers were lying open on a pile of discarded clothes. He looked at the picture of himself sitting at "21" with Gilda Greenway and the slim Texan, and shook his head. Then he hurried back to the kitchen, to the front door, to listen for the hall phone.

He knew he had to return the clothes he'd borrowed. He'd do it right after she called, King promised himself. Twice he thought of phoning Deauville Tolin and telling him he'd be there before four, not to worry, and by the way, had he seen the *News* yet? But he wanted to keep the phone free. And then he began to notice what a mess the place was.

He had to clean up. He kicked the shoes and old socks under the bed and cleared off the threadbare armchair. He hid the girly magazines behind the curtain that covered his closet. He emptied the fridge of old cardboard containers of half-eaten Chinese take-out, a pint of sour milk, and a slice of stale pizza. He found in the clutter the missing insurance forms the taxi company he applied to had told him to fill out, and an apron they'd docked him for at the bakery where he worked from five at night to five in the morning three nights a week. He even found a chewed-up rubber ball of Lucky's, which had to be three years old. Alvin Beamer had never returned, so King had sold the dog to Hannah when she moved to Vegas with Margie and a couple of her other girls.

After he swept up, he stood there, looking around the apartment in frustration, and disgust. For the first time he noticed the peeling paint and the dirty linoleum floor. Sure, it was clean. But it wasn't his place and it wasn't his furniture, and it wasn't good enough for a classy girl like Devon Barnes. It was just digs—an interim dump where he was bunking, waiting for his life to begin. Standing there with goosebumps suddenly prickling his skin, he got a crazy idea that what he'd been waiting for all along was Devon Barnes.

He couldn't believe he'd just thought that. After all, he was the hot young stud who'd seen all and done all, wasn't he? And yet . . . somehow he knew it was true. Devon Barnes was going to be a part of his life for a long, long time.

It had worked.

Inez could scarcely believe it.

In chapel that morning, she prayed the way she'd learned to pray in the fifth grade in Brooklyn. It was the first time her prayers had ever been answered.

She was the first one back to the room. Seeing the note pinned to the door with Scotch tape, she crossed herself and kissed her thumbs for Christ. Then she ripped down the note and ran to the phone.

He answered on the eighth ring, just when she was beginning to think he wasn't home. His voice was breathless. He must have run to the phone. "Yeah, hi there," he said.

"Hi there yourself." She said it the way Harriet taught her, sexy and slow, like Gloria Grahame in *The Big Heat.* "I got your note."

Silence. Then, cautiously, he shifted gears. "My note?" There was no mistaking his disappointment. "My note. Oh, yeah. Well, uh. How ya' doing, Inez?"

It hit her right in the belly. She bit her lip. Her prayer had no magic. Gloria's sexy voice hadn't pleased him. She hated Harriet. "I'm okay," she said, too injured to try to be sexy or clever or sweet.

"Is Devon around?" King asked.

"No," she sulked. *He wanted Devon. How stupid of me. I'm such a bimbo.*

"Well, uh . . . I mean, when do you think she'll be back? I mean, did she leave the school? Go someplace?"

"Yes." She'd gone for a walk with May. May had invited Inez along, but Inez could tell Devon wanted to be alone with May. She could see they wanted to whisper and gossip and share secrets. They were best friends. The way she and Harriet had been before Harriet ran off without even saying goodbye.

"Did she say where she was going?"

"No." Oh, God, she was practically whimpering. He'd think she was a jerk, a whining loser.

"Was she . . . I mean, did she go . . . alone?"

Why was he doing this to her? Why did he keep asking questions about Devon? He was taunting her.

"No," Inez snapped. "She did not go alone. Is there anything else you want to know?"

"Hey, babe, sorry. Jeez. What're you so riled up about?"

"I've got to see you," Inez blurted out, surprising herself. "I mean, I want to talk to you."

"Me?" He couldn't disguise his surprise.

"There's no one else. No one I can really talk to. Harriet was my best friend and now she's gone. I need to talk to someone. I feel so . . ." She looked down the hall, through the window at the end of the corridor, and took her inspiration from the stark treetops and snow clouds looming low and bleak.

"Depressed," Inez finally said. And suddenly it was true. "I feel so damned depressed. I've got to get out of this place for a little while and talk to someone who isn't wearing a pony tail. Please,

King, could I just come see you? I can get a pass. Please, for just a little while?"

"Well, sure, if you want to. But maybe you ought to—"

"Oh, thank you, thank you, King." She ran to her room for a pencil, took down his address, then looked at the timetable and told him what train she would catch. He gave her directions from Grand Central. And before he could tell her about the picture in Ed Sullivan's column, she hung up.

She signed out to her parents, Maureen and James Hollister. Destination: Brooklyn, New York.

Over her dead body.

Destination: anyplace but.

For one dumb minute, Inez considered phoning her parents at Aunt Mary's, which was where they got their calls, and making up some story to be sure they wouldn't call the school while she was gone. And then she thought, what was she, crazy? Her mother had phoned exactly three times in the three and a half years that Inez had been at Westbridge.

The first phone call was to say that her brother Terry had been arrested for cutting someone in a street fight, and did Inez have any rich friends she could borrow money from? The second call, months later, was to let Inez know that Terry had jumped bail and Jimmy, Jr., had gone with him. The third and final call, filled with shrieking and tears, had been about "Big Jim" getting drunk and telling her the most terrible lies, stories he made up just to break her heart. Filthy tales of mortal sins. They *were* lies, weren't they, Inez?

Soon after, "Big Jim" himself phoned. He was drunk and said he missed her. He lay awake nights just thinking about her, he said, about her titties and her sweet juicy little pussy. He was her father, he said, suddenly indignant, and he wanted her to come home, right away. Or he'd take the strap to her again—she wasn't so big that he couldn't still give her a good licking.

That night, Inez told Harriet about everything, including Jim's drunken phone call. The next day, Inez standing behind her, terrified, Harriet phoned Aunt Mary, pretending to be the dean. She told Mary that she would swear out a warrant for Mr. Hollister's arrest if he ever used obscene language over the school phones again. All phone calls to the school were monitored by the FBI for obscenity and threats, she explained to poor addled Aunt Mary, whom Inez could imagine crossing herself and clutching a gold-plated crucifix safety-pinned to her housecoat. If Mr. James Hollister ever phoned again, he'd be immediately arrested.

Inez never heard from him again.

Through the train windows, Inez looked out at the snow that was beginning to fall—big and fluffy, like Ivory Snow flakes. Ninety-nine and forty-four one-hundredths percent pure. Not like Brooklyn, where the snow was as dirty as atomic fallout, even before it hit the ground.

Well, here she was, Inez Hollister, going to meet a real hunk in New York City. This train was carrying her away from Brooklyn, not Connecticut. This ride was carrying her toward her true destiny. She knew it.

At the age of eleven, Inez had known what it was like to be alone, to scratch for her own space in the chicken yard of life. Her father was good-for-nothing shanty Irish trash who had charmed her mother into marrying him with false promises and bogus dreams of grandeur in the restaurant business, then couldn't afford to send his three kids to decent schools on the wages he made as a waiter. He worked at Gage & Tollner, an elegant old-world restaurant with real gaslights on Fulton Street that served gigantic lamb chops to the regular customers and sent its employees home with serving-cart scraps for the dogs. Except that the dogs in Jim Hollister's family were his scrawny wife and hungry kids. Some nights he didn't come home at all and Inez would be sent to the Volunteers of America for paper cups of cold chili to feed four ravenous mouths. It was always a treat on Sunday after mass because then the kids got Kool-Aid.

Exhausted from long days of working in the laundry above their basement apartment, Inez's mother had no time to take care of her only daughter. The boys could watch out for themselves and if they failed, there were reform schools that could do the job. But Inez needed supervision. She was poor in her studies (always a snob, Inez had told her mother arrogantly, "Who needs to pass Spanish? There isn't one Spanish-speaking person in the subway I want to speak to!"), and when left to her own devices, spent all of her time at the movies or the public library, devouring books as if they were steaks and she hadn't eaten for a week.

It was Jim Hollister, a hypocrite to the manner born, who suggested the convent school at St. Ignatius. Behind the stone walls, Inez found herself with fifty other girls in blue blazers and white pleated skirts. She paid for her uniform with money she earned washing dishes in the school kitchen.

The nuns were a far cry from the weeping and shouting at home. Next to her mother's fatigue and her father's psychotic mood shifts, they seemed pallid and cold. Yet, as time passed, Inez learned that most of the girls came from poor homes and were as terrified as she was, and she sensed that the sternness of the sisters hid a genuine concern for their young charges. Outfoxing two brothers and always having to dance a neurotic tango to stay six feet ahead of her father had prepared Inez for a graduate degree in cunning and self-preservation, even at the still tender age of thirteen.

In no time, she was running the convent school and designating the pecking order for her classmates. With other students bullied into doing her homework, Inez's grades improved and she had free time to read and write the imaginative stories and heavy-breathing romance novels that fueled her daydreams.

One nun took a particular interest in her. Sister Marcus had herself been an aspiring writer at an early age, before she joined the order. In Inez's aggressive personality, she saw the remnants of her own lost cause and was determined to help the girl. Sister Marcus encouraged her to put her thoughts on paper, made her editor of the school paper, lavished her with friendliness and praise. Inez wrote wild and pretentious short stories for English class about rich society girls who shopped at Wanamaker's and committed suicide in the ladies' room at Schrafft's. Sister Marcus just smiled affectionately and said she could turn out to be the next Dorothy Parker.

"Have you actually ever *been* to Schrafft's?" Sister Marcus asked.

"No, Sister, but everyone in J. D. Salinger stories eats at Schrafft's in their Brooks Brothers polo coats," replied Inez. "It must be a very glamorous place."

Sister Marcus took her to Manhattan one Wednesday for a field trip to Schrafft's. Inez took one look at all the little old ladies with blue hair eating chicken sandwiches on cheese toast and after that all of her characters dined at the Stork Club.

One weekend, when Inez returned to the filth of the family basement, her mother was hiding her face in her raw hands, tears smudging the edges of her fingers. Jim Hollister was gone for good, her brothers would have to go to work, and there wouldn't be enough money left from her meager wages at the laundry to keep Inez at St. Ignatius.

Inez was panic-stricken.

Instead of sleeping in the cool gray-walled dormitory, she'd be back in the dingy room with her brothers. Instead of Sister Marcus encouraging her to become the next Dorothy Parker, there would be her mother, forcing her into a grueling life of washing and ironing.

"I won't leave school, I can't!" Inez wailed.

"We haven't got a cent, honey!"

"Then I'll talk the sisters into letting me work full-time!"

Sister Marcus, rushing to her defense, prevailed upon the mother superior to assure Inez hot meals and a free education. In exchange, she would set up the tables for breakfast, lunch, and dinner in the dining hall, help out in the kitchen, and serve. Inez didn't care. Anything was better than a full-time life at home—with or without her father—in the basement under the laundry, choking on the smell of lye and detergent and starch. She hated the apartment with its crucifixes and candles and Virgin Marys. It looked like a goddamn Anna Magnani movie.

Inez hated her mother's drabness, resented her inability to use men the way women in the movies did. When she came home on weekends, she lapsed into long periods of hostile silence. She tried to confide in her mother, tell her about her ambitions.

"Honey, you're just climbin' Fool Hill," was the standard reply. "You better come to your senses before you fall off and break your head wide open."

Eventually, her father returned and things got worse. Sometimes he'd meet her at school and take her for an egg cream on Fulton Street. But then he'd touch her knee under the table and his fingers would move up her thigh to the soft forbidden places the nuns always warned her about. Inez hated him for that, but it was the only physical contact she had. She dreaded it, but she needed it, too.

The first time was the scariest. Some of the girls at St. Ignatius were going to a Saturday night dance at Erasmus Hall High and had even pooled their resources to buy Inez a pink gabardine dress marked down to $9.95 at Gimbel's. It was her first dance, her first grown-up dress, and she was wearing her first lipstick—orange sherbet Tangee, from Woolworth's.

Her mother was at Aunt Mary's, saying a rosary for a neighbor who'd been run over by a taxicab on Delancey Street in the rush-hour traffic. Her brothers were riding the Cyclone at Coney Island. And Jim Hollister was already into his second bottle of Jack Daniel's when his daughter emerged from the bathroom, ready to leave.

Maybe it was the first time he really saw her. The toadstool had turned into a truffle. Her shoulders were broad, her hips narrow. Even at thirteen, she was growing tits. The pink dress bulged in all the right places. Inez wore a green bracelet and a gardenia in her hair, like Dorothy Lamour in *Road to Rio*.

"Where do you think you're going, dressed up like a Chinese whore?" His breath was foul. He loomed over her like a hairy, grotesque spider.

She edged away, but he was too fast. "Don't you want to give your old man a good night kiss?" He lunged. It happened fast, but the next few minutes seemed like an eternity.

She thought her heart would explode with fear. She fought him, but he pinned her arms behind her while he ripped her panties. A fire leapt at her thighs where his strong beefy fingers clawed her flesh. And then she felt the scalding pain between her legs as something big and rough tore into her until she thought she would vomit.

He was breathing heavily and coughing his raspy cigarette cough as he plunged faster and harder, his hair rubbing against her mouth. Inez had never experienced such pain.

It was the pain she would always remember—even when the humiliation and the smells were forgotten. But then she closed her eyes, pretending it was happening to somebody else in a movie or a book, and she knew, even in the terror and pain, that she would survive.

Suddenly it was over. Jim Hollister grunted, rolled over, and made moaning sounds.

"You bastard!" Inez cried, but her father wasn't listening.

Her legs ached, but they were still there. Her arms were still hers. She was the same girl, even though she looked and felt battered and old with shame. The same mirrors she had peered into with such impish satisfaction when she was dressing for the Erasmus Hall dance now seemed clouded and disapproving. Her makeup was smeared. There was a lump on her forehead and an ugly brown bruise on her arm. Her hair looked like mattress stuffing. The gardenia was on the floor.

She wrapped her bloodied dress and panties in newspapers and buried the bundle in a garbage can in the alley. Her father was snoring now, with no regret. She thought for a fleeting moment about burying her mother's butcher knife into his sleeping body, nude below the frayed hem of his torn undershirt, until it severed the arteries around his heart and broke off at the handle.

Then she thought of more important things, like the movies she'd never see, the books she'd never read, and the fame she'd never have. So she pulled on a pair of jeans and a blue cotton shirt that belonged to one of her brothers, and left home.

A policeman found her at one in the morning, wandering near Prospect Park, and asked her where she lived. He drove her back to the convent in a patrol car and she slipped into her dormitory room. She didn't fall asleep until dawn.

It happened several times after that. Always on weekends, sometimes when her mother was sleeping only a few feet away. She learned to endure it in silence, without tears. She hated her father. She hated all men. But after each submission, there was a reward. First, it was a purse, then a parasol. She was acquiring quite a wardrobe and her father was not the groveling, guilt-ridden, crimson-faced coward he once had been. He seemed contented and fulfilled. Inez's mother remarked on the change that came over him. "You must be doing something to please him," she said one day between rinse cycles. "It can't be that he's found God. I still can't get him to mass for a hill of beans."

Inez winced, but there was a half-smile on her face. She had discovered the key to unlock the hearts—and pocketbooks—of men. And she would use it on them all. The invitations came often now, and many nights Inez would sneak out of the convent to accompany boys to parties.

"Inez, you're trying too hard to have fun," said Sister Marcus. "That's understandable. You're young and beautiful and a compliment to any boy, but don't try to catch all the gold rings at once or they'll cease to have any value at all and you'll fall off the merry-go-round."

Her father's advice was even stricter.

Don't wear so much rouge. Don't laugh so loud. Don't talk too much. "Don't use forty-dollar words if all you've got in your pocket is forty cents" was her favorite. She ignored it all. She was on a roll now. She wasn't yet sure what she wanted, but she knew she could get it. And she didn't much care, as long as it took her as far away from Brooklyn as her long, shapely legs could carry her. Sure, she sometimes felt helpless and afraid. Alone. But she was learning fast.

When she graduated from eighth grade, Inez was informed that she had finished her schooling at St. Ignatius. There were no more courses for her to take. High school seemed out of the question, college an even more remote possibility.

Once again Sister Marcus stepped in. She took upon herself the liberty of assembling a portfolio of Inez's short stories and newspaper editorials, and secretly mailed them to Nicholas Pryor, a former English professor of hers at Stephens College who was now the secretary at the Westbridge School.

Mr. Pryor wrote back. Things looked promising for a scholarship.

Inez pleaded with her mother, who argued that there were four years of expense ahead, and times were still financially ruinous. Inez was experienced at serving meals, and she could earn spending money waiting on tables. Jim Hollister went on a rampage. Where did she get off thinking she ought to go to a fancy boarding school? They couldn't do without her to help out at home, he bellowed, but Inez knew he meant *he* couldn't do without her at home.

She stood her ground and bit the bullet. "Listen to me, Daddy. Either I go or I *tell*. That means Mama, the nuns, the convent, everyone in goddamn fucking Brooklyn! I wonder what they'd say at Gage & Tollner. As a matter of fact, I wonder what they'd say at the local precinct station."

Jim Hollister was speechless. His mouth began to move in little round gulps, like a goldfish. "You tell and you won't live to get to that fancy school of yours."

"Terrific!" She spat back, fearless now. She already had one power. She decided to see if she had another. "In addition to rape, incest, and child abuse, we'll add assault and battery and attempted murder. Let's see. By my calculation, nobody in Brooklyn will lay eyes on you again for at least eighty-five years!"

Sister Marcus gave her a goodbye speech on the train platform in Brooklyn about how men took advantage of teenage girls, her mother gave her a prayer book and a rosary, and her father didn't bother to show up at all. But she was on her way. And once she was installed at Westbridge, she swore, smoked, and drank smuggled old-fashioneds made with drugstore cherries. It took her about three weeks to figure out how to terrify the other girls into doing her chores.

And she survived. She wrote three of the school plays, edited the the campus paper and the yearbook, and had the male professors eating out of her hands like dumb pigeons.

She would never, *ever* go back to Brooklyn.

If only they could see her now. The kids who had worn the same uniform at St. Ignatius but thought she was inferior because she washed their dishes and ran their errands. The nuns who fluttered like trauma-tized penguins, unable to figure out which girl had mixed up the laundry lists or left a condom in the chapel or ordered 300 pizzas to be delivered to the mother superior. The father who didn't mind feeling her up when his dick got hard but laughed at her dreams of being a writer like Dorothy Parker. And all the jerks who laughed if you said your life story would someday be made into a movie and maybe Ava Gardner or Gilda Greenway would star in it opposite Patrick Wainwright or Cary Grant.

You weren't supposed to have any ambition at all in Brooklyn— except maybe to move to Queens, which Inez's mother thought was paradise. Well, it was goodbye to all that, as Robert Graves had written, and goodbye to the stink of Dreft and Trend and Oxydol and her father's Cremo cigars. And hello—to what? She still didn't know what or whom, but from the thumping in her heart and the gurgle between her legs, today was as good a time to start as any.

The snow had turned to sleet by the time the train plowed noisily through the tunnel into Grand Central Station, but Inez felt almost feverish thinking about all of the things she wanted to do to King Godwin.

Inez looked like an ice cream sundae by the time she reached King's apartment. The rouge and the cherry-red lipstick had melted into a crust of pink slush on her face, and the rest of her was covered with a half-frozen layer of snow.

She hadn't realized how far it was from Grand Central Station to Tenth Avenue, and her thin dress-up clothes were poor protection against the winter storm. Beneath a beret of ice, her hair was soaked. So was her coat. The ladylike white gloves she wore were translucent with moisture and frozen to her fingers. She looked like Lillian Gish in a silent movie.

"You must be freezing," he said, opening the door to his apartment. She nodded, but her teeth were chattering too hard to smile. Inez waited at the threshold in a puddle of melting snow, the dye from her glamorous high-heel shoes staining her stocking feet blue.

"Come on in." King was torn between pity and laughter. "What happened to you? Did you get lost?"

She stuttered, but couldn't answer. The next thing he knew, though he couldn't imagine her wetter than she was already, tears were streaming down her cheeks.

King took her in his arms. He felt her breasts heaving against his flannel tartan-plaid shirt with great wracking sobs. "Don't you know your way around the city? I should have met your train. I'm sorry. You poor kid."

Inez lifted her face to him. The snow had melted from her eyelashes, which were thick and shiny. Her eyes were shining, too, looking up at King with forlorn gratitude. Her lips trembled, puffy and red. King wondered if they were still cold.

He was surprised by the intensity with which she returned his kiss. By how sweet her lips tasted and how warm they had become. He felt himself stir. Her coat, still cold and wet, rubbed against his pants, and he strained toward her, pressing toward the warmth beneath her clothing. She was the wrong girl, but the contours of her body fit him in all the right places.

Her face was warming now, but her hands, touching the back of his neck, sent shivers through his groin. King peeled off her icy gloves and put her cold hands inside his shirt, pressing against her again, her nose brushing the hairs of his neck.

"I love you," Inez said, hiding her face shyly in the flannel warmth of his shirt collar.

His stomach was in a knot. This was Devon's friend, for chrissake.

"Do you?" he whispered, moving her hand toward his waist. He felt her pull away. "Do you?" he asked again, holding her wrist until she stopped resisting. Then he moved her hand down again to the great lump bulging against his fly. Her eyes grew large when she felt it. In her fantasies, she hadn't imagined anything quite so . . . *amazing*.

"Could I borrow a bathrobe until my clothes dry?" She shivered violently.

"Here." She handed him a paper bag she'd carried under her coat. "I brought us a picnic from the country. I'll be right back. I gotta take off this dress and my stockings."

She came back in, drying her hair with a towel and wearing King's Marlon Brando sweatshirt, a gift from a girl he'd met waiting tables in the Village.

"What do you think?" She modeled the sweatshirt, which hung to her mid-thighs. Then she hugged herself. "It's warmer in your bedroom," she said, huskily. "Bring the food. We can eat in there."

King followed Inez into his bedroom and watched her settle, crosslegged, on the bed. She said she needed to talk to someone, but here she was, wearing nothing but his sweatshirt, looking unbelievably sexy and inviting. She's just an innocent schoolgirl, King told himself. She doesn't even realize what she's doing to me.

"I'm still cold, King," she purred, half closing her eyes. "Please warm me up."

He sat down next to her, wrapped both arms around her, and pulled her close. She rested her head on his chest. Then after a minute he turned her chin up and kissed her very gently. Inez moaned almost inaudibly, then slowly ran her tongue over his lips and into his mouth. King could hardly believe what was happening; he felt as if Inez was fucking his mouth with her tongue, twisting it in and out, then teasing him by nibbling his lower lip with quick sharp bites.

"Inez," he whispered, wanting to warn her, to give her the chance to stop him now, before he tore the sweatshirt away to expose her breasts, before he ripped his pants off and slammed himself into her.

"Please, King, make love to me."

She brought his hands up to her mouth, bit into the fleshy part of each of his palms, then guided his fingers underneath the shirt, up to her breasts.

Since his porno adventures in the loft with Hannah and Margie, King had slept with other girls, mostly aspiring actresses whose eyes he caught as he walked by the theaters where they waited to audition. He sometimes missed Margie's expertise and Hannah's imaginative forays, but the gypsies were pretty and sweet and warm, with no strings attached. And they seemed to enjoy his energy and enthusiasm.

But Inez was a confusing mixture of innocent kid and horny vixen. As she lay back on his bed, her legs spread slightly apart, she seemed a willing, inviting pupil. Yet he couldn't help feeling that she knew just what she wanted, that she was totally in control of what was about to happen to him.

King yanked off his jeans, almost embarrassed by the size of the ol' tallywhacker springing to attention. It grew very large and Inez pulled him to her with one hand and stroked his balls with the other.

"Touch me everywhere," she said. "Make me feel your soul."

He pulled at her underpants, but she pushed his fingers away. "No, not yet."

King understood. She was nervous, wanted to be ready for him. He ran his tongue over her nipples, already taut with excitement, and remembered her tongue in his mouth as he bit down on her left breast hard enough to leave a tiny red mark.

"Oh, yes, King." Inez thrust her other breast into his open mouth, her squirming body giving him permission to claim them both. Then she pushed him away, opened her legs wider, and touched herself over her panties.

"Feel how wet I am," she whispered. He put his hand where hers had been and could feel the tropical steam through the wet silk. She guided him over the elastic waistband and down into the sticky, moistened tangle of her hair, panting as together they explored her with their fingers.

When she withdrew her fingers, coated with her own syrupy

liquid, and slid them over her tongue to lick them clean, he suddenly saw Hannah, fingering herself that afternoon in the loft. He ripped off Inez's underpants and tried to shove himself inside her, but before he had a chance to plunge and thrust as he wanted to, she twisted out from under him.

"Inez, please, I promise I won't hurt you," he groaned. He was on his knees, his hands pulling at her hips, urging her to satisfy his craving. And then her mouth was there, beneath him, and she was pulling him down closer so her tongue could lap the silvery-white drops of liquid at the very tip of his cock.

She smiled up at him. "I know I'm taking a long time, but I want this to be very special, King. Please," she said, pleading, pulling him farther down into her throat.

The throbbing pressure in his groin was too intense.

"Now, Inez, *now.*"

He guided his cock into her effortlessly and he felt her insides reaching up around him, contracting and expanding as his explosion came, building slowly at first, then erupting with a fury that was unlike anything he'd ever felt. This was different from acting out Margie and Hannah's erotic movie scripts or the friendly, good-time sex he'd had with the chorus girls. Now he understood what the other guys meant when they talked about real fucking. He was fucking Inez and if he died at the very moment he came way down deep inside her, he didn't care if he didn't go to heaven, because he was already there.

Later, still lying on top of her, he wondered whether she would tell Devon what she'd done this snowy afternoon, and hoped she would return and do it again. And he wondered how in hell a sixteen-year-old kid, from Westbridge School, knew the things Inez Hollister knew.

"You don't think I'm a tramp, do you? You haven't lost respect for me, have you, King?"

Lost respect? You're a goddamn sexual genius, King wanted to tell her.

"Of course not. I didn't hurt you, did I?"

She snuggled up close to him, massaging his thighs. "Oh, no. That felt so nice." She buried her face in his chest and said, "I really liked it when you put it in my mouth, King. You are so . . . *enormous.*"

Devon. Jesus, he didn't even want to think about her, but he couldn't help it. He'd wanted to see Devon, to talk to her about acting. But Inez was here, lying in his arms, and he liked what he was hearing.

The room was suddenly chilly and the growl in his stomach reminded King that he hadn't eaten all day.

"Let's get under the covers and eat your picnic," he suggested. He took out one of the pimiento cheese sandwiches she'd made in the Westbridge kitchen and offered her half.

Inez stared straight ahead, ignoring him. "First, I have to tell you why I'm not a virgin."

He didn't want to hear it. He got out of bed, trying to swallow the sticky cheese spread that clung to the roof of his mouth, and picked up his flannel shirt from the floor where he'd flung it.

"About what happened with my father . . ." She was still talking. My God, thought King, this girl is some *yenta*. The newspaper was under his shirt. He wanted to show her the photo in Ed Sullivan's column. *Hey, look, Inez, we're a couple of celebrities,* he wanted to say.

But he heard what she was saying now. About her father, and the fear, and the blood. He let the newspaper lay there on the floor and crawled back into bed. "You poor kid," was all he could say.

She told him most of it, leaving out the part about the strange control it gave her over the father who raped her. Then she put her head on her knees and began to sob.

"I should've gone easy on you," King said, not knowing what else to say.

"Oh, no. *This* was different. You understand me. We love each other. It wasn't like with *him*, just because I was there and he wanted somebody. It wasn't like that at all."

It was. It was just like that.

She took a big bite of her sandwich. "I'm starving. Can I have a root beer?"

God, thought King, this girl is incredible. Just told me a story so fucking depressing it would make *Stella Dallas* look like a slapstick comedy, and now she's hungry.

There was a knock at the door.

"Shit. I hope it's not the cops. How old are you, Inez?"

"Seventeen," she lied. "I'll be eighteen soon."

He kissed her forehead. "Well, hurry up," he said, pulling his pants on. "I'll be right back. Maybe you should see if your clothes are dry."

It was the old man with the tubercular cough from the front apartment. "For you." He jerked his thumb at the hall phone.

"I'll be right back," King shouted to Inez. He knew who it was before he touched the receiver.

Devon had just gotten his message. On the other end of the line she was standing, twirling the phone cord around her finger. She was in complete bliss.

"Hello?" he asked.

"King, it's Devon. I just got your message. I'm—I'm so glad you called."

He could practically see her smiling. He hopped around to keep warm, grinning like Harpo Marx on the trail of a blonde. "Are you?" he asked.

"Oh, yes, I'm just sorry it took me so long to call back." *Cawl bay-ck.* He loved that southern voice. "You see," she continued, "I just ran into Roberta Stevens, the girl who answered the phone. She told me she'd left a note on my room door. That a boy with a funny name called. But when I got to the room, the note wasn't there." She was laughing.

"You think I have a funny name?"

"Yeah." She laughed her terrific hooting laugh. "I do. And listen, I'm sorry about asking you that damn fool question."

"What question is that?"

"You know, about whether you were telling the truth. Lord, you blessed me out for that. And I deserved it, too. I told May about it today—"

"You did?" She'd been talking about him. To May Fischoff. He liked that. He liked that it was May she'd been talking to, May she'd gone out with today. And he liked the thought that probably at the same minute he was phoning her, she was talking about him. "Kismet," he said.

It meant fate, Deauville had told him. Kismet, like the movie Deauville had dragged King to see, and then spent half the picture grumbling about how they tried to make Howard Keel look colored. Shit, Deauville had said, whenever there was a decent part for a Negro in a movie, Hollywood would slap Max Factor "Egyptian" on a thick slab of white bread like Howard Keel. "Except for Paul Robeson. He was no cakewalking minstrel clown. He was a chunk of truth that stuck in honky craws like a fishbone."

King didn't know who Paul Robeson was, but the girl he'd taken to the picture show did, and she'd gone home with Deauville. When King ran into him the next day, Deauville grinned and said the girl had been a credit to her race.

"What's that?" Devon asked.

"Nothing. Kismet. You know, fate. What'd you tell May?"

"Oh, just what you said about truth, about how, for an actor, that's all there is. I agree with you. I just never thought of it before."

"You ever heard of The Workshop?"

"Well, of course. If I had the nerve, I'd try out for it—"

"Audition," King corrected her. "Maybe I can help you. Maybe we could go over some scenes together when you're ready. I'm going to audition for them soon. You know who Avery Calder is?"

"The writer?"

"Playwright. I met him last night. He wants me to read for him. He says if I'm as good as I think, he'll help me get into The Workshop. He says Gilda might give me a recommendation, too."

"Wow!"

"I almost forgot," he said. "Did you see today's *News?* Our picture is in the paper. That's what I called you about."

"No kidding? Oh, Lord, I've got to tell May and Inez! They'll freak out. I wonder if Inez knows."

"Devon, wait—"

"I don't know where the heck she is. I haven't seen her since this morning. I hope she's okay—"

"She's okay." He had no choice. He would not lie to her.

"Oh, I'm sure she is. She's probably just gone to the library—"

"She's here."

Silence.

For what seemed like an eternity.

King could hear her breathing.

"I'm sorry," she said, and hung up.

King put the receiver back on its cradle and rested his head against the metal phone box. When he looked at the doorway to his apartment, Inez was standing there, wrapped in a blanket. Christ. He should have known this was going to get him in trouble. He felt like shit.

"Hi," she said. "I missed you. You're not mad at me or anything, are you?"

"Aren't you cold?"

She nodded. "I was afraid you'd leave me."

"Naw," he said, depressed and suddenly tired. "I wouldn't do that."

It was the first lie. Because, though King didn't leave Inez, he meant to. He meant to just bundle her up, get her over to Grand Central, and send her back to Connecticut. He didn't think he'd see her again, not then, not ten minutes after he'd made the biggest mistake of his life by telling the naked truth to the laughing Texan.

When he followed Inez back into the seedy, godforsaken dump he called home, what followed—and his response—was a mystery to him. She turned, opened her arms, and pulled him down on the bed, under the blanket. His defenses crumbled. He didn't know whether it was out of despair over Devon or simply anger. But Devon . . . beautiful, southern Devon was at the heart of it. He put his arms around Inez's body and squeezed her so hard he bruised her rib cage. She tried to protest, tried to push him away and catch her breath, but King didn't let her. Goddamn it, she was part of the reason he was in this and she was going to take *all* of him. He dragged her down to the floor, pulled his hard cock out of his pants, and roughly throwing up her legs over his shoulders, just started banging her. And when Inez whimpered and then tried to scream, King clamped his mouth over hers until their teeth scraped, and rode her brutally until he was done.

This time, King didn't bother to apologize. Not even to himself. On the way to the train, he was wrapped in a numbness that was safer than rage. His hands were plunged into the pockets of his leather jacket. His shoulders were hunched against the cold. He watched his thick boots plod resolutely through the gray slushy snow.

Beside him, Inez shivered in silence, glancing at him with eyes tear-stung by worry and weather. She clutched his arms with two hands, like an orphan on Christmas, afraid someone would take back her new present and give it to another child. After she bought her ticket and he walked her to the gate, King said, "Well, take care now, okay?"

"Am I going to see you again? I mean, could I come in again next weekend?"

He shrugged and shook his head in wonder at her persistence. This bitch had nerve. "I'll call you," he lied.

But the next weekend, after telling Deauville about this chick he'd found who couldn't get enough of his big ol' tallywhacker, after saying, "You ought to meet her, Deau, she'd gobble you up and spit you out, man," King phoned Westbridge and told the girl who answered to put a note on Inez Hollister's door that King said it's okay to come down on Sunday.

Had he really imagined that Devon Barnes might answer the phone if he called? Would he have said, "I fucked your roommate but I'm in love with you"?

Years later, King realized he'd used Inez as a link to Devon. He knew Devon would never go out with a guy who'd slept with her roommate. But if Inez became his girl, he could call Devon Barnes and say, "Hey, remember I promised you I'd help you with the Workshop audition? Come into town, and we'll do some scenes together."

And the more he thought about how Inez had kissed him and touched him and held him, the more he wondered what else they could do together. So he left the note for Inez.

And, of course, she arrived that Sunday, and the next. After that, she came late Saturday afternoons and stayed over. Then she started coming in some weekends after classes on Friday. Sometimes he'd tell her he couldn't see her because Avery was taking him to the theater, or Gilda wanted him to be her escort at a party for Patrick or at an opening night. Inez never begged to come along, and King never suggested it, not even when Patrick Wainwright asked whether King knew a discreet, attractive girl who might join them, just to even things up a bit. Inez said, "That's okay. I'll just wait at your place. I'll see you when you come home. I'll be there, waiting for you."

She became a habit. He found he liked having her waiting up for him. It was comfortable to talk about what he'd learned about the structure of a play from Avery Calder's analysis, what it felt like to be mistaken for Gilda's boyfriend by Dorothy Kilgallen. He described how the fans screamed, "Oooo, there he is, King Godwin! Oooo, King, King!" Inez was a good listener. And it was good to know that when he brought home the buzz of Gilda's presence and the sexual tension between her and Patrick, Inez was sitting there reading, the blanket thrown back and her knees bent so he could see she was wearing nothing but his Brando T-shirt, which looked sexier on her than any lace nightie.

He was hard even before he walked in the door. Occasionally he'd just say "Hi," pull off his clothes, push her down on the bed, and shove himself inside her. More often, he'd wait to see what new game or position Inez wanted to try. After they had been sleeping together for a few months, he finally asked her how she knew about doing it from behind, or about chewing on pieces of ice before she used his mouth on him, or tying his hands above his head like a prisoner so she could tease him until he begged, "Please."

"I'm a writer, King," she said, as if that were the most obvious thing in the world. "Imagination is everything."

"Kiss me down there," she said the third time she visited him. She could only climax if first he held her legs apart and used his mouth until she was wet and groaning with pleasure. He had stopped telling Deau what a good lay she was because he figured they were now a team. Locker-room talk made him feel disloyal.

But one Sunday afternoon when they hadn't bothered to get dressed and had just finished a late breakfast, Inez was sitting on the kitchen counter, her legs dangling over the side.

"What about dessert?" she said.

She reached for the banana that was ripening above the sink.

"You eat it," King said. "I'm full."

Inez giggled and said, "Watch me, King."

She broke the banana in half and squeezed it onto a plate until it was soft and mushy. Then she moved herself forward to the edge of the counter.

"Come play with the food," she said, scooping it up with her fingers and stuffing it inside herself. She ran his fingers up and down her fruit-coated opening. "See? A real banana split."

King went wild. Before he penetrated her, he licked away every morsel the two of them had smeared over her outer lips. And after he slid the ol' tallywhacker inside her, through her juice and the thick banana pulp, just before he began to thrust so violently that he lifted Inez clear off the counter, he couldn't help thinking, "Wait until Deau hears about this!"

One night he finally introduced Inez to Deauville, and the three of them went bar hopping. Deauville knew the brick-walled basements of the Village where some of the world's most eloquent musicians jammed after hours. They drank whiskey from a flask hidden in Inez's purse because they couldn't afford the watered-down drinks at the Half Note or the Vanguard. They went to a gay bar called Lenny's Hideaway and rode uptown with two queers on the back of a milk truck. And at 5:00 A.M. they smoked a reefer with a skinny alto sax player from the Basie band they picked up in front of Birdland.

When the sun filtered through the dirty, broken shutters, they fell asleep together, strewn across Deauville's bed like discarded rag dolls, listening to Lee Wiley records on his new hi-fi. They faded out and crashed, three of them bundled together, while Lee Wiley's beat-up voice sang "Livin' for you, is easy livin . . . " Later, when King woke, he caught Deauville's black hand stroking Inez's pink ass. King forced a grin. "Hey, man," he whispered.

"You mind, man?" Deau lifted his big hand, held it aloft, opened wide. "No problem. Didn't know you cared."

He didn't. But he had grown so sure of Inez that on weekends, when he was busy with Avery or Gilda, he'd tell her to give Deauville a call and hang out with him so she wouldn't be bored. Deauville introduced her to the Broadway actors who hung out at Downey's, took her to the beat coffee shops on Bleecker Street, exposed her to jam sessions at Birdland. Once he asked her why she never called her parents in Brooklyn. It was so close, he said.

"The bridge to Brooklyn might as well be the Bridge of San Luis Rey," she countered. "It's two different worlds. And I found the world I want to be in."

One weekend, when King was driving Avery Calder down to Philadelphia to catch the tryout of a new Bill Inge play, Inez brought May and Devon into the city and introduced them to Deauville. When King got home, late Saturday night, Inez told him his best friend had fallen for Devon in a big way. "Deauville invited Devon to the Workshop, to see the piece you guys have been working on. She's coming next week. Isn't that solid? We can double."

King didn't answer.

"What's the matter? You look terrible, hon."

"I'm sick," he said. "Car sick. It was a long ride." He stumbled into the kitchen and doubled over the sink.

It should have been perfect. Avery had written a glowing letter of personal recommendation. "Tennessee said he always depended on the kindness of strangers," Avery drawled. "But in this business, baby, it never hurts to depend on the kindness of friends."

And King and Avery had indeed become very good friends. Avery taught him how to play bridge, strip a lobster in thirty seconds, and mix a perfect Rob Roy. He gave him plays to read—Genet, Beckett, Chekhov—and introduced him to giants on Broadway, people King had only read about: Elia Kazan, William Inge, Josh Logan.

Avery had kept boys in ten states, but King wasn't one of them. Since that first night, nothing physical had happened between them. And if their entrances at Sardi's were greeted with raised eyebrows and knowing giveaway smiles from the jaded crows who lived on gossip and scandal, Avery would just say, "The carrion birds are out tonight. They've been feedin' off my heart for years. Smile, baby. Give 'em their money's worth."

And now this. King was up for a real part in a new Avery Calder play and a chance to introduce it at the Workshop. Gilda, who had never seen King act, phoned Serge Malinkov and Denise Auerbach, who ran the Workshop, who had guided the careers of Brando, Clift, and Jimmy Dean, and told them of King Godwin's remarkable natural talent.

King was astonished that Gilda Greenway had made the calls. "What are friends for, baby?" she said. "You'll learn soon enough who your enemies are."

King worked hard on the audition, a scene Avery hadn't shown to anyone from the new play he called *A Day in the Quarter,* about a one-armed war veteran who made a living as a deformed but dazzling hustler in the Vieux Carré. By the time *A Day in the Quarter* had its first full-scale production in the spring of 1957, the title had been changed to *Barracks Street Blues* and it made King Godwin a star, though Avery always graciously insisted it was not his words, but the right actor in the right part that made the play.

Before *Barracks Street Blues* went into rehearsal, the part Deauville had read with King at the Workshop—the role of a black sailor who picks up the hero one night in a New Orleans bar—was changed to a white whore. Avery begged King to explain to Deauville Tolin that the playwright's friends, his agent, even the producers had insisted that he remove any suggestion of homosexuality from the play.

"I've got enough problems already," moaned Avery. Then he took one long look at King, his muscles bulging under the army fatigues he wore for the part, the ol' tallywhacker thumping against the khaki fly. "No need to gild the lily, baby."

Avery decided to showcase the play off-Broadway in a theater on Sheridan Square. On opening night, Devon Barnes sat beside Deauville and heard his sigh of resignation when the actress playing the whore stepped onstage from the shadows. She saw Deauville bow his head and cover his eyes. Later she watched him stand to tumultuous applause and cheer King Godwin's electric performance with the other first-nighters. He nudged Devon to catch the smile on Walter Kerr's face. "He's got it made," he whispered. Watching him applaud his lost chance with a radiant, compassionate smile for the moving drama, love for his friend, and tears streaming down his face, Devon felt something move inside herself, softly as a rabbit shifting positions in a warren.

Gilda threw a party for King and Avery, and the reviews justified the champagne. When they burst through the doors at Sardi's with the first editions, it was Inez who ripped through the pages to the *Times* review.

"My God, listen to this," she said. " 'Last night Mr. Avery Calder opened a new play in our town, called *Barracks Street Blues*. They may be singing the blues on Barracks Street this morning, but all I can hear from where I sit is the music of success.' Mr. Calder, is that typical of the *Times?*"

"Not in this lifetime," said Avery, uncorking another bottle of Dom Perignon.

"Listen to Walter Kerr," gurgled May, waving the *Herald-Tribune.* "He says, 'If *Barracks Street Blues* doesn't make a full-fledged, first-cabin star out of an actor named Kingston Godwin, then there is no God!' "

"I'll drink to that," said King, who already had.

While the glittering entourage at Sardi's crowned the newest member of theatrical royalty, Devon Barnes was downtown on Jones Street, in bed with Deauville Tolin. Her grandmother in Texas would have dropped dead if she'd known. As her grandmother had said more than once about whites and Negroes together, "I don't give a damn what they call it elsewhere, girl, but here we call it *wrong.*" But that night Devon surrendered to another man what King had longed for—her innocence and love.

Somewhere, in the sun-parched earth of the San Joaquin Valley in California, she knew she had a daddy who would understand.

NINE

DECEMBER 26, 1979

"S eems like old times," Billy Buck said.

"Does it?"

He glanced over at Devon. Her profile was silhouetted against the sweltering sunshine streaming through the car window. They were driving down the Pacific Coast Highway in Billy's XKE.

"God, you look good," he said, eyes back on the road. "I don't know what I expected. Margo of Shangri-la, I think. You know, *Lost Horizon* syndrome—once you leave Lotus Land, you're supposed to prune up, turn into Sam Jaffe."

He hoped she would laugh. He was longing to hear that ridiculous laugh of hers, though he'd happily settle for a smile.

"I thought you'd change. At least, I *hoped* you would. But, woman, you're almost forty, and you're more beautiful than ever."

Devon was curled into herself, staring out at the Pacific, out past the Santa Monica Pier. She hadn't said much since he'd rescued her from the chapel.

"I don't have any plans for this afternoon. You can tell me all about it as slowly as you please."

"No, I can't actually," Devon said. "There's someone waiting for me. And I need to talk to King."

"You're not still carrying a torch for him, are you?"

Devon looked stricken.

"Honey, I'm just teasing you," Billy said. He reached over and patted her hand. Unexpectedly, Devon clasped his hand in both of hers and pressed it to her heart.

The gesture shook Billy Buck, because it was just what Gilda would have done. "God, you remind me of her," he said. "The way she was—before she made *Cobras.* When she still needed people."

Devon stiffened. Releasing his hand, she turned back to the window. "She still needed people right up to the end, Billy."

"I know. It's hard. I know how much you loved her—"

She cut him off. "Did you know Inez lived here once?" Devon said as they approached Venice. "Around here somewhere, when she first came out to California."

Billy noticed a barefoot girl perched on a motorcycle. The kid was nodding out.

Well, there you have it, Billy thought, watching the young junkie, thinking of Inez's losing battle with drugs and alcohol. Nothing changes.

"Poor Inez," said Devon.

"Much may be said of Inez Godwin, but poor?"

"Do you remember Deauville, Billy?"

It took him a minute. He tried to remember if she'd lived in Deauville, or made a movie there during her first exile, when she'd fled to France. Then, he recognized the name. "Deauville Tolin? Is that who you've been with for the past two years?"

"Is that what you think?"

"I never think out here. I keep a pied-à-terre in New York for that."

"I was just thinking about him, of days gone by," she said in her now famous southern drawl. "The year after graduation, when Inez came out here, and May was at the University of Chicago. I was living in the Village with Deauville, and we were at the Workshop together."

"What about King?"

"King was there, too. I know people from back then who still believe that was where he got his name—because he was a king of sorts. They'd never seen anything like him. His looks, that shaggy blond hair and self-effacing manner. He was embarrassed about the remnants of his southern accent and he took to mumbling and kind of talking with his head down. Like he had a mouth full of wet Kleenex. And pretty soon there was this shaggy-haired, brown-leather-jacket mumbling epidemic at the Workshop. Billy, he was *so* good. Everyone thought Avery had paved the asphalt ahead of him and that King was just using him—"

"And they were wrong?" Billy asked cynically.

"Of course. King adored Avery. He worshiped him. But he worked all the time. Wherever he went, he watched people, he tried on gestures and voices and walks. He'd turn up at Deauville's at suppertime with a new scene he'd practically torn out of Avery's typewriter. That was before Deauville and I lived together. Before Avery wrote Deauville's part out of *Barracks Street Blues.* King would drag Deau away from the table to read with him. It didn't matter if we were at Deauville's place, or at the Café Figaro or the Automat. Or he'd phone at dawn from one of the all-night movie houses where he'd just seen some incredible film for the first time, and you'd try to stay awake while he gave you a plot analysis of *The Cabinet of Dr. Caligari.*

"Later that spring, after *Barracks* opened downtown, when Deauville and I were living together, it was Inez who phoned in the middle of the night. She was at Bennington that year on scholarship. May was already at the University of Chicago. And I was broke in Greenwich Village, learning how to make espresso and carry four plates at a time while moving *sullenly*—"

"You? Sullen? I don't believe it."

She looked over at him, smiling faintly. "It was 1957, the days of beatniks and bongos. I was an actress. Sullen came with the territory. So I struck my sullen pose and glided between the coffeehouse tables in my black flats and black turtleneck and black tights. Between classes at the Workshop, pumping espresso at the Figaro, running with Deauville to catch some late-night poetry reading or jam session, I was lucky if I averaged three hours' sleep. And whenever I was most wiped out, Inez would call. She'd try King first—and if he wasn't in, she'd phone us. If I said I didn't know where he was, sometimes she'd take the train down from Vermont and show up at our doorstep just as we were leaving for an acting class. She'd be red-eyed with exhaustion and worry."

"Or vodka and Ritalin."

"No, not in those days. Sometimes she'd smoke a joint with King and Deau, but that was about as wicked as she got. It took me a while to figure out why she always phoned me. Why she always showed up wild-eyed and strung-out at *our* door."

"She wanted to make sure King wasn't under *your* bed."

"Journalists are so perceptive."

"Comes with the territory."

"Deauville figured it out before I did."

They were well past Venice now. "How did Inez wind up out here? In Venice, of all places."

"Gilda sent for her. Avery was preparing to move *Barracks Street* to Broadway. It was summer, and without school to occupy her, Inez was getting into everyone's hair. She'd hang around the theater, the Workshop. She'd phone King twenty times a day. He'd walk out on her and she'd tell everyone how devastated she was, how desperately in love with him she was. She scared people. Serge Malinkov rushed to our apartment one night while Inez was sleeping over. She'd phoned him and told him she was taking an overdose. He even threatened to throw King out of the Workshop.

"They always got back together, though. There'd be these dramatic reunions. They'd walk down Bleecker together, hand in hand, and people would practically cheer. But it was hard on King. Finally, Avery got Gilda to send for Inez."

"And she went? Just like that?"

"There was some talk of her doctoring a script for Gilda, or writing one. I don't remember."

Devon was silent for a moment. Then she turned toward the window again. "Could anyone refuse Gilda?"

Her bitterness took Billy by surprise. Perhaps, he thought, it was Devon's way of expressing grief—grief at the desertion of a loved one. Surely, her sudden appearance at the memorial service, after a two-year absence, testified to her relentless devotion.

But he couldn't stop the nagging questions in his mind. Where had she been? What had she been doing? And how had she heard of Gilda's death?

TEN

D etective Lionel Biggs left the West LAPD headquarters on Butler Avenue, headed for Coldwater Canyon, and turned _____ onto the side street that led to Gilda Greenway's fabled mansion, The Pearls.

He watched as the gate swung open, automatically triggered by an electronic eye. Talk about shoddy security, Biggs thought. If she was so security-conscious, where was the gatekeeper? Then he remembered it was the day after Christmas. She'd probably given him a few days off. He steered the car up the steep, winding drive, the windshield of his Plymouth shaded by the overhanging magnolias.

He parked in front of the mansion and appraised the place for the first time by daylight.

It was some movie star hideout.

The Pearls loomed over him, three stories high, completely skirted by meticulously groomed hedges. Jesus, he thought, the place looks like something out of a Selznick picture.

On two beautifully hand-carved white wooden doors under the pillars in a recessed entry was a very large brass knocker with the initials "G.G." Above him, a cut-glass lantern held securely by a long brass chain swung gently in the breeze.

Biggs turned around.

Beyond his car, the driveway curved like a horseshoe down both sides of a long, sloping hill that spilled onto the street beyond. He couldn't see the entry and the exit gates from the driveway in front of the house. If King Godwin had arrived just after the murder occurred, it's possible the killer had heard his car or seen his headlights coming up the drive and fled. The killer could have coasted down the exit drive without King seeing or hearing him.

It was just a thought. He'd wait for the coroner's report to check the exact time of death.

He turned back to the house. The front doors had been sealed with tape stretching across the crack between them. It read: CRIME SCENE—LAPD POLICE SEAL. DO NOT BREAK!! ENTRY IS PROHIBITED.

Biggs extracted from his pocket the Gucci key ring found in Gilda Greenway's purse the night of the murder.

Choosing a key that looked the right size, he inserted it in the lock. The lock's chambers made small clicking sounds. After a minute the detective felt it work. He turned the knob and entered. The door had not been wired. For a woman terrified of intruding fans, Gilda had a security system that was out of the forties. All that money, yet the alarm system was probably the original one that came with the house.

The silence was startling. Normally, it would have also been creepy. Not for Biggs. He welcomed the chance to move around uninterrupted and unobserved to see if there was anything here they might have missed. A clue, a fingernail. *Anything.*

He surveyed the entry hall. Almost as big as his fucking apartment. He was truly impressed. On both sides of the hall were staircases as grand and expansive as the ones he'd seen in *Gone with the Wind.* Any moment he expected Butterfly McQueen to come shuffling down, whining, "But Miss Scarlett, I don't know nothing' 'bout birthin' no babies!"

To live in a place like this required wealth beyond his imagination. In the center of the hall hung a magnificent seven-tiered cut-crystal chandelier, casting off a sea of prisms from a beam of light that shone through a small window at the very top of the wall above the entryway. The chandelier must have been specifically designed to catch the light like that, Biggs told himself. Amazing how the old stars thought of everything.

The other night when Biggs had been here, he'd been so busy on the crime scene it never really hit him exactly where he was. Now it did. He'd been a fan of Gilda Greenway for years. Had seen almost all of her old movies when they'd originally been released, and still tried to catch as many as he could on the Late Show. He had, like so many men, loved this woman vicariously through the magnified magic of the silver screen.

And now, here he was, in her house. Alone with the ghost of her all around him in the silence. He felt like Martin Balsam in *Psycho*—cautious but determined.

He moved to the living room just off the entry hall. There, a red plastic tape had been strung from one side of the living room's entry frame to the other. The sign that hung from it repeated the words on the police seal. He stepped over it and into the scene of the crime.

Biggs pulled out a packet of Camels. Despite his wife's repeated nagging, he was up to four packs a day. He'd tried everything—hypnosis, acupuncture, carrot sticks. Now, when he left for the office, he'd find packs of Dentyne in his jacket pockets. To the annoyance of his wife and his fellow officers, he had now developed the double habit of chewing wads of gum and smoking at the same time.

On either side of the fireplace, two identical white chaise longues faced each other. In front of them and the fireplace, was a royal purple silk velvet sofa. A burled walnut cocktail table was the centerpiece for the three pieces. The chaise longue where Gilda Greenway had been found was stained a deep brown, like dried chocolate. A stain about eight inches in diameter, but one that had obviously run, as evidenced by the drip marks. In the middle of it, a small, barely perceptible hole.

Biggs looked around the immediate area where the body had been found. Black fingerprint dust covered much of the furniture, giving the living room a morbid look. Next to the chaise was the unwatered Christmas tree, now dropping dry spruce needles on a multitude of bright, very expensively and extravagantly wrapped presents.

For an instant he thought of robbery again as a motive, but his gut instinct, the one *true* bet a cop can stake a case on, told him no. Besides, nothing had been stolen. None of the jewelry Gilda had so prominently worn on the night of her death had been removed. There were no signs of forced entry. No signs of struggle.

No, Biggs thought, looking around. This was something premeditated. A murder with a reason. But what?

He moved away from the chaise longue and walked over to the Steinway, which stood right in front of two large windows. Elaborately framed photographs covered almost every inch of the piano top. Biggs recognized many of them. Elizabeth Taylor. John Wayne. Ronald Reagan. Lucille Ball. Joan Crawford. Lana Turner. Deborah Kerr. Most were autographed with inscriptions: "To the Queen of Hollywood, love . . . " "To Gilda, without you I couldn't have done it . . . " "Here's to many more years of friendship, Merry Christmas . . . "

Biggs picked up a color photo right in front.

Billy Buck.

Journalist to the stars.

There he was in a white suit, a white shirt, a pale pink tie, and a gold Cartier love bracelet on his wrist. He was smiling that famous dimpled smile. The inscription read: "To the only genuine American beauty I know in a town full of thorns—with undying admiration, Billy."

On Christmas day, before Biggs had driven to the morgue, he'd gone over to Billy's house in Bel Air, rousing him at 7 A.M. If anyone knew what Gilda had been doing the previous night, it would be Billy. They were as tight as any journalist and star could be without compromising positions.

Billy Buck had sleepily answered the door in a checked houndstooth polo robe.

"A little early for eggnog, isn't it, Detective?"

"Gilda Greenway's dead."

Billy's eyes widened. His heart fluttered. "What? I don't believe it. Is this a poor cop joke or what?"

Biggs shook his head, finding it hard to believe himself. "She was murdered, Billy. Late last night."

Billy leaned heavily against the door, feeling dizzy. Finally, he motioned for Biggs to come inside. Biggs stepped in, following the columnist to the back of the house.

The sun poured into his terra-cotta-tiled kitchen. Billy took out two mugs inscribed with the logos of 20th Century Fox and Columbia, spooned coffee into the Mr. Coffee, then filled the cream pitcher.

Everyone reacts differently to news, Biggs thought. Especially when you bring news this bad. Some people are calm, like King Godwin, some clam up and just sit there, building slowly into a catatonic state, and others start moving around, making themselves busy, so they won't have to concentrate on the grim, devastating, but inevitable truth.

"Billy," Biggs said, watching him prepare the coffee, "I need to ask you a few questions. You've got to help us. Somebody murdered her."

Billy was numb.

It was a nightmare.

On Christmas morning.

Billy knew Gilda had cut herself off from a lot of people in the past year or two, especially the Four Fans. Like every other survivor in Hollywood, she of course had an enemy here and there. But certainly nobody hated her enough to *kill* her.

Or did they?

He shook his head. God, he needed caffeine.

"Why Gilda?" he asked no one in particular.

He had been with her just the night before, he told Biggs.

"What were you two doing?"

"Why, we had dinner at Chasen's. She was supposed to go to this party, this get-together that Inez Godwin was throwing over in Holmby Hills, but she changed her mind. She decided she wanted to go to a restaurant instead."

"Did you take her home?"

"No," Billy Buck said, massaging his head, gazing out at the pool, reeling from the news. "She got this phone call during dinner and said she had to leave. There was something she had to take care of."

"Did she say what?"

"No, I didn't hear the conversation. Usually you can have a phone brought to your table at Chasen's. But the maitre d' just came over and said, 'Miss Greenway, you've got a telephone call,' or something like that."

"And you have no idea who it was?"

"No."

"Billy," Biggs huffed, lighting a cigarette, "you wouldn't be with-holding information would you? You know that's a federal offense."

"Oh, come on, Biggs, you've been watching too many *Kojaks*. I just found out the woman was murdered this very minute. Christ, you cops are all the same."

"So how did she finally get home?"

"The maitre d' phoned for a taxi."

"And when was this?"

"Around ten-thirty."

"Did she say anything at dinner last night that would indicate she was having problems with anyone?"

Billy immediately thought of May. Gilda had told him May was livid because she had decided to back out of a television deal May had been diligently preparing. They'd had the worst row of their lives. May had threatened her, called her a cunt, whore, and bitch, and that was just for starters.

He wasn't *about* to tell Biggs anything without checking it first, on his own. If May had killed Gilda . . . No, that was just too ridiculous. But he remained circumspect.

"No, not really. I mean the usual bitching about Hollywood, deals made, deals broken, people, you know. Just gossip."

"And she was in good spirits."

"Yeah," Billy said nodding. "She seemed to be."

"Do you know anything about this?" Biggs asked, pulling a piece of paper from his coat pocket.

It was a Xerox copy of the photograph they'd found on Gilda.

Billy shrugged, fanning away the offending smoke from Biggs's cigarette. "Yeah, what about it? It's a pretty famous photograph. Sur-prised you haven't seen it before. The Pearls Girl and her Four Fans," Billy said, confirming for Biggs what King had already told him.

But why, Biggs wondered, was she holding it when she died? He wasn't about to ask. There was some information you had to withhold until the right moment.

"Would there have been anyone else at The Pearls that I can talk to? Servants? Guests?"

"No, she'd given Mrs. Denby the week off. None of the other servants live in."

"Who is Denby?"

Billy yawned. "Her housekeeper. She's been with Gilda for years and years. She runs that place like a battleship. She looks a bit like one, too. Gilda told me last night that Mrs. Denby had left in the late afternoon. I presume the other servants left then, too."

"Do you know where I can reach her?"

"Yeah, Transylvania."

Lionel Biggs stood in Gilda Greenway's living room holding the picture of Billy Buck. He put it down thinking that guy is foxy as a gold digger on the scent of new money, and in this kind of investigation, just as dangerous.

Biggs was snapped out of his reverie with a jolt. Behind him, in the tomblike stillness of the empty house, he heard the front door open.

ELEVEN

SUMMER 1957

T he telephone rang. Though it was on Deauville's side of the bed, it was Devon's job to answer it. She scampered across the sheet-draped mountain of his sleeping body and, hanging across his hips, lifted the receiver. His breathing rocked her gently as an ocean wave. She peeked at the alarm clock and knew that if it wasn't a wrong number or an emergency, it would be Inez.

When she had first moved into Deauville's Jones Street apartment, the late-night phone calls were invariably for him, from women oddly undisturbed at the sound of her voice. "Oh, hi," they'd say, "can I speak to Deauville?" Their accents ranged from regional to exotic, their voices playful or desperate, their desire politely disguised or defiantly obvious.

At first Devon was hurt, then resigned, and finally outraged. Deauville loved to tell his friends about the night the telephone interrupted their lovemaking twice within an hour. When it rang a third time, Devon rolled off him, snatched the receiver from its cradle, and holding it to his cock, said, "It's for you."

She knew there were girls. She just didn't know how many. If she was going to live with Deauville, she told herself, a sense of humor was a prerequisite. Once, while they were watching the Loretta Young show on a Sunday night, Devon answered the phone, listened for a moment, and without uttering a word, briskly hung up.

"Who was that for?"

"The Coast Guard."

"The—wha'?"

"Well, it was some woman wanting to know if the coast was clear."

They looked at each other silently for a fleeting second, then burst into laughter, as if on cue.

Now it was only Inez. And the words were familiar. "Devon? Oh, God, I don't know what to *do*. I need your help."

"It's three o'clock in the morning, Inez. Where *are* you?"

"Home. I mean at King's. He just left."

"Did you have another fight?"

"No," Inez said, sounding affronted by the notion. "He went out for a nightcap. Listen, Devon, this is serious. Gilda Greenway called me today. From Hollywood."

"And—?"

"And she wants me to fly out there right away. She called *me*— not King. Can you believe it? I mean, she said, 'Baby . . . ' Actually called me 'Baby.' She said, 'Listen, baby, I want you to think about coming out here. Out to Hollywood. And soon.' That means like right away! Like next week if I can."

"For what?"

"Jesus, Devon, you can be so obtuse at times." Inez liked that word. *Obtuse*. It was a writer's word. *She* was a writer.

"So . . . what?" Not understanding.

Deauville stirred beside her. His eyes opened, squinting at the clock—then at her. "Inez," Devon mouthed. Smiling sleepily, he dozed off again, leaving his cock awake to keep her company.

"Never mind. Anyway, she wants me to write for her! She's got a project she thinks 'may interest' me. Can you believe it?"

"Wow," Devon whispered, "that's fabulous."

"But there's one thing that bothers me. It means leaving King."

"Oh. Well, yeah, I didn't think of that."

"Well, Gilda Greenway sure did. With King getting ready for Broadway, and Patrick doing a movie in Europe, she said we could sort of keep each other company out there."

"What's wrong with that, Inez?"

"Nothing, I guess." But Inez sounded depressed. After a moment, she said, "Devon, do you think he's just trying to get rid of me?"

"Who, King? Don't be silly, Inez. I mean, would Gilda invite you to Hollywood if that were the case?"

"If he asked her to, she would."

"Inez, a movie star like Gilda Greenway isn't going to jump just because a promising young actor asks her to. She must really need you."

"I don't know, Devon. . . . Still, I want to go. Let's face it. King will end up in the movies eventually. And this way, instead of being left behind in New York, I'll already be there waiting for him."

Like a spider for a fly, Devon thought. Deauville had begun to stroke her back. She wriggled happily under his hand, on top of his warm body, loving the feel of him hard against her belly.

"You don't have to decide tonight, do you, Inez? I'll call you back later."

"I've already decided," Inez said. "I'm going. I mean, she said she'd wire a round-trip ticket. Who would pass up a free trip? I can always come back."

"Great. Listen, Inez, let me call you back in a couple of hours, okay?" Deauville's hand was sliding around her bottom.

Summer. It must've been 90 degrees outside. One hundred and one in the Jones Street garret. The thin cotton sheet beneath them was already soaked. Devon's stomach was wet. The inside of her thighs were wet. Deauville's big hand was slick with sweat. She was trying to keep her wet thighs locked because once he pried them open, she knew she would drown. There was no way she'd be able to hold back the flood. She was having a hard enough time now. Oh, and he was having a hard old time, too.

"There's just one thing I need, Devon. One thing I need from you," Inez insisted. "Promise me you'll leave King alone."

"I'll call you back."

"What kind of a friend are you?" Inez cried.

The plane ticket was waiting at the travel agency on Waverly Place. It was first-class, round-trip, just as Gilda promised. "I can always cash in the return if I decide to stay," Inez said. Devon could see the wheels already turning in the turnstiles Inez called a mind.

"Then why the gloomy look?"

"Dev, I'm scared. I've never been any farther away from New York than Bennington, Vermont. You and May always know just what to do with strangers; I try to imitate you, but it just doesn't always work. You're real Stork Club material. I'm still hogging it up at Walgreen's. You can take the girl out of Brooklyn, I guess, but you can't take Brooklyn out of the girl," she said, biting her lip.

Devon sighed in exasperation. Sometimes Inez was such a pain. "You did just fine at Bennington this year. Anyway, you can damn well *try.*"

"You bet I can. You know what they say about Hollywood— everybody out there lies, but it doesn't matter because nobody ever listens anyway. God knows I can bullshit my way through anything."

"Any idea what you'll do for money?"

"I'll be staying with Gilda," Inez chirped, her previous doubts erased, feeling more cheerful now that she'd voiced her fears and insecurities. "But after a while, I guess I'll get a place of my own. In Venice, probably. Everyone says Hollywood is utterly square and Venice is where the writers are—all the beats, you know, Kerouac, Anger, Lawrence Lipton. You don't need as much money in Venice. And of course I want to pay my own way."

"Naturally," smiled Devon. They had a cup of coffee and walked to the theater near Sheridan Square where King was rehearsing the new rewrites for the Broadway version of *Barracks Street Blues.*

"Well, kiddo," Inez said with the finality of a junior executive who has just rid the firm of a senior partner by handing him a gold watch, "it's the end of an era."

"I guess so," Devon said, feeling suddenly sad. "Hey, I'm going to miss you."

"Yeah, like menstrual cramps. Anyway, don't worry. You'll be hearing from me. I'll write. Hell, I'll phone you. There's a three-hour time difference. If I get it right, I can catch you and Deauville—at least, I hope it'll be Deauville. I sure wouldn't want to catch you with King."

Always nipping at my heels, Devon thought. They said goodbye at the stage door. Inez watched Devon fade in the traffic. Then she smiled her Gioconda smile, patted the airplane ticket in her purse, and rummaged around for the apartment listing she had torn from the *New York Times* and circled with red eyebrow pencil. She hailed a cab uptown. It was Thursday and she had to hurry.

The apartment, in a luxury building on East Sixty-fourth off Third, was perfect. "The former occupants left in a hurry. Two months left to go on their lease," said the super. "I don't know why young people today are in such an all-fired hurry. They left their TV and a couple of wicker chairs. Phone company's cutting off the phone this weekend. If you take it, you can have the TV, I guess. I already got two of my own."

Inez felt the pulse throb in her temple as she wrote the hot check for one month's rent and one month's deposit. She knew it wouldn't reach her bank until Monday. The super, innocent as a Thanksgiving turkey following sunflower seeds all the way to the kitchen door, gave her the keys right there.

"I won't be moving in until Sunday," said Inez.

"Whatever suits you. I probably should wait till your check clears to give you the keys, but you signed the lease and all, and—well, you look like the honest type."

Ha! Inez laughed to herself. *If only you knew.*

As soon as the door closed behind him, Inez phoned in her ad to the *Times.* They required payment in advance. Damn. She hadn't counted on that. She cabbed it over to the newspaper, forked over the cash, and prayed. The ad was too late, they warned, to make the Sunday real estate section, but promised it would run on Saturday.

Everything was going just as the story in the *Daily News* had described: COPS WARN RENTERS: BEWARE OF PHONY APARTMENT DEALS.

With the housing shortage, an increasing number of prospective renters are victimized for large sums of money; an average half-dozen are showing up for the same apartment, all paid for in advance.

Here's how the scheme works: A swindler rents or subleases an apartment, investing a month's security and rent. Then he advertises in a newspaper or asks a broker to find tenants willing to cough up six months' advance rent for the same apartment.

A spokesman for the Police Department's Special Frauds Squad reports that the con artist then tells prospective tenants he is making an illegal sublet that will result in a swift rent hike if the landlord finds out about the transaction.

Inez included the phone number of the empty apartment in the *Times* ad. She didn't want King's phone to ring. On Saturday morning, she arrived at the new apartment at 7:00 A.M. The telephone was ringing when she turned the key in the lock. She sat there all day. By 11:00 P.M., when she raced home to meet King after the Saturday evening performance of *Barracks,* she had already screened and made appointments for twelve eager applicants. They started arriving at 10:00 A.M. on Sunday.

By dusk, she had pocketed almost $20,000 in personally endorsed checks. Two people had even given her cash. The phone was still ringing Sunday night when she locked the door and looked for the final time at the apartment she would never see again. "Y'all come again," she giggled, blowing a kiss to the silent TV set in a poor imitation of Devon's Texas accent.

"I love you, honey," she said in bed, biting King's earlobe while he tried to sleep. "And don't worry about taking me to the airport tomorrow. I can get there on my own. After that, it's 'Hooray for Hollywood.'" But all she got in response was a snore.

Monday morning, before King was awake, she left a perky note smeared with violet lipstick and headed for the banks. Five of them. With almost $23,000 in her pocket, she took a taxi to LaGuardia to catch the three o'clock flight to L.A. Her heart was beating like a conga drum.

The driver, sensing her nervous agitation, offered her his *Daily News. "Nobody* reads the *Daily News,"* she smiled arrogantly, crossing her fingers. "You are looking at someone who is in a position to know *that* for a given fact."

And that's how Inez Hollister got to Hollywood.

It was Deauville who caught Devon with King.

In the first weeks after Inez left, King was busy working with Avery to get *Barracks Street Blues* ready for Broadway. Then, in August, King phoned to invite them to a run-through of the doctored play. It had been changed so much, he said, they'd hardly recognize it. He wanted their reactions, their feedback.

Deauville refused. He couldn't bear to sit through it again, to see the changes, to watch the role that had once been his now played by someone else.

A week later King phoned again. Devon assumed he was calling Deauville. "Hi," she said, "Deau's not here. He's working tonight."

"Yeah, I know," he said, having just called the Five Oaks where Deauville waited tables, to make sure he wasn't home. "I feel like a shit calling you, but I had to. I've been wanting to all week."

And how. Ever since Inez had flown the coop, Devon was all he could think about. Night after night he dreamed about her, waking with a raging hard-on. All he could do was beat off in frustration.

"But listen," he said after a pause, "promise me you won't say anything to Deau, okay? He's still my friend."

Devon pressed her back against the wall and let herself slide slowly to the floor. "I don't feel right about that," she said weakly, trying to quiet her mind, which had gone wild scrambling for a place to hide. Her hands on the receiver were sweaty, her face burning. A mad voice whispered in her head; *Talk to me, I won't tell him. Tell me what I know is true. That it's me you want, have wanted always.* Oh, God, what would she do if he really did say it?

"I've missed you," King said. "Have you missed me?"

"Well, sure. But I know how busy you've been. How's it going? How's the play?"

"Devon, listen. There's something I want to talk to you about. I've talked to Avery about you, and to Oscar. I want you to meet me at the theater in an hour. Can you do it?"

"Who's Oscar?"

"Oscar is Oscar McGrath, the director. Come to the theater. Will you do that?"

No, she wanted to say. No, I'm sorry, that's impossible.

"It's important," King said, "trust me. Have I ever lied to you?"

"Well, no," she admitted.

"Then just trust me. This one's for you, Devon. It's one I owe you. Don't say anything to Deauville, and get over here fast, okay?"

She arrived at the Longacre Theatre an hour and a half later. It took her that long to shower and reject half a dozen costumes, to settle on her everyday skinny black pants, which she wore with one of Deauville's white shirts, the tail trailing to her knees like Audrey Hepburn in *Funny Face.* She had to towel-dry her unruly hair and iron it straight, then spray it with water again so it would spring back into the wavy raven tresses she loathed and Deauville loved. She put on so much makeup she looked like T. C. Jones doing an impersonation of Bette Davis, then scrubbed it all off again, until her face was clean and shiny. It took her an hour and a half to prove to herself that she was making no special effort to look special for King.

"God, you're beautiful," he said. "I always forget." He kissed her cheek, put an arm around her waist, and hurried her down the aisle toward the stage, where Avery Calder was waiting with beefy, bald Oscar McGrath.

McGrath puts his hands on his broad hips and chewed his thumb. "Okay," he said, circling her, "not bad. You wouldn't find her in a seed catalogue, I admit. We'll see."

Avery Calder was slumped in a front-row seat. Though it was seasonally sluggish in the theater, he wore a cashmere jacket across his shoulders. Pale and sweating, he squinted at Devon over the top of his bifocals, through the smoke curling in patches from the cigarillo clamped in his teeth. He sipped from a paper cup filled with bourbon. Studying Devon silently for a moment, he raised the paper cup to her in greeting, then looked over at King.

King was pacing behind McGrath, moving lightly on his toes like a prizefighter. Finally, he said, "Devon, how'd you like to read for us?"

"Read what?" she asked stupidly. All this attention was making her nervous. She felt like a calf in a county fair.

"Barracks," King said. "The play. Avery's been doing some serious

rewriting. There's a perfect part for you. Will you read it? Right now, cold?"

Avery removed the cigarillo from his mouth, took a sip of Jack Daniel's, and stood up. He seemed shorter than Devon remembered, and anorectic. Devon had met him twice before—when Deauville was reading the role of the sailor, and the night the play opened on Sheridan Square, the night she'd made love to Deau for the first time.

"Gilda sends her love. She believes you're right for this role," said Avery. He was weaving now. He stood in the front row, his jacket over his shoulders, the contents of the paper cup sloshing precariously against its sides.

"Gilda?"

"I read it to her on the phone this morning," King explained.

"This morning? Did you speak to Inez?"

"She's not there anymore. Gilda thought you'd be perfect."

"Of course, Miss Greenway hasn't read the entire play," said Oscar McGrath, leaning against the stage. "Not this version, anyway. It makes a difference."

"And, of course, my illustrious nephew here—" Avery waved his cup at King, who jumped back, out of the way of the splashing bourbon. "Well, he says you're splendid. Is that so? Are you a splendid actress?"

Devon laughed. The robust sound echoed in the empty hall and Avery Calder straightened abruptly. "My, what a big noise," Avery said, squinting at Devon. Then he grinned, turning to King. "Where we come from, baby, every hurricane begins with a small drop of water."

They handed her pages with the part they wanted her to read underlined in red. She began alone. Then King was on the stage beside her, reading with her. He was right. The part was wonderful. The musical cadence of the speech was feisty southern and easy for her.

King made a perfect foil, letting her do the work, letting her be aggressive, which was what the role required. He looked away from her, mumbling. He made her come after him, playing it at such a quiet pitch that she had to strain toward him to hear, move close to him to be heard. He was the trembling field mouse. She was the predatory falcon. The chemistry was volatile.

When she finished King said, "Oh, man," and walked into the

wings. Avery Calder was sound asleep in the first row, his shirt stained with the bourbon he'd spilled.

McGrath plunged his hands into his pockets and paced in front of the stage while Devon waited, rolling the script in her hand, not wanting to say, "Well? How was I?"

Finally, McGrath scratched his bald head and looked up at her. "You know Miss Greenway long?

Devon said, "No. I met her about a year and a half ago. And saw her again at the opening."

"She ever see you act?"

"No."

"She must be psychic, then," Oscar said. "She said you were the one for the part."

"Was she right?"

"Damned close. I was thinking blonde, but that's no problem. I've got to read a couple of girls tomorrow, but unless one of them is Julie Harris, it's yours."

"Thanks," Devon said, feeling her nose sting, knowing she was close to tears. "Thanks a lot, Mr. McGrath. But I can't do it. I loved reading for you, but . . . " She grasped for words. "I . . . just . . . can't."

"Can't do it?" the director asked, incredulous. McGrath turned around to find Avery snoring and King gone. "What is she talking about, 'Can't do it'?" He was talking to the air.

"I can't explain," she said meekly. "It would take too long."

"What do you mean you can't explain?" he raged. "Do you know how many young women your age would *kill*—kill, mind you, for this fucking role?"

Devon rubbed the back of her neck nervously. "I know, Mr. McGrath, but . . . do you know Deauville Tolin? This role was his in the original play. Before they changed it from a sailor to a hooker. I just can't do it."

"Tolin? The nigger? That's history, honey. Let him get a calypso shirt and sing 'Day-oh.' What's it got to do with Broadway?"

Devon opened her hand and, suddenly composed, let the script fall onto the stage. "Good night, Mr. McGrath," she said, and walked into the wings, then out the stage door.

King was already waiting for her in the alleyway, on his new Yamaha. "You were unbelievable. You're the character."

"Take me home."

She knew she should hate him. That she should walk past him out of the alley and never look back. How could he have done this to her? Setting her up to take Deau's original role. God, a Broadway role. But the wrong role. Damn King.

"What's wrong? Didn't McGrath offer you the part?"

"It's Deau's part, King. You know I can't take it."

King didn't turn around to look at her. "Bullshit," he said, starting the bike. "Is that what you told McGrath? A role that's been completely rewritten, which you're perfect for. You can't take it? Did he offer it to you?"

"Yes," she said as they drove out of the alley. "But it's the wrong role and you shouldn't have called me."

"Right. King's a real bastard, huh? You get a fantastic break, and I'm the heel? I figured you deserve a chance to choose. What the fuck is the matter with you? You chose wrong, Devon. You chose with what's between your legs. What are you, an actress or a piece of ass?"

"Shut up!" she yelled over the noise of the Yamaha and the city streets. But she didn't jump off. The vibration churning against her thighs made her itch. She felt angry. Angry and elated.

And . . . *sexy*.

It was so strange, but it was true. Riding on the back of that bike, hugging his warm, wonderfully smelly leather jacket, Devon felt different than the way she felt with Deauville. With Deau she was always a little girl. But with King, she felt strong. Mature. She'd walked away from a goddamn leading role in a Broadway play. Partly because King pissed her off. But mostly because she felt a surge of strength and maturity. Out of nowhere, she thought of Inez saying "It's the end of an era" the day she left for Hollywood. Well, it damn well *was*. That first day when Inez had ridden away from Westbridge on the back of King's motorcycle, perched right where she was sitting now, Devon had been hurt and helpless.

She wasn't helpless now.

She was strong.

And talented.

"I was good, wasn't I?" she shouted above the din, wrapping her arms even tighter around King's chest. "I mean, I can really act, can't I?"

He didn't answer, but she knew the answer was yes.

Deauville was waiting for her. He'd heard the motorcycle and seen her from the window. When she got upstairs, he said, "What were you doing with King?"

"Nothing." Her euphoria had made her dizzy. She wasn't ready to surrender the feeling yet.

"What do you mean, *nothing?*"

She felt her heart still racing through the steamy night, powerful with triumph and desire. *"Nothing,"* she snapped at Deauville. "Just what I said. *Nothing!"*

He flinched. She saw his beautiful, dark eyes wince with pain. They they glazed over, locking her out. Deauville turned away from her and slammed out of the apartment.

He stayed away all night. When he returned the next afternoon, sullen and cloudy, she begged his forgiveness. She'd gone to watch a rehearsal, nothing more, she said.

"Never mind. Let's not talk about it. Let's not talk about it *ever* again."

"Okay," she said.

But it was never the same between them again. Inez was right. It was the end of an era.

TWELVE

AUTUMN AND WINTER 1957

B arracks *Street Blues* opened on Broadway the second week in September. King sent them tickets to the opening, but Devon tore them up before Deauville checked the mail. Still, she couldn't stop herself from going out at midnight to buy the morning papers and pour over the "money" reviews. They were all enthusiastic about the play and ecstatic about King. Walter Kerr called him "a Broadway improvement on off-Broadway perfection."

"Your pal Gilda Greenway called about ten minutes ago," Deauville said, when she returned. "She and Calder and that fritzy bunch are uptown. His play opened tonight. They're celebrating. She wanted us to come up."

"What did you tell her?" Devon asked.

"I said I'd give you the message," he answered. Then, climbing his army jacket, he walked out.

The morning after the opening, Gilda was still in bed in her sumptuous Sherry-Netherland apartment, an apartment she and Patrick Wainwright kept for trips to New York. It was furnished with Louis XIV furniture, Ming vases, a Cézanne, a Van Gogh, even a pair of priceless Jean Michel Frank lamps executed by Diego Giacometti. Since The Pearls, her Beverly Hills home, was done in "strictly Hollywood" style, Gilda thought at least *one* place should have some *real* class. "Besides, if I've got to put my money in something," she would joke, "it might as well be in a *few* things older than me."

Patrick lay sleeping beside her, snoring off a long night of drinking, and Avery and King were passed out in the living room. It had been a hell of an opening. She only wished Devon, May, and Inez had been there. They were the children she and Patrick would never have. Liz ... Janet ... Debbie ... they all had at least one kid now. Gilda had none.

But these four, they were smart, bright, ambitious, and in desperate need of a mother figure. A mother with the connections and balls of a Samuel Goldwyn. Well, she snorted to herself, at least she still had *that.*

On an impulse, she picked up the phone and called Devon, thinking, I'm beginning to feel like I need them as much as they need me. "Hello, baby." She spoke as if she and Devon talked regularly. "I'm so sorry you missed the party last night. The boys are hung over as hell and I'm not exactly Miss America myself. When are you coming out to the Coast to see us? Inez is always talking about you. She's doing fine. Has her own bank account and everything. And I'd love to see you again. You know, Oscar McGrath told me about that reading you gave. He was terribly impressed—even if you didn't take the part. What are you doing in New York anyway? You're an actress, baby. I mean, what do you have to keep you here?"

Devon wasn't sure. Deauville said, "Hollywood is the only place in the world where you can die from encouragement." But she was beginning to think it might be a lovely way to go.

Two weeks later Gilda called from California. It was late in New York, nearly 3:00 A.M. The sound of the phone was shrill, but not as shrill as the ring of terror in Devon's head. Deauville's side of the bed was empty.

"Devon? Hello, baby," Gilda said, in a voice warm as a bedtime quilt. Suddenly Devon realized she'd been dreaming about her mother —that was what had terrified her, leaving her feeling abandoned and alone. "I've been thinking of you," Gilda said, in that Hershey syrup voice. "How are you, baby? Are you happy?"

"No," Devon whispered, closing her eyes against the shadowy darkness and wrapping herself in the flannel voice at the other end of the line. "Oh, Gilda, I'm so glad you called."

"Are you, baby? I am, too. I saw Inez this evening. She sends love," Gilda sighed. Safe and warm now, Devon waited for Gilda to tell her a bedtime story. "It made me think of you. Well, really, I thought of me, seeing our poor Inez, so hungry for life, so desperate for love . . . " Gilda chuckled. "Christ, will you listen to that dialogue? If this was a picture, I'd walk out on it. Do you know how I got into pictures, baby? Have I ever told you about that?"

The photograph, Devon remembered sleepily. She'd read about it in a fan magazine, years ago. Or had May told her about it at school? A talent scout for MGM had seen a picture of Gilda in the window of a photographer's shop. A high school graduation picture, Devon thought.

"The talent scout who saw your picture in the window?"

"Talent scout," Gilda said ironically. "That's rich. It's kinda complicated, honey. Pimp was more like it, but a nice pimp, if you know what I mean. I was seventeen and I had never been out of Hilltop, Oklahoma, in my life. Six kids, orphaned when our folks died. I was ten years old at the time and the baby. My sister Vy raised me, with nothing to eat but mustard greens and cornbread and you were lucky to get that.

"In those days I had no ambitions to be anything but dead. It was Vy who had the dreams. Vy's husband, Orval Scribner, worked in the Purina Feed Store and took pictures of everything in his spare time. Chickens, freight trains, even a thirty-pound watermelon he entered in the county fair in Norman. And me, of course. I guess I was something of a looker, even then, before the miracle of MGM and plastic surgery. Anyway, Orval showed Larry Malnish the picture of me."

"In the photographer's shop?"

"F. X. Ryan. The only professional photographer in Tulsa. Orval talked him into showing some of his pictures in the window. And there I was, between a two-headed calf and the bald, toothless baby they found one morning in the back seat of the Henryetta High School bus. The baby was adopted by the minister of the Henryetta Pentecostal Church and I was adopted by Larry Malnish."

Devon was confused. "How did Larry Malnish get you to Hollywood?"

"Malnish was from Tulsa. He went to high school with Orval. Orval worshiped him. Malnish was the one who escaped, the one who left the Oklahoma hills and went to Hollywood. Orval and my sister Vy thought Hollywood was better than Heaven. Everyone went to Heaven. Only Larry Malnish went to Hollywood. Anyway, Malnish was on his way to some meeting in New York. He was working at MGM out in Culver City and he stopped off in Tulsa to see his mother, who was dying of cancer. Orval and Vy drove over to see him and he bought them a porterhouse steak at the Roundup Grill and they showed him my picture in Ryan's window and asked him if he thought they might be interested in me out there at MGM. I guess Larry was impressed. I was just a skinny brat when he left. He told Vy he could make me the biggest star since Joan Crawford."

"And he did."

"Legend has it. But not right away. Hang on a sec, baby, will you? I gotta get a cigarette."

Devon couldn't believe she was talking to a movie star, intimately, all the way from Hollywood, just like two long-lost school chums talking over old times. Gilda's story was as glamorous and amazing as Lana Turner on that soda-fountain stool. Suddenly the voice was back on the line, reassuring Devon that she was not dreaming.

"Did Inez ever tell you about her family?" Gilda asked. "She told me tonight, poor kid."

"Yes," Devon said cautiously, not sure how much Inez had told.

"I think that's what got me on this kick. This 'sentimental journey.' I was once just as desperate to be somebody, to escape the goddamn emptiness of being a nobody from nowhere, pressing my nose against the candy store window with my stomach growling. Larry Malnish, with his manicured nails and camel's hair coat, I thought he was Christ sent to Oklahoma to rescue me. He made about fifty copies of that silly picture and passed them around to everyone at MGM and I almost dropped dead when they asked me to come to New York for a screen test. Vy went with me. I was seventeen and I hadn't even finished high school yet."

Devon could hear her drawing on her cigaratte.

"But Larry Malnish and Vy both said I was gonna make it, and I believed them. I didn't know what a star was. Hell, I didn't even know if I wanted to be one. I think I just wanted to be whatever a guy like Larry Malnish thought I ought to be. When we got to New York we stayed at the Taft Hotel and ordered chicken sandwiches from room service and waited three days for MGM to call. Meanwhile, Malnish dressed me up and took me to Billy Reed's Little Club and Lindy's and the Latin Quarter while Vy waited at the Taft. He told me what to drink and what to order and how much to tip the girl in the powder room. He spent a fortune and never made a pass at me. I started to worry. I thought maybe I wasn't classy enough. And then he introduced me to Big Ted Kearny, and that was it. Bing. Bam. Alakazam. I was blown away."

"Big who?"

Gilda laughed. "Of course he was before your time, dear. Morgan Edward Kearny. He was a Wall Street wheeler-dealer with a taste for young show girls, and Larry Malnish was his talent scout. Kearny owned a theater chain in which Sam Durand was a silent partner. If old L. B. Mayer had ever found out, Sam would've found himself on a soup line. Kearny had a lot of clout in Hollywood. He was big physically, too —he was the biggest man I'd ever seen. Huge, handsome, very rich. According to Malnish, Ted Kearny was going to be my ticket to the big time. All I had to do, Malnish said, was make him like me. Ah, but I screwed up. I fell in love with him."

"With Big Ted?"

"I was seventeen years old, and Ted Kearny was forty-five, and from the moment I laid eyes on him, I was lost. I never wanted anything so much in my life as I wanted him to like me. Malnish took me to his town house on Gramercy Park to see him. We went up to his dressing room. A servant was helping him into a white dinner jacket, brushing his suit with a whisk broom. I took one look at him and just like that, I fell in love. He had thick black curly hair, just touched with gray here and there. And big hands, and ice-blue eyes, which were always half smiling. I've thought about it so much, for years and years, and I still don't know why I fell for him that way."

Devon thought of King. She remembered the first time she'd seen him from the window at Westbridge. "It happens like that sometimes, doesn't it?"

"Maybe it was the feeling of security I got from being with an older man. Maybe it was the house, those dark polished mahogany bookcases and thick carpets. Even the flowers everywhere were huge. Towering bouquets. Brilliant colors. First peonies I ever saw. And cabbage roses. For a man, he sure loved flowers. Everything about him was bigger than life.

"Ted Kearny watched me in the mirror. 'Larry tells me you want to be in pictures. Do you know what it takes to be in pictures?' he said. I was sitting on the window seat, velvet pillows against my back, ignorant as a hillbilly. I didn't now shit from Shinola. 'It takes beauty, which you've got,' Kearny said, watching me in the mirror, 'and style and brains. But most of all it takes ambition, a willingness to do whatever you have to do to get where you want to go. How ambitious are you?'

"I was only seventeen, but I knew exactly what he meant. The servant had disappeared. Larry was long gone. 'Oh, I'm plenty ambitious,' I said." Gilda laughed. "I had to convince him. He was trying to make me, and all I wanted was for him to succeed. I didn't care a damn about being in pictures. I wanted *him*. Hell, as far as I was concerned, I was already *in* the most romantic movie ever made. Gilda Greenway—only it was Quinn back then, Gilda Rae Quinn—and Big Ted Kearny. I was madly in love with him and two months pregnant before I found out he wouldn't marry me."

"Oh, no!"

"Vy stuck it out with me. Malnish got her a job selling candy at the Fannie Farmer's on Forty-second Street and somehow we managed to pay the rent at the Taft while we waited for the screen test. I did a couple of bits in teenage flicks. Larry Malnish got me an abortion and with Ted Kearny's help I finally got an agent and a screen test, too. And Sam Durand gave me a contract and a new name. I became a star about two years after that. First, I had to be groomed, coached, and taught how to lose that goddamn Oklahoma accent, which I never quite learned. Hell, I didn't even know how to walk. I walked across the screen in my first picture like a mule with hemorrhoids.

"I was only worth a hundred bucks a week to Metro. They didn't know what to do with me, so they stuck me in a couple of Andy Hardy pictures. I played a lot of cigarette girls and typing-pool secretaries in Norma Shearer pictures.

" 'Is my husband in?' Norma would ask me, and I'd say, 'He's in conference, Mrs. Andrews,' or something dumb like that. And she'd barge in and find him with Ruth Hussey.

"Mostly, I just hung around with the grips and tried to fight off Howard Hughes."

"You're kidding!"

"I wish I was. He was after me like a hound dog on a trail of bacon grease. One night he grabbed me on the ass at Ciro's, and I knocked him out cold with a copper ashtray. His press agents tried to tell the press he was in the hospital with stomach trouble, but I spilled the beans to Winchell when he called from New York, and that's when I got my first important press. Mayer hit the fan like a sack of goat manure, but parts got better.

"Hell, I wasn't looking for publicity. But I wanted Ted to know I was keeping my legs crossed, waiting faithfully for him. He found out. And the parts got even better. I got a raise. Then came that stunning little bit with the pearls in *Night Anthem.* It made me a star.

"Now those film scholars write long-winded articles about how I tossed those pearls over my shoulder and changed the face of American womanhood. It makes me laugh. The truth is, I was trying to swat a goddamn fruit fly that had landed on my back and was chewing the hell out of me. The director was so mad he shot it over again, but when they saw the rushes they tossed a coin and the take with the action won. Accidental history, that's all.

"That's the story of this whole fucked-up industry and most of the careers in it. If it hadn't been for a fruit fly, I might be slinging hash today at Barney's Beanery. After that, I was a hot property called Gilda Greenway. Howard Strickling and the whole MGM publicity department started treating me like a hot property and *then* Big Ted Kearny fell in love with me. The rest, as they say, is history."

"What a story. It's so sad."

"No, baby. It's just what happened. The only sad part, I guess, was the abortion. It was 1939, for God's sake, and they went in with bamboo shoots and messed me up pretty good. If I'd known it was going to screw up my chance of ever having kids, I'd never have agreed. I'd kill before I'd let one of you girls go through that. But what the hell? It got me out of Hilltop, Oklahoma. It changed my life and Vy's, too. She gave up her marriage for my career. I owe her a lot, may her sweet soul rest in Heaven."

"You mean you can't have children?"

"Sure I can," said Gilda. "May's my baby. And Inez. And how about you, Devon Barnes? Could you use an extra mama?"

"Well, mine lives in a condo in Dallas. She used to sell oven mitts and mayonnaise lids. Now she supervises about a hundred other women in a tri-state area who sell them for her and she lives on commissions. I haven't seen her in years. I was raised by my grandmother, and she sent me five dollars in a Christmas card last year. Since I left Westbridge, she refuses to send me one more penny unless I go home to Texas for the rest of my life."

"Well, it's a deal then. The rest of your life can be an awfully hell of a long time, baby. I'd hate to see you spend it milking Jerseys."

"I dreamed about my mother tonight," said Devon sheepishly. "I woke up soaking wet and feeling so alone without her. I think I remind her of my father, who was a dreamer and a drifter."

"Aren't we all? Listen, Devon, can you hear me? Now you've got *me*. Get your ass out to the Coast and I'll teach you how to play one helluva game of double solitaire. You'll never be lonely again."

Deauville laughed derisively when he heard about it. "Lonely? Gilda Greenway? Even Hedda Hopper lost count of the men in her life. Why would she need *you?* Hell, *I'm* lonely, Devon. You don't see *me* wasting a dime trying to get warm next to you."

Gilda phoned again a week later. And then the following Tuesday. "Just to chat, just to get to know you," she said. She didn't mention the 3:00 A.M. call, nor did Devon. She just began checking in regularly, like a surrogate mother.

"I spoke to Denise last week—Denise Auerbach of the Workshop, Serge Malinkov's partner," she'd say. "Denise thinks you'd be swell in pictures. I worked with Denise out here years ago. She's a fabulous actress, but the camera hates her. Eats her up and spits her out. You do a scene with her and she'll have you crying, weeping, drooling. And then you take a look at the rushes and it's not there. Whatever it was she did that tore your heart out, it's not up there on the fucking screen. She's like Dietrich. It's hard to light her and she's got bad teeth. She thinks *you* could do it, though. They *both* do, Denise and Serge. They think you could go the whole way, Devon."

"You won't believe the craziness," Inez told Devon.

In late November, King and Avery flew to California for twenty-four hours to discuss a film deal on *Barracks Street Blues*. Inez called Devon to tell her all about it as soon as King returned to New York.

Inez was sharing a house near the beach in Venice with a couple of guys Gilda knew. One was a hairdresser apprenticing with Bud Dahlripple at Metro, the other a boy from New York who was writing a movie for Rock Hudson at Universal. Inez made it a threesome. Inez had bought a second-hand Chevy, without which, she assured Devon, you could not survive in Southern California. The house was "upscale beatnik," with stucco walls, rubber furniture shaped like sex organs, the smell of clove incense, and marijuana growing in the window box.

Inez spoke to Gilda every day; they were working on some movie ideas together. And she talked to King about once a week, usually from Gilda's place, which was a "goddamn palace." It was called The Pearls.

"Twice a day buses cruise by the gates with pasty-faced tourists hanging out the windows trying to see past the magnolia trees. And she's got this zoo out back behind the pool with birds and dogs and three horses and a zebra—"

"Come on, Inez."

"No, I swear it. Gilda is crazy for animals. Remember how she told us about her dog, Tallulah? Well, that's just the one that *travels*. She has four more that stay at home."

"Who takes care of them?"

"Devon, she has a staff, *of course*. And this awful housekeeper, who cooks special meals for the whole menagerie in a special kitchen. Gilda's dogs eat better than I do.

"Anyway, King and Avery came out to talk to some movie people about a film version of *Barracks Street Blues*. But he didn't even call me!"

Instead, King had shown up in the middle of one her roommates' famous Sunday night free-for-alls. "Talk about a party!" Inez laughed. "The house was filled to its peeling purple ceiling with weird types— belly dancers and bearded cellists, Hell's Angels, hairdressers, muscle- men, starlets sitting on the laps of poets and actors, coffeehouse free- loaders. I didn't even see King come in. He just waded through the frankincense and myrrh, honey, and tapped me on the shoulder. Then he dragged me into my room and cleared the place."

"He didn't."

"Oh, yeah," said Inez. "He did. My hero. He emptied the place and we didn't get out of bed until an hour before he had to get to the airport on Monday morning. Poor baby. He could hardly walk to the door. His first trip to Lotus Land, and all he saw was the ceiling."

May was in New York for the Christmas holidays. Devon met her uptown at Rumplemayer's, where a butterscotch sundae cost as much as a week of waitress tips. May had chosen the restaurant. Now she was ordering the ice cream, hot cocoa, and peanut butter cookies, asking for double nuts on the whipped cream. "But skip the marshmallow, please. I'm on a diet."

"And you, miss?"

"A rare cheeseburger and hot tea, please," said Devon.

"Are you sick or something, Dev? This is Rumplemayer's. Order anything less than three thousand calories a bite and they send you to Bellevue."

"I know where we are, May," she said, watching the waiter leave, "and Bellevue is cheaper. Deau and I are so broke that I haven't eaten anything but Kraft macaroni for a week and a half. Don't worry," she said, seeing the remorse on May's face, "the role of poor, struggling actress suits me. I promise to order a hot fudge sundae for dessert. Now tell me everything about school."

"Okay, here's my biggest news. I'm not a virgin anymore," she giggled. "Now all three of us have finally discovered the meaning of the words 'Open, Sesame!' Well, don't look so shocked. Some of us have fatter doors than others, Ali Baba. They still open."

"May, this is super. Tell me all about him."

"Actually, it's *them.*" May waited until the waiter set their food down and returned to the soda fountain. Then she plunged on, between slurps of hot butterscotch. "I met these two boys one night at a fraternity party and we got drunk on Black Russians and I went back to their dorm and slept with both of them."

"At the same time? Together?"

"Well, there's more than enough of me to go around," May said defiantly. "Devon, do you think I'm a whore?" May still wore white stockings and flat-heeled shoes, and enormous knit sweaters over wool skirts to hide her bulges, but she had definitely changed.

"Don't be a goose. I just never heard of doing it with two boys at once. Doesn't that sort of break the concentration?"

"It's fun, and nobody gets left out. You sort of get upside-down, if you know what I mean." May was halfway through her sundae. "See, one of them is chewing my boobs while the other one is kissing my pussy . . ." She scooped out a spoonful of syrup and slowly licked it off the surface of the spoon. "And this is what I do to both of them."

Devon could not believe what she was hearing. Deau often used the word *pussy* when they were making love, knowing she hated it. Sometimes he teased her into saying it herself because he got excited when she talked dirty. But for May to pronounce the word, here in the middle of Rumplemayer's, while they were *eating* . . . She was acting just like Inez!

May seemed to read her mind. "Don't tell Inez, okay? You know how she gets off on dirty books. I'm not a pervert. Devon, I feel like I'm somebody special when I'm with these two boys. They actually *like* me—*and* my body." She swallowed the last of her cocoa, licked her lips, and grinned. "Tell Deauville instead. Maybe he has a couple of friends who'd like to meet me. Have pussy, will travel."

Devon was not amused. "I think we'd better get the check."

"Just kidding," May said, touching her arm. "It's my Mae West routine. But I am dying to meet *him.* Mother has invited both of you to spend Christmas Day with us."

"Damn white of her," said Deauville. "See what you get when you go to a liberal ratfuck like the University of Chicago? You get to be a limousine liberal and invite a nigger home for egg nog. No, thank you, y'all jes' have to make do with one turkey for Christmas. Invite Harry Belafonte."

He decided instead to go South to see his grandmother, who lived in Alabama. He hadn't been "down home" since he was a boy. Devon tried to talk him out of it, afraid of what would happen to him there. That autumn the National Guard had been called out to end the riots that erupted after the Supreme Court's school desegregation order, when nine Negro students tried to enter Central High in Little Rock.

Deauville wouldn't listen. He needed to get away, he said. He had enough bread to get to Alabama and back. His folks down there would take care of him for a while. Devon suggested California as an alternative. "Inez loves it out there. You could stay with her."

"Sure," he said sarcastically. "Is Gilda running a special on the underground railroad? The Harriet Tubman of Beverly Hills? Where the hell would I get the bread to go to California? I'm not doing six nights and two matinees on Broadway, baby. I'm doing *Emperor Jones* in a pisshole garage on Fourth Street for a motherfuckin' ofay director who thinks I ought to be paying him for the privilege."

He was at the door, leaving again, ready to burn the world to an ash heap. He'd slammed out so many times since the hot summer night when King had brought her home that Devon suggested they install swinging doors to make it easier on the neighbors. But now he paused with his hand on the doorknob.

He turned, broken and exhausted.

"Devon," he cried, then slumped at the table they had dragged down to Jones Street from the Salvation Army.

Devon rushed to him, stroked his head, rocked him in her arms. "I'll call Gilda. She'll lend us the money, Deau. You must get away. I don't care about anything but your happiness and safety."

They made love that night with the passion of their halcyon days. He caressed her in all the secret places they had explored together. As he held her in his strong, dark arms, she stroked his lips and earlobes, his determined jaw and long, graceful neck. She brushed her hand across his chest and across his belly and up and down his muscular thighs until she memorized his body. When he eased himself into her, she melted around him.

"I love you, Deau," she whispered. "But I'm afraid you'll never come back. Please, please don't ever leave me."

In the morning, he was gone. He left a note by the bed, saying he'd phone from Alabama. May came down to spend the night with Devon and keep her company, but the phone didn't ring.

On Christmas Eve, Devon surrendered. She took the IRT uptown to the Fischoffs' luxury apartment on West End Avenue and stayed with May. She was tired of being alone and, as May kept reminding her, "Even stray dogs need a friend on Christmas."

Norma Fischoff had turned the seven-room apartment where May had spent her childhood into a model of Victorian opulence. "My mother is the only woman in the world who even puts doilies on the toilet seat," said May, and Devon could see what she meant. The rooms were rich and dark, but the furniture seemed to dwarf the door frames. Polished mahogany armoires loomed over curved six-legged tables not wide enough to serve a dog biscuit on, and there was fringe on everything.

There were glass breakfronts for heirloom china, gold mirrors, and Devon had never seen so much wallpaper—vertical red patterns on silver backgrounds, mottled green clouds nestled in skies of pink, and eggplants in the kitchen. The living room had a black wall-to-wall carpet with pink cabbage roses. "She likes everything, so she just buys it all," moaned May, rolling her eyes.

Framed photos of Frankie's clients crowded every tabletop. In the center of the grand piano was, of course, a picture of Gilda and her famous pearls in a burgundy velvet frame, and next to her, Frankie's latest client, King Godwin. An enormous painting of Norma by Augustus Johns dominated the room above the carved oak fireplace. There wasn't a single photo anywhere of May.

"Mama keeps me small and delicate, the way she always sees me in her mind, hidden away in her wallet."

May's room was from another, distant planet. James Dean posters, Yale pennants, dead carnations in a milk bottle, crumpled Milky Way wrappers under the brass bed, and blue and white gingham wallpaper were the order of the day here, a sharp and lived-in contrast to the oppressive formality of the other rooms.

Devon sighed with relief. "I'm glad there's a real person living here. I was beginning to feel out of place without a shawl and an oil lamp."

"My mother is really very young at heart," May said, "but Daddy has erected this candy box as a shrine to her and she just sort of goes along with it. I know the day he dies, she'll sell all this creepy stuff that belonged to old Grandmother Fischoff and move to a glass house in Miami Beach. So welcome to Molly Goldberg's Whitman's-Sampler-on-the-Hudson."

The Fischoffs were Jewish, but they were also show business. Norma had Chanukah candles *and* a Christmas tree. "Daddy gets so much graft during the holidays from producers, actors, and movie people that he'd convert to the Holy Rollers before he gave up Christmas."

May's parents greeted Devon with warm, sincere hugs. They spent Christmas Eve stringing popcorn and cranberries, listening to the Norman Luboff choir sing carols on the phonograph, and assisting Estelle the cook with last-minute preparations for the next day's feast. Estelle, who had clucked over May since the day she was born, was spending Christmas Day with her family in Far Rockaway, so they had to eat early.

Devon spooned mince filling into the tarts while May busied herself with the marshmallow topping for the sweet potato casserole, popping one in her mouth for each marshmallow in the dish until she ran out. The sweet potatoes arrived at the table the next day with a big space in the middle. The Fischoffs retired early on Christmas Eve to make holiday phone calls from a bedroom that May said "looks like Marie Antoinette died in it" and the girls curled up under the blankets, watching the lights of New Jersey across the Hudson from May's bedroom window. When Devon fell asleep, May was still talking about the magic of her first orgasm.

On Christmas morning, Devon woke to the sound of Bing Crosby singing "Jingle Bells." She wore a red velvet dress with white lace cuffs, while May climbed into an oversized tunic over a pair of Claire McCardell culottes big enough for Lou Costello.

"Good morning, good morning," beamed Frankie as he kissed Devon on the cheek. May angled hers for the same response, but her father turned and headed for the kitchen to get the coffee tray.

"He hates me every other day of the year," shrugged May. "Why should Christmas be any different?"

They sipped coffee and nibbled breakfast brioches by the tree. Then Frankie ceremoniously announced the opening of the presents. Devon gave Norma a bottle of half-price Ma Griffe perfume and presented Frankie with a money clip shaped like a dollar sign which she had bought for $10 from one of the waiters at the Figaro. For May, she had found a diary. From what May had already told her, she'd need one.

The Fischoffs gave Devon an antique cameo—"Something suitably old-fashioned for an old-fashioned girl," said Norma, brushing back the long black strands of hair that fell over Devon's face and hid her tears.

"And now for *my* old-fashioned girl," Frankie glowed, "the bestest of the best!" From a silver Bergdorf-Goodman box, Norma extracted the most breathtaking sable coat Devon had ever seen.

"Frankie, have you gone berserk?" Norma lost her composure. Her always delicate mouth hung open like a broken gate.

"Try it on," insisted her husband, grinning foolishly. "Gilda can eat her heart out when she sees you in this, honey." Norma didn't take it off the rest of the day.

May produced her gifts. For Devon, a handsome Gucci script holder "for your first starring vehicle." For her mother, a delicate candlestick holder made of pale green sandwich glass. And last, she handed her father a gift, which he unwrapped with great fanfare. From inside the silver gift wrap with the silver pine cones, out tumbled a photograph of his daughter in a silver frame with the inscription, "Dear Daddy—I love you with all my heart. Love, May."

"What's this?"

Frankie couldn't hide his disappointment. He didn't even have the grace to try, Devon thought. She resented him bitterly for it.

"It's for your office, Daddy. You have pictures of everyone else. I posed for it at school last month. I had my hair done and everything."

"Frankie, how absolutely exquisite," said Norma, wrapping her sabled arms around the crumbling May.

"Very nice," Frankie said. "When's the turkey coming out of the oven? I'm hungry."

"We're eating at one o'clock, like we always do. Just hold your horses. May, I think you've thought of the loveliest presents of all. Now open yours."

"I'll open them later. I—I feel—" May leapt to her feet and fled to the sanctuary of her room, choking on a lump in her throat as big as a golf ball.

"Frankie, you've spoiled everything. I want you to apologize to that child at once. I mean it."

Devon was surprised by the sudden authority in Norma Fischoff's otherwise sweetly demure voice. She was even more surprised by the abrupt change in Mr. Fischoff's manner. Arrogance and irritation had been replaced in an instant by a pouting, hangdog petulance. "Yes, lamb," he said meekly, so softly Devon could scarcely hear him, and ambled off toward May's room.

Later, when they were alone, May told her he had all but begged her to forgive him, promising to hang the photo in a place of honor on his office wall as soon as the holidays were over. "Then he looked around this room and I thought he was going to puke. Honestly, Dev, every time I leave I think they hold a family conference to see if they should just burn my room down."

"At least give him credit for trying."

"He just gave a doomed martyr performance because my mother would make his life a living hell if he didn't. He knows which way the mop flops."

"What did they give you for Christmas?" Devon changed the subject before the tears returned.

"Same old shit. Clothes that will have to be returned because I gained ten pounds since last year and none of the sizes fit. And a diet book. I figure by this time next year I can lose forty pounds. According to this book, all I have to do is eat nothing for the next 365 days but 4,928 grapefruits."

King called while Devon and May were at Radio City Music Hall watching the Rockettes and "The Nativity" Christmas show, with Marlon Brando in *Sayonara* on the big screen. "He and Frankie are flying out to California first thing tomorrow morning," Norma Fischoff told them.

The movie deal Frankie had been holding out for had come through, and King's understudy was taking over his role in *Barracks*

Street Blues for a few days during the holiday doldrums. "It's a phenomenal deal, really, for a first picture," Frankie said proudly. "One hundred thousand on a play-or-pay contract. The perks and the escalation clause for overages could earn King a cool quarter of a million in no time. Swifty Lazar is always bragging about his deals. Wait till I tell him about this one."

May flew back to Chicago—"I've got a hot date for New Year's Eve," she told her mother, winking at Devon—and Devon returned to her empty apartment on Jones Street, feeling more abandoned and bewildered than ever.

The holidays made her blue. Maybelle was a constant irritant, badgering her to desert "that sordid life" and come back to Texas. Devon's mother hadn't even bothered to wish her a Merry Christmas at all. On New Year's Eve, Devon celebrated by taking a long walk alone in Washington Square, dining solo on black-eyed peas and falling asleep before midnight.

The phone awakened her at dawn. "Wake up, it's 1958!"

"Good lord, Inez. What time is it out there?"

"Who knows? Who owns a clock? I've been up for days. I just put King on the Red Eye. Dev, I've got top-drawer news." Inez sounded drunk. "Hold on. I'll let Gilda tell you. It's all her fault, really. It's all just too *outré.*"

Where did she find these words?

Gilda's voice was creamier. "Inez and King are getting married, darling. Isn't that wonderful? Naturally she wants you and May to be bridesmaids."

"Inez—and King?" Devon burst into tears. "Yes, yes . . . wonderful."

Inez was back on the line, gurgling and giddy. "And Miss Gilda Greenway is orchestrating everything. Devon, we're going to be married at The Pearls! Gilda says Frank Fischoff got King the best contract they've ever heard of out here. The whole town's talking. King can afford me now. God, he could afford Elizabeth Taylor! But he's marrying little old *moi!* I don't understand money. You know me. I'm just a struggling but passionate writer. Devon, aren't you thrilled for me? Isn't it romantic? Gilda's arranging everything. Are you sitting down? My wedding dress is being designed by Edith Head!"

THIRTEEN

1958

I nez and King were to be married the second Thursday in March.

The producers of *Barracks Street Blues* weren't thrilled to release their meal ticket from his one-year contract, but after Frankie Fischoff cited everyone from Ben Gazzara to Paul Newman as precedents, Avery Calder intervened and another actor moved into the role. "He doesn't own the part; he's only rentin' it for a little while, baby," said the playwright. "You can return any time the sun fries yo' brains out in Cuckooville."

King didn't want to leave New York.

He didn't want to marry Inez Hollister.

He wasn't even sure he wanted to do the movie version of *Barracks Street Blues.* His two brief visits to California had made him dizzy. But he was restless. He couldn't sleep. Success was a piranha, nibbling at his nerves. He was tired of playing the same role night after night with one arm tied to his back. He had to make a movie. And considering the circumstances, Inez didn't leave him much choice. Gilda was running her life now and an abortion, she insisted, was unthinkable. He wouldn't run from this mess. He'd face it like a man.

He worked out every day at the Hudson Health Club on Fifty-seventh Street, pumping his pecs, molding his thighs for Cinemascope, and every night he'd freeze the same muscles into spasm, walking through the snow on his way to the theater. If a career meant waiting for the next chess move, lying on a beach was a better way to wait, and the chess board in Los Angeles was cleaner.

King played through the end of February, sold his motorcycle, finished his 186th performance on a Saturday night, and turned over his digs the next day to a hooker named Glenda. By Sunday night, he was in the clouds, reading the trades, on his way to a new kind of Russian roulette—the role of a would-be star with a would-be marriage to a would-be woman in a never-was town called Hollywood. He watched part of a Doris Day movie in first-class, threw up what TWA shamelessly called dinner, and fell asleep clutching the *Hollywood Reporter* with one hand and rubbing his dick with the other, convinced that if anyone ever wrote a movie about a guy driven impotent by loneliness and confusion, he should get the part without even audition-ing. Just as Oscar Levant had predicted, when he woke up in Los Angeles the next morning, he had turned eighty.

Inez had changed.

When she picked Devon up at the Los Angeles airport the follow-ing Sunday, she had bobbed her hair into a fashionable pageboy, like June Allyson or Ella Raines, and was terribly sophisticated in pink cashmere and pearls. Devon felt awkward and liverish in her dirty New York raincoat. It had been snowing when she left, and the unseasonably warm sunshine of California made her skin sticky.

Inez unlocked the door of Gilda's blue Bentley and said, "You remember Tallulah, don't you?"

Gilda's cocker spaniel lay sprawled across the back seat of the car.

"I believe you two were introduced at '21.' She's spent so much time in limos with Gilda that she gets crazy if she doesn't have her daily drive, but Gilda's too busy with the wedding arrangements so she asked me to do the honors today."

"Cute," said Devon.

"I *told* you she had this fixation on animals. Wait until she insists on introducing you to the rest of the family."

Inez babbled all the way to Beverly Hills and she didn't always make complete sense. She was using words like "jejune" and "recalcitrant," and Devon knew she hadn't picked them up before she bailed out of Bennington.

"And just wait till you see The Pearls. Honestly, Dev, it's something right out of a Joan Crawford picture. King and I are staying there until our apartment is ready on Doheny. Of course I had to relinquish my share of the Venice house. King doesn't want to live so far away from the studio. We don't know when he'll start the picture. It could be months. You know the red tape out here. You could drop dead just waiting for somebody to return your phone call. I'm sure when King starts shooting and those positively *insouciant* per diems roll in, the studio will find us a house, a pool, another car. All that stuff is strictly *de rigeur* out here, *naturellement.*"

"*Naturellement,*" replied Devon, trying not to bite a hole through her tongue.

"Meanwhile, we're at The Pearls, living like Charlie Chaplin and Paulette Goddard. Honestly, this place makes Pickfair look like Gasoline Alley. Gilda did the whole first floor in navy blue and white, which can get kind of *doloroso,* if you get my drift. But there are fifty rooms, so you can always just escape to another ambience if you get the willies. And there are nine guest suites, all named after and decorated in the style of her early films. I think you're in the Daisy Ashley suite, so get y'all's southern accent dusted off, Miz Scarlett, the plantation's gonna hum this week."

Inez bubbled with information. During the next five days, Edith Head would be fitting Devon and May at Paramount, where she was working on a new Audrey Hepburn picture. Inez would wear oyster white with Gilda's pearls, the bridesmaids would wear yellow chiffon with bouquets of daisies. Extra servants were hired, but there was one problem.

"Gilda has this housekeeper named Mrs. Denby who positively rules everything and everyone who sets foot inside the place, morning, noon, and night. God, Devon, this cow is the living epitome of a total creepburger. King calls her Mrs. Danvers. She is the queen of the pickle people. If that woman ever smiles, you know one of your kittens has been poisoned in the scuppernong arbor. The expression on her face is *quel* doleful. She makes Gale Sondergaard in *The Spider Woman Strikes Back* look like Sparkle Plenty."

"Why does Gilda keep her around if she frightens the horses?"

"God only knows. King says she knows where all the bodies are buried. I think it's because she buried them herself."

Devon thought Los Angeles looked like a temporary town in which everything had been stripped of its natural color and reshot with a filter lens. "Inez, I haven't seen a soul on the streets since we passed the Beverly Hills sign."

"You won't, either. You could be arrested here for walking to the post office. This place is so exclusive even the police have an unlisted number. The palm trees are infested with rats and at Christmas they sell pink and black Christmas trees. Gilda spent a fortune at The Pearls bringing in bulldozers to rip up the palm trees and had them replaced with magnolia trees just to make her feel more at home. Since her contract ran out at Metro in 1952, she's been box office poison, but she still lives like the last of the genuine movie goddesses, I am here to tell you."

"Is it always this hot?"

"Honey, you haven't seen anything yet. Eighty degrees is a cold front out here. And one more thing. I hope you brought earplugs. Every morning you wake up with the same sound in your ears." Inez sucked in her cheeks, then popped her tongue in and out of her tight mouth, making a sound like "thwop, thwop, thwop."

"What in the hell is that?" Devon giggled.

"Tennis balls, dahling. Tennis balls."

Inez sounded as if her dialogue was written by Anita Loos, but she hadn't exaggerated about The Pearls. Turning abruptly off Coldwater Canyon, they came to a crunching halt before a menacing electronic gate. "THE PEARLS" was engraved, next to the speaker box in the stone walls, in mother-of-pearl. Inez said, "Open Sesame," pressed the electronic remote-control box clipped to the sun-shield visor, and the gate swung open, admitting Devon to a verdant paradise kissed by chlorophyll. Lush carpeted lawns as green as a golf course spread out like quilts on both sides of the giant magnolias that bordered the rock-lined drive. They climbed, as though wafting toward Shangri-la.

"Where's the moat?" she joked, but it wasn't funny. Peacocks pecked and clawed under grape arbors. Hollyhocks high as split-rail fenceposts sparkled in the sun. Lavender clusters dripped honey from wisteria vines. Then the columns of Tara rose from the azaleas, guarding a brick veranda of chintz-covered wicker. A lantern above the door swung gently in the still heat. A large golden retriever barked a greeting.

Mrs. Denby met them at the door. "Another New Yorker," she sniffed, leading the way to Devon's suite while a Haitian girl named Creola struggled with the luggage. Devon and Inez exchanged looks, like new arrivals at the scene of a lurid crime.

"I dreamed last night I went back to Manderley," said Inez, *sotto voce.* Devon shrieked.

Mrs. Denby whirled around, the hairpins in her braided bun shivering with annoyance. She had the face of a hammerhead shark. All angles and no curves. "This way, please." The voice sounded like a chain saw.

"Definitely right out of *Rebecca,*" said Devon when they were alone.

"Are you kidding?" Inez countered. "She makes Judith Anderson look like Thelma Ritter on Mother's Day."

They both agreed "Mrs. Danvers," as Edna Denby would forever be called, was no wisecracking housekeeper in Thelma Ritter rabbit slippers. She was no Land's-sakes-alive-I-smell-something-burning-in-the-oven type, either.

"More about her in the second reel," poked Inez. "Come on, let's find Gilda."

Devon had never seen anything like The Pearls. It was as vast and beautiful as a museum, but more exciting. From her room, she could see King on the tennis courts, already brown as a walnut. Beyond, she had a view of the croquet courts and what looked like a maze.

"That's the gardener's cottage," said Inez, pointing to a Spanish tiled-roof hacienda drowning in bougainvillea. And beyond that, there was an Olympic-size pool presided over by a marble Venus and encircled by fourteen Corinthian columns.

"They actually filmed a scene from an Esther Williams musical in that pool. Gilda had it copied from the Hearst castle at San Simeon. *Très extraordinaire, n'est-ce pas?*"

A row of carpeted cabanas with lemon yellow and white striped awnings bordered one side of the pool; on the other, the beginnings of the meticulously landscaped English gardens were nestled under a symphony of French lilacs. Behind the house, hidden from view by a jungle of eucalyptus trees, was Gilda's "zoo."

"Dinner's at seven-thirty. There's a bubble bath from Floris waiting breathlessly to caress your skin in a bathroom so filled with perfumes and milk solutions you couldn't get through all of them in a month. Every morning you get the *L.A. Times* and the *New York Times* delivered to your bed with fresh grapefruit juice and croissants, and every night you sleep on Porthault linen. If you want anything, just pick up the phone and dial any room in the house. Honestly, Dev, we're gonna spoil you rotten while you're here."

"I don't know whether it's jet lag or catatonia," said Devon, pinching her elbow. "But I don't have a very clear picture of what's going on here."

"Neither did I when I arrived, but I got used to it. 'You can take the girl out of Brooklyn but you can't,' et cetera, et cetera," winked Inez, mocking herself. "Well, I didn't even have to try. Everybody in this town's from Brooklyn, it seems. Just relax. Pretend you're Alice and you just fell into a rabbit hole and the next week of your life will be the maddest tea party you ever dreamed of. Honey, even the tea in this house has a name you can't pronounce. Later, 'gator."

In the starched innocence of the Young Daisy Ashley suite, Devon felt as if she were drowning in ruffles and tears. The irony did not escape her. Just like Daisy, she thought, jiggling the pronged gold-plated receiver of the alabaster phone, an exact duplicate of the one on which Gilda, as young, idealistic Daisy, poor but proud, had received the crushing news that her beau was marrying the richest girl in town, played by Marsha Hunt.

Not that Inez Hollister was the richest girl in this or any other town. Not that King Godwin was Devon's "beau." And certainly she was no jilted *naif*. Still, she wondered if Gilda, always perceptive, had not suspected her feelings for King and intentionally assigned her to this ruffled pink paradise to relive an old movie script out of—what? Empathy? Cruelty? Maternal compassion? Somewhere, in the back of her mind, perhaps Gilda was harboring the same twin poisons of *maybe* and *someday*.

The Montgomery, Alabama, operator came back on the line. "Ahm tryin' to hep ya, honey, but ah cain't find the potty y'all lookin' foh. It'd hep if yuh haid a fust name."

"Tolin's the only name I know." Her tears flowed again and she gulped for breath. "I'm sorry. I don't even know if that's the name the number's listed under. Thank you for trying."

She had left Deauville a note in their apartment and messages for him at the Workshop, the Living Theatre, Riker's on East Eighth Street, with the waiters they knew at the Five Oaks, the Cafe Reggio, the White Horse Tavern, and on the bulletin board of the *Village Voice*. If he wanted her, Deauville knew where to find her. And she desperately hoped he would, though she didn't imagine for a moment that she deserved his loyalty.

The next three days spun by fast as pinwheels. May flew in from Chicago, forty pounds overweight. "Nice of you to get married during my spring break, Inez," she said, hugging both her friends at once. Then she pulled Devon aside and whispered, "Remember, not a word to her about you-know-what."

The three of them shopped Beverly Hills like Louisa May Alcott's "little women" on Christmas Eve ("No money but lots of enthusiasm," wrote Devon in her diary)—sighing over the Irene suits at Bullock's Wilshire, fingering the Jean Louis gowns at I. Magnin, checking the price tags at Don Loper.

May protested she would probably be arrested. "Fat is illegal on Rodeo Drive."

The girls stared at the pink house on Sunset Boulevard where Jayne Mansfield posed naked on a pink patio near a swimming pool filled with pink water. They lunched at the Brown Derby with Gilda and almost fainted when Natalie Wood joined their table for coffee. Patrick treated them to a movie at Grauman's Chinese and, afterward, to hot fudge sundaes at C. C. Brown's.

Through her father May arranged a trip to Burbank's Warner Brothers lot and Devon watched Paul Newman film a scene from *The Young Philadelphians*. The world of make-believe seemed crummier than ever as Devon gazed at the boat Spencer Tracy rowed for an eternity in *The Old Man and the Sea* against a backdrop of fishnet and cardboard. The sets from *Auntie Mame* were peeling, and in the commissary Inez pointed out the zits on Tab Hunter's face.

In the mornings, the girls were fitted for the wedding day ensembles by the frisky Edith Head. "Just as I thought," said May, pins protruding from her ruffled yellow gown as she peered into a full-length mirror from under a wide-brimmed, pale-yellow straw hat groaning with fake daisies. "Devon looks like a cool dish of sherbet and I look like a banana that just exploded."

"Nonsense," said the Oscar-winning Paramount designer. "Grace Kelly said the same thing about her *Rear Window* costumes until she saw how I pulled her together. Judy Garland was the worst. I had to *invent* a whole new dress figure to fit *her.* She had the strangest waistline I ever saw. Thunder thighs from here to Santa Monica, legs like toothpicks, and a waist that started at her tits. The only role nature ever intended her to play was Josephine, and she never got the chance. Leave it to me, girls. By Thursday, you'll all look like Audrey Hepburn."

Devon liked Edith Head, a petite woman with sunglasses, ricocheting among her dress dummies in her chic Chanel suits, a tape measure in her mouth and priceless sketches in her hands. She liked the bagels and lox at Nate and Al's, where Doris Day breakfasted every morning, arriving and leaving on her bicycle. She liked the Cobb salad at the Polo lounge, where Shelley Winters threw a glass of milk in a man's face at the next booth and a midget in a Philip Morris suit plugged pink telephones into everyone's table while they talked to their shrinks. She liked the electricians and the grips on the studio sound stages who puffed on unfiltered Camels without ever exhaling, so jaded that an actress could undulate across the set in a see-through slip, her cleavage undulating several steps ahead of her, and they never looked up from their *Daily Varietys.*

King was right, of course. Hollywood was just a "series of hick towns, all connected by freeways," but she was seeing it for the first time, not through the eyes of a tourist, but through the ideas of an insider with privileges. She was sent by Gilda Greenway, and the name still opened doors.

"When I hit this burg," Gilda said at dinner one night, "I knocked on all the right doors." She shot a sideways look at Patrick. "And when the right doors didn't open, I walked into the wrong ones."

In the evenings, Patrick took the ladies to swanky restaurants like La Rue or the Bistro, where the subdued lighting even made May's pudgy skin look like a camellia petal. King was always absent from these festive forays.

Since the first night, when Devon extended her hand during cocktails at The Pearls and he held it too long, escaping the attention of no one, King had avoided Devon. During Gilda's entrance that night at dinner, he had spilled a glass of red wine on the white damask tablecloth, and he rarely made anything more than an obligatory appearance after that. During the day he was playing tennis or doing interviews, Inez reported. At night, he was off somewhere "paying dues" in his rented Thunderbird.

On the eve of the wedding, everyone dined at The Pearls on oysters and caviar and the eggs of quails on beds of shredded radicchio. "Just pick," whispered May in Devon's ear. "Later, we can make peanut butter sandwiches."

As always, Patrick was the genial and dashing host. Usually sanguine in Gilda's presence, he was especially jubilant and witty as he toasted the bride and groom. "We've laid the cornerstone in this town for a younger, brighter generation—like all of you present tonight. I propose a toast, first to the newlyweds, and then to each of you— friends, family, and future. The industry is in your hands."

The crystal goblets clinked twice in succession. Then Gilda urged him on. "Patrick, tell them your Marlene Dietrich story."

"Oh, no. They've got years to form stories of their own. They don't want to hear about the good old days."

"Please, Patrick," nudged Inez. "Let's hear about Dietrich."

"Well," he began, straightening his bow tie with his enormous leathered hands, tan and rough as a catcher's mitt. "When I first came to this town, she was the most glamorous, alluring creature on the face of this earth. Small, sleepy eyes that didn't miss a trick and that guttural German lisp that drove men to self-destruction. Godawful teeth, which is why she never smiled on camera or anywhere else, but who cares? With a face like that, who needs Shirley Temple? The Lonely Kraut, they called her."

"Patrick made the Lonely Kraut a little less lonely, didn't you, dear?"

"Gilda, you're getting ahead of me," he said, blushing. "Anyway, I had built up quite a reputation as a stunt man and John Wayne sort of adopted me. We used to sail and fish together off Catalina and he made up his mind I was ready for the big transition into acting, so he bamboozled them into giving me a pretty juicy part in a frontier epic he was making with Dietrich. I was so tongue-tied the first day I met her that I stepped on her foot. I don't think she was amused. Anyway, we're two weeks into the picture and she pulls out a cigarette and turns to me and says, 'Geeve me fire' and I was so excited I whipped out my Zippo and burned her eyelashes. I was almost fired from the picture, but the Kraut liked me. She said, 'Ee's got sahmtink, thees one.' She invited me to dinner. I scrubbed everything for hours, but all the big shots who were there spent the whole evening monopolizing her. Dietrich just yawned all through dinner and at 9:00 P.M. she got up and said, 'You all must leave now, I need nine hours sleep.' At the door, I kissed her hand and she asked me again for the following week."

Patrick paused and took a sip of wine. "Patrick has never known the value of a punch line," chided Gilda. "Go on, darling, we're on the edge of our seats."

"I asked her on the set if I could give her a little token of my appreciation for being so nice and she yawned—she was always yawning, that broad, I think she was the most bored woman in Hollywood in those days—and she said, 'Don' send me woses, dey only wilt and die and you have to twow dem out.' I talked to Duke Wayne about it and he said, 'Give her a pocket knife.'

"I spent days finding the perfect one—mother-of-pearl, with a silver star on the handle. And then I went to dinner again up at that old house she lived in that looked like a spider web. I gave the gift to her, and she tore off the wrapping paper and dropped the satin ribbon on the floor without batting an eyelash. She took one look at the pocket knife, opened a long drawer in an antique chest in her entrance foyer, and tossed it inside with about a hundred pocket knives of every color and description you can think of. I was so wrecked I couldn't eat. After dinner, when she ushered me to the door, I glanced at the chest and screwed up my courage and asked her, 'Won't you explain why you have so many pocket knives in that drawer?' The Kraut just yawned and looked in the mirror. 'You see me?' she asked. 'I am vewy boootiful, yes? Vewy gwamowous. I don' need no car. I got cars. I don' need no fuhs. I got fuh coats. I don' need no woses. But some day I know I will not be so boootiful, so gwamowous, so desiwable as I am today. And when dat day comes, I will be pwepahed. Deh ain't notting a sixteen-yeah-owd boy won't do for a good pocket knife.' "

Everyone roared, including King. After dinner, they saw a new print of *Marjorie Morningstar,* and when the lights came on in the screening room, King was missing.

"He's drinking an awful lot," May shuddered as Devon lay across her bed, her head resting on the inside of her elbow. "He sleeps in the room next to Inez, and honest to Pete, I don't think they ever say a civil word to each other when Gilda's not around."

"When she touches him, he freezes. I've noticed."

"You can't miss it. He's not even subtle. I think they're both sweating darts."

"Then why go through with this charade? For Gilda's sake?"

"I shouldn't say this," said May, "but the torch he's carrying is burning at both ends, and you might as well face it. You're the one he wants to marry."

Devon's face turned crimson. "Then why—" She never finished the sentence. She suddenly knew why.

May nodded. "Don't be surprised if the Daisy Ashley suite turns into a nursery by Labor Day. No pun intended."

Shortly after dawn, Devon watched a crew from Chasen's erecting a huge candy-striped tent on the flawless green lawn. She hadn't slept a wink all night. She was attacking the half-moon circles under her eyes with Erase when she heard a knock at the door.

"Devon? It's me," May said. "Are you all right?" May was the only girl Devon knew who wore flannel pajamas twelve months a year.

"God," said May, surveying the Daisy Ashley suite. "Every time I walk in this room it looks like Miriam Hopkins died in here. I've never seen this much organdy in a Betty Grable picture. Now, my room is named 'The Bridge' suite. Remember *The Bridge?* That's the one where Gilda played a nun in the bamboo swamps of Sumatra. Everything looks like the skin of a goddamn pomegranate. Even the sheets are red. I feel like the Bride of Fu Manchu."

Devon plucked a pink tissue from the Young Daisy Ashley tissue box and wiped the streaked mascara from under her eyes. And then she realized that May had been crying too. Under her usually cheerful eyes were black smudges of mascara and her nose was red. She was clutching at a wet, crumpled handkerchief.

"What are *you* crying about?" she asked.

"It's my parents. They're not coming."

"Oh, May, that's no reason to suffer! What in the world's wrong with you?"

"My mother's sick, Devon." May tugged at the buttons on her pajamas. "Gilda didn't want to tell me until after the ceremony, but I kept bugging her about why they weren't here yet—"

"Maybe they just don't think King and Inez's wedding is important enough for them to fly across the continent. If Gilda hadn't begged and bullied me, I wouldn't have come either."

May sniffled loudly. "Well, that sort of makes sense. I've been phoning the house all morning and there's no answer. That's what got me so upset. I mean, if my mother's too ill to fly, then they ought to be at home, right?"

"They're probably window-shopping on Fifth Avenue right now, on their way to lunch," Devon said, remembering how King had looked that very first day at "21", how she had hoped he liked her and had only given Inez a ride into town on his motorcycle because she'd spoken up first.

"Oh, don't you start, Devon," May said, handing her a wad of pink tissues. "What's the matter? Did something happen to Deauville?"

Devon wept anew.

And dear friend that she was, May joined her. They sat side by side on the ruffled pink bedspread under the ruffled white canopy of the fruitwood four-poster, wailing and howling as if they were a pair of deranged hounds, until they took a look at each other. And then they began to point and laugh and hold their stomachs.

As they were gasping and gulping for breath, Gilda suddenly appeared carrying Tallulah and began to scold them. Inez was crying, she said, and they ought to be ashamed of their selfishness. Sitting there having a high old time, while the bride-to-be was falling apart.

"Get your rumps on over to her room," she commanded. "This isn't fun. This is marriage." Then she winked at them and rushed off to make certain Mrs. Denby was supervising the hot hors d'oeuvres.

Devon, May, and Inez weren't the only ones who cried that day. The three of them sobbed through the entire ceremony, as did Avery Calder, who escorted the bride down the aisle.

The girls looked splendid in their yellow chiffons, and for Inez, Edith Head had come through with a wedding gown that made her look as radiant and virginal as Elizabeth Taylor in *Father of the Bride:* a white satin Peter Pan collar governed a bodice of see-through chiffon that led from the collarbone to the satin tuckered waistline, covering the satin bra. The full skirt of oyster-white satin was gathered behind in an eight-foot train and covered with enough net and tulle to send forty girls to the senior prom. The bridesmaids carried daisies, and the bride held a small army of white lilies tied with a train of white satin ribbons that dragged on the floor.

There had been a noisy scrap between the bride and groom in the middle of the night. May had heard doors slamming and quite a few "fuck you's," but when she switched on the Chinese lamp in the Bridge suite, the house seemed quiet as a church. Inez gave no indication of it now, carrying off her wedding like a pro, her eyes moist with anticipation and what looked like love.

For something old, Inez carried a lace hankie Sister Marcus had given her for a going-away present the day she left Brooklyn for Westbridge. Something new was the Edith Head gown and the white high-heel satin shoes Devon and May chipped in to buy her at I. Magnin. For something borrowed, she wore strands of Gilda's famous pearls, and for something blue, a hidden lace garter threatened to cut off the circulation in her left thigh.

Gilda had thought of everything. A string quartet played Rodgers and Hart songs while formal ushers showed the one hundred guests to their seats. Devon spotted Rosalind Russell and the Jimmy Stewarts in the crowd, and somebody said Louella Parsons had to be escorted to the powder room after she pissed all over herself with excitement.

Avery led them all down the aisle of the blue ballroom at The Pearls in his white tails like a proud general commanding what was left of his defeated troops, on their way to sign a declaration of surrender.

John Wayne ambled up to Patrick and Gilda and said, "Ya gotta wonnerful weddin' here, guys. Ya oughta be proud."

"Thanks, Duke," said Gilda, beaming. "They're like my own kids."

The event was covered by the trades and the society editor of the *L.A. Times,* and a photographer from *Life* snapped pictures from every angle.

Gilda had opened her purse and her heart for this one. The ballroom overflowed with white orchids, white tulips, and white lilies, and a menagerie of white doves cooed sleepily in white wicker cages imported for the occasion from the MGM prop department. Everyone wore faded spring pastels except Gilda, who, always mindful of Technicolor, wore emerald green silk moiré and a green emerald necklace that caught the sun's rays whenever she moved. The ever-watchful Mrs. Denby added a threatening Margaret Hamilton presence in a black jersey dress with a black shawl that seemed to be chewing her skin in the California heat.

"She forgot her broomstick," May whispered, poking Devon in the ribs as they started down the aisle.

Tallulah wore a yellow ribbon around her neck, as did three of Gilda's clumsy white ducks named Huey, Dewey, and Louie.

Glancing at Patrick, who sat across the room next to Sam Durand, Gilda's boss at Metro for twelve halcyon years, the woman in green shed a tear for what never could be. And Patrick, tanked on Dom Perignon, put his arm around Durand, sighed heavily and whispered, "If not for circumstances, old buddy, that coulda been Gilda and me."

King, too ossified to cry at his own wedding, had to be held erect by two brawny young contract players who were recruited for the occasion and ordered to attend by the studio publicity department.

When the preacher pronounced them man and wife, King caused a murmur among the crowd by pinning back Inez's veil and turning her head aside roughly to avoid her mouth. Stunned, she recovered quickly and offered her cheek. The guests flowed through the French doors onto the lawn for a lavish buffet of what King called "fairy food" and a five-tiered cake topped with a marzipan motorcycle and a white chocolate typewriter for the bride and groom. May ate the carriage return all by herself. There was dancing to a swing band and the Four Freshmen sang "Graduation Day."

Everyone was misty-eyed except King, who had vanished in the blaze of noon.

* * *

After the ceremony, May went up to Inez's room to help her change into the beige linen suit she would wear to Palm Springs. Devon gulped down two glasses of champagne on an empty stomach, then took the remainder of the magnum with her on a tour of The Pearls. She intended to drink a toast in as many of the mansion's rooms as possible and leave to chance which one she'd pass out in. She was four toasts down when she opened the door of the screening room, where someone was watching Road Runner cartoons. She squinted into the shuttered darkness.

"Come on in," a man's voice called to her.

Devon picked her way carefully along the side aisle, down the carpeted sloping length of the room. She stopped and tried to focus on the figure seated with his long legs stretched before him in front of the movie screen. He was sunk low in an enormous tartan-plaid club chair, staring up at the noisy animated violence on the screen. In the hand dangling over the arm of the chair, she saw a champagne bottle.

"Hello," she said, steadying herself with effort. "I'm Devon Barnes, a friend of the bride's. Who are you?"

The bottle dropped with a thud onto the floor. "Fuck you mean, frien' of the bride's?" the man said, slurring his words.

" 'Scuse me," Devon said and started back up the aisle.

"Devon Barnes, get back here, girl. Fuck you mean, frien' of the bride's?"

"King?"

"Whazzat s'posed to mean?" he demanded. "You ain't *my* frien'? You still pissed off at me 'bout tryin' to do you some good, you bitch?"

"Shut up," she said, startling herself.

"C'mere." He waved his arm at her. "C'mere to me, Devon. I missed you so damn much."

When the cows come home, she thought to herself. And all the while, her feet, in the yellow silk slippers, moved toward him.

He gestured to her to join him in the club chair, then seemed to realize, as she stood with her hands on her hips, looking down at him crossly, that it was not wide enough to accommodate them both. "Oh," he said, trying to haul himself up out of the chair.

"Never mind," Devon said, annoyed. She sat down in a heap of yellow ruffles at his feet. His face was alternately illuminated and obscured by the light and shadows reflected off the screen. In the light, King's blue eyes were pale.

"What do you want?" she asked.

She meant to sound forceful. She'd have settled for petulant. But she heard her voice and in a second realized that King had heard it too —the throaty sigh. A submission. *What do you want? . . . It's yours.* Appalled, she began to gather together her skirt, the magnum of champagne, and the will to stand up again.

"Don't go," King said softly. "Devon." He sounded sober. "Do you forgive me?"

"For trying to help my career?" She knew that was not what he'd meant.

King reached out his hand and she offered him the magnum of champagne, knowing that was not what he was asking for. Ignoring the bottle, he carefully lowered himself onto the carpeted floor, and sat with his back against the front of the club chair. He studied her, his head tilted, staring straight into her eyes.

"Cut it out," Devon said, trying to turn her head but unable to tear her eyes away from him.

"It's too late, isn't it?"

She nodded, thinking, Oh, King, I want you so badly. I've loved you for so long. Why couldn't I ever admit it to you? And now it's all over. Tears filled her eyes and rolled down her cheeks, ruining her carefully applied makeup. She started to sob.

"It is, King . . ."

"Shh," he said, catching her wrist and pulling her toward him. "Not for us. It'll never be too late for us, Devon."

He pulled her against him, then wrapped his arms tightly around her as she sobbed into his chest. Then he pressed his whole body against hers, holding her, locking her to him.

Devon began to pull away. "Don't," he said, tightening his hold.

When she stopped resisting him, he tilted her face toward his and waited until she opened her eyes. He watched until the protective fantasy she'd wrapped herself in cleared like vanished smoke. When he saw in her eyes that she knew what was happening between them, he kissed her.

Devon's lips clung to his, as he fumbled with her buttons. She held onto him, dimly aware that once she succumbed, consciousness would overtake her, consciousness *and* conscience, and she would never allow herself, never forgive herself, for what they were about to do.

The silk buttons on the back of her gown flew open and he impatiently pushed the top down to her waist. Her breasts were free against him. He tilted her back, looking for a very long second at her bare breasts, then pulled her tightly against him again, letting the full weight of his chest crush her breasts.

His hand moved down her spine, pressed against her backbone, drawing her tightly to him. There was no room between them, no space to breathe. He lifted the bottom of her ruffled gown, reached under the silk lining and the satin petticoats, and touched her so deftly that she quivered, arching forward against his probing fingers. He was hard, thrusting himself against her thigh, but before his hand could reach the zipper of his striped trousers to free himself, Devon came, clinging to him, clutching at him, writhing spasmodically against his body. Her teeth were clenched to suppress the growling noises in her throat. Her face was buried in his neck.

The lights in the screening room snapped on with blinding, ice-cold brightness.

Devon gasped and tried to sit up, but King forced her back down. Hands pressed against her naked shoulders, he held her pinned beneath him. "Wait, wait," he groaned, grinding against her, jolting her into the prickly carpet.

"Shut that fuckin' light off," he growled at the unseen intruder, who obeyed instantly. As he rubbed and bucked against her, Devon kept her eyes on the carnation wobbling in his lapel, until it tumbled down onto her chest only moments before King did.

As soon as he sat up, she pushed him away, pulled and buttoned her dress into place, and ran down the sweeping marble staircase, not daring to glance behind her at the balcony, at the carved wooden doors of the projection room. She did not want to see King again.

Not ever.

May was upstairs, helping Inez out of her elaborate wedding gown when Frankie Fischoff made the call that would change her life.

"Where's King?" Inez had asked, reaching impatiently behind her to help May unhook the tiny pearl buttons. "And why isn't Devon here?"

Later May couldn't recall what she had said. Had she teased Inez, asked her if she thought they were off together somewhere? Or had she just said, "I don't know," or "What does it matter?" Maybe she'd made a joke about so many torrential tears at the wedding that one of them had gone out to buy a canoe. She didn't remember, it was so long ago. Still, all the rest of it was burned into the part of her brain where memories are stored.

Gilda had appeared suddenly at the door, red-eyed, clutching a lace-trimmed handkerchief. "Your father's on the phone, baby. Take it in my room." Gilda took her arm, walking her down the hallway, past the screening room with its massive door slightly ajar and merry cartoon music playing within.

She's crying about the wedding, May told herself. Maybe she's thinking about how she can't marry Patrick and it's making her sad. She looks so frightened. It can't be about me. There's nothing wrong with me. Or my mother. No. Nothing serious. A cold, the flu—oh, God, pneumonia maybe? I hope not, she told herself, as Gilda pointed to the receiver of the French phone, which lay on the lovely French provincial quilt on Gilda's huge bed.

"I'll be right outside the door," Gilda said.

"No, that's all right." May shook her head. She'd even tried to smile. "Better go help Inez. I want to be alone."

"May? May, is that you?"

Who was speaking? Not her father. No, it was a familiar voice, similar to Frankie's, but deeper and desperate-sounding. Frankie was never desperate. Never as eager to speak with her as this man on the phone seemed to be.

"Yes. Who's this?"

"It's Daddy, May."

There, she thought. That was proof it wasn't Frankie. Frankie would never identify himself like that. He'd say, "It's me, May, what the hell's the matter with you?"

"She's sick, May," the man continued. "My Norma. They opened her up yesterday. Exploratory, they said. They took one look and sewed her up again." Then, in a furious whisper, he said, "They're crazy here,

May. They're telling me she's going to die." The man was talking loudly now. "You believe this crap? She wants to talk to you. She's right here. She told me to call you and I said, not now. But she's not herself. She hollered at me. She never hollered at me in our whole lifetime together, but now she wants to speak to you, so she yelled at me. So I phoned, only, May . . . she . . . fell asleep. I asked Gilda to find you. Just like Norma told me. I did exactly what she wanted. I dialed. I told Gilda to hurry. And she—wait. Wait! Here's Dr. Vogel—"

"Daddy," May hollered. "Wait, don't talk to him now, Daddy. Talk to *me!*"

She heard her father say, "She fell asleep, like that." He was shouting. "One minute we're talking, the next, I make a telephone call, I turn around and she's fast asleep. What the hell's going on here, Vogel? Cancer, all of a sudden, you tell me. She's fine one day, a couple of cramps, a headache, that's all. I bring her to you and all of a sudden we're dealing with cancer!"

"Daddy," May screamed. "Daddy, what happened? Tell me!"

"*No!*" she heard Frankie shout. "What are you doing? You butcher bastard! What are you covering her face for? She's not dead! You're crazy, you're all crazy!"

And then May heard, indistinctly, Dr. Vogel telling the nurse to alert the heart unit, that Mr. Fischoff seemed to have had a stroke.

May shouted into the phone, over and over, "Doctor Vogel, it's me, May! What happened? Doctor Vogel, tell me! Help me!"

On the plane back to New York that night she and Devon drank Smirnoff straight out of the bottle. May described the phone call from her father over and over again, meticulously coming back to the moment she'd realized her mother was dead and her father needed her.

And she tried but couldn't bring herself to talk about how she'd raced crazily through the house looking for Devon. How she'd run into the screening room and turned on the light and seen Devon half-naked and panting beneath King Godwin on his wedding day.

Surrounded by a crowd of mourners that comprised a Who's Who of Broadway and Hollywood, May stood in the middle of a manicured Southampton cemetery that had once been a potato field and buried her mother. Gilda sent a huge arrangement of roses, tulips, and soft white baby's breath, Norma's favorite flowers, the ones Frankie had given her every year on her birthday. She wished she could be there to see May through the funeral, but she was in the middle of filming a new movie, a sweetheart of a deal that Frankie had put together, and she begged May to understand.

Devon held her friend's hand as she wept through the ceremony and watched the mahogany casket being lowered into the grave in Southampton.

Still in mourning for her mother, May took charge of her father's recuperation, as well as his complicated but lucrative business. Frankie healed slowly, almost unwillingly, but never fully regained his health. Partially paralyzed, he was left with just enough strength to tell May what needed to be done. Frankie would listlessly sign his name to contracts in a shaky, spidery hand. His eyes were perpetually glazed, like the crab apples on a bourbon-baked ham, and he often confused May with his dead wife.

His friends and cronies—even his competitors—lent a hand to teach her the fine points of the bargaining procedure known to every ten percenter as *hondling*. At just eighteen, May was a quick study. She didn't choose the business, it chose her. But once she got the hang of it, it came to her naturally.

Every night after feeding Frankie the supper Estelle had prepared, May would settle into her father's favorite reading chair, her mother's doilies still resting on the arms, and pore over contracts, studio deals, licensing agreements, and overdue commissions. She'd make notes, writing questions to ask her father on a large yellow legal pad, absorbing everything she could.

She was fascinated. Not just by the structure of the deals and the terminology—such as points, gross, net, turn-around, options, and pick-ups—but by the actual mechanics of what makes a bad agent bad, a good agent better.

Frankie had been good. May, with a mind sharp as a razor blade, saw a few areas where he could've been better. Up to that point, she had never given agenting a second thought. Now she knew exactly what she was going to be.

The best goddamn agent in show business.

* * *

The day after Norma's funeral, Devon returned to Jones Street.

Deauville had come and gone. He left no message, just took his clothes and books, and the photograph of W.E.B. Du Bois tacked up on the kitchen cupboard next to the clippings about the bus boycott in Birmingham and the riots at Central High. There was an eerie white patch on the bedroom wall where the autographed 8×10 sepia of Paul Robeson had hung. Guilt tore at Devon whenever she looked at it. And she looked at it often in the sleepless nights that followed her return to New York. But when guilt tore at her, she thought, of course, of King.

King called several times from California, but she hung up on him. Inez phoned too. A New York publisher who'd been at the wedding had suggested she work with Gilda on an autobiography of the star. Inez thought she might. She sounded lonely and aimless. She began phoning at odd hours again, saying she was looking for King, had Devon heard from him lately?

In April, a month after the wedding, Gilda phoned and told Devon that Inez was pregnant. "Four and a half months pregnant, to be exact. It happened Thanksgiving weekend when King was here for twenty-four hours. I knew about it on New Year's Day. That's why I rushed the wedding. I thought it would solve everything—but I guess I was wrong."

Devon could hear Gilda drawing on her cigarette.

"I probably shouldn't tell you this, but back in December, Inez skipped her period, and she went looking for a doctor to give her an abortion. When she couldn't find anyone, she tried to kill herself. She swallowed a bottle of Miltown. Luckily, one of the guys she was sharing the house with in Venice came home early and found her in the kitchen, passed out on the floor, with the bottle next to her. Thank God he called me instead of the police."

"Gilda, how horrible. What did you do?"

"Took care of everything, baby, as usual. I still got plenty of connections in this town. And then I sat her down, read her the riot act, and told her what that butcher had done to me. There was no way I was going to let one of my babies go through what I did."

Devon tried to imagine how awful Inez must have felt. Poor Inez. . . . And she hadn't said a word the whole time Devon had been in Los

Angeles. . . . Went through with the wedding as if she were the happiest girl in the world.

"I've got her here with me at The Pearls, so I can keep an eye on her and make sure she doesn't pull another stunt like that. Now she's obsessed with the loss of her figure. She's convinced King will leave her. She's driving Mrs. Denby crazy. She needs a friend, Devon, desperately. She's longing to see you, baby, and so am I. Come visit us."

"Oh, Gilda, I—I don't know." How could she face Inez after what she and King had done?

"What have you got to keep you in New York?"

"Nothing," Devon said, knowing that was the absolute truth.

She phoned her mother in Dallas, but there was no reply. Then, biting her lip, she called Maybelle. The voice on the phone was stern and uncompromising.

"Return to Texas immediately. I haven't been well and I need you here. Do you want to inherit your share of your worthless father's land or not? You won't get a plugged nickel out of me if you don't return to Mills County this very day. Stay in New York and you'll go straight to hell, Miss Know It All. You're just like your foolish, wasteful father."

From a box under the bed, Devon retrieved the half-finished pillow she'd been needlepointing all winter. It was a simple design— bold black letters on a white backdrop that said SIT ON IT. She finished the final stitches, mailed the pillow to her grandmother, gave Deauville's Billie Holiday records to a girl down the hall, and blew a farewell kiss to the cockroaches. Before she turned in her keys, she phoned May to say goodbye, but had to leave a message with the answering service. As the taxi pulled away from Jones Street, she was astonished that she wasn't even crying.

A few months later she received a phone call at The Pearls from an attorney in Austin notifying her of Maybelle's death. She had left each of her grandchildren except Devon a trust-fund inheritance. What, the executor of the estate wanted to know, should he do with the broken antique sewing machine she'd willed to Devon.

"Burn it," she said, in a voice that needed defrosting, and listened serenely to the dial tone.

* * *

On August 15, 1958, Gilda phoned May to announce that Inez had given birth that morning to a six-pound boy.

"When are you coming out to meet my grandson?" she wanted to know. "We're dying to see you."

"Are you kidding? I'm up to my double chin with work."

May had already built up her father's business to fifty clients and was aiming for the 100 mark. Everybody had a price and she knew it. But unlike most wheeler-dealers, she knew not only the price tag of all things, but the value, too.

"I can't come out to see some kid. Besides, who's going to look after my father and the business? Everything's casting for fall production right now. No, it's impossible. The kid'll have to come meet me in New York when he's old enough."

A week later, a housekeeper showed up at the West End apartment with a Vuitton overnight bag and an air of cheerful competence. While May was trying to convince the woman she had the wrong address, the phone rang.

"Did the housekeeper show up?" Gilda wanted to know.

May sputtered with laughter and irritation. There was simply no stopping Gilda.

"Listen, honey," said the maternal voice on the other end, "you now have a practical nurse and a housekeeper there, compliments of Artie Donovan. He says the least he can do for his old business partner is to help out. This woman has impeccable references. Now you have no excuse whatsoever to miss the 'Welcome to the World' party I'm giving Hollis Avery Godwin."

Devon picked May up at the airport in a station wagon she rented from Hertz. She looked more relaxed than May had seen her since their junior year at Westbridge. Or maybe it was just that May was so frazzled and overworked everyone looked calmer. Gilda had been right to make her come. She knew that as soon as Devon handed her a bag of tangelos from one of Gilda's citrus trees. She was overdue for some fun and sun.

Devon gave her a huge hug and said, "Wait until you see the little quarterback, May. You're absolutely gonna fall madly in love with him."

May paid no more attention than if she had just been promised the latest flavor of the month at Baskin-Robbins. If only she knew . . .

FOURTEEN

DECEMBER 26, 1979

"A ren't you going to eat anything?" Devon asked, pointing to Billy's untouched plate of guacamole.

They were sitting on the patio of a little Mexican restaurant, overlooking the ocean at Hermosa Beach, where the food was much more interesting than the straw hats and strolling mariachi band. As sunlight bathed their table and a nice crisp breeze came up from the beach, Devon devoured her enchilada special and was now on her second Carta Blanca beer.

"I seem to have lost my appetite," said Billy, shielding his eyes from the sun with Givenchy sunglasses. "God, I hate the sun. It's so depressing. I prefer New York, where the weather is like the plot in a Doris Day movie—if you don't like it, just stick around. It's bound to change."

"Well, you could use some sun. You're beginning to develop screening-room pallor."

"You sound like Gilda, Devon."

"Don't. If I start crying now, I'll never stop." She rubbed the back of her neck with the palm of her hand, a mannerism he had seen onscreen in each of her films.

"I'm sorry. But I miss her so much."

"We all do."

"Lionel Biggs told me she was found holding that famous Four Fans picture of all of you at '21.'"

"So?"

"So I think it's time for another margarita. Before I start asking you questions like whether you think King killed her or where you've been for the last couple of years or why I always had the feeling that Gilda knew where you were or how you happened to be in town the day of her funeral . . ."

"Hold on. Is this a game of Twenty Questions?" Devon took a long sip of her beer. "Gilda was good at keeping secrets. She had lots of practice—all those years with Patrick, and with Big Ted Kearny before that."

"You know, years ago, when I was the new kid in town, I put an item in my column about her and Kearny and got into a helluva jam."

"He fucked her up," said Devon. "The big bastard. She said he broke her heart. 'First he broke my cherry, then he broke my heart.' Billy, I just remembered a couple of calls I have to make. Order me another beer, will you?"

Devon walked unsteadily into the restaurant. Billy could see her through the window, talking animatedly to someone, looking as if she were trying to make a point. Then she hung up, dialed again, and spoke for several more minutes. She came back and said, "We have to go soon."

"Not that it's any of my business, but was that our friend, Lieutenant Biggs?"

Devon waved away his question. "Where were we? Oh, yeah, Gilda. She married the sweet ones and fell in love with the rats, didn't she?"

"Oh, I can think of at least one rat she married, too. A rat so big he could've started the bubonic plague."

"The singing matador from Brooklyn," Devon said, making a gun of her fingers and pointing it at Billy. "Right?"

"Artie Bender," Billy remembered. "They called the two of them 'the Battling Benders.' Lasted a whole year. He gave her nothing but black eyes, but he's the type who'll send roses to Forest Lawn now that she's dead, every year on their wedding anniversary. Didn't she ever show you her rat collection? She had a bookcase filled with rats, mice, rodents of every size and description. The way some women collect charms for bracelets, Gilda hauled in rats. Ceramic rats, wooden rats, stuffed rats, Mickey Mouse, rats of rare sandwich glass, Wedgewood china, you name it. She used to point to the bookcase and say 'I have always been surrounded by rats; I even married a few.' "

"Who else was there?" Devon asked. "The soccer jock. The guitar player from the Stan Kenton band . . ."

"She never married the guitar player. She just lived with him a few months in a mobile trailer in the Palisades. The soccer jock was something else, however. He was her first husband. His name was Herman Gehrig, and the big jerk always claimed he was Lou Gehrig's second cousin. Gilda called him Hermann Goering because he only had one ball."

Devon almost fell off the chair. "And then," Billy added, "there was Chunk Williams. What a sweet kid. Big, gorgeous discovery of the guy who found Rock, Tab, Lance and all the others with names like carbonated drinks. And Chunk was on his way to stardom when the shit hit the fan in Louis B. Mayer's office. Gilda married him as a favor to Avery Calder, you know."

"I didn't know it. What's Avery have to do with Chunk Williams?"

"Do you remember *Barracks Street Blues?*"

"Yeah," said Devon. "I sure as hell do. Didn't you know I auditioned for the part of Rose Ann, the hooker?"

"That was Chunk Williams!" said Billy.

"What the hell are you talking about, Billy Buck?"

"Chunk Williams was this gorgeous young hustler Avery fell in love with in New Orleans. You know, hustler-with-a-heart-of-gold type. *Barracks Street* was practically a love letter to him. Avery wrote him in first as a black sailor, then changed him to a white lady hooker. But a lot of folks knew it was Chunk Williams, the ex-Mr. Gilda Greenway. Avery sent him out to Hollywood, in the forties. The kid did some musicals. Chorus stuff. Loyal blond buddy in a war movie or two. You know, the type Phyllis Thaxter and Teresa Wright waited for on the home front at the kitchen sink. Then he got nailed in a raid on the Fantasy Club."

"I thought the Fantasy Club was a whorehouse."

"It was. Male only. They caught the kid in the kip with another contract player who was moonlighting at the club. I forget the other kid's name now, but a director of note had the hots for him. The director and Avery were called in on L.B.'s orders by Sam Durand— you know, like parents to the principal's office. L.B. was a horny old bastard for the ladies, but he *hated* fags. These boys had portrayed GIs, remember. Uncle Sam's pride and joy. If it came out they were gay, the scandal would have rocked the industry. So Sam Durand, who was L.B.'s right arm, called in the 'interested parties' and Gilda married Chunk."

"As a favor to Avery."

"And to Kearny, the way I heard it. He wanted her married. When you think about it," Billy said, "she was only married three times —twice during the years she was Kearny's mistress. Remember, he was almost thirty years older than Gilda. And a Brooks Brothers New York coat-and-suitor. He had a reputation to keep clean. So what if they called him 'The Pirate of Wall Street'? Robbing the rich was one thing. Robbing the cradle was another."

"What happened to Chunk Williams?"

"He killed himself in 1944. Swallowed a bucket of lye from the potting shed in Gilda's garden and washed it down with weed killer. Ted Kearny paid for the funeral."

In 1944, *Photoplay* asked ten of Hollywood's most glamorous female stars to sum up their definition of romance with one word that best described their own experience. "Fulfilling," wrote Bette Davis. "Tantalizing," wrote Hedy Lamarr. "Challenging," said Joan Crawford.

Next to Gilda Greenway's name was the word *Goodbye.*

FIFTEEN

D etective Lionel Biggs hid next to an ebony inlaid nineteenth-century sideboard in Gilda Greenway's living room. It was near the Steinway grand, against a wall, just tall and deep enough to keep him nicely concealed.

He had heard the front door open in the entry hall a few seconds ago, and then close. Someone locked the front door. A chain slid into place. Whoever it was had not only ignored the seal, but had a key and did not want to be interrupted.

The shadow moved in the hall. Rather large, more rotund than tall. The shadow moved closer to the living room. Biggs pressed himself as flat against the wall as he could. He froze, willing his sinuses not to wheeze the way they did when he slept or breathed through his nose.

Then he saw her.

She moved slowly, like a cat stalking a rodent, into the living room. She was an older woman, with salt-and-pepper hair, dressed completely in black. A frumpy black dress, black patent leather shoes and a patent leather purse to match.

Biggs's mind was racing. Should he step out, ask her what the hell she was doing? Or wait and see what happened?

She answered for him.

The woman shuffled over to the white chaise longue where Gilda Greenway had been found. Biggs narrowed his eyes. The woman gently held her purse next to her breasts and sat down on the chair. She leaned over and started weeping softly, staring at the bloodstain. Biggs felt uncomfortable. Like a voyeur.

"Oh, Gilda . . . why? Why did they do this?"

Biggs stepped away from the curio cabinet. He spread his coat open in the front so the mystery woman would see his holster and service revolver under his arm.

"Police," he announced louder than he meant to.

The woman jumped a foot, screaming at the top of her lungs.

Biggs rushed over and said, "It's all right! Police. I'm with the police."

The woman clutched her chest, gasping. She looked terrified. Tears had streaked her pathetic attempt at cosmetic regeneration. Her rouge was wet, her powder running. She had definitely been mourning.

He waited. After a moment, her breathing returned to normal. When she was shaking less visibly, he said, "Lady, I'm sorry for scaring you like that, but who are you?"

The woman arched an eyebrow and looked him dead in the eyes. "The question, I would think, is who are *you?*"

Biggs presented his badge. "Detective Lionel Biggs, LAPD Homicide."

The woman's eyes filled with tears again. "Oh, of course . . . Homicide. You investigate murders."

She was crying again, with muted little gulps.

Biggs touched her shoulder. "Listen, lady, I'm asking you again, who are you?"

The woman tried to calm herself. She squared her shoulders and lifted her head. "Why, I'm the housekeeper," she sniffed.

Of course.

The one Billy Buck had mentioned.

She'd been given the week off.

Biggs felt like a blockhead. Thank God Monahan wasn't here. He'd kill Biggs for scaring the old lady like that.

"I see," Biggs said gently. "What's your name?"

"Denby. Mrs. Edna Denby."

"I'm sorry. This must have been a terrible shock for you. When did you find out?"

Mrs. Denby took out a handkerchief from her purse, then snapped it shut. "I was at my house"—suddenly weeping—"and heard it on the news."

"But what brings you back now?" he asked, lighting another Camel.

She stiffened, composing herself. "The animals, of course. I'm the only one who ever remembers to feed them. And I came back to get my things."

"Animals?"

"Miss Gilda was famous for that. Didn't you know? This is such a terrible thing," she said, weeping again.

Biggs looked at her and couldn't help but feel sorry for her. Poor old thing. Wakes up one morning, finds out the woman she's been working for for years, one of the great legends of our time, is blown away on Christmas Eve. There were moments when he hated his job. He studied her as she dabbed her eyes. She might have been a handsome girl when she was younger. And then there was something about her face and her eyes that reminded Biggs of his mother. This lady was probably very sweet.

"Do you know who did it?" she asked, already forgetting that he'd just told her they were still investigating.

Biggs shook his head. "We're working on it. In fact, I think you could probably help us. If you don't mind, I'd like to ask you a few questions." He blew out smoke and took another drag.

Edna Denby averted her eyes from the big brown spot of blood right behind her. Tears rolled down her cheeks again. "I just can't believe they'd do this to her," she said forlornly.

"Who?"

"Whoever did it."

"Why do you say 'they'?"

"Oh, I don't know," she said sadly. "I'm just not using the right English. Sorry."

Biggs shifted on his seat. He leaned forward, taking another drag. "Mrs. Denby, can you tell me if anything unusual happened recently?"

"What do you mean?"

"Anything out of the norm."

Mrs. Denby sighed. "Well, Devon Barnes made a grand reappearance here the other day, after being away for two years." Her voice had a trenchant tone. "It completely surprised Miss Gilda. They hadn't spoken in two years. In fact, she hadn't spoken to any of the four in almost that whole time, except her agent, May Fischoff."

"The four?"

"The Four Fans."

"Right. I know all about them. You were saying Miss Barnes completely surprised Miss Greenway?"

"Right out of the blue. I imagine she's the last person Gilda would have wanted to see. But there she was. Marched herself right into the house and went upstairs to the bedroom. Brought some kid with her. I don't know what they talked about, but there were words exchanged."

"Anything else?"

"Then," Mrs. Denby said coolly, "everything seemed okay. In fact, Devon Barnes talked her way into staying here over Christmas. Her and the kid. And I was told to take a week off."

"You're sure Miss Barnes was staying here the night Miss Greenway was killed?"

"Of course. Devon Barnes mooched off us whenever she could. They all did."

"Why do you say *us?*"

"I'm sorry. I meant Gilda, naturally."

"You don't know where we can find Miss Barnes, do you?"

"No idea. But she certainly made an entrance at the services this morning." Mrs. Denby was weeping again. "Those kids! It was as if they were all trying to upstage that funeral. Damn them all. Especially Devon."

Biggs stood up and put his hand on Mrs. Denby's bony shoulder.

She clutched it and cried some more. Poor thing. She *was* a lot like his mother.

"Mrs. Denby, I'll leave you for now. Go ahead and feed the animals, but please don't touch anything in the house. Especially in this area. Then, I'm afraid, you'll have to leave. We've got to keep the place locked up."

"I understand," she said tearfully.

"Do you have a number where I can reach you if I need to talk to you again?"

"Oh, I—isn't this awful?" She seemed embarrassed. "I can't remember it. If you hadn't asked, I probably could have told you. Let's see, it's—no, it's—oh, I *am* in the phone book, Mr. Biggs."

Biggs smiled. "That's okay. If I need you, I'll just call you."

On his way down the exit drive, Biggs radioed an All Points Bulletin for Devon Barnes. He wanted to bring her in as soon as possible for questioning. No wonder she had fled the funeral scene so quickly. She probably had good reason to. Funny. According to the old woman, she was staying here. After the murder, poof! No more Devon. Well, he'd find out where she'd been soon enough. Or why she'd left.

When he reached the exit gates, his car triggered the electronic switch. The gates swung back to let him through. After he rolled past the gates, and was about to pull onto the side street that led to Coldwater Canyon Road, Biggs noticed something peculiar.

A palm tree was bent, chunks of its bark on the ground in splinters. All the others in the row in front of The Pearls' gates were okay. But this one . . . this one looked as if it had sustained some heavy damage. He put his car in park and climbed out.

Walking over on the grass, he came to the tree and noticed it was broken. Just at the bottom of the trunk. He glanced over at the street. The grass was marked with tire tracks from the curb all the way up to the tree. Biggs bent down and ran his hand over the grass by the tree. Particles of glass. He picked one up. It was clean. The accident had occurred very recently. The tire marks in the grass proved that as well.

Biggs shrugged. It might not be anything, but you could never tell. He made another entry in his notebook to check with the LAPD

Traffic Division as soon as he got back to the office. But first he had a few more stops to make.

At Chasen's, the maitre d' who had been on duty Christmas Eve greeted Biggs and pleasantly answered all his questions.

". . . And then you called a cab, right?"

"That's correct, sir. It arrived and she left, and Mr. Buck stayed and had a few drinks until we closed."

"And when was that?"

"We officially close at eleven. That's when we take our last reservation. On Christmas Eve there weren't a lot of people here at the time. Those who stayed after dinner had a few drinks and lingered. I believe Mr. Buck was here until around midnight or so. In fact, he said something about it turning into Christmas Day. He wished everyone Merry Christmas and left."

"You remember the cab company you called for Miss Greenway?"

"But of course. The Checker Cab Company.

By one that afternoon, Lionel Biggs was at the Checker Cab Company on Argyle. It took the owner a few minutes to locate the driver who'd driven Gilda home. He was on the premises having his taxi serviced. He was a young man of about twenty-two with boyish good looks and a pleasant demeanor, wearing a T-shirt that said, "I GOT MY CRABS . . . AT SEA WORLD."

"I picked her up," the cabbie said. "It was around ten-thirty, or so. We drove straight from Chasen's to the house off Coldwater Canyon Road."

"Did you see any cars coming either way? Anything that looked a little strange?"

"No," the young man said, shaking his head. "You've been out to the place. If there was anything on that little side street, you can't help but notice it."

Then Biggs remembered the broken palm tree. The glass around it. "What about right in front of The Pearls' gates? Did you see a car up on the grass, by any chance? Wrecked into a palm tree?"

The driver laughed. "No way. Because I remember pulling up to the gates, seeing them swing open, thinking, 'This is one loaded lady.' Shit, I didn't even know it was Gilda Greenway at first. And hey, I'm supposed to be an actor? And I didn't even recognize her when I first picked her up."

"So then what happened? You went through the gates and—"

"—and went up that long drive. The whole time I'm thinkin', 'How do you ever get money like this?' Even for Beverly Hills and all, that place is pretty damn big. We're talking big bucks."

"Enough to murder her?"

The young man bolted upright on the couch in the cab owner's office. "Hey, no way, man. Like, I *loved* that woman's films, man. I *studied* them at UCLA in my film classes. No way, Sam Spade. Uh-uh."

Biggs believed him. "Okay, so you went up the drive—"

"—and we pulled up to the front. She had some trouble finding her keys. I asked her if I could help. By then, I knew who she was. She said no, sort of drunklike. It was quite obvious the lady was plastered. She was rummaging through her purse, and I kept getting flashes of all this damned jewelry she had on. Diamonds out the kazoo. Finally, she finds them, and stumbles out. She makes it to the door and after a minute or two, unlocks it and goes in."

"So it wasn't open when you pulled up?" he asked. King had said he'd found the door open, there'd been no sign of forced entry—which again ruled out robbery as a motive.

"No. The light on the porch was out, which is why I think she had trouble finding her way in. But when the door opened, lights were on inside. Then she disappeared in the house."

Biggs sighed. "Okay, kid. Thanks."

At that moment, across town, on the second floor of the Los Angeles County Forensic Science Center, Dr. Alice Wong, a young toxicologist, read the graph provided by the chromatograph machine on Gilda Greenway's blood.

The GC machine, unlike the ultraviolet spectrometers that had been used up until the late sixties and early seventies, was much more exact in its hematology analysis. Several years later this very machine would turn out to prove critical in the determination of John Belushi's death. Analysis was done by heating a blood sample in a tiny oven. As it heated, the blood would emit gas that contained the various chemical elements in the blood. As the GC measured the speed of movement in the various elements, toxicologists could tell—knowing the precise speed the elements are *supposed* to move—exactly what was in the blood and how much of it was there.

Alice Wong was reading Gilda Greenway's chart as it came off the machine. She could already see that Gilda had had a fair amount of alcohol in her blood the night she died. There were also minor traces of Valium and Seconal.

But none of these killed Gilda Greenway.

She had been shot.

Or at least that's what Alice Wong thought. Until she studied the graph more closely.

Her eyes grew bigger. Reading the chart, she felt her pulse quicken. Something was wrong. Unthinkable. She couldn't believe it. But there it was . . .

Alice Wong's adrenalin was pumping.

She had found what killed Gilda Greenway.

She picked up the phone and called the coroner.

PART 2

SIXTEEN

MARCH 18, 1965

O ne night in 1965, Billy Buck ran into May Fischoff at Don the Beachcomber. The party was like every other party in Hollywood. Somebody made a movie, somebody else opened a bottle, and everybody made money on everybody else.

The privileged and exclusive glamor of the golden era was reserved for very few. The studios had dropped their stables of contract players. Kids who, a few years earlier, were parking-lot attendants at Chasen's or mailroom clerks at William Morris were now running the show. The czars like Jack Warner and Harry Cohn were soaking up the sun in St. Jean Cap-Ferrat, and the living legends like Gilda Greenway were picking up checks at the Polo Lounge.

It was a whole new ball game, but Billy Buck wasn't watching from the bleachers.

A twenty-seven-year-old wunderkind from the *New York Times*, he was, in the world of show-business journalism, as much a star as the people he wrote about. When he moved west he knew he'd sacrifice a few IQ points, but a nationally syndicated column read by 80 million people and a network radio show in the bargain spelled POWER to the survivors of a sinking ship called Hollywood.

He was feared and he was despised by the people who once knew how to deal with Hedda and Louella. Now the rules were different. Hell, there were no rules at all. You couldn't buy a good review with a dozen yellow roses in 1965.

Billy Buck appeared in the middle of the chaos fresh out of the Columbia School of Journalism. He had imitated the stars of the New Journalism like Gay Talese and Tom Wolfe in *Esquire* and *Playboy*, winning friends and enemies on both sides of the typewriter. His sassy, irreverent Sunday pieces in the *Times* caused one fading Hollywood legend to utter the widely quoted opinion that "this sonuvabitch is either at your feet or at your throat." Billy laughed all the way to Chase Manhattan.

But Billy was different from the other first-person journalists who got rich and famous in the sixties drawing blood. What his enemies didn't know was that Billy Buck had a place in his heart, soft as a macaroon, for the good old days of Hollywood's golden era.

He was a fan.

He had grown up at the movies in the days when movies meant something. He saw them all, and remembered most of the lines. Let the others knock themselves out following Warren Beatty around. Billy got juicier copy out of Bette Davis.

He looked different, too. Unlike the traditional hacks Hollywood had come to expect, with their seersucker suits, dirty fingers, and bad teeth, Billy Buck was suave, self-assured, well-dressed. He wore honey-colored tortoiseshell glasses, penny loafers, Eagle shirts with button-down collars, Bill Blass blazers with antique gold buttons, and striped Bert Pulitzer ties. With his swimmer's physique and his straight blond lemon-streaked preppie haircut, he had both the California look of a sun-kissed surfer and an East Coast mind that snapped like a bear trap.

He knew his job, he did his homework, and he didn't suffer fools or hypocrites easily. Pretentious phonies who treated him like a copy boy lived to see themselves barbecued in print from coast to coast. He wrote that Sandy Dennis entered a room "like a Volkswagen with both doors open." He described Barbra Streisand as a "banana split night-mare." He offered the opinion that Louella Parsons "is so mean and ugly, it is the general consensus among Those Who Know in Holly-wood that she should never appear on the street before dark, and not even then unless heavily veiled."

This kind of polished arrogance had led Billy Buck from $125 Sunday features to a $50,000 syndication deal. And May Fischoff had been one of the first people in Hollywood to welcome him with cellulite arms wide open. From the day he arrived in La La Land, May let it be known that in the world of agents she was as big a star as Billy was in the world of ink-stained wretches.

"She's tough," warned an editor at the syndicate. "In the eight years since she arrived in Los Angeles, she's turned her father's busi-ness into a $30-million-a-year corporation. The pressures of being a superagent have turned her into a cunt. You'll think you're talking to a man."

The first time they met, he had a reason. She had agreed to help him with a story he was writing for *Harper's Bazaar* about Hollywood society. He had expected a rock-hard tootsie with dyed hair and a Joan Crawford formality. Instead, the rotund woman with long, tapered fingernails and shoulder-length hair soft and fair as corn silk was funny, warm, and instantly chummy.

"You look surprised. What did you expect? Eve Arden in *Our Miss Brooks?*"

"Well, you're not Madame Bovary," he shot back. "But you're not exactly the girl next door, either."

"You want to see the girl next door? Then go next door."

He liked her immediately.

Billy knew about Gilda Greenway and her famous Four Fans. He had already researched part of the story. May filled him in on the rest.

He had interviewed King Godwin in New York, when the movie version of *Barracks Street Blues* opened at the Rivoli, to smashing reviews. Godwin had loped through the lobby of the plush Carlyle Hotel in his lizard-skin cowboy boots, ranch jeans, and a 10-gallon Stetson looking like the Marlboro man. But underneath, King was just what Billy wrote in the *Times:* "A freak in the chrome-and-rhinestone jungle of Manhattan, and just another sensitive actor with a bruised ego, a confused image, and a Holmby Hills address in a lethal industry already overcrowded with all three."

It hadn't been easy. With a new baby, a nagging wife, and a career in slow gear, there had been money problems from the start. Inez had rushed into the stucco-sprayed apartment building on Doheny, and with the help of the bodybuilder who lived next door, painted it orange. Then she set about living the life of a movie star's wife.

Barracks was postponed for a year while the studio made budget cuts. Inez paid the rent with her savings from the New York rent scam, further emasculating her unemployed husband. He started avoiding her and the baby, which infuriated her. She tried the old power-through-guilt trip, whining that she had put her own writing career on hold to give King a son, and now he was ignoring them both.

Most nights, she stayed at The Pearls, where Gilda had decorated a nursery with Disney cows doing a conga line on the lilac walls, hand-painted by an animator from the Disney studios who owed her a favor.

King appealed to May, who had opened a West Coast branch of the Fischoff agency and was on her way to her own special kind of power. May got him an interim job on a TV series playing a kind of revolutionary Buffalo Bill. With a gang of great character actors like Ben Johnson, Harry Carey, Jr., and Don "Red" Barry lending ace support, King made an immediate impact with the TV critics, although the series was dropped after thirteen weeks.

King didn't care. He got to spend seven weeks on location in Santa Fe, away from Inez's carping. His hair grew so long he had to tie it up under baseball caps for interviews. He badgered his way into guest shots on *Felony Squad* and a creature-feature series in which he played, over May's objections, a marine biologist attacked by man-eating frogs.

"Today the frog pond, tomorrow the world," consoled Avery.

When production began on *Barracks Street Blues* in 1960, the deal money Frankie had promised before his stroke finally came through. Inez promptly began an arduous search for a home properly befitting the life-style of a major Hollywood star, settling on a three-acre spread in the fashionable Holmby Hills section, and using up all of King's earnings on Plexiglas furniture and mortgage payments.

At no time during his early Hollywood days could anyone call King Godwin's life-style pretentious. He avoided the party scene and worked long days at the studio. He put in more ragged hours at night as a caretaker for an old apartment building in Westwood in exchange for low-overhead rent on a one-room bachelor paid without a phone, where he spent most of his time escaping from Inez.

Barracks Street Blues was the critical and commercial success May had predicted. King gladly toured the country making personal appearances to stay away from home.

In New York he told Billy Buck, "When people say I'm lucky because my career is working out so well, it pisses me off. Things have come my way because I *made* them come my way. I believe you create your luck in this business. If you like yourself you can survive. You have to learn how not to personalize all the negative crap they throw at you. The bottom line is dollars and cents—how much are you worth to those vultures and how much can they sell you for? I can get employment doing all their TV crap and all their dumb horror flicks. It's trying to find the quality roles that's hard. When a guy walks into that town with a moustache, the first thing they say is, 'He's another Clark Gable.' Then the minute they see you on a horse they say, 'He's another Gary Cooper.' You have to run before you start believing all that crap yourself. You cannot believe the casting-couch stories I've been through, man, with women *and* men. All the clichés are true. Turning down propositions has hurt me, but I'm the one who has to live with guilt. My conscience is clear. The story of King Godwin in a nutshell is this, man." He propped up his long legs and scratched his balls while Billy took notes. "I've learned one thing. You can't count on anything in fucking Hollywood. You've gotta count on yourself."

King's second picture, *Hanging On,* was a prizefight picture. He played a boxer inherited by a cosmetics queen. The boxer enters a big championship fight to pay off the lady's corporate debts and is blinded in the final round.

He was no pugilist, but he trained like one. He went on another publicity tour and gave the press a pretty good imitation of Sugar Ray Robinson, punching sofas, collapsing on the backs of overstuffed hotel chairs, and pulling down his jeans to show one obnoxious lady reporter the ol' tallywhacker up close.

The press clippings, always unflattering, called him hostile, sardonic, defensive, arrogant. One reporter wrote in *Esquire:* "He appears feverish, excitable, as if he tends, always, to run a temperature consistently higher than normal, like a dog's."

May cautioned him, but he only laughed in her face, saying, "All I owe the press is a performance. I don't care what they call me as long as they stay out of my private life." And the money rolled in.

Hanging On was huge.

"It grossed more than ten million in its first week of general release," bragged Sam Durand, "topping even *Barracks.* It's going through the roof in the Midwest."

By 1963, King had made six films, all of them successful except a Biblical epic about John the Baptist filmed in Rome. Even King got panned for that one.

"To my knowledge," wrote one acid-penned critic in *The New Yorker,* "neither the Disciples nor anyone else in the Old Testament ever said, 'What's happenin' in Galilee, man?'"

Billy Buck wrote that King seemed to walk through the role in a trance, "as though he were always looking just beyond the camera, to make sure nobody had stolen his motorcycle."

"He got half a million bucks just to prove he doesn't look good in sandals," sighed May.

And Inez was going through the roof at home.

"All I know about my husband is what I read in interviews," she complained to May. "They're all based on his image, whatever the hell that is, but the image has nothing to do with King. Half the women in America think he's the stud of the world, and his own wife hasn't been laid in almost two years. The only thing that changes is the money. But I've still got anxiety attacks, I feel rejected, I'm nervous, my hands are clammy. Last night I dreamed my father was climbing the stairs stark naked with an axe in his hand. If I don't find something to do with myself, I'll end up in a nuthouse."

Through Gilda's persistence, an editor at the *Herald-Examiner* agreed to give Inez some free-lance assignments. An appointment was made for her to interview Sean Connery, who was in town promoting the James Bond pictures. "He's only giving me fifteen minutes," she told Gilda, "but I've got a plan."

"Don't do anything to make an ass of yourself," warned the woman who had herself experienced every reporter's trick. "The man isn't stupid. And for godsake, use a tape recorder."

Inez studied her wardrobe, picked a low-cut, see-through white crepe blouse and a full skirt, and left her bra at home. During the interview at the Bel-Air Hotel, she leaned forward earnestly and played with her nipples. Then she crossed her legs like a man, hiking her right ankle up to her left knee with her steno pad on the edge of the hem.

There was no way her subject could avoid it: every time he glanced at the notes she was taking he was forced to look up her dress. The distraction prolonged the interview, the subterfuge got Connery away from his standard "party line" PR chatter and into more personal areas, and the interview lasted one hour, forty minutes. The resulting piece was unprintable.

For one day, she was a restaurant critic. She was sent to a small French restaurant in Santa Monica.

"The food is so bad here," she wrote, "that it's hard to tell one dish from another. The sauces taste like wallpaper paste, the shrimp are like petrified toes doctored with iodine, the strawberry soufflé is flat as a spatula and half as tasty. The only thing in the whole place with any character and appeal is the bread, and it's not even on the menu."

The restaurant had thirty-five dinner cancellations the night her review appeared, and the owners, who had studied with Paul Bocuse in France, threatened a lawsuit.

"Do me a favor," said the editor to Gilda. "Lose my number."

Grounded as a journalist, Inez spent money on her rapidly developing new career in upward mobility. She was determined to join the ranks of Hollywood's Group A hostesses, ignoring the cruel fact that it was King everyone wanted at their dinner parties, not his talky, manic wife.

"If God had meant you to talk more than you listen," Gilda scolded, "he would have given you two mouths and one ear, instead of the other way around."

Inez, undaunted, became convinced that if she couldn't achieve King's fame or Gilda's legend or May's power in a town where those were the only three things that counted, she'd make it through what she called "trendy osmosis." Devon, who hadn't made it either, was the one who was most often chosen to listen. Inez dragged her along on shopping excursions, lectured her on social amenities, and burdened her with the emotional baggage she carried around like produce from Gelson's.

First, there was the house. Outside, it looked like a Louisiana plantation. Inside, it looked like a set from *Lost Horizons.* Twenty-foot columns appeared at awkward intervals throughout the living room, leading to cottage-cheese ceilings. Glassed-in patios nobody used irritated King, especially when Inez always insisted he call them "lanais." Half of the living room was a gigantic, rectangular-shaped goldfish pond that forced everyone to take long walks to get from one end of the pond to the other in order to cross the room. "Goddamn booby trap," groused King, who had fallen in drunkenly on more than one occasion.

The furniture was an amazingly random hodge-podge of unmatched wire, glass, rubber, suede, and wooden doweling. There were concrete clocks and pineapple lamps; a table made of a bowling ball, a rubber hose, and three cue balls; and a chunky pop-art console built of Corian, a synthetic marble usually seen on kitchen counters. The floors were all carpeted wall-to-wall with white shag.

"Holy Christ," cried Gilda, when she first toured the place. "No wonder King never wants to come home. It looks like a Himalayan monastery. I can't decide whether it's all white because of a sadistic decorator or because of all the cocaine Inez spills on everything."

Inez sniffed. "Trouble with you, dear, is you don't understand California *upscale creative.*"

Driven by a desperate craving to join the ranks of Hollywood's elite, Inez made a study of all the Group A hostesses written about in *Women's Wear Daily* and Joyce Haber's column in the *L.A. Times,* imitating everything they did, purchased, and wore.

"Keeping the status going is all that counts," she ranted at May and Devon over omelettes at the Derby. "To be like Betsy Bloomingdale, Fran Stark, or Edie Goetz, you have to follow the rules. You've got to sit at the correct tables at the Bistro, spend a minimum of $30,000 a year on clothes and $50,000 a year on jewelry, preferably from the David Webb catalogue, and work for *acceptable* charities like Dorothy Chandler's Blue Ribbon 400 or the Frostic School."

"What the hell is the Frostic School?" asked Devon.

"I don't know, but it's important," said Inez, ignoring her skepticism. "The Thalians is strictly *déclassé* because it's run by Debbie Reynolds, who isn't even Group B.

"Rosalind Russell is definitely a Group A star, but her husband, Freddie Brisson, is just tolerated. They call him the 'Lizard of Roz.' Ross Hunter is the Group A producer, Denise Minnelli is the Group A scorekeeper, and Nancy Sinatra is the Group A martyr. Frank Sinatra is the Group A singer, but you can't invite the Group A martyr and the Group A singer to the same party. The torch gets so hot it melts the Rigaud candles."

"I wonder what group I fit in," laughed May. "Probably Group Therapy."

"Nonsense," shot Inez. "Below Group A and Group B, there's nothing. Then you just stay home and read about it."

"Everyone sounds so old," grinned Devon. "After they wear themselves out giving inventive Group A parties, do they get Group A blood transfusions? What do they do on the most horrible night of the year, when there's an earthquake on the San Andreas Fault and they have to stay home?"

May shrieked. "Nobody knows, but there are no Group A babies."

Inez pursued her goal with unquenchable zest. She spent $800 for a nightgown, and considered herself naked without custom-made lingerie from Juel Park. She had her hair done by Hugh York, her legs waxed at Elizabeth Arden, and her false Juliet nails fabricked and splinted at Grace's.

She bought a custom-padded, back-slant board from Marvin Hart, the Group A exercise instructor, ordered Porthault linen from the Staircase and Shaxted, and refused to speak to anyone who lived in the San Fernando Valley.

"She'd better be careful," said Gilda, "or she'll give herself a trendy little nervous breakdown."

From the start, King would have none of it. He ate pizza, refused all invitations to parties and premieres, and peed in the swimming pool. Inez complained every time she was forced to park her Rolls in the same driveway with his Volkswagen. "Don't you care about anything?" Inez wailed. "I am trying to save your image."

"Sorry, Inez. You must have me confused with somebody who gives a damn."

In many ways, the demands of Hollywood status had forced May Fischoff to make the roughest adjustments of all. "It's you, sweetie," said Inez in her infuriatingly patronizing manner, "who needs the most infinite number of changes."

First, there was the chin lift, which was like the cart before the horse. When the scars healed, the cart looked better, but she was still dragging the horse.

After the cosmetic surgery, she put her pain on the market. "What do I do now?" she wailed, like Agnes Gooch in *Auntie Mame*.

"For God's sake, May, don't you know anything?" Inez was exasperated. "Don't you ever read *Vogue* or *Harper's Bazaar?*"

May bought them at the Beverly Wilshire. The beauty ad, in boldface type in *Harper's Bazaar*, advised: "Layer your eyeshadow in related shades, apricot on violet, up to the brow. The effect's like looking through a deep, clear Aegean pool, and it's irresistible . . ."

She haunted the makeup counters at Bullock's and Saks. Her nails were spruce and teal. Her eyelids were chartreuse. Her "easily achievable sensuous mouth" shimmered with cashmere-red lip gloss by Estée Lauder. Her hair was turned spicy saffron by Vidal Sassoon. "I look like a hotel room in Las Vegas," she moaned to Inez, who urged her on to more time-consuming financial madness.

Dutifully following *Vogue*'s fall fashion palette for "colorful seduction," she shelled out $3,700 for a hot pink silk chemise with black cuffs, a tulip-shaped scarlet parka with a hood and two flap pockets, fuchsia gloves and hot orange earrings. "I look like somebody just threw up a banana split," she sighed, touching her mirror to see if there was anybody home.

Plunging farther, she tried everything *Women's Wear Daily* told her Candice Bergen did. Nothing worked. Oatmeal scrubs and papaya cream rubs for her complexion gave her a rash. Two-hour gym classes and a three-hour session of floor calisthenics for the thighs and abdomen threw her back out of joint. Shiatsu massage from a Korean sadist named Akita gave her so many migraines she almost got hooked on Percodan. A visit to Marilyn Monroe's nutritionist resulted in a ten-day "rejuvenating diet" of grapes and raw almonds that gave her a month of diarrhea.

"Can you believe Joan Collins spends three hours a day with a gallon of milk in her bathwater?" ventured Inez. "She must curdle in a heat wave." May tried it and discovered she was allergic to dairy products. Cucumber shampoo and avocado rinses prescribed by the most expensive trichologist in Beverly Hills to "oxidize the follicles" taught her the true meaning of the heartbreak of psoriasis.

One day she decided she'd had enough. Like the unwelcome ants at a family picnic, her advisers and friends were finally told, "Everybody off! The hypocrisy of fashion writing is the biggest sick joke ever perpetrated on the American female!" That was the day May Fischoff canceled her subscription to *Vogue,* gave up being another amusing casualty in the morgue of fashion victims, and announced her Declaration of Independence.

To prove her point, she wrote a feverish article on "Using the Body You've Got to Have Better Sex," sold it to *Cosmopolitan* for $1,000, and celebrated with a hot fudge sundae with toasted macadamia nuts and double whipped cream.

As Inez's attempts to invade the social scene became increasingly futile, Devon's empathy became increasingly less reliable. Inez had always been an adventurous, aggressive climber, while Devon was a cautious, passive observer. Inez was caviar and Dom Perignon; Devon was meat loaf and Coors.

For Devon, California was a place where fate had sent her. She adjusted to its constant surprises as though it were an amusement park where each day introduced a new ride. She took Hollywood's licorice pizzas and drive-in funerals in stride, but she never adjusted to the exhausting strategy of its social war games.

Inez, on the other hand, was willing to do anything. To draw attention, she had actually considered, at one point, filling her swimming pool with baby sharks. Each morning when she woke, she sipped a bloody mary and scanned the trades to see if her name had been mentioned, while Devon rose, brushed her teeth, and ate a bowl of granola. They were different—too different for Devon to catch up. And she soon lost the energy to try.

May, on the other hand, was too busy to care. Her agency business was growing so fast she had to put in six new phone lines in the first year. Between staff meetings, board meetings, and story conferences, she attended production meetings, lunched with clients, and signed checks. "It never occurred to me how an agent should be," she said. "The rules were here before I took over. My job is just to keep everybody happy."

She met the press, and she met her clients, seating her opponents in a pink canvas white-fringed deck chair with the word MAY written across the back while she stood facing them, placing one hand on each ample hip, or crossing her legs with the weight of her arms resting on each of their chair rests, staring them straight in the eye, while puffing away on cigarettes people were constantly offering her from crumpled little packs lying around the office. When she thought of something, even in the middle of a sentence, she would jot it down and stick each message to herself on the steering wheel of her cream-colored Corniche with Scotch tape. It wasn't unusual to find ten of them taped on at the end of the day.

Inez realized Devon was too dull and May was too busy. She turned to her old friends in Venice—the leftover beats from the Kerouac days, the disillusioned poets and unpublished composers who had befriended her on her arrival in 1957. They befriended her again, with drugs.

Devon had her classes at the newly organized West Coast branch of the Actor's Workshop and charity work in the ghettos to occupy her time. Inez had nothing. And at night, neither did May. She became a perfect accomplice for Inez's forays into recreational drugs.

It started with an occasional Quaalude to relieve the loneliness of nights at the beach with a bag of Fritos. Then the Acapulco gold relaxed the tension of negotiations that were going badly, relieved the pressures of frustration over a client's faltering career. For sex, there were only the hustlers from the call service she used—sometimes two at a time. And the older she got, the younger she liked them.

When May smoked dope she got hungry. She'd wake up after a stoned evening and cry when she saw the crumpled bags of Cheezits on the floor, the discarded Baby Ruth wrappers under the bed, or the empty cans of salted cashews in the kitchen sink. Then she'd wash her face in crushed ice to reduce the swelling, swallow a diet pill, and head for the office to make some more money, often tossing a mysterious jock strap from her car seat into the middle of Sunset Boulevard.

Then, one night, she came on to a saxophone player who was in town recording some sessions with a film composer she was handling at the time. Ace didn't have a friend, but he was cute and lonely, so when he invited her back to his room at the Tropicana Motel, she said yes.

"How about some coke?" he asked.

"Sorry, I only drink orange juice and beer."

"Coke for the nose, May—nose candy. Got a small makeup mirror?"

From his TWA bag, he took out a tiny glass bottle filled with white powder and spilled out a small amount across the surface of the mirror. Using his pocket knife, he formed the finely cut powder into four straight lines. "This is good stuff—it wasn't cut with baby laxative or any of that shit."

May was fascinated. She'd heard Inez talk about "blow," but this was the first time she had actually *seen* cocaine. Ace held up a hundred-dollar bill that was rolled into a tight cylinder. "Watch," he said. Then he bent over the mirror and, inhaling deeply, sucked one of the lines through the dollar bill into his right nostril.

"Welcome to Coke Heaven," he said, offering her a turn at the mirror.

First she felt the roof of her mouth and the inside of her nostrils go numb. Shit, she thought, I'm having an allergic reaction to this stuff. Then she tasted the bitterness on her tongue and in her throat.

"Relax," said Ace. "You're cool."

And suddenly she was. She felt wonderful: beautiful and then happy, absolutely positive she looked like Audrey Hepburn.

"You are sharing your cocaine with one of Hollywood's most important agents," she said, hardly believing it was May Fischoff bragging to this blasé kid.

"Far out," Ace said, offering her another line. "But how do you rate in bed?"

"One of Hollywood's top ten in the Sealy posturepedic poll."

They ripped their clothes off and fell on each other, touching, kissing, biting whatever their mouths and fingers came across. May felt the coke kick in. She was possessed of a raw sensuality she'd never before experienced.

"I've got it where it counts, Hollywood agent," said Ace. His hand was between her legs, his middle and index fingers exploring her front and back. With his free hand he squeezed her inner thighs and breasts. May grunted with uninhibited abandon, as he pulled away from her and reached for the gram bottle . . .

"Welcome aboard, Dorothy," cracked Inez the next day, when May told her about it. "You're not in Kansas anymore."

Billy Buck hadn't actually run into May Fischoff at Don the Beachcomber. Bored and restless, he had sought her out. In the crowded room of basic-black anorexics, May stood out in her embroidered caftan like the front of the Imperial Hotel in the Tokyo earthquake.

She introduced him to one of her new clients, saying, "Kiss ass, darling, he *writes!*" Howard Sundance was a handsome, quiet sort of kid who projected more juice on stage and screen than in real life. He'd won a Tony for his role as a young lawyer in the hit Broadway comedy *Two Can Do*, and had just won an Oscar nomination for recreating that role in one of the year's most popular pictures.

"Congratulations," Billy said, shaking the kid's hand. "I saw the movie. I thought you and Devon Barnes were wonderful. I must tell you, I was surprised she wasn't nominated as well."

The kid stiffened. "Yeah, I know. Well, thanks."

May winked at Billy. "Poor schmuck, he's been hearing that all night. Listen, Devon's over near the door, with Inez Godwin. They're baby-sitting for me. Why don't you go on over and tell her yourself?"

He found Devon and Inez at the bar with two blond boys in dinner jackets, ruffle-yoked shirts, and identical plaid cummerbunds. Inez was perched on a stool, her tight-fitting suede skirt slit up the sides nearly to her waist. Her legs were spread and one of May's "babies" was standing between them. The other boy stood behind her, massaging her neck and shoulders. Devon was watching them with a look of glazed boredom.

"I wish I could say you look radiant, Miss Barnes," he said.

"Oh, Billy. Hi. Too much champagne. Too much—" She waved her hand at the crowd he'd just plowed through. Then, dutifully, she straightened up. "Billy, do you know Inez Godwin?"

The boy between Inez's legs seemed to be sucking his initials into her neck. "Hi," she said, blinking at him over the boy's head. "The bitchy writer, right?"

"Haven't got a pen on me tonight," he said, on the slim chance she cared. He knew that most of the principal photography was finished on the epic King Godwin was shooting in Rome—a gladiator movie that had him paired with Italy's new dish of ravioli, Claudia Leone. He considered asking Inez when her husband would be returning to the States. But the neck sucker and the back massager might find the question tasteless. They were burly brats. Billy had no desire to offend them.

He turned to Devon. "I just stopped by to say I think it's a crime you weren't nominated for *Two Can Do*. Without you, I'm afraid it would have been a thoroughly silly waste of ninety-seven minutes and eight million dollars. You've come a long way. Gilda was absolutely right about you."

"Well, aren't you nice. Thank you so much. You didn't happen to see her on your way over, did you?"

"No. I ran into your agent and your co-star, but I haven't seen Gilda tonight."

"I was hoping she'd give us a lift out of here. I came with May and company." She jerked her thumb at the boys. "But May's gone off to do her bit for Howie Sundance, and Inez is too tanked up to drive herself home. And those two probably aren't old enough to have a license."

"I'll give you a lift, if you like. I'm about ready to leave."

"Really? Lord, that'd be great, Billy. Are you sure? I wouldn't want to drag you away."

"I don't think I'm the one you're going to have problems with," he said, as Inez wrapped her legs around the neck sucker's thighs.

"She's had a rough week. Take my word for it, Billy. She's not herself tonight. Inez," she said, taking hold of the boy's hair and pulling him off her friend's neck. "Time to go. Billy here has kindly offered us a ride home."

"Oh," said Inez, surfacing as if from a state of deep hypnosis. "Well, isn't that cozy." Her head reeled back. "Oh, God, I'm awfully drunk. Who's he?" She tried to focus over her shoulder and seemed startled to see the boy massaging her back.

"Friend of May's," said Devon. "Alley-oop, baby. How are your legs working?"

"I can't feel them." The boy behind her caught her as she began to crumble. "I'm in no condition to leave. Go on without me. I'll be all right. And anyway, I'm not half as drunk as I want to be."

"*Mrs.* Godwin," Devon whispered, "you are making a spectacle of yourself."

"*Miss* Barnes, you seem to forget that it's my fucking husband who is making the fucking spectacle. My husband, King-Fucking-Godwin, in case you've forgotten. The biggest fucking spectacle Rome has experienced since Burton nailed Taylor on the set of *Cleopatra!*"

"Is she taking language courses at Berkeley?" Billy sniffed.

"Inez," Devon said sternly, "don't you know it's rude to repeat yourself?" Billy and Devon each took one of her arms and nearly carried her to the parking lot.

As they waited for Billy's Jaguar, Inez began to weep. "Oh, Devon, it was such a good script."

"She can't mean the Roman epic," said Billy.

"That cow! That smelly Italian cow!" she sobbed. Then she cackled again. "Did you hear about the happy Roman?" she asked Billy. "Gladiator. Get it? Glad-he-ate-her! Oh, the filthy fat-titted cow! I hope his fucking pizza-dipped prick falls off!"

"No," Devon said, as they dragged Inez down the steps and bundled her into the back of the car. "She means her script. The one she wrote. May's been trying to sell it. Even Gilda tried." Devon shook her head sadly. "It's no use. They can't find anyone who'll tackle it."

"Cowards. Filthy town full of yellow-livered cutthroats. Oh, God, Devon, do you have a Miltown or anything? These damn pep pills my doctor prescribed are making my teeth tap dance. It takes two of them to get me out of bed in the morning, then I need a couple of Miltowns to stop the shakes. And two of those green-and-black capsules to fall asleep. I've been living on pills and booze all week."

Billy handed Inez two aspirins. "Oh, make the world go away," she said, kissing the tablets and tossing them into her mouth. "All that work. All that bloody work. I put my heart and soul into that script, Devon. You know I did."

"And it was good, Inez. Everyone said it was good. Everyone knows how talented you are. She's an excellent writer, Billy. Did you know that? It's just the material. The story—"

"They're afraid to make it, can you believe that? I lived the story, but they're afraid to make it! Oh, the cow," she screeched again suddenly. "I'm dying. I'm fucking dying of rejection here and King's laid up in some Italian villa giving that cow hot beef injections!"

It was only 10:30 when they left Inez with her housekeeper. "How about a cup of coffee?" said Billy.

"I'll make you some," she offered, as they drove to her place at the beach. "I get tired early these days. I've been waking up at 5:00 A.M. We don't start production on the Glenn Ford picture for two weeks yet, but someone forgot to tell my body about it."

Devon turned on the radio. The news was on, something about a confrontation between police and civil rights marchers. "Do you realized that Negroes in this country still can't vote without taking their lives in their hands? It's disgraceful," she said with uncharacteristic anger. "Everyone says, well, that's just the South, you know. But it isn't. How many Negro actors and directors did you see at the party tonight?"

"It's getting better," Billy said. "I mean, there's Poitier, and—"

She cut him off. "The fact that you can name them, proves my point! Oh, Lord, Billy, I'm sorry," she apologized. "I'm just tired and cranky. Don't pay any attention to me." She changed the radio to a mellow music station and stared out the car window into the blackness of the night, listening to Tony Bennett.

Billy was surprised by the old-fashioned farmhouse charm Devon Barnes had managed to pour into her battered little two-room beach rental. He was even more startled by the house itself. In a town where thatched-roof Hansel and Gretel cottages cozied up to thirty-room Spanish haciendas, he had come to expect everything to look like Disneyland. But Devon's beachfront hideaway was unique, like Devon herself.

The exterior was once a double-decker London bus, imported

twenty years earlier by a film company for a World War II saga with Irene Dunne. A studio grip had sawed it in half and turned it into an eccentric beach house, retaining the bottom half of the bus for a living room. The spiral conductor's steps led, Frank Lloyd Wright–style, to the upstairs bedroom, renovated with California redwood shingles.

"Welcome to my Toonerville Trolley," said Devon, ushering her guest into a snug den with bus windows open to the crashing Pacific. Billy whistled. It was obvious the Gabor sisters didn't live here.

Against walls of knotty white birch, Devon had hung needlepoint samplers and American Revolutionary tavern signs. A faded 1780 pie cupboard with its original paint made of buttermilk and crushed blueberries displayed a collection of pale blue and white Staffordshire china. Pots of yellow mums snuggled at the base of a black, loop-back Windsor rocking chair occupied by an enormous Raggedy Ann doll. The sofa in front of the fireplace was covered with an authentic appliqué Baltimore quilt in a series of colorful block motifs—floral cornucopias, blue eagles, red baskets, a brown ship with yellow sails, green stars on a white background. Mallard duck decoys rested on the kitchen windowsill.

Far from the flashy coffee table books he found in most movie star homes, the reading materials resting on the miniature William and Mary table under a lamp converted from an old green fire extinguisher were further proof of Devon's unpretentious but eclectic tastes: Steinbeck, Douglas MacArthur's *Reminiscences,* poems by Rimbaud and Verlaine, a pasta cookbook, the stories of J. D. Salinger, a yellowed copy of the defunct *Vanity Fair,* and the autobiography of Malcolm X.

"Disappointed?" asked Devon.

"Far from it. I could live here myself. I've been in a lot of houses in L.A., but nothing like this. We *are* in New England, aren't we? That *is* the sea off Nantucket I hear, isn't it?"

She laughed that Texas tumbleweed laugh he found so appealing. "Actually, it's a bit of Connecticut. I went to school there. I probably should have been a band singer. I've always felt like a transient, just passing through. It's only natural that I should end up living in a bus."

"This bus looks like a real home. Most Beverly Hills homes look like a bus."

"I found it quite by accident, really. The story of my life. Everything has been a series of accidents. May and Inez consider me a source of never-ending irritation because I tend to trivialize success and the things people have to do to keep a career going. I never thought much about it. Inez would kill her grandmother for a dinner invitation to George Cukor's house. I went there once with Avery Calder and was seated next to Katharine Hepburn. We spent the whole evening exchanging brownie recipes. I thought she was just like one of my aunts in Texas."

"I've eaten enough catered Group A dinners to write a book," Billy said. "Believe me, you're better off with brownies."

"I've been in California seven years and I've only made three pictures, so obviously I'm a late bloomer. I drive a rented Mustang, wear gingham shirts and sneakers, and prefer hot dogs at Pink's to flaming Polynesian pineapples at the Luau. You can see where my money goes. I'd rather buy a Hepplewhite table than a new Mercedes."

"I know a lot about Gilda's other three fans, but you're still a mystery, Devon Barnes. I think there's a story there somewhere."

"Not really. We all arrived about the same time. King and Inez were already here. May arrived with her work cut out. I just sort of wafted. I lived with Gilda for a while, answering the phone and doing silly secretarial work. You know, writing letters of advice to fans, mailing autographed photos. She paid me a salary so I wouldn't feel like a leech, living off charity up at The Pearls.

"Then Denise Auerbach moved out here from New York to open up a West Coast branch of the Actor's Workshop and she hired me to teach a class in scene study. I got tired of hanging around the pool at Gilda's, so I took a variety of jobs during the day. I was a waitress for one day but I couldn't wear starched napkins and high hats, they made me look like the Jolly Green Giant. I got a job as an elevator operator in Century City that lasted one week because I got carsick between the second and third floor. I taught swimming. They hired me as a secretary at Paramount on a Friday and I learned how to type over the weekend.

"Then the Workshop did a production of *Sabrina Fair* and May talked John Frankenheimer into coming to see me. He put me in a "Playhouse 90" and things just sort of happened from there. I got a nine-line part in a picture with Anthony Quinn and they started writing that I was a hot new dish. Then I played the school dyke in a thing called *Reform School Girls* and somebody wrote I was half dish, half dishtowel. I refused to work again until I could do something fulfilling. I worked at the Workshop at night, did charity work in Watts during the day. And then May came up with *Two Can Do.* I still don't know what kind of blackmail she pulled on the director to get me into that one, but it paid off. Inez is finally speaking to me again."

"Tell me about Inez's writing," Billy said, setting into the patchwork pillows.

With Gilda's encouragement, Inez had been working on the script almost eight years, almost since she'd first come to Los Angeles. "It started out sweet enough, a bit like *A Tree Grows in Brooklyn,*" Devon said, handing Billy a mug of coffee laced with Kahlua. "Strong young Peggy Ann Garner type, struggling to survive in a harsh poverty-ridden environment."

"Is that why they turned it down? Was it too similar? Too sweet? I mean, why all that ranting about our local cowards?"

"Because it evolved into a much more harrowing story. The closer Inez got to making the script real, the less chance she had of getting it produced. Gilda tried to warn her. May did, too. But she kept going. It's a good script, Billy—a tough, hard, sad story. The right director and cast—it could be great."

"What's the hard, sad story?"

"The whole thing centers on an incestuous relationship between the girl and her father."

Billy whistled. "Nothing too controversial."

"They said she had to change it, make the father lose his temper on booze, hit her—but no sex. Inez went nuts and told May to withdraw the whole project. Gilda's been trying to change her mind all week. Problem is, just when Inez needs King most, he's on another continent. Rumor has it that he's shacking up with his co-star. Can you believe it?"

"With 'the cow'?"

"Claudia Leone."

"I begin to get the picture."

"The fade-out is what worries me. I've seen Inez mad and I've seen her morose and self-pitying. But she was practically suicidal this week. I never thought I'd pray for her to explode. That anger she let loose with me tonight is the first healthy thing she's done all week."

Devon looked at her watch, then turned on the TV. "Watch the news for a couple of minutes while I get more coffee."

The anchorman said, "Tonight, another confrontation in the South. They're calling it 'Bloody Sunday.' The toll of the injured has not yet been taken, but it could run into the hundreds. The confrontation broke out as Alabama state police today tried to turn back Dr. Martin Luther King's freedom marchers on the road from Selma to Montgomery."

On the screen was a film of four black men in hats and overcoats, arms linked, walking down a bleak highway. Behind them, four and five abreast, marched the demonstrators. The side of the road was lined with club-wielding troopers.

Like robots in a science fiction horror movie, the Alabama state police began moving toward the unarmed demonstrators. The camera swung away from the blur of black boots to the twisted legs of a fallen marcher, then focused on one of the victims. Blood was streaming down his dark face as he was dragged out of camera range by five uniformed troopers who seemed to be kicking and clubbing him as they ordered the cameraman back.

"Deauville!"

Billy hadn't realized that Devon had come back into the living room. She was staring aghast at the television set, her face mirroring the expression of pain and outrage on the face of the bloodied man.

Now the local newscaster was back, promising good weather and a sports update right after a message from Bullock's Wilshire.

Devon was frantically switching the dial from one station to the next, looking, Billy supposed, for more reports on the civil rights demonstration.

"Devon," he said, "what's the matter?"

She turned off the television with an angry curse and slumped on the couch, sobbing as if she were personally affected by the violence on the screen. He sat beside her, and leaned her head against his chest. Finally, she stopped crying and began to breathe more normally.

"You know that man," he said, with sudden understanding. "The one with the bleeding head."

"Deauville. His name is Deauville Tolin. I lived with him in New York. I was in love with him. Did they say whether he was dead?"

"No, darling. No, he's not dead. He'll be all right. Don't worry, Devon. Don't worry, he'll be fine and so will you."

"But I've got to do something. If he's alive, he needs help. I have to find him."

"First of all," he said, sounding calmer than he felt, "it may not even be the same man. You can't be sure—"

"It was Deauville, Billy."

"When was the last time you saw him?"

"Last summer, on the news. And I saw his picture in the papers a few years ago, too. She suddenly thought about all those long, hot summer nights that she'd spent with Deauville in New York. So long ago . . . so much love. "Wait," she said finally, "I'll get it."

"It's all right, I believe you."

"He was with a busload of Freedom Riders. I was so proud of him," she said, raising her voice as she disappeared up the stairs. "So glad he was doing something. He'd gotten so depressed. He'd been so choked with frustration when I saw him last."

Billy followed her up the stairs to the bedroom.

She pulled a battered suitcase from the closet and was dumping its contents on her bed: old theater *Playbill*s, love letters, her beloved Gilda paper dolls, a dog-eared map of California. "And then, last year, on the news, they showed him making a speech up at Berkeley, recruiting for SNCC. They wanted kids to go down to Mississippi to register voters. Last summer when those boys from New York were murdered . . .

"Here!" She held up a batch of photographs, head shots of a smiling, handsome young black man. Then she pulled a newspaper clipping from the pile of papers on the bed and waved it at him. "This is all about Deauville. Now do you believe me?

"Billy, I have to call the police in Alabama. They'll know who I am—someone there *has* to have seen my movies. I'll tell them I want to put up bail for him. Maybe I can go down there, or send someone down to get him out of the hospital or jail or wherever he is. I could take care of him here . . ."

It took him nearly half an hour to dissuade her.

"Devon," he said, "it wouldn't work. And what's worse, it would mean the end of your career."

"I don't give a damn about my career, Billy. Deauville was my lover, my friend. He took care of me. I have to do something. I can't let him rot in jail or die. What's the point of a career, of being famous, if I can't do something about this, if I can't make a difference?"

"You can. You will. But in this case, it's *because* he was your lover that you can't help him now. Think about it, Devon. Think about telling some Alabama redneck that you lived with a Negro. That you were in love with him. You're right, they *would* know exactly who you are. And they'd use it against you. Do you know interracial marriage is illegal in most states? Cohabiting with a Negro is probably a felony in some. Going public with that kind of admission is for damn sure a punishable offense in Hollywood. Do you want to turn a love affair into the butt end of dirty jokes and hate mail? Think of telling those troopers we saw, the ones with the boots and helmets and sunglasses."

"They'd kill him," she said suddenly. "Oh, Lord, Billy. They'd beat him to death, wouldn't they?"

"They might."

"I'll call May. Maybe she knows someone who can help. Or Inez. Inez always liked Deau." She caught her breath abruptly. "King," she whispered. "*He* can do it."

"King Godwin? Does he know your friend, too?"

"King introduced me to Deauville. There were at the Workshop together. He's a man, so there'd be no sexual complications. He's a star now, isn't he? It couldn't possibly hurt his career to help Deauville. They'd listen to him. If anyone can find Deauville and get him out of that mess, it's King."

Billy tried to imagine the temperamental star as a good samaritan. Since King had skyrocketed to stardom in the movie version of Avery Calder's play, he'd developed a quirky reputation. He was a fine actor, electrifying, in fact. But he was also unreliable. He'd been suspended twice in five years, and he'd walked off the set of his last movie, a fast-paced detective story based on a Ross Thomas novel, citing "artistic differences" with the director.

Around Beverly Hills, he was beginning to be known as a bad boy, along with McQueen, Beatty, and Brando. More than once the Beverly

Hills Police had been phoned about the rows between the Godwins when King came in late for the third or fourth night in a row. Or when King had found Inez in bed with the pool boy at lunch. Or when Inez had found King in the cabana with Miss January, one of Hugh Hefner's playmates.

King Godwin had recently been traveling the international fast track. He'd become good friends with Michel Weiss-France, the French filmmaker and former *Cahier du Cinema* critic, whose professional dedication was equaled only by his personal decadence. Weiss-France had launched half a dozen young actresses with what Billy had heard was quite a formidable rocket. In fact, Billy seemed to recall that Weiss-France was supposed to have "discovered" Claudia Leone, and lived with her briefly.

No, he couldn't see King Godwin playing the offscreen hero here. And then he remembered something else.

"Devon, wasn't there a problem of some sort between you and King? I seem to remember hearing something about you two having a chilly relationship."

"But this isn't about me. This is about Deauville."

The idea didn't sound promising, but he agreed to help. It didn't take long to find out where King was supposed to be staying in Rome. And from a PR man Billy knew at Cinecitta Studios, he managed to get Claudia Leone's private number.

"Cara," she said, handing him the phone. She draped a soft white arm across his chest and fell back to sleep.

It was 8:00 A.M. in Rome. King's head felt swollen with last night's wine. They had dined on *pollo alla cacciatora* at the insanely expensive El Toula and finished off three bottles of Pinot Grigio Felluga ("the wine of angels," Claudia cooed drunkenly, biting his ear). If he remembered correctly, he had ended the evening chasing her up and down the curved stone steps of the Tivoli Gardens.

He reached for the glass of stale chianti on the marble-topped table beside the bed. By the pale morning light, he saw the crumpled telegram from Gilda, the scripts May had forwarded, and the little framed photograph of Hollis that had become his traveling talisman.

He took a sip of wine and swilled it in his mouth for a moment before swallowing. Wine had become his morning mouthwash. He glanced at Claudia. Tangled pitch-black hair framed her pretty cameo face. Her full lips were generous, like Devon's. Her arms were shapely, but plumper than Devon's, and soft where Devon's were well-defined and athletic. He loved her marvelous white breasts, big and full, and amazingly firm, with nipples as pink as a kitten's nose.

They were in Claudia's apartment, a richly appointed duplex on the Via Margutta. His hand reached down to stroke her mossy black hair.

"Yeah, this is King Godwin."

And the voice at the other end of the transatlantic tunnel said, "King? Oh, thank God. It's Devon."

His heart kicked over, like a motorcycle catching, suddenly ignited, ready to roll.

"Devon?" He wondered whether he was still drunk.

He'd been shit-faced the night before. Maybe he was dreaming.

Suddenly he envisioned her beautiful, soft face . . . remembered her long, coltish body, and felt a stirring in his groin. Since his wedding day, when he and Devon had shared that one, brief moment upstairs at The Pearls, he'd tried to stay away from her. She and Inez were still friends, but he couldn't be.

She was the one woman who stripped him of his self-control.

"Devon, where are you?"

"L.A., of course. Oh, King, it's so good to hear your voice. It's been too long."

He sat up and took another sip from the wine glass. He felt as if forty Russian soldiers had just spent the winter inside his mouth. But Devon was on the phone and if this was a dream, he never wanted to wake up.

"You're telling me," he said, desperately rummaging through his foggy head for something to say that didn't make him sound like a dumb cracker kid.

Claudia stirred against him. All he needed was for her to wake up.

"How are you, Devon? And how'd you get this number?" he asked quietly.

"Okay, I guess. Billy Buck found it for me."

"I should've known. The rhinestone cowboy of journalism. Anyway, I've been thinking about you. Thinking about you a lot. I've missed you."

"King—I'm not calling for me."

"Well, if you're calling for Gilda, tell her I've got her telegram right here. It's *my* marriage and *my* life."

"It's Deauville, King. He's in trouble. He needs help."

"Who?" he asked coldly. He reached for a cigarette.

"Deauville. He was beaten up down in Alabama. I saw it on the news out here—"

"The news," he said flatly. "Excuse me." He drained the rest of the wine.

"The police in Selma. They used tear gas and truncheons. It was horrible. Makes me embarrassed to be from the South."

"I didn't know," he said, setting down the glass, "that you two were still in touch."

"King, it's a bad scene here. There was a riot at a bridge. Hundreds of people were gassed and beaten. I was watching the news, and there was Deau. They were beating his head in with clubs and fists. They were kicking him, King, and dragging him away."

"Hang on, will you? I've got this killer hangover."

He nudged Claudia awake. "Hey, get me some water, baby. Mineral water, and a couple of aspirin." She nodded with a fuzzy smile, kissed his nipple, and slipped out of bed.

She was shorter than Devon, and plumper. Her ass jiggled when she walked, her breasts bounced. Her legs weren't as good as Devon's. Her laugh wasn't as deep and wild.

"I'm sorry, King. I don't mean to disturb you. But I'm not calling for me. It's for Deauville."

"Yeah, you told me that. Jesus, it's cold here. Claudia, hurry up. Get back here, baby. I'm freezing."

"King, please, you've got to help. He was your friend, too."

"I'm thinking about coming home soon," King said, looking at the picture of Hollis in its silver frame. "How's the weather in L.A., Devon?"

"It's warm."

"Yeah. It's fuckin' freezing here."

"What about Deauville?"

Claudia hurried back to bed. She put the aspirin on his tongue and held the water glass for him to drink. She curled herself around his body, but she was cold from having walked naked in the big chilly apartment.

"I'm sorry," King said. "Devon, really, I'm sorry. And I'm sorry you didn't get a nomination this year."

"Are you going to help him, King?"

"The movie was shit, but you were terrific. Better than the red-head, what's his name? Sundance?"

"What about Deauville, King?"

"You're a hell of an actress, Devon."

He hung up. Claudia wriggled against him. He reached out to touch her, then stopped. And stopped himself from pushing her away.

"I have to make a phone call, *bambina*. You get some more sleep. I'll use the phone in the living room."

"You are going home soon, yes?"

"Soon," he said. She pulled the big quilt over her head. He heard her weeping as he left the bedroom.

It took a while for him to get through to Paris. The girl who answered Michel Weiss-France's phone told him the director was out of town for the weekend. "The little bastard followed his cock south," she said. "If you find him, and the girl answers the phone, her name is Gilles. She's a little redheaded whore. Tell her Marianne say hello. See if the bitch has a conscience, *bien?*"

King rang the Hotel du Cap in Cap d'Antibes and asked for Michel Weiss-France. A girl answered the phone, but King was in no mood to pass along messages.

"I need a favor, Michel," he said when Weiss-France took the receiver.

"Babee. It better be good. As good as what you interrupted, babee."

"Did you hear anything on the news about Alabama? A riot in Selma?"

"Are you mad? This astounding bitch was giving me the greatest head on the Cote d'Azur. The first amateur to get three-quarters of my cock down her throat, and you want to talk politics with me?"

"Michel, this is urgent."

"King, you prick. Having a pair of gorgeous lips inching toward your balls, that is urgent."

"A friend of mine is in trouble in Alabama. I need someone who can go down there and bail him out."

"So you call on a Frenchman in Cap d'Antibes."

"Your modesty is uncharacteristic and ill-timed, Michel. What happened to the fiery Marxist *auteur,* the *enfant terrible* of the left-wing cinema? Listen, you little frog, you're the best-connected revolutionary I know. I want you to call that lady lawyer friend of yours in Washington—"

"Ah, I'd almost forgotten. Now, she give the great head, babee."

"Michel, the guy's name is Deauville Tolin. I want him out of there fast. He's a Negro, Michel, in a place where they've been gunning down whites lately just for walking alongside a Negro—they've been killing kids, bombing churches, blowing up cars. I want him found and yanked the fuck out of there, fast."

"Tell me his name again, Kingston. I call her *tout de suite.* She's a good girl. She do anything for me."

"Deauville Tolin." He spelled out the name.

"You must love this guy, babee. He's a lucky man, no?"

"Luckiest motherfucker I know," King said. "I hate his guts."

"Okay, I call my fiancée in Washington. She know everybody, babee. If it can be done, she do it for me. She is *fantastique,*" Michel said. "Whew! This lawyer give the blow job *fantastique!* I give you her number."

"Size of your pecker, she'd have to have jaws hinged like a python."

"No." Michel laughed. "She practice on the Washington Monument, babee. She got the technique, you know. But not the passion like this one I have here, under the covers. This one is a treasure. A secret, babee, I cannot even share wis you."

"If she's a cute little redhead named Gilles, tell her Marianne says hello."

"King, you so funny, babee."

Devon hung up the phone looking utterly defeated. Tears stung her eyes. She wouldn't repeat what King had said, only that he had refused to help.

Billy brewed her mint tea with honey and brandy—a good stiff belt of brandy, and then another and another, as she racked her brain trying to figure out how she could help Deauville. Finally, at two in the morning, worn out with exhaustion and alcohol, she phoned The Pearls.

Gilda was still awake—and how. She was pacing the floor of her lavish bedroom ("the Tara Suite"), livid with Mrs. Denby. She'd just had another of her ongoing fights with the housekeeper about whether Tallulah and the other dogs should get boiled chicken or canned meat.

"Boiled chicken, goddamn you, you old battleaxe! And pick out every bone."

Mrs. Denby curled her lip. "Dr. Pritchard says canned meat. It gives them more protein."

"*I* know what to feed those fucking dogs!" Gilda raged. "*Not* the vet! And I don't ever want to find you feeding them canned dog food again! I couldn't believe it when I saw it in their bowls."

Christ! Gilda fumed. *Nobody* knew more about her animals than she did. She'd read every book she could find. These creatures were her babies. Her children. Almost as much as Inez, Devon, King, and May were.

The phone rang. Gilda grabbed it and paused, trying to lower her blood pressure before answering.

"Hello?" It was suddenly the voice of a film star, low, languid, and ready for quadrophonic sound.

She listened for a few minutes. "You're sure it was him, baby?" was all Gilda asked. "Okay, you get some sleep. Mama'll take care of everything. Now let me talk to Billy.

"What the fuck is the time in Alabama?" Gilda asked. Her voice cut through the knot of tension in Billy's stomach.

"Four A.M.," replied Billy.

"All right," she huffed. "Put her to bed and I'll try to handle this fucking mess."

Devon was in her room gathering up the pictures of Deauville scattered all over her bed as gingerly as a child picking dandelions.

"Bedtime, beauty," Billy said, confiscating the 8×10 glossies and tossing them into the suitcase. She was soused and weaving slightly. He walked her to the bathroom and propped her up on the toilet seat while he ran a tub, adding a soothing cupful of Crabtree and Evelyn jojoba gel.

"It's like the lion with the thorn in his paw, isn't it, Billy?"

"What is, darling?"

"Gilda and me." She closed her eyes and leaned her head against the cold wall tiles. "I'm the mouse," she explained. "The one who gnaws through the ropes or takes out the thorn, or whatever the little mouse did to repay the lion."

"Yes, precious." He began to unbutton her shirt. She raised her arms like an obedient child. She was almost twenty-six, but at that moment looked more like sixteen, a remorseful, tired teenager who'd had too much to drink at the high school prom.

"And I'll repay her someday. Someday she'll need me, Billy. And I'll help her. You'll see. When Gilda's got a thorn stuck in her paw, I'll take it out. I'll gnaw through the ropes. Oh, Lord, Billy, I love her so. She's my one true mama. The one who'll never desert me, right, Billy?"

"She loves you very much," he said.

"She wouldn't leave me standing in the dust, would she, Billy? Not Gilda. She loves me." He tugged off her shirt and she opened one eye and peered up at him. "Do you?"

"Do I what? Love you? Darling," he said, "I'm undressing you, aren't I?"

She thought about it, squinted suspiciously at him for a moment, then gave him a dazzling, drunken smile.

"You're irresistible. Can you manage the rest on your own?" he asked.

She nodded a little too vigorously but assured him, finally, and he went back to her room to turn down the sheets.

He noticed that a photograph had fallen face down on the floor. Billy picked it up and found himself looking at a much younger Gilda Greenway, smiling her dazzling "I love all of you out there" smile. She was surrounded by four good-looking kids, wearing starry-eyed, slightly astonished expressions. He studied the photograph for a few seconds before realizing why their faces looked so familiar.

"Devon," he said, standing in the doorway of the bathroom, "when was this picture taken?"

Devon squinted at him. "A very historic occasion," she said, underlining each word with mock formality. "The first meeting of Gilda Greenway and her Four Fans—and the first time I met Kingston Godwin. Unfortunately, he preferred Inez's tits to mine. Remind me to tell you about it someday when I'm sober."

"Can I make a copy of this? I'd love to have it for the collection in my den."

"Oh, take it, Billy," she said, waving bubbles at him. "I must have two or three others to remind me there once was a time when I believed that life turns out the way it does in fairy tales."

SEVENTEEN

1968

D evon became one of Hollywood's major fund raisers for the civil rights movement. She marched at rallies and demonstrations, and helped organize an interracial committee to prevent riots like the one that raged in Watts for six days that August in 1965. She was forever getting Billy and everyone else she knew in Hollywood to write a check—"Even a small check helps"—for a defense fund, breakfast program, or peace march.

Two years after *Two Can Do,* Devon received a Golden Globe Award as the year's most promising newcomer for her role in *Emma Blandish.* Devon played Emma, an illiterate southern girl who is taught to read by a compassionate Negro schoolteacher. The man, a northerner, has come South to teach in the local segregated school. When a rejected boyfriend finds them together one night at Emma's house, all hell breaks loose. The white man is accidentally killed. Emma helps the innocent schoolteacher escape and stands trial, alone, for murder.

Devon campaigned for the title role.

From the moment she heard about the project, she wanted to play the dirt-poor southern martyr. May agreed the part was a plum, glamorless and difficult, but just the one—after two comedies back-to-back—to showcase Devon's full range as an actress. They enlisted Gilda's help, and she arranged a dinner party to which she invited, among others, Billy, May, Inez, the film's producer, and Axel Mordus, the director.

After veal medallions with sorrel and kiwi tarts, Gilda screened *Two Can Do* for her guests. Everyone commented long and loudly on Devon Barnes's talent, and how she'd really deserved a nomination for turning a contrived featherweight romp into a film of substance. May talked about Devon's charming down-home "southern" accent and how hard she'd worked to lose it. Inez said that Devon had the same wonderful, catlike quality, only less genteel, that Vivian Leigh had in *Gone with the Wind.*

"Earthier, more vulnerable. Do you know what I mean?" she asked the director.

Billy Buck delivered the *coup de grâce.* King, on location in Mexico, had called him earlier in the day to say he'd heard Devon was interested in the movie Axel Mordus was making and that he thought she'd be wonderful in the role. And, of course, Billy could quote him.

He wasn't at all surprised when Devon phoned that night and made him repeat every word of what had been said at Gilda's. When he told her King thought she'd be perfect as Emma, Devon sounded shocked.

"King? He called you from Mexico to say that? Well, what do you know!"

"Oh, come on, Devon," he'd said skeptically. "This is me, Billy."

"Honestly, this is the first I've heard of it. Why would he . . . Oh, Gilda probably got him to do it. God knows what pressure she exerted."

"Well, he was pretty convincing for a man under pressure. I believe he does think you'd be the best actress for the job. He talked *me* into it."

"Are you going to join up?"

"You can read about it in my column tomorrow. I think I'll run a shot of King, though. Not you. Did you know he's now among the 'Ten Most Recognizable Faces in the World'? Some poll I just read. You owe him one, Devon."

"You think so?" she laughed. "No. We're about even."

Whatever King's motive had been, he was right about Devon. She was a perfect Emma Blandish. For thousands of moviegoers, Devon, barefoot, in blue jeans and a flannel shirt, became Emma, a girl of passionate convictions. It was the pivotal role of her career, the one people identified her with for years—Emma Blandish, a plucky but vulnerable girl who is thrust into a dangerous notoriety for protesting injustice.

It was the role Devon had begun to play in real life before the screenplay even existed. And not everyone applauded.

The scene in which Emma Blandish kissed the compassionate black teacher goodbye was part of Axel Mordus's final cut, but was edited out of the release print. Interviewed on a late-night radio show, Devon briefly mentioned that she'd protested the editing. The studio got venomous phone calls and letters calling Devon a "nigger lover" and a "traitor to her race and country."

She was threatened with everything from a boycott of her movies to murder.

But it had become fashionable to invite blacks and long-haired street people into one's Holmby Hills estate and to pass a mink-lined hat for them, along with joints of Acapulco gold. Hollywood stars and scions in flowered shirts and Nehru jackets were photographed engaged in earnest dialogue with men in dark sunglasses, exploding Afros, hand-dyed dashikis, and Algerian beads. Screen goddesses and society matrons let down their hair and raised their hemlines.

Swathed in fringed and beaded suede, Inez Godwin was one of Hollywood's most ubiquitous hostesses. Even if she never cracked the barriers of Group A, even if Inez's busy hunk of a husband wasn't home, there was always lots of free-flowing booze, great grass, the right ratio of money and glamor to passion and artistic poverty, and an assured appearance of the fiery Devon Barnes.

"Darlings, you've just *got* to come!" Inez would say. "Mick's supposed to be here, so's Keith and a couple of other Stones. Maybe Grace Slick and Timmy Leary. My connection just delivered the *best,* absolutely *fabu* Colombian cut crystal. And Janis is bringing some Acapulco gold. The maharishi says he'll come if he gets his Rolls fixed. Can you imagine the swami walking? With poor John, Ringo, George, and Paul trailing along behind him? Should be a hoot."

Laughing hysterically, she'd take a toke, snap for a servant to fetch another vodka stinger, and dial the next number . . .

During one of Inez's 6:30 cocktail shindigs, Devon confided to Billy she thought she might be pushing too hard, taking on too much. She'd begun to feel the strain lately. It wasn't the hate mail that was bothering her, or the increasingly vicious swipes by the conservative press.

"Tell you the truth, Billy, I've been getting just a touch paranoid. Lately I think there are strange men following me."

"Look at you, beauty. Of course there are."

She smiled at him. "I'm serious. I'm jumpy as a hound dog in a lightning storm. Hell, I only *hope* I'm paranoid."

She took his arm and asked him to walk outside with her. The twilight was humid and overcast, the threat of rain hung in the air. They moved away from the blaring music and loud voices, toward the tennis courts, where a man in tennis whites was practicing his serve alone.

"How awfully Fellini," Billy said, gesturing toward the solitary player. "Do we know him? Something familiar about him."

Devon saw a compact, athletic man moving with grace and intensity. His face was square and sculpted, lit by deepset eyes, black as currants, beneath heavy eyebrows that gave him a perpetually brooding cast. His thick straight hair fell forward across his brow. He kept flinging back his head, as if to get the hair out of his eyes.

"It's Michel Weiss-France," said Billy. "Do you think he's attractive? He's supposed to be a ladykiller. What does he have, do you suppose? And don't answer in inches."

"I think he's extremely attractive."

"That's nice. You're just his type."

"What is his type?"

"Female. Actually, he's quite a connoisseur. I think you'd give him a run for his francs. Very political. They're calling him 'Sartre *du cinema,*' or some such idolatry. All you'd have to do is crook your little finger, kiddo. Now, *he'd* be thrilled to follow you. So who's his competition?"

"I don't know. That's what's driving me crazy. It's different guys in boring cars. The most sinister thing about them is they're so boring-looking. Men in golf sweaters and polyester slacks. Guys in business suits with white socks and wingtips. One of them even has a crewcut."

"Sounds like the FBI."

"No, really, Billy. Do you think I'm just being crazy? Should I call the police?"

"In L.A.? There are police in L.A.?" They both laughed. "And tell them what? That you're being followed by boring men?"

In the humid stillness, her husky laughter cracked and rumbled, echoing on the tennis court. Weiss-France looked at them sharply, his concentration broken.

A bolt of blue lightning lit the sky. Devon's face was briefly illuminated in the eerie glare. "*Ça va*, Emma!" he shouted, breaking into a sudden grin, waving his arm at her. And then, a rumble of thunder erupted. Billy grabbed Devon's hand and raced with her to the equipment shed near the tennis court.

Michel Weiss-France shrugged with Gallic resignation and gathered up the tennis balls as pea-size drops of rain began to fall. By the time he joined them inside the wooden shed, he was soaked to the skin.

"Ah, I was right," he said, grinning again, licking the water streaming down his face. He shook her hand enthusiastically. His arm was brown and muscular, and slick with rainwater. "You are Emma, *oui? Jeanne des Jeans.* Joan of the Blue Jeans," he explained, still clasping her hand. "It's what I call you. Like Jeanne d'Arc, you understand?"

"Joan of Arc?"

"Yes, yes. That's it. How *fantastique* you are. Ah, *ça va. Monsieur* Buck," he said, nodding to Billy, patting Devon's hand. "We have met in Cannes, no? At the festival."

Weiss-France turned to Devon. "He say a very funny line at Cannes. Billy is introduced to the Princess Grace in front of many people. She say, '*Ah, oui, le critique Americain.*' Very phony, *oui?* So Billy say, '*Ah, oui, la princesse de Philadelphie.*' I applaud that kind of arrogance."

"Monsieur Weiss-France, how kind of you to remember."

"But you wrote splendidly of my film. Can I forget such eloquence and good taste, eh? I must change," he said, releasing Devon's hand to demonstrate how wet his white Lacoste shirt was by pulling it away from his body and shrugging apologetically.

"Voilà! You will wait, yes? I may not lose you? I will go fast, okay? Ten minutes, yes? I have the Porsche. Kingston's prize, you know. He is in the wilderness, in Oregon, my poor friend. He suffers for his art. And I have the pleasure of his home and friends and magnificent car, which in any case, I sell to him one year ago. So!"

Michel Weiss-France backed out of the shed into the rain. "You will meet me, yes? In my car? Ten minutes, no more. I beg of you. I have only thees night. I return to Paris tomorrow."

"Yes," Devon laughed.

Weiss-France sighed and clasped his hands prayerfully. "Bravo. *Encore.* Laugh at me again. I have dream about thees laugh . . . the laugh of Emma Blandish. *Merveilleuse!"*

He backed away, throwing kisses at her, a delirious Daffy Duck smile on his rain-soaked face. Finally, he turned and ran back to the house.

"I think he likes you," Billy said.

"No shit, Sherlock," said Devon, laughing anew.

"I begin to understand what he has going for him—besides rumors of 'sufficiency,' which I suspect he started. He's supposed to be hung like a donkey, you know?"

"Ah, Beelee," she said, "you 'ave such eloquence and good taste."

"Never mind, dear." He patted her arm. "Just call me in the morning with the blow-by-blow. To the centimeter. And don't forget your tape measure."

Michel made an illegal U-turn on the Pacific Coast Highway and swung the beat-up black Porsche into the parking space in front of her London bus. Through the rear window, Devon could see the blue Ford parked across the road. The crewcut was at the wheel, drinking coffee or soup from a paper container. The golf sweater was asleep on the seat next to him.

"Who are they?" Michel asked.

"I don't now. But they've been parked out there a lot this week. When I get paranoid, I think they're watching me. When the paranoia turns to terror, I imagine all sorts of things. They could be following an unfaithful husband or taking a coffee break. Or they could be hit men with a contract on my life. Who knows?"

"I think they are FBI."

"Hefbeyi? Oh." She laughed. "FBI. Do you really?"

"I will find out."

"How?"

"Like this," he said, opening the car door. He crossed the road, buttoning his blazer. In the side mirror, Devon watched him lean down to talk to the driver of the blue Ford.

He nodded gravely.

Then he shook the man's hand and hurried back across the road.

"What did they say?"

"He say he is waiting for his friend. His friend live here. He is full of shit, you know?" He opened her door and helped her out. "He is FBI. I can smell them. They follow me in New York and in Washington. They all look just the same. Little gray men with the look of mediocrity. Gray men. You understand?"

"Yes, perfectly. Michel, I think it's me they're watching. Do you want to go somewhere else? I don't know what to do."

He grinned at her. "Here, I show you. The least we can do is to be amusing for them, no?"

He took her in his arms and kissed her. It was a warm and gentle kiss, with a sincerity that surprised her. His arms were strong. His body fit hers wonderfully.

He had big hands, big enough to reach down and caress her backside. Devon felt her short skirt riding up. She wondered if the crewcut or the one with the golfing sweater could see them in the fast-fading light. She wondered if the FBI could see Michel as he slipped his thick hand inside the back of her panties. She arched her back to bring her buttocks within his reach.

"Enough," he said, withdrawing his hand suddenly. She followed his gaze across the road. It was too dark now to tell whether Tweedle Dum and Tweedle Dee had enjoyed the show. She had. She took his dark, brooding face in her hands and kissed him.

"*Ça suffit, cherie.* They can do mischief. They can cause you pain and trouble. I go home tomorrow. But you, my sweet Emma, you are here."

"My name is Devon. You must call me Devon."

"My sweet Devon."

"You're so funny," she said, stroking his face, brushing back the hair from his brow.

"Yes?" He threw back his head and opened his arms and hugged her. "But this is exactly what I dream. Exactly to make you laugh. Yes." She was laughing again. "Yes! To make you laugh. Will we make love? I will delight you. I will make you laugh."

"Come on inside. Let's talk about it."

They sipped Courvoisier by the fire and listened to the waves. He thought she was naive not to know she'd been under surveillance because of the speeches and activities she'd been engaged in.

"I haven't done anything illegal," Devon said. "I haven't advocated violence of any kind. If anything, I've tried to use my influence to promote and equilibrium. A lot of terrible things are happening in this country, Michel."

They talked into the night. Devon trusted him. Never mind the stories and statistics. She was living them, and they weren't in the scripts she was acting, either. She had been to the Watts ghetto and she had rung doorbells of white liberals asking for aid to establish jobs for Negroes. She'd gone to a huge party at Marlon Brando's house on Mulholland Drive to raise money for Resurrection City and alienated everyone by being the only one present to ask where the money was going. She signed her name to a list of prominent liberals volunteering to go to prison if Dr. Benjamin Spock was convicted. She supported Bobby Seale and marched in "Free Huey Newton" rallies. She sat on the floor at John Frankenheimer's beach house and talked half the night with Bobby Kennedy, windburned in Bermuda shorts and a Howdy Doody T-shirt, while his dog Freckles ate her porterhouse steak off her plate.

She was on a soapbox for the minorities. As her liberal views became known, she was solicited for money and her signature, both of which she gave so willingly that even Gilda, an old limousine liberal herself, was forced to admonish her. "Your whole life, baby, is turning into one damn crisis after another."

"And what have you done for the underdogs lately?" Devon retaliated.

"Don't give me that condescending holier-than-thou shit. Mama gave at the office. For years. But I gave with charm."

She did, too. On more than one occasion, her cornpone charm had come in handy.

"Do you know how Gilda got through the McCarthy witch hunts

in the fifties?" asked May one day at lunch, wolfing down three entrees. "She was one of the biggest pinkos in town. Every blacklisted Red in the industry played poker at The Pearls after Dore Schary took over Metro and kicked Gilda off the lot. But when the Committee called her, she invited them over to the house for a barbecue, and served spare ribs, potato salad, and watermelon by the pool. They were like some-thing out of Archie comics. The matter was closed and nobody ever mentioned it again."

"God," said Devon. "Lillian Hellman faced them all like a tiger, while our girl Gilda just dished up some more cole slaw."

Devon was different. The alienation in the streets and on the campuses bred a seething social unrest that mattered to her in a way her movie career did not. The roots of her compassion were complex, the price she knew she might be forced to pay was treacherous and costly, but she could not watch the world ignite while she languished under artificial watercolor clouds and neon moons, waiting for someone to yell, "It's a wrap!" She had to dance on the lip of that volcano.

"You are a teepical American idealist," Michel said, kissing her index finger. "And that means an easy mark."

"What do you know about it anyway?" she shot back, stunned at his callous indifference.

A lot, as it turned out.

Michel confessed that despite his service to France and his own war record, he was having grave doubts about the transitions in his own country. He had worked for DeGaulle, but the recent strikes in riot-torn Paris made him even more keenly aware of the validity of the questions raised against the French leader. He knew American history, reminding her of long-ago persecutions and inequities she had never considered: the incarceration of Japanese-Americans in concentration camps during World War II; the Bonus Army, a group of ragtag World War I veterans who marched on Washington to demand the benefits and pensions they'd been falsely promised, who were beaten and chased out of the capital by the U.S. Army.

He knew about sin and mendacity in France, too. He talked about the French Vichy government and Nazi sympathizers like Maurice Chevalier, who performed willingly with shit-eating grins for Hitler and the invading Germans. He knew even more about the French intervention in Africa and Vietnam. They talked about colonialism and Ho Chi Minh. And how the French, like the Americans now, had underestimated the intelligence and commitment and fighting skill of colonialized races.

By the time the fire went out and they'd drunk the last of the Courvoisier, Devon was in love.

"Ah," he said. "I must make an apology. I tell you I will make you laugh, but then I talk so seriously."

She smiled and kissed his palm. "I love listening to you. In America now, we're a country of gaps—generation gaps, communication gaps, political polarization gaps. I feel with you, this moment, there is no gap."

"I have not disappointed you, eh? Ah, well." He pulled her to her feet. "I hope I shall not."

He didn't want to touch her again until they were naked and lying in bed together. He wanted, he told her, to lie beside her and explore her body.

Devon waited under the patchwork quilt. "So now I must tell you my secret," he said, returning from the bathroom, drying his arms with a towel, naked but for his French bikini briefs. His tan was the color of cumin. His arms and legs were stocky but wonderfully defined, athletic and muscular. He smelled like cloves.

"I have, in France, the reputation of being a superb lover, yes? And you must know, I work hard to achieve such fame. But the secret is that I have a partner in the crime."

She grinned.

"This partner, ah, a pig, a selfish dog, a whimsical beast." He tossed the towel across the room and slipped off his briefs. And then he turned to her. "May I present the partner in crime. As you see, he is without distinction. He is, perhaps, a disappointment?"

She looked him over at his invitation. He had a lovely cock. It was proportionately as stocky and well-formed as the rest of him, if momentarily less muscular.

"He is a very adequate partner, I think."

"Merci." He slipped into bed beside her. His body felt very solid and warm. She loved the feel of her own body, nipples straining, belly undulating slowly against him, making him grow.

He carefully, slowly, moved his hands over her like a feather, feeling every texture of her body. *"Cherie,* I like this," he said huskily. "I want to kiss you everywhere. But now I like this, to be with your lips. You taste so good."

She moved her hand over the curve of his torso, his waist, his hip, feeling the warm muscular thickness of his backside. With his hand guiding hers, she felt him grow, heavy and loose in her hand.

"You must be patient," he whispered. "I tell you the secret. I trust you with this secret, my Devon. With someone I love, it is more difficult for me."

But as she touched him, he was building, to a size she never imagined. Slowly, he filled against her palm.

He kissed her breasts, then licked her belly and along the crevice of her thighs. Now he was kissing her body with the same warm intensity with which he'd kissed her lips.

"I want to hold you," she said. "I want you in my hands again."

"You will. I will be gentle, yes. I want to make love with you. Trust me, it will not work any other way."

Soon she found out what he meant. She became incredibly wet. Whether it was his mouth's wetness or her body's, she didn't know or care.

"Devon," he whispered, moving on top of her, "I have never ask this of anyone. Tell me. You like me, yes? Tell me."

"I *love* you."

"I know. *We* know. My partner and I. You see," he said, rubbing against her wet thigh, parting her with his fullness. He was large and round and hard as a lead pipe. She reached down to touch him again.

"Guide me into you," he said. "I go slowly. I try not to hurt you. I have made you ready?"

"I think so," she gulped. Then she felt the pain. She closed her eyes, trying to relax, as the pain turned to pleasure.

Michel moved deeper into her. She felt herself opening to him, her warmth and wetness engulfing him. "I love you," Michel said, thrusting into her, filling her. "I will not leave. I love you."

They lay spent with emotion, physically and mentally united in an apex of ecstasy. Michel lit a Gaulois as Devon stroked his chest and fingered his navel.

"I'm about to start a new film," said Devon. "And you have to leave for Spain, don't you? Bad timing for us, Michel."

"Yes, but perhaps we will be free in the summer? Perhaps we can meet then. I know the wonderful, perfect place to meet—a small village in Normandy with apple orchards sloping all the way to the sea . . ."

There was a violent crash of glass in the living room and then the sound of angry footsteps on the staircase.

Before Devon could scream, the door to the bedroom flew open with a loud splintering crack.

Four men, two with guns drawn, burst into the room.

They're not wearing masks, Devon thought.

The crewcut was there, taking orders from a man in a suit the color of baby shit. "Okay, check the closets and the bathroom." His gun was pointed at Michel. "Get your hands above your head, Frogman," the man in the ugly suit commanded. Devon hugged the covers against her chest.

"Who are you?" Michel demanded. "Where are your papers? Do you have a warrant for this? Or are you just criminals?"

"We know who *you* are, buddy," the leader said, shaking his gun at Michel. "And you're in deep shit if the nigger's here. Your government will have an easier time getting the Statute of Liberty back than trying to spring you, if we find the nigger here. And if we don't find him, well, we might just find something else to keep you right here in the good old U.S. of A."

Devon was trying to button her shirt, but her hands were shaking.

The crewcut thrust a picture in her face.

"You know this guy?"

It was a photo of a black man, his eye puffy and distended with dark scar tissue. Another scar extended from just above his swollen eye into his scalp.

"No," she said, hesitantly, still examining the picture. "Who is he? What do you want?"

"Look again, honey," said the crewcut.

One of the man's eyes in the photo was familiar.

It was Deauville.

"Clean," one of the men called from downstairs.

"Did you check the kitchen? Anything in the garbage can?"

"We've covered the whole place, Phil."

The leader grabbed Devon's arm. "You're on the wrong side, lady," he said with a menacing sneer. "We're the good guys."

"You're hurting me," she winced.

He waved the picture of Deauville at her again. "This guy's a murderer. A vicious nigger. You see him, you run the other way, lady. 'Cause one of us is going to be right behind him shooting."

They were gone almost as suddenly as they'd appeared.

It took Devon the rest of the night to convince Michel he must return to France immediately. If he lingered she was afraid the men, whoever they were—FBI, CIA, maybe worse—might come back and arrest him. He had a film to make, didn't he? He could do more that way. With freedom, he could do more than tying up his time fighting in the American courts. And no, she couldn't go with him. Not now.

He reached for her, but she was despondent—and breathless with fear. "I'll call," he said with his hand on the door. All she could manage was a tentative nod. She believed the madness afoot; she just couldn't believe it was happening to *her*.

EIGHTEEN

1969

I t was the worst year of Devon Barnes's life. Harassment was as much a part of her daily routine as boysenberry yogurt. On the morning Michel flew back to Paris, the front-page headline in the *San Francisco Chronicle* shrieked "THREE SOUGHT IN MARIN COURTHOUSE SLAUGHTER."

One of the three was Deauville Tolin.

According to the *Chronicle,* the FBI wanted Tolin and two other Black Berets in connection with the attempted kidnapping and subsequent murder of a judge and four policemen at the Marin County Courthouse. FBI sources claimed Tolin was the leader of a five-person Black Beret execution squad. Two members of the radical black power group were already in custody, while the search for the remaining three continued.

The "gray men" returned to her beach house time after time, with telephotos and mug shots of black men with bushy Afros, shaved heads, and reconnaissance berets. They asked her if she knew them. They showed her photographs of buildings, some of them razed to rubble, in San Francisco, Cleveland, upstate New York, which they said were, or had been, Black Beret headquarters. They grilled her about pictures of charred bodies and faces splattered with blood.

Coffee grounds and dairy containers littered the path from her house down to the beach. For weeks she thought there was a wild dog or a coyote loose in the neighborhood, but late one night she saw two men in business suits examining her garbage by flashlight.

They followed her to The Pearls. When she drove through the exit gates after visiting Gilda, a dark car blocked the road. One of the men in the car got out and came over to Devon.

"Is she in on it, too?" he asked.

Devon saw herself, mirrored and reduced in his silver-tinted glasses, shaking her head.

Not all of them wore suits. There were men in beards and bell-bottoms, in love beads and cowboy boots. Long-haired hippies came up to her at peace rallies and offered her joints, mescaline, acid.

A thirtyish flower child with a single earring waited for her outside Giorgio's on Rodeo Drive.

"I hear you're hot for nigger dick, Devon," he said, falling in step with her. "How do you like the pecker on this one?"

He showed her an 8 × 10 blowup of a dead black man, sprawled naked, in a pool of blood.

Devon successfully managed to conceal the turbulence in her life from her industry friends, confiding only in Billy. Her movie career had been galvanized by *Emma Blandish* and she was in high gear. But she was relying more and more on Valium to maintain her public composure.

When Michel's documentary *The Children* received an Academy Award nomination for Best Foreign Film, Devon was thrilled. Weiss-France had tried to return to the United States several times but had been denied entry by the Immigration and Naturalization Service. Both he and Devon hoped the publicity surrounding the nomination would persuade the bureaucrats at the State Department to change their minds. Finally, Michel asked Devon to accept the award for him, if he won.

"And the winner is *The Children.*"

The presenter's voice boomed through the tense stillness in the Dorothy Chandler Pavilion. "Accepting on behalf of Michel Weiss-France is Devon Barnes."

Devon's pride and love for Michel willed her to her feet. She had so desperately prayed for him to win, wanted *his* movie to get the recognition it deserved, that for a moment she worried that she'd only imagined his victory.

As she began the speech Michel had dictated to her over the phone, the paper shook visibly in her hands. His strong, brave words, thanking the Academy and everyone involved in the film for their behalf in and support of his work, rang out through the star-filled auditorium.

And then, suddenly, there were boos and catcalls.

Bobby Kennedy and Martin Luther King were dead, Richard Nixon had been handed the keys to the White House.

Either the times were changing and Hollywood was shifting toward conservatism, or the whisper campaign mounted against Devon had started to take effect. The atmosphere in the Dorothy Chandler Pavilion was tense and hostile.

Devon took a deep, steadying breath and tried to continue over the escalating outcry. Then, just as suddenly, the booing and catcalls subsided, giving way to a buzz of questions. People were turning around, rising to their feet, straining to see the figure coming from the back of the hall.

Trapped in a center seat, Billy Buck stood on tiptoe trying to see what was going on. Finally, he caught a glimpse of King Godwin, striding toward the stage. Billy hadn't noticed him earlier in the audience. In fact, he was sure that Inez had been escorted to the ceremony by her son, Hollis, and a dark-haired young man wearing blue jeans under his white dinner jacket. Billy also seemed to recall reading in the trades that King was in London, working "golden hours" to finish the new Stanley Kubrick picture.

But there he was, marching down the center aisle, in civilized evening wear, looking like the cover of *Gentleman's Quarterly*.

And, suddenly, there was Inez, in flowing, fringed chamois, her long chestnut hair bound with a leather headband, moving along the row of seats toward the aisle. Her head high, her eyes flashing, whether with pride or fury, Billy could not tell, Inez stepped into the aisle behind King and began to applaud.

May Fischoff, in a black Pierre Cardin caftan sequined as an oil shiek's tent, pushed her way into the aisle, also applauding heartily.

And then Billy saw Avery Calder, startlingly frail, reach out to pat King's back as the blond actor passed. King stopped briefly and embraced the ailing playwright, who, a moment later, was joined in the center aisle by Patrick Wainwright.

But it was only after Gilda made her way into the aisle—Gilda, at forty-seven, a luscious vision in cranberry velvet, still all cheekbones and cat's eyes, still wearing her fabled rope of pearls—that the center aisle filled with actors, agents, writers, and technicians, standing for Devon, cheering her and what she stood for.

It happened fast. King was suddenly onstage, kissing her in front of the Academy of Motion Picture Arts and Sciences and 40 million television viewers.

"That was my first message from Michel," he announced, as the audience grew vocal again, cheering and booing in a cacophony of muddled emotions.

King put one arm around her and with the other, triumphantly lifted the Oscar, which had been sitting on the podium in front of her.

Somehow, she managed to babble a few words. "On behalf of Michel Weiss-France and the children-turned-soldiers in North Vietnam . . . and in America . . . *our* children, *all* of them . . . we thank you!"

Jane Fonda was screaming, "Bravo!"

Hand in hand, Devon and King walked into the wings. "Thank you," Devon murmured, overwhelmed. "Thank you for being there for me."

"Hey," King said, "it's all I ever wanted to do."

He rushed her past the waiting reporters. No, he told them, they would not be staying for the post-Oscar photo session. Yeah, maybe there'd be a statement later.

Tomorrow.

See May Fischoff about it.

"Where's the frog prince?" a local show biz reporter called as they hurried toward the stage door. "How come Weiss-France didn't show?"

"He was denied entry by the government," Devon responded.

"Not the way I heard it," the reporter shot back. "There wasn't a casino or whore house he didn't hit. What about it, King? What happened to your pal? Where'd he get that shiner he was sporting out at LAX?"

"What's he talking about?" Devon asked King as they stepped outside into a chaos of trucks and portable canteens, television cables, security guards, and technicians talking through crackling walkie-talkies.

"Beats me. Old times, probably. Over there," he said.

Devon saw the new motorcycle.

She remembered the stage-door alleyway they'd stepped into years ago, when she was high on the excitement of having read for Avery Calder and his director. King had called her a fool and worse for giving up the role to save Deauville's pride. She'd felt powerful in the recognition of her talent. Powerful and excited.

King jumped off the loading platform and held his arms up for her. "Speaking of old times," he said. Laughing suddenly, she descended into them.

"What's so funny?" he asked, grinning with her, as they hurried toward the motorcycle.

"I was thinking about New York, about that midnight audition for *Barracks,* and how you've still got your bike and here we are in an alleyway again."

"You gave it all up for Deauville. Yeah, I think about that, too, sometimes. I was so pissed at you. You were a spunky kid. Would you do it again? Blow acting for a guy? Could you just walk away from it again?"

"I don't know. After tonight, I may have to."

He secured the helmet on her head and lifted her chin so he could buckle it. "Yeah," he said softly. "You just might. Jesus, for an actor my timing sure stinks. Devon—there's a surprise waiting for you back at the house."

Then he tapped the top of the helmet and gave her a grin. "Climb on, Tex. It's party time."

Devon saw him through the glass doors, framed by pots of hanging white geraniums. His back was to her, but it was definitely Michel.

He was standing on Inez's cherished lanai with a scotch in one hand and a Gaulois in the other, in animated conversation with a bosomy bleached blonde. No other guests had arrived yet. There were just the two of them, with the caterer's staff, the bartenders, and the white geraniums.

The blonde saw her first, smiled, and said something. Michel whirled around. His face was lit with such irrepressible joy that the momentary hurt of finding him with another woman vanished instantly, and Devon's heart swelled with love. He wore a small bandage above his left eye. His face looked bruised.

Then he was at her side, hugging her and lifting her off her feet. He crushed her against him, whirled with her in his arms.

"I love you. You are more beautiful than I have remembered. I love you, Devon. Yes? You understand me? I love you. You understand what I am saying? I love you."

She kissed his cheeks.

"Aow! *Merde alors,*" he howled.

"Michel, what happened to you?"

"I will tell you everything," he promised. He kissed her lightly, then murmured, *"Merde!"* again, gingerly touching his swollen upper lip. "Ah," he said, as King entered. "Here is the villain. And the hero, too! Yes, it is so. He get me into the country, with his fabulous connections—which I must add he has made through me! Ah, yes, the lady lawyer in Washington. She is *fantastique,* yes, my good friend? And then, he kidnap me to Nevada and try to kill me. As you see."

"I don't understand," Devon gasped, breathless with love and excitement.

The blonde was standing in the doorway of the living room, looking awkward and out of place. She was wearing a low-cut tube top showing the upper part of her breasts, red hot-pants revealing the lower part of her cheeks, and high-heel Joan Crawford fuck-me pumps.

Wherever she came from, thought Devon, it wasn't the Academy Awards. Or Miss Hewitt's school for girls.

"Hello, I'm Devon Barnes. I'm afraid we haven't been introduced."

"Ah," said Michel, "I'm so sorry."

"Yes, I know," said the bosomy tomato. "I mean, I know who you are. God, I mean, I've seen all your pictures."

"Devon, this is Margie," King said. "Margie's an old pal from New York. We ran into her in Las Vegas. Come on, Marge, I'll show you around."

Michel took Devon's hand and pulled her toward the stairs. "I am hungry for you, babee. Will you come with me now? Will you let me make love to you again?"

She had a million questions that would wait.

"I will tell you everything," he promised again. "And how proud you make me. I watched you on television. I thought to myself, Oh, I die for her. I mean to say, Oh, I *am* dying for her. And then, I think, But, no, Michel. She is dying for *you*. Right there, in front of the world, she stands up with courage and pride, in your place, she receives the homage, the hatred you have not dared. Truly, you are my Jeanne, I think. My *Jeanne des Jeans*. I have miss you like a crazy person, Devon. I have never love anyone like this."

They made love on the double bed in the purple guest room.

"A depressing color, purple, no?" Michel asked.

"Please, dahling," said Devon, imitating Inez—*"aubergine."*

Laughing, they tore the clothes off each other and fell back onto the bed in a tangle of wet flesh.

"I remember you," Devon said later, stroking his body, his warm, damp penis.

Michel brought her hand to his lips and lightly, wincing, kissed it. "Devon, *écoutes*. Listen to me." He raised himself on one elbow and looked at her. His dark eyes were ablaze with pleasure. His thick hair was falling over his brow. Devon felt his breath on her face, wanting to kiss his soft, swollen lips until they melted.

"I'm listening," she said.

"But you are crying." He leaned forward and licked from her cheeks salty tears she was unaware of. "Have I done this? Have I caused you *tristesse?*"

"No, not you. It's been a terrible year, Michel. And I've missed you so. I couldn't cry before. I think it's only that I feel safe now. Michel, you have no idea what's happening here. I couldn't tell you everything long distance. My phone is tapped. I've been threatened with blackmail several times. One night I found a loaded pistol in my bureau drawer. It's something out of goddamn Kafka around here.

They even poisoned my cats. Everybody in the movie business is so confused politically that they're acting schizophrenic. Have you heard what they're doing to Jean Seberg?"

"Yes, my pet. I met her in Paris. She's ready to crack. But I will not let the same thing happen to you. I am taking you away from this monstrous insanity."

"Did I forget to tell you how much I love you?"

"See. Just see what you do to me." He moved against her. "You tell me you love me. And, *voilà,* the beast stirs. We will make love again and again, yes? But, Devon, must it be here? Can you not return to France with me? You said you feel safe, yes? You are safe with me. You are safer still in France. You have no idea how you are loved there. How people know you and admire you. Just as I do."

"France?"

"Yes. I have thought about it for months. This is what I return for, to be with you like this, to tell you this. I want you to return with me to France and live with me forever."

"The girl is actually smiling," Inez said, sucking the last of a Stoli out of her glass as Devon came downstairs. "We are sick with worry and now Public Enemy Number One is grinning like a Disney cow." She whipped the leather headband off her forehead and threw it at the dark-haired boy in the white dinner jacket and jeans.

"Eddie, get me a fresh Stoli, would you? It's in the freezer in the kitchen. Carmella can show you where."

"Oh, there you are," May said, thundering in. "Nice work, kiddo. I hope you've got a bikini with a holster in your closet. I have a hunch we're going to be reading nothing but beach blanket movies and Westerns for a while." She gave Devon a big bear hug. "I'm so proud of you, Devon, and fuck 'em all. And no cracks from you, kid," she warned Hollis Godwin, who was waiting sulkily for the women to clear the stairway so he could get up to his room and out of the suit his mother had made him wear.

"Har-dee-har-har, May," he said, trying to look bored. "You were great, Devon. You should have seen Bob Hope when you were giving your speech. He nearly had a heart attack. Hey, where's my dad? Was he upstairs with you?"

"Hollis," Inez snapped. "Give it a rest, will you? I've got a split-ting headache no Excedrin will cure. I've had enough excitement for one night."

"But all I said—"

"Where *is* King?" Inez asked Devon. "Oh, my God, Michel!" she shrieked. "When did you get here? Darling, your eye. What happened to you?"

She looked from Michel to Devon.

"So *that's* what you were doing upstairs. Jesus, no wonder you were smiling."

Michel kissed May and Inez in turn. "Your husband, he did this to me," he said.

"You're kidding. What happened? No, don't tell me. It was over a broad, right? It had to be. I hope she was worth it, whoever she was."

"Aw, Mom, come on," Hollis said, embarrassed.

"Hollis, shut up and get me another drink. Eddie seems to have gotten lost."

Michel ruffled the boy's long blond hair.

The dark-haired kid in the white dinner jacket returned with Inez's vodka, just as the doorbell rang.

"I'll see you later, Michel," Hollis said. "Maybe we can hit a couple of balls down on the tennis court, huh?"

"Carmella, the door!" Inez screeched. "Eddie, gimme a 'lude." She downed the pill with a slug of vodka, then lifted her glass. "Let the Olympics begin!"

Devon looked around for Gilda, wanting to share her joy with her maternal surrogate. Michel had already told King of his intention to take Devon back to France with him. That was why, Michel explained to Devon, King had dragged him off to Las Vegas. For a bachelor party. King had insisted.

Margie, the girl, the blonde woman? She was a whore King had known in New York, an old friend, down on her luck. They had run into her at the Sands. And King had decided to bring her out to Hollywood where, she said, she'd always dreamed of working.

"I can see the murder in Inez's eyes," Michel said, strolling arm-in-arm with Devon toward the pool, where King and the blonde were talking. "So I'm afraid we'll have to entertain Kingston's old friend, just until enough of the guests arrive. Do you mind?"

"Of course not."

"She's very amusing, actually. It will not be difficult."

"Hello, Michel," the blonde called.

"Ca'va, Margie? How do you like this life, eh?"

"I'm so proud of him. For years I been telling the girls I knew him when, you know? They never believed me. Why should they? Hannah knew, though. You remember Hannah, King? She used to talk about you and that dirty dog of yours all the time. She ran away with a show girl, five, maybe six, years ago. Honest to Christ, the girl's husband came down to the ranch and tore the place apart looking for them. All the girls were screaming bloody murder, trying to tell him they were long gone. Took the dog and Elyse, that was the girl's name, Elyse's two kids and a fluffy cat with no tail, and off they went up to Washington State. I was thinking of going to see them this summer. Hannah said, sure, come on up. They got forty acres."

"Hannah," King said, shaking his head. "And what was his name?"

"Russian George, the sleaze bag. Georgie O. I could never pronounce his name."

"No. I meant the dog. Lucky. Yeah, Lucky. If he's still alive, he's probably living the good life."

"Not as good as yours, doll. Ain't this a dream come true? Only need one last thing to make me happy."

"Name it," King said.

"Directions to the powder room."

"Allow me," said Michel, extending his arm. "I'll walk back to the house with you. And we leave Kingston to explain my wounds to Devon. I still don't know how his fist fell in love with my eye."

For a moment King stood silently next to Devon, watching Michel and Margie walking away. Then he turned to her.

"You're going to do it," he said. "You're going to Paris with him."

"You knew about it all the time. You knew when you asked me if I'd give everything up, didn't you?"

"Yeah," he said, taking a sip of whiskey. "He's my best friend. I knew."

"Is that why you tried to discourage me? Do you think I'm not good enough for him, King? I am. I love him, you know."

He looked up at the house. Michel and Margie were on the terrace with Inez. "Walk with me," King said.

Between the oval pool and the tennis court was a latticed grape arbor. They walked toward the cool tunnel of vines.

"What happened between you two in Las Vegas? Michel claims you kidnapped him. He says you insisted on throwing him an instant bachelor party. It must have been some party. He can't remember what got you angry, why the two of you came to blows."

"Do you want to know the truth, the whole truth and nothing but?"

"Is it so awful?"

"Depends on your point of view. I told him to leave you alone. I told him it wouldn't work, that he should forget it."

"You told him as a friend, of course. You were only looking out for his interests."

"No," King said slowly. "I was looking out for yours."

"Mine?" She whirled around. "Liar! You arrogant liar. I love him—"

"I know you do, Devon. I love him, too. He's my best friend. But I know him better than you do."

"I'm going to marry him, King."

He winced. "Marry him? He asked you to marry him?"

She felt like a fool. She hated King for knowing Michel had never mentioned marriage at all.

"Well, he didn't exactly *ask* me. Does that make you feel better? Honestly, I don't understand you, King. I never did."

"I know. I wish we had more time, then maybe you would."

"We'd better go back—"

He pulled her to him. How many times had he wanted to do this since his disastrous wedding day? He had never been able to get her out of his system, and looking into her pleading eyes, he felt the same magic, as strong as ever.

He wanted to kiss her, but she pushed him away, into the shadows of the grape arbor.

"Before I go, I just want to tell you . . . I was in love with you once, King. I always meant to tell you that. It's too late now . . ."

She saw Inez walking toward her from the pool.

"*Darling,*" Inez purred unconvincingly, a fresh tumbler of Stolichnaya in her hand. "Where on earth have you been?"

Devon had a sneaking suspicion she already knew.

"Gilda and Avery just arrived. Everyone's asking for you."

The Quaalude Inez had taken earlier had kicked in. Vodka splashed over the sides of her glass, wetting her diamond ring. "You haven't seen King, have you?"

King stepped out of the shadows of the arbor.

"Well, well," Inez said sweetly, "this *is* a first. Even for one of *my* parties. I thought it was that blonde trash you were hot for, King. Have you and Michel decided to trade off again, like you did with Claudia Leone?"

"Inez, don't," said Devon.

"Oh, Michel always scouts for King, Devon. I thought you knew that. Poor King. Sloppy seconds again. Or is this one of those rare times that King got there first? Is that it, darling? Have you been pimping for Michel?"

Devon walked past her. "You're drunk, Inez."

Inez reached out unsteadily and clutched Devon's shoulder. "No, puss. I'm stoned. High and dry. This"—she waved the tumbler of vodka again—"is only a prop."

"Let her go, Inez," King said.

Inez threw up her arms. The glass fell out of her hand and rolled on the manicured lawn. "Yes, master," she said.

Devon rushed past them and headed for the safety of the brightly lit house.

"Just for the record, nothing happened, Inez. Not that it matters."

She walked past him and sat down on the wooden bench under the grape vines. "Damn you," she hissed, and hid her face in her hands.

"We've got to talk, Inez."

"No," she shouted, shaking her head, her face still hidden. "Fuck you. Fuck around all you like. I don't care. I won't stop you. I never have. But not here." She looked up at him, glaring. "Not here, not right under my nose, not with my best friend."

"She's in love with Michel. She's going to Paris with him. And it has nothing to do with this, with us. Not really."

"She's in love with *you*. Always has been. And it's not fair, King. She's got everything. She's free and independent and celebrated. She doesn't have a home, a husband, a child. She can go wherever she likes and do whatever she damn well pleases."

"So can you, Inez."

"I tried, didn't I? I wanted to be a writer, but Gilda made me marry you. I wanted an abortion. She wouldn't let me. She said I could write movies for her. And I did, King. I wrote a wonderful script from first-hand experience. I told the truth about everything—about my life, my goddamn father, what it was really like. I told the truth and they said no one would pay to see it, no one would believe it. Incest isn't hot. Nothing in it for Barbra Streisand. No one cared, no one wanted to know about it. Cowards. Fucking cowards!"

The leaves of the arbor rustled. "Who's there?" shrieked Inez, suddenly terrified.

King peered into the bushes. Shadows fell across the grass behind him. He missed seeing the slim figure, poised to flee.

"You're stoned," King said. "There's no one there."

"No one. No one's there. That's right," she said, turning on him, tears streaming down her face now. "I'm stoned and no one's there. Not you, that's for sure. You were never there, King. When I needed you, really needed you, where were you? Shacked up with that Italian cunt. I needed you then, King! And all I got was a kid and a house full of fucking Chinese gongs!"

"I'm sorry."

She looked up at him, in disbelief, in disgust. "You're what? Is that it, is that the payoff? My whole life in the toilet, and all you can say is you're *sorry?*" She swung at him. He caught her wrist. "Are you always like this? Stoned, drunk?"

"You'd never know. You're never here, Mr. Fucking Movie Star."

"What'd you take? What are you high on, Inez?"

"What are you high on?" she mimicked him, wild-eyed. "Hey, I'm high on life. My fabulous life. I'm Mrs. Kingston Godwin. God-damn! Envied by millions, secret guardian of the ol' tallywhacker. Well, I've seen a lot of tallywhackers lately, but I haven't seen yours. Is it still there, King? Let's have a look."

She clawed at his fly and lost her balance. He grabbed her shoulders to steady her.

"Inez, for God's sake!"

She fell against him, burying her face in his chest and sobbing uncontrollably.

He stroked her hair.

"I'm sorry, Inez. Please believe me. I wish it'd been different for both of us."

"No," she moaned. "Oh, God, no. Don't say it, King. You're all I got, baby. Don't say it. Not now."

"We've been avoiding each other for years. I'm tired, Inez, aren't you? Why don't we call it quits? Ten years is long enough to be dancing this neurotic tango. We've got to get out of it—to save ourselves. It's time."

"Not now. Not yet. Oh, God, King." She put her hands over her ears. "No! I'm not ready. I'd *kill* before I let you go."

"Where's Inez?" May asked.

"She went looking for her old man," the dark-haired boy said. "I hope she found him. She was pretty ripped. I got some far-out smoke, man. You wanna hit?"

May looked him over. He was an inch or two taller than she was, with a surfer's shoulders, a bull neck, and jeans bulging in the crotch, worn thin with friction. Either gay or a hustler or both. Or may be he just liked touching himself where the sap rises. He was either stuffed with tube sock or ready for the saddle.

"Love to," May said. "My place or yours?"

"You live around here?"

"The colony."

"What, Malibu?"

She eyed him up and down.

"Nice," she said. "You looking for love or money?"

He was stoned. "You look like you got a lot of both."

"What pebble did Inez find you under?"

"Hey. Be nice. I'm here on business, man. I brought the joints, the 'ludes. I got a little coke on me, a little meth. I can score some skag, if you're into it."

"Thanks, anyway."

"You straight, or what?"

"I was wondering the same about you."

"What?"

"You got a friend here? A guy who'd like to join us?"

"Hey, wait a minute. What're you talking about? You talking about, like, getting it on with two guys? You into double-headers?"

"Come here." She took his hand and walked him into the guest bathroom.

They surprised two men groping each other—an agent in a dark dinner jacket and red cummerbund, and an actor in a flowered shirt, buckskin bell-bottoms, and a Peter Max tie.

"What the hell?" the man in formal wear said.

"This is a bust," May said. "Come out with your hands up."

"Christ, May," said the agent, a rival of May's. "Why didn't you knock?"

"Why didn't you lock?" She pushed them outside. "Like this," she said, locking the door.

"You're funny," the boy said. "What're we doing here? You want a joint now?"

"Yeah." May put her hands on his waist and slid them up and down. "Solid. You surf?"

"Yeah. I work out, too. Over in Venice, man. Muscle Beach. Here, feel this." He flexed his forearm.

She ran her hand over it. "Like a rock. *Very* nice."

"Here, look at this." He rolled his shoulders for her. His chest danced. She touched it, rubbed his nipples.

"Hey, man, you better watch out," he grinned. "You're liable to get me excited."

"Watch this," May said.

She slipped the caftan down over her shoulders and let it fall below her breasts, which filled her corset bra to the bursting point. She pressed her arms against her breasts and they rose in the bra, nipples tumbling out.

"Oh, wow," the boy said. "Can I touch them?" His hands were rough and calloused. He pinched her nipples. "You like that?"

"You promised me a joint."

"Oh, baby, I got one for you, too. Right here." He rubbed his crotch. "Touch me, will you? I'm going to pop, I swear."

The doorknob rattled. "May, are you in there?" King Godwin asked.

May ran her hand over the boy's crotch. It felt as good as it looked. It stirred. No socks. The real McCoy. "Yeah," she said.

"May, is Hollis with you?"

She took her hand off the boy and shimmied into her caftan. "No," she said, and unlocked the door. "Why? What's the matter?"

"Oh, shit," the boy groaned. "What're you, crazy? Come *on*, what's going on?"

"I can't find him. Inez and I were arguing, and suddenly there he was. He must have overheard us. Then he took off. She was in rotten shape. I couldn't leave her. Now I can't find him."

"I haven't seen him. I'll look around."

"What about me?" the boy in the bathroom asked.

"Start without me," May said.

"Forgive me for interruptin', children," Avery said, taking Gilda's arm. "My sincere congratulations to you, Monsieur Weiss-France, for your impeccably made yet deeply disturbin' film, and to you, Mother Courage, for a myriad of things that go without sayin'."

"Michel, may I present—"

"Monsieur Calder." Michel inclined his head. "I am a great admirer of your work."

"You're sweet. Excuse me, pressin' business. My dear," Avery whispered dramatically to Gilda, "somethin's got to be done about the local color." He rolled his eyes in the direction of Margie, who was tottering away from them on the stiletto heels of her plastic springolaters. The voluptuous blonde glanced over her shoulder at that moment, recognized Avery, and gave him a little wave. When he waved back, she giggled and put a finger to her lips and mouthed, "Shhhsh."

"That's right, pumpkin." Avery put a finger to his lips and mouthed, "Shhhsh."

Margie winked at him, then pretended that she was locking her lips with her finger, and dropping the key down the front of her dress.

"Who the fuck is that?" Gilda asked, watching as Margie made her way unsteadily through the crowd. "A student of Marcel Marceau's?"

"You remember, she is the friend of Kingston's who we meet in Las Vegas," Michel said. "I have introduce you to her."

"I thought she was a hooker," said Gilda, "but in Hollywood anyone who dresses like that could be somebody's mother, on her way home from the Safeway."

"Honey," said Avery, delicately extracting a silver pill case from his breast pocket, "with friends like that, the boy don't need no enemies." He offered the pills around. They all shook their heads. "Don't get me wrong. She's perfectly sweet. But soused to the gills. My dear," he confided to Gilda, "she has just been tellin' me the most *peculiar* stories." He selected two tablets and washed them down with a gulp of Gilda's drink.

"Oh, God, what are you drinking?" he asked, clutching his throat.

"Ginger ale, Avery. You'll live. What stories?"

"We were just going," Devon said, giving Gilda a peck on the cheek.

"Baby," Gilda said, hugging her. "You'll call Patrick before you go, won't you? His wife's back in the hospital. He drove up right after the awards. He won't be back in town till tomorrow. You're not leaving immediately, are you?" she asked Michel.

"I am afraid I must return in two days. I have left a film and many people are waiting. But when they see for what reason I have left them, they will understand."

"I'm sure they will. I'd have given you a party, a dinner, at least."

"I'll phone you in the morning," Devon promised her. "Say our goodbyes for us. Good night, Avery."

"Is it true? Has Patrick gone to see Marie?" Avery asked, once they'd gone.

Gilda nodded. "How's my eye makeup?"

"Splendid. Why, have you been cryin' over him?"

"Why should this time be any different? And now Devon. God, I feel old as the hills tonight. I wish Pat were here."

"What if she dies, Gilda? Have y'all talked about that?"

"Who, Marie? No, not for years."

"I don't know how you can stand it. I'd get so awfully jealous. I mean, I know she's paralyzed, weak as a newborn kitten, and livin' from dawn to dusk in a state not unlike that of a boiled asparagus. But it would bother me, the times he's visitin' the vegetable patch. Never there when you need him, like tonight."

Gilda put her arm through Avery's. "I've got you, tonight, baby. I'm just fine. Now, what happened with you and Margie? What was that coy pantomime all about?"

"My dear," he whispered, eyes sparkling with mischief, "the girl knew him *when.*"

"So she said."

"Gilda, do I have to write out the lines for you? You're supposed to say, 'When *what?*' "

"When what?"

"When they were doin' porn loops together in New York."

"Porn loops?"

"You know, darlin'. Those little snippets of film you chuck quarters into machines to watch on Forty-second Street. They're usually shown in little curtained booths at the back of shops sellin' dildoes and vagina sprays."

"Blue movies? King Godwin did stag films?" she giggled.

"Not stag, exactly. Canine."

Gilda's eyebrows raised. "Canine?"

"As in bow-wow. As in Rin Tin Tin. Only their co-star's name was Lucky. Oh, Gilda, I know it's beastly of me, but I asked what's-her-name, Margie, if she happened to know whatever became of their work together. It seems her lover, some bull dyke named Hannah, still owns the reels."

Gilda whistled softly. "Jesus. Does anyone else know about this?"

"If we don't get her out of here presto-pronto, lamb chop, they bloody well could. Someone gave her a tab of speed. Inez's little friend in the jeans and dinner jacket, I think."

"Well, pardner, shall we escort our little friend out of the House of Usher before it falls?"

They strolled toward the bathroom.

"Gilda," May called. "Have you seen Hollis?"

"Hello, baby." Gilda extended her cheek for May's kiss. "In the time I've been here everyone seems to have aged considerably, so I'm not sure when I saw him last, but I distinctly remember he was looking for *you.*"

"Oh, shit. Well, God only knows where he is now. I've been all over this madhouse. If you run into him again, tell him I tried to find him, will you?" She had her hand on the bathroom door.

"I believe the pissoir is occupied," Avery said.

"Yeah," said May. "I hope his motor's still running. She opened the door. "Oh, sorry."

Eddie was facing the toilet, his muscular thighs spread, his jeans around his knees.

"Oh, God, not now," he groaned. "Wait."

And then May noticed the knees between *his* knees, the blood-red fingernails gripping his white jacket.

"Oh, shit, don't stop. What is this? What the fuck is going on here?" he cried, as the disheveled blonde who'd been sitting on the toilet seat in front of him stood up and squinted at the spectators in the doorway.

"Oh, hi, Avery," the blonde giggled, pushing past the half-naked kid with the jutting purple cock in his hand. "Hello, Miss Greenway. Hello everybody. I was just going to throw up but Eddie, here, said that would be a pitiful waste of the crystal meth he'd given me before, right, Eddie? So, I said, what are we doing? He says he's got this hard-on here, waiting for the big broad to show up who left him, like, in the middle of a diddle. So I said, like Eddie, hey, you want to talk about a pitiful waste, I said—"

"At least, her mouth was occupied," Avery said to Gilda, as they led Margie toward the vestibule coat rack.

"What a trip," the boy said to May. "I really wanted *you.*"

"It's the thought that counts. If you can hike up your jeans without breaking anything, I'll meet you out front. In the white Rolls."

"So where'd you disappear to?" the boy asked a little while later, as May pulled into her beach house driveway.

"I was looking for true love."

"Another guy?" he asked, as they walked up the side steps to the kitchen door.

"You're so quick," she said curtly, tossing her bag onto the wicker chair. "A boy," she said. There was just enough light to see him. He was taking off his white jacket. "A *little* boy."

"Yeah?" he said, throwing his jacket onto the chair. "You like little boys?" He pulled her caftan down over her shoulders.

"Not *too* little."

"Oh, man, there they are again," he said, reaching for her. "You got fantastic titties, you know that?"

She unbuttoned his shirt. He reached into the corset bra and pulled her breasts out over the cups. "Oh, my God, it's just like before. Oh, shit, I gotta feel them. You like that? You like when I squeeze your titties?"

She put her arms around his neck. Her breasts rose.

"Here I go again." Clutching her, he kissed her neck and throat and licked her breasts and bit them. Then he kissed her lips. He kissed them hard at first, biting and licking the way he had done to her breasts. Then, he slowed his pace. She could feel him mellowing into it, getting lost, falling for her. Slowly, she licked his lips and sucked them. Expertly, she moved against him, brushing his chest with her nipples, brushing his groin with her belly.

"Oh," he sighed, pulling away for breath. His hands moved down from her breasts. "Take that off, that girdle or whatever it is. Oh, please," he moaned, reaching down below the waist-cinching merry widow to the naked flesh below.

She unhooked the long bra and took it off. Her big breasts sprang free. He grabbed them, tried to scoop them all up in his palms, but he could barely hold one in two hands.

"You're so big. Oh, mama, I could die between your titties."

She pulled her caftan back onto her shoulders.

"Let's go into the bedroom," May said.

"Oh, yeah, let's. Gimme a kiss. Hey, listen, I never was with anyone like you. You're so big. You got so much, of everything. Even your lips. There's plenty, ain't there? But, I want it all. I want to fuck you everywhere there is, you dig me?"

"The bedroom," May moaned.

"You really like to do it with two guys? Come on, tell me." He pulled her hand against him and moved it up and down. He was very hard. "You don't really need two guys to get off, do you? Not with me, you don't."

They moved into the bedroom groping at one another.

"Oh, shit," he said. "I can't see, I can't see you. I want to look at you, again. I never seen so much woman in my whole fuckin' life."

May flicked on the light switch. "Like what you see?"

But the surfer was staring beyond her at her rumpled bed.

"A guy! Another fuckin' guy!"

"Shhhsh," May said, "you'll wake him up."

Somehow, Hollis Godwin had hitched a ride to Maibu and there he was, in May Fischoff's bed.

"I'm already awake. Hi, Eddie," said Hollis.

"Oh, Christ. It's Mrs. Godwin's kid! Oh, man, you people are too sick for me!"

"What are you doing here?" May demanded, pulling her caftan back in place, covering her breasts.

"I needed to talk to you. I looked all over the party for you. I thought you went home."

"Oh, shit," Eddie said, "this is worse than bad acid. This is, like, unhealthy. You can't keep getting boners and never getting off, not without winding up in the hospital or something."

"What did you want to talk about that couldn't wait till morning?"

"I think my dad's going to leave—for good, this time. I think they're going to split up, May. You gotta help me. I don't want him to go."

"Go?" Eddie shouted a moment later, as May led him to the door. "What're you, crazy?"

"You're a big boy, Eddie," she said, stuffing a fifty-dollar bill into his shirt pocket. "Here." She handed him the *Playboy* with the Patrick Wainwright interview in it. "You won't believe the tits on Miss February. Just don't get the piece on Wainwright all sticky, okay? It would be like desecrating the flat." The boy was still sputtering when she slammed the door in his face.

She poured herself a Stoli and a glass of milk for Hollis. She cut them each a slab of Sara Lee cake, then went back into the bedroom.

He'd been crying. His hands were dirty and he'd rubbed his eyes with them and now his face looked like a road map in mud season. He looked up at her with his runny nose and dirt-streaked face and his long, blond hair, all sweaty and sticking out like off little wings from his scalp.

"You mad at me?" he asked.

"For what?" she said, handing him the milk. "I'm hot stuff. I can get laid anytime." She broke off a big hunk of cake and put it into her mouth.

"Come on, don't say things like that."

"You want help or you here to lecture me again?" May said.

He put down the glass of milk and stood up. "I hate when you do that. Why can't you be cool? Why do you have to talk dirty all the time?"

"You want your cake to go, or what?"

"Yeah, sure!" he shouted. "Boy, what a godmother you turned out to be." He pulled a joint out of his shirt pocket and stuck it behind his ear. "I'm going, and you can shove the cake, okay?" He started past her.

"Whoa, baby," she said, catching his belt loop. "What have we got here?" She reached for the joint. "Hollis, you're too young to start in with that shit."

"Oh-ho, now who's giving a lecture, huh? Know where I got it? From your dumb boyfriend, that's who. He rolled it for me himself. Off of my mom's Thai stick. I got a couple of her downs, too." He reached into his pocket and pulled out two pills. "She takes these all the time. She was stoned tonight, when they were fighting. I was listening in the bushes. She said these really stupid things to my dad. These really far out, unbelievable things, you know. Lies. Crazy stuff. Like how she never really wanted to marry him. Or you know, like, have a kid. Stuff like that. That's not true, right? Man, May, she was wild tonight."

"She said that?"

"Yeah." He looked up at her, with his big blue eyes.

May started to laugh. "You're kidding. Wow, Hollis, she must have really been ripped, huh?"

He began to smile. "Yeah, wow. She was really out of it. Right?"

"Sounds like it to me."

"Yeah. That's what I thought, too. But, May, Dad looked funny. I think he, like, believed her. Or maybe he was just mad about her being stoned." He opened his grimy little hand and held out the two pills. "You want one?" he asked.

She took them both.

"Why don't you wash up? I'm going to call over there and tell your dad you're here, okay? He was looking for you."

"He was?"

"Why are you so surprised?"

Hollis shrugged. "I don't know. I don't see him that much."

"You miss him?"

"Naw. I mean, I know he's, like, really busy and all. He's always away on location. I don't mind. Only, I don't want them to break up, May. I don't think I could handle that, you know? I mean, I know my mom. She acts real tough and all, but I think she'd really crack up if he split, you know?"

"What about you?"

"What do you mean? You know my dad. He's always splitting. It'd be the same between us, wouldn't it?"

"Get washed. And take off that shirt, too. You stink."

May phoned King.

"Hollis is here," she said. "He hitchhiked over. You were right, he heard your little scene from Virginia Woolf. He thinks you're going to leave her, for good."

"I am," King said.

Inez was vomiting in the next room.

"No, you're not. Not until we have a talk, King. Not unless you're planning to take your son with you. You are not going to leave him holding the bag. You walk out, Inez falls apart. Hollis gets left trying to put her back together. No way."

"May, it's over. It's been over for years."

"I know, Tiger. But it's just beginning for your son. He loves you. He's been doing your dirty work for years, King. While you've been working and traveling and screwing your brains out in every hotel room in Europe, he's been at home trying to take care of her. You're not going to walk out without so much as a thank you. He hasn't even had the time to be a kid. You owe him that, you bastard. Ten years old and he's already turning into a pothead. He's like an old soul in a Boy Scout uniform. Give him a childhood before you disappear on him again."

"I'd take him with me, May, but that's no kind of life for a kid. I know. I did it."

"Talk to me. Let's just get together and talk before you pack up, okay?"

"What are we going to talk about?"

"Getting Inez back on her feet. Getting her away from drugs and into something that'll give her a sense of pride. Hollis needs you now, and if you are going to leave Inez, she's got to be in better shape. Maybe she won't ever be able to take care of him, but at least she ought to be able to take care of herself, so he can do something besides worry about her."

"What do you want me to do?" King asked.

"Negotiate. Let's have breakfast tomorrow. I'll drive Hollis back in the morning and pick you up. We'll take a meeting, okay?"

"Yeah," King said softly. "Okay. Jesus, May, you are something, you know. A piece of work."

May smiled. She could hear tap water running in the bathroom and, rising above it, Hollis's reedy voice singing in solemn imitation of Bob Dylan: ". . . how does it feel, to be without a home, like a complete unknown, like a rolling stone?. . ."

"You think I'm a piece of work. Wait till you meet your son."

NINETEEN

D etective Lionel Biggs rode the elevator up to the second floor of the West LAPD headquarters on Butler Avenue and walked into his cluttered office. He was weak in the knees and his corns were killing him. Talking to the maitre d' at Chasen's and smelling that wonderful food had also aroused his appetite. After questioning the taxi driver who'd taken Gilda home on Christmas Eve, he'd grabbed a Big Mac at McDonald's and gobbled it down in the car on the way back to headquarters.

Now he thought he was going to be sick.

He belched, then farted.

Just as he was about to shove some reports off his chair and onto the floor, Detective/First Grade Larry O'Brien called out from the office opposite Biggs's.

"Hey, Lionel, you got a call on line two. You'll never believe who it is—Devon Barnes!"

"She's just the person I want to talk to," he said, feeling his stomach groan. "Hey, meanwhile, do me a favor. Get hold of someone at Traffic. Run a check on any accidents they might have had in front of The Pearls the night Gilda Greenway was shot."

"Will do," O'Brien called out, picking up the phone.

Biggs pressed line two.

"Biggs, here."

"Detective Biggs? This is Devon Barnes. I need to talk to you."

"I bet."

"Detective Biggs, I was at The Pearls the night Gilda was shot."

"I'm one ahead of you. In fact, I've got an All Points Bulletin out on you right now."

"Oh . . ."

"Are you coming in?"

"Yes. I can't right now. I'm down the coast lunching with a friend. Can I come in around five?"

"That's awfully late, I'd make it earlier."

"I *can't*. There are some things I've got to take care of first."

"You know there's a chance you'll be spotted, then they'll bring you in anyway. That wouldn't exactly look great in the press."

"I'll take my chances. But I promise—I'll be in at five o'clock."

Biggs had no sooner hung up than O'Brien called out, "Hey, Lionel, Monahan is on the phone."

Biggs swallowed. Now he really felt sick. Great, this was just what he needed. Why couldn't the guy be in traction or something so he couldn't use the phone? Biggs couldn't have been so lucky. Instead Monahan was laid up in a hospital bed—missing one of his balls.

These particular gunshot wounds couldn't have happened to a more deserving prick.

"Biggs," Monahan shouted over the phone. He always shouted. Being ball-less, Biggs figured, probably made him want to shout louder. "Where are you on the Greenway murder? And don't tell me every little detail. Just the facts, man. Just like on "Dragnet," got it?"

"Got it," Biggs said, feeling like smashing the phone with a hammer. He repeated the main points to date: the anonymous phone call tipping them off to the murder; finding King standing over the body; questioning King; questioning Billy Buck; going to the morgue yesterday; the funeral today where Devon Barnes showed up, then suddenly fled with Billy Buck; his APB on Devon after learning from the housekeeper that she was staying at The Pearls; questioning the maitre d' and the taxi driver.

"Listen," Monahan shouted, "this is a disaster! Just what I was afraid of. Amateur night! You're undermining every inch of credibility my division has, you imbecile. The broad has been dead thirty-six hours and this is all you've got? I *knew* this would happen. If it was *me*, I'd have the thing wrapped up by now. Any *decent* detective worth his badge knows the first twenty-four hours after any homicide are the most crucial. You've had that plus more, and what've you got? *No leads!*" He screamed.

Biggs took a deep breath. Too bad they hadn't aimed higher. Like right in the mouth.

"And," Monahan continued, "you haven't even *mentioned* the autopsy report. Where the fuck is it?"

"It's coming. I'll have a preliminary any minute, then the toxicology later this afternoon."

"Christ, you've got to kick *ass* over there. You should have had it this morning!"

Biggs drummed his fingers on his desk.

"And," Monahan said, "I want to ask you how in God's name did the press find out she was holding that fucking picture? It's all over the news. Who leaked it? Who have you been blabbing to? What sort of investigation are you running there? Where's the control? Where's the—"

Biggs hung up. Screw him. Ball-less Monahan was going to be in the hospital another two weeks. He'd worry about the repercussions then.

Larry O'Brien called out, "How was the old bastard?"

"Rabid as ever."

O'Brien laughed.

A few moments later, an envelope arrived by messenger from the Los Angeles County Forensic Science Center.

Biggs tore it open and quickly scanned autopsy case #79-3064. There was, typically, a lot of medical jargon and drawings. The coroner's initial observations, which he'd made earlier that morning in Biggs's presence, were enclosed as well.

One bullet had entered the victim's body, just above the left breast. It had exited through the middle of the right shoulder blade. Because of the dimensions of the tissue damage, and several slugs they'd retrieved that had missed the body, the coroner had established that hollow-point, copper-jacketed, Remington-Peters .38 caliber bullets had been used. This would also explain the extensive tissue damage done to Gilda's back, since hollow-points ricochet on impact in equal dimensions.

Biggs smiled. The old .38 special, that's what the killer had used. The easiest gun in the United States to buy. And one of the most effective.

According to trajectory estimates, the gun was fired from a distance of approximately ten feet, and held at a level approximately one-fifth of a foot higher than the victim's position, suggesting the killer had been standing while firing, and the victim had been seated.

He continued reading.

> Because blood settles after the heart stops pumping, it has been possible to determine wounds made before and after death, and whether such wounds were fatal or not.
>
> In this case, the tissue and organ damage done by the .38 bullet would have been fatal. However, it is in the best judgment of this examiner that the gunshot wound was made *after* the victim's death. Approx. time of death: 10:30 P.M.–11:45 P.M., December 24, 1979.

Biggs bolted upright. His mouth suddenly went dry. He reread the last paragraph.

Gilda Greenway was dead *before* she was shot?

Then what the hell killed her?

He read on.

> This examiner also found two small wounds on inside right wrist, approx. 1″ above the hand. Wounds were ⅛ of an inch in diameter, and approx. 1.5″ apart. Pending toxicology report, however, no final conclusions will be made as to cause of death.

He didn't believe it. They had to wait for some goddamn blood tests?

He called the coroner's office.

"How long before those toxicology results come back on the Greenway murder?"

"You should have them late this afternoon. I'm having Alice Wong run them through a second time."

"What do you think killed her if it wasn't the gunshot?"

"Read the report."

"Goddamn it, I'm running this investigation. What was it?"

"Read the report."

At the other end of the line, the coroner hung up the telephone and resumed dictating an autopsy report he'd been working on before Biggs called. Because of the noise from other autopsies going on in Room A—electric saws, fluid suction equipment, brains banging on metal scales—the coroner had retreated to a soundproof booth in a corner of the room where he could work undisturbed.

Suddenly, he stopped dictating. He thought about the Greenway case. Yesterday, when he'd done the physical autopsy, he'd come across something. . . . Biggs had obviously seen it in his initial report. And though the coroner hadn't included his suspicions about the *real* cause of death in his report, he had thought about it overnight. He *knew* his instincts were correct.

If so, they had a bombshell on their hands.

But this coroner in particular had already experienced more than his share of controversies. He wasn't about to create another until the toxicology lab confirmed it. He had patience. He could wait.

Back in the Homicide Division, Larry O'Brien called out from across the hall to Biggs, "Hey, you wanted me to call the Traffic Division. They've been running some checks on accidents Christmas Eve. They're on line three."

Biggs picked up the phone.

"Detective Biggs? There was an accident on Christmas Eve in front of The Pearls. That's the only recent date we have on our records of anything like that."

"There *was*? Why the hell didn't you people call us right away? Don't you read the papers? There was a *murder* at The Pearls that night. This could have expedited the investigation! Jesus! What time was the accident?"

"We don't know. The call came in from a private neighborhood patrol. They spotted it around 11:00 P.M. We had a tow truck out there and took it away about 11:20. It wasn't called in because we don't report towaways."

"Eleven?"

It was getting worse. Gilda Greenway's approximate time of death was in that time range.

"Right."

"I hope you've run a registration check on the car," Biggs snapped.

"Yes, sir. It belongs to a Mrs. Inez Hollister Godwin."

TWENTY

DECEMBER 26, 1979

"Time to go," Devon said, signaling the waiter in the sunny yellow poncho for the check. "Let's do this again, Billy, under happier circumstances."

"This one's on me." Billy paid with his Gold American Express card, meticulously tearing up the carbons while Devon inspected the damage from the Carta Blancas in her compact mirror.

They were on their way to the exit when an overweight matron wearing pink sunglasses and a blouse stained with taco sauce blocked them.

"Miss Barnes . . . Miss Barnes, can I please have your autograph?" She thrust a broken eyebrow pencil at Devon, who obliged politely, smiling weakly. "I'm awfully sorry 'bout Gilda Greenway, Miss Barnes. I read in the *National Enquirer* you two was real close. That's just awful 'bout King Godwin murdering her. He did it, you know. The *Enquirer* psychic predicted it. Just as sure as John F. Kennedy's still alive on that island—"

"Buzz off," Billy said, pushing the woman aside and ushering Devon out the door. "Christ, I thought all the fucking fruitcakes were at Knott's Berry Farm," he said, starting the XKE.

Devon wiped her eyes and touched him on the shoulder. "It's all right, Billy. It will probably get worse."

They headed north on the freeway, back to Los Angeles.

"Devon," Billy said after a few minutes, "I saw you on the pay phone when you went to the john back at the restaurant. Would you mind telling me what the big mystery is all about? Who did you call?"

Devon smiled. "May Fischoff."

"And here I was, thinking you were calling someone special."

"Clever fellow. I was, actually. But I wanted to speak to May, too. Gilda was her godmother. She played backup mama to her from the day May was born. This has been very difficult for her. She's in more pain than you can imagine."

"Do you think May could have done it?"

"Do *you?*"

"Well, she was angry at Gilda. That night at Chasen's—the night she died—Gilda told me she'd turned down a television deal May had been working on for over a year. All she said was she had re-examined her priorities and there were now more important things in life than fame and money. I thought she'd gone born-again on us. When I asked her, she howled. Said she sold her soul to the devil forty years ago. All I know is May could have retired on that commission."

"To do what? Stay home and give herself a coronary, worrying that Hollis might be off somewhere in the sack with a teenybopper?"

"From where I sit, they look like one of the longer-playing couples in town."

"They are. Poor Gilda—I don't think she ever understood that. She was forever going on to May about the age difference. And May didn't know about the abortion that wrecked Gilda's life. She just thought Gilda disapproved of the age difference. She figured Gilda considered her too screwed up to make Hollis happy. But the truth is, Gilda was always convinced that Hollis would disappear one day with an eighteen-year-old, the way Ted Kearny left *her.*"

"Devon," said Billy, "how do you happen to know that?"

"Billy," said Devon, "you should take over the Carson show. You ask much better questions."

Devon turned on the radio, dial-doodling for a music station.

"Police in Los Angeles are still investigating the death of Gilda Greenway, one of Hollywood's most famous leading ladies of the 1940s. The star, whose body was found in her Beverly Hills mansion on Christmas Eve, was buried today at Forest Lawn Cemetery. Paying tribute at the service were several hundred of her friends and fans, including King Godwin, who is being questioned about his presence at Miss Greenway's home when her body was discovered.

"Police will not comment on whether the woman who called to report the alleged murder was the same caller who contacted the late actress at Chasen's where she was dining the night of her death with Billy Buck, columnist and confidant of some of the screen's most celebrated performers.

"Police do say they are planning to question Devon Barnes, the actress and political activist who made a surprising appearance today after a two-year absence from Hollywood. They are not confirming a report that a key witness in the case claims to have seen her with Miss Greenway the afternoon of the star's death. More developments on "News at Six."

Billy checked his rearview mirror, switched off the radio, and pulled the car over as calmly as he could to the shoulder of the freeway.

"I wonder what my reading public would think if they knew the 'confidant of the stars' has the surprising Miss Barnes here by his side while the rest of the world is searching frantically for her whereabouts, and I can't get a word out of you. Is that true, Devon? Did you see Gilda that day?"

"Billy, I swear I am not being coy. Yes, it's true. I was at Gilda's, but I was not alone."

His overtaxed brain made one last calculation. "You are protecting someone," he said. "The person you were with at Gilda's the night of her death is the same person you're hurrying back to now. I'm right, aren't I, Devon?"

"Please, Billy, I have to talk to King and Detective Biggs before

I can say anything else." She looked at her Cartier tank watch. "Please, it's getting late."

"Just one final question," Billy said, maneuvering the Jag back into the flow of traffic. "Where is it that I'm taking you now?"

"East L.A.," she said. "The *barrio.*"

TWENTY-ONE

1976–1977

F or Devon, the body count just kept adding up.
  She was visiting a children's hospital in Hanoi when
she found out, several weeks late, that Patrick Wainwright
had stuck a 12-gauge shotgun in his mouth and blown his brains out.
Devon had been feeling the strain that day, had been exhausted and
depressed by the heat and destruction she saw all around her.

She had traveled to Southeast Asia many times in the seven years
since she'd left the United States with Michel. She'd done two films
for him—*Amerique* and *The Innocence.*

In *Amerique,* a sci-fi parable on American involvement in the
Vietnam war, she played a twenty-first-century warrior-courtesan
named Amerique, who vaulted about looking like an earless *Playboy*
bunny decked out in brass.

As a symbol of America, the corrupt aggressor, she'd gotten to
rape five of her six co-stars, including Marianne Veranne and Claudia

Leone, two of Michel's golden oldies. And had been raped by the sixth, a 250-pound British dirigible with terminal halitosis and blubber lips whose arch delivery made Charles Laughton look butch.

The Innocence was a sequel to Michel's Academy Award winner, *The Children.* Devon narrated the documentary and appeared in it as one of a team of observers visiting Hanoi during the American bombing of Cambodia.

Now she was sitting by the bed of a beautiful little girl without legs. She was holding the child's hand and nodding as the doctor, a child herself despite the white hospital coat she wore over black peasant pajamas, tried in halting English to explain what had happened to the girl and her family.

Devon wasn't really listening. She was thinking, I want to take this child with me. Out of here. I want to make it up to her, replace the family she lost, the parents who thought they could change the world and were killed trying.

It suddenly occurred to her that she was thinking and feeling angry at her own parents. She still hadn't forgiven them for leaving her. She was tired and wanted to make peace with them, too. She was thirty-six years old. She wanted children of her own.

Just then a pretty British journalist—the latest member of Michel's ever-changing cast of paramours—entered the ward. Seeing her, Devon realized that she would never have children with Michel. He couldn't tolerate the competition. He was the bright and mischievous little boy whose transgressions she was supposed to endure, understand, and love. She had become his wise and forgiving mother.

And she was sick of the role.

She was sick, too, of being typecast in France as the fresh-faced symbol of America's anti-war movement. Cartoons showed her as a cowgirl Joan of Arc. Michel's *Jeanne des Jeans*—Joan of the Blue Jeans. They called her *la belle Americaine,* the antithesis of "the ugly American."

"Did you know Wainwright personally?" Sheila Farraday, the British journalist, asked Devon in her grating, perky accent. They had walked back to Devon's hotel and were sitting at the bar, drinking whiskey neat. Devon wore khaki army fatigues, having long ago abandoned her wardrobe from Giorgio of Beverly Hills. Sheila had on a crisp, perfectly tailored linen dress and looked more like a British Airways flight attendant than a serious journalist.

"I'm sorry, I didn't consider the possibility you might have known him. I just thought it was news from Hollywood you might not have heard."

"What did the wire say about Patrick?" Devon asked quietly.

"He committed suicide. Bloody mess, I bet. I expect it had something to do with his wife's death. Mmm, yes. I'd almost bet on it. Apparently he was quite devoted to her. Married to her for eons, though she was ill most of the time."

"His wife?" Devon asked dully. "When did she die?"

"Half a year ago, at least. Oh, God, there's Michel." She brightened considerably. "I *am* sorry, Devon."

Michel waved and approached the table. He kissed Devon's cheek. "*Ça va,*" he said, looking at Sheila Farraday, then back at Devon.

"I was just telling Devon about Patrick Wainwright."

"Ah, then you have heard?" Michel said, kneeling beside her. "I wanted to tell you. It is very sad, no? And very strange. One does not think of a man like that to crumble. To kill himself."

"It has a rather ironic edge, I think," Sheila interrupted. "I mean, he was the archetypal American, wasn't he? Pat Upright, they called him, didn't they? And now Saigon has fallen. America has lost the war. The Khymer Rouge are invading and Patrick Wainwright commits suicide." She smiled brightly at them. "The spirit of America, you see? That incessant irony."

Devon threw her drink in Sheila Farraday's face.

The journalist shrieked.

"Devon! Are you mad? The girl was merely making an observation." Michel began wiping Sheila's dress with his handkerchief.

Devon left the two of them and went back to the suite she shared with Michel. She tried to phone Gilda but couldn't get through to Bangkok, much less to Hollywood. It didn't take her long to pack and go through Michel's pockets and drawers. She came up with a great deal of cash, with which she was able to cut through every inch of red tape that might otherwise have kept her in Hanoi for hours or days.

When she arrived in Paris seventeen hours later, a dozen messages from May were waiting for her. Some of the messages were a month old. The more recent ones were from London.

May had called the last two times from Paris, from the elegant little L'hotel, not even a ten-minute walk away from Michel's apartment on rue de la Seine. Without bothering to phone, and despite the lateness of the hour, Devon hurried—ran like a track star—to May's hotel and called upstairs to tell her friend she was waiting in the shoe box lobby. May's shrieks of joy over the house phone were still echoing in Devon's ear when May stepped off the elevator in a floor-length black mink, her blonde hair disheveled, her round face half-hidden behind huge, dark Porsche glasses.

"My God, Devon, they told me this is the hotel where Oscar Wilde died. Don't believe it. He's still in my room."

They flew into each other's arms and bawled like babies.

"May, you haven't changed a bit!"

"How rude. And look at you. Still good enough to eat. You'll tell me who's been getting *that* priviledge as soon as we find a drink. God, girl, I was beginning to think you'd disappeared into the rice paddies forever. But your timing is still impeccable. I'm leaving Paris tomorrow. I've had it with prehistoric plumbing. I want to hear all about you and Michel, but I get to talk first. I have the hugest favor to ask."

"Anything, May, anything," Devon said, hugging her oldest friend and crying with the relief of seeing her face in the City of Light.

She took May to Brasserie Lipp on the Boulevard Saint-Germain, ordered two scorpions, and plowed right in. "Before anything else, tell me about Gilda."

"Before anything else, isn't that Yves Montand under the mirror? My God, he's the only man in France I'd let feel me up. At the moment. It's still early. Oh, yes. Gilda. She's in rough shape, Devon. I've never seen her like this."

And she hadn't.

May remembered what Gilda had looked like just before she left for Europe. Sunken eyes, pallid complexion.

Mrs. Denby, in a rare moment of concern, had confided, "She's not herself. Last night I found her wandering the grounds, almost sleepwalking. Night before that I heard her playing the piano in the ballroom at 3:00 A.M.—with all the lights out. She doesn't even know *how* to play the piano. She's totally ignoring the animals. Won't go near them. They're *her* creatures and she won't touch them."

May repeated it to Devon.

"How awful."

"Damn Patrick," said May. "He had Gilda wrapped around his pinkie finger. Then he does this. And so unexpectedly. He'd been depressed about Marie, which was natural enough, but this time he wouldn't snap out of it. Got worse and worse. He spent the weekend at The Pearls with Gilda. They had a very loving, romantic weekend. Then he drove up to the ranch and killed himself."

"No wonder she's taking it so hard. Who's with her? Who's taking care of her?"

"Well, old Dill-face Denby, of course. Mrs. Danvers. But Inez kind of stepped into the breach as well. She even went to A.A. and gave up drinking. She's back on the sauce now—with due cause, I'm afraid —but nothing like before. But Devon, would you believe it? It was Inez who came up with the solution."

"Solution to what?"

"Getting Gilda out of her depression before she turns into a Thorazine special. Back to work. Something to bring her back alive."

"But is there any work for her?"

"Not really. And if things keep going the way they've been, she won't be getting any, either. Aside from everything else, some moron ran a full-page ad in the trades a couple of months ago, saying, 'HAPPY FIFTIETH BIRTHDAY, GILDA!' "

"Fifty? Is she really?"

"Fifty-four, actually, but she stopped counting years ago."

"I haven't kept up."

"Well, you haven't missed any good news either. There are days when she looks seventy. The fan who ran the birthday greeting didn't know he was running an obituary. But that's the effect this fucking thing has had. I had drummed up a few decent scripts for her the past few years. Nothing great, but dignified. We were even looking at a love story between a widow and a young boy, which Gilda could play the hell out of. The script needed work, but the part was close to perfect."

"What happened?"

"The day after the trades hit, with that Happy Birthday shit, the producers called back the script. It was written for a thirty-nine-year-old, they argued, forty tops. Didn't matter that Gilda could have played years younger than that. On good days, with the right makeup, she still looked better than Jacqueline Bisset. But all of a sudden, she was Mrs. Methuselah and box-office poison."

May polished off her scorpion.

"Baby, you would not believe the shit they're sending me now for her. Dyke prison matrons, ax-murdering grandmothers, zombies from outer space who attack the city of Pittsburgh."

Devon ordered another round in French while May kept on talking.

"And the worst thing," she sighed, "is she may have to actually take one of these godawful things. I think she needs the money. Patrick didn't leave her a penny. Not that he had one. Pissed it all away at Santa Anita. He couldn't resist the track. And Gilda has no earthly idea what running that fucking San Simeon ripoff she calls home has been costing her all these years. I've begged her to let me handle her finances instead of the German Nazi accountant she's had since the old MGM days, but forget it. So now I've got a 'Love Boat' contract on my desk, and a $350,000 deal for her to star in a piece of trash called *Motorcycle Mama.* I'm actually mulling it over."

May shook her head. "Add to that Patrick's suicide, about a quart of tequila a day since he died, and her natural insecurity about acting —the woman actually thinks she got by all those years on looks alone, are you ready?—and now you begin to get the picture."

"Oh, Lord, how awful. But you said Inez has come up with the solution?"

"Bless her self-serving little heart. No, really, I shouldn't be cruel. God knows, she got a swift kick in the teeth for her efforts. I owe her. Gilda owes her, too—not that Gilda would see it at the moment." May shrugged. "It's simple, really. Inez suggested we commission our own screenplay, get one tailor-made for Gilda."

"Well, of course," Devon said.

"But here's the rub. King and I have talked it over and come up with a plan. The only way to guarantee a hit is if Gilda co-stars—with King, and *you!* Can you imagine the publicity? It'll be the event of the year. Never mind the plot. Gilda loves you. She loves King, too. If it was the life story of the Andrews Sisters, she'd ask King to play Maxine. Now the only question is—are you ready to go back to work?"

Devon ignored the question. "How is King?" she asked. "I saw him a few years back. He and Michel had one of their infamous nights on the town that ended two weeks later in Mexico."

"Actually, he's terrific. He's turned out to be a wonderful father to Hollis and a wonderful friend to me. Hollis is living with me now, did you know that?"

"No. Well, lucky him. He couldn't have picked a nicer god-mother. How old is he now? Must be about—"

"Eighteen. Six-two, about one-fifty, shoulders out to here, and a beautiful head of hair. Don't get me started on Hollis or we'll be here all night. Oh, God, have I got *lots* to tell you. But business before pleasure. King's trying to talk Gilda into doing the picture. He's already committed, sight unseen, script unwritten. Soon as the Western he's doing with Howie Sundance is finished . . . which is about, let's see, three months, max."

"He's doing it for Gilda?"

"Hey, we're all doing it for Gilda. But, listen, we *need* you. You and King are really the only ones who can talk her into it. Right now she's staring mortality in the face. Patrick's suicide has done that. She thinks she's getting old, worn out. A has-been. A dusty memory. She isn't going to convince easily. She's easy to piss off, and she doesn't trust anybody.

"Devon, you want to make a movie? You want to act again? No offense, but no one in the world could run around in that set of brass knockers you wore in *Amerique* and still make people cry, kiddo. For that, my unending admiration. Never mind that you did it for peanuts and I didn't even get a shell."

"You're not mad at me, are you, darling? I did that little camp epic for love. It was my dowry."

"Some dowry. I heard the pattern was registered at Bullocks Peking. No, Dev. I don't know what it would take to make me angry at you." She shook her head and reached across the table to take Devon's hands. "I've missed you so much. Say you'll do the movie. We'll be together again, all of us."

"Oh, May, if you only knew how good that sounds to me. How

often I've thought about going back, working in America again. But what's it like there now? Really. It's hard to tell at this distance. Last I heard, the tabloids were calling me Ho Chi Minh's daughter."

"So what? What do you care? You're a woman of conviction and commitment. A real chip off the old block. I think it's wonderful. And wildly brave. Your father would have been proud of you."

"My father? May, when you said 'chip off the old block' I thought you meant Uncle Ho."

"Him, too, then. Devon, you've been to Hanoi. How can you be afraid of Hollywood?"

Devon laughed her violent Betty Hutton laugh.

"Listen to that, would you?" May said, grinning goofily. "You know how long I've waited to hear that ridiculous laugh of yours? Devon, think of it. The comeback movie of the century, starring three Hollywood greats who, for some unfathomable reason, have never acted together before. The press'll eat it up. Maybe there's a book in it. Who knows?"

"This is either the best or the worst offer I've had in years—and I don't know which. I have to think it over."

"No problem. You have until three o'clock tomorrow. And I hate to pressure you, kiddo, but you're on my shopping list—without you, there's no movie. No movie, no Gilda. Hey, no pressure, Devon." May smiled sadly. "I'm sorry. I know I'm being a bitch. But I've got a reputation to keep up. I really don't know any other way to blast her out of her rut. She needs help. She's always been there for us. And anyway, wouldn't it be fun? All of us, working together on one project."

"The Pearls Girl and her Four Fans," Devon said. "Together again, folks—as you've always loved them."

"Oh, God, that picture of us. What a memory you have. Wait, I almost forgot to tell you—talk about the best and the worst—Avery Calder's agreed to do the screenplay. I stopped in London to see him. He's absolutely thrilled at the prospect. He's been terribly ill. Had a lung removed. He's quit smoking, that's something. But he's drinking harder than ever and still popping pills. He says he's too old to mend his ways now. He's convinced he's got breast cancer. I said, 'That's very strange isn't it—breast cancer in a man?' He says, 'Baby, strange things been happenin' to me all my life.' "

They roared.

"But he can still write like a bitch. Come aboard, Devon. Just imagine, you, King, Gilda, screenplay by Avery . . . If I can't get us a deal with that package, I might as well quit this fucking rat race and open a doughnut shop."

"What about Inez? You said the *four* of us, didn't you?"

May bit a cuticle. "Devon, I don't know what I'm going to do. You've heard the best, now here's the worst. This whole damned thing was Inez's creative brainstorm. And she was so excited about it. Andy Hardy time, I swear. 'Hey, kids, let's all get together and make a movie, right here in my garage.' But Gilda's too scared right now. She doesn't want to take any chances. She wants Avery or nothing. And it makes sense, of course. Who's going to bankroll a movie by Inez Godwin? I mean, who is *she?* King's wife. Period. Oh, yeah, also Hollywood's 'hippest' hostess. Swell, right? She passes out cocaine on Lalique etched glass, honest to God, with gold straws. She stashes it in Fabergé eggs. Well, one egg, anyway. Very elegant. And don't think half the hotshots with whom we've got to cut our deal don't adore Inez's generosity. They do. But are they going to bank on it?"

"Can't she work with Avery?"

"He's never collaborated on anything in his life. I hinted at it when I saw him. Not even if it was Mankiewicz, and he *loved* Mankiewicz. I didn't dare mention Inez in the same breath."

"What a fix. It's rotten, isn't it?"

"Please, I can't think about it without getting sick. I have to come up with something for her. Not just because I love her, which, God knows why, I do. But because, get this—no Inez, no King."

"You're kidding."

"I wish I were. Me and my big mouth. I kept telling him he'd be a real prick if he split before she was on her feet. Before she'd accomplished something on her own. Well, this was going to be it. Her big chance. His passport to freedom. No Inez, no King. No Avery, no Gilda. No you, no nothing."

Devon looked out at the quiet, dark street. The sky had changed from indigo to pink. A young couple strolled by hand in hand, oblivious to the early-morning hour. The café was half empty. Even the Parisians had to go to work in the morning.

An aproned waiter appeared at their table.

"I guess we'd better go," Devon said. "With all the time changes, I don't even know what day it is. *L'addition, s'il vous plaît,*" she told the waiter.

"It is already paid, Mademoiselle Barnes," the man said in French. "The children, there. From America. They have insisted to pay. They ask me to say they adore you."

Devon turned. A few tables away, several young Americans, dressed in sweatshirts and jeans, were whispering and smiling at her. She lifted her glass to them and called, "Thank you."

A beautiful young girl stood up and called out, "Devon, we love you! When are you coming home?"

May raised an eyebrow. "I'm asking the same thing."

Behind the carved hunter-green doors of the apartment on rue de la Seine, Devon could hear the insistent ringing of the telephone. She rummaged in her bag for her key, unlocked the door, and automatically rushed toward the angry sound. But she didn't pick up the receiver. The big apartment was stuffy. She went to the windows and opened them to let in some air. She was in the bedroom, opening the French doors, when the ringing finally stopped.

She thought, How do I know it's Michel? It could have been May. Or Adele, Michel's assistant. Or Perry L'eaise, of *Cahier du Cinema.*

Maybe it was Gilda . . .

But fifteen minutes later, the phone rang again.

She ignored it.

And fifteen minutes after that, when it rang again, she knew it was Michel, because that was what he did after their long-distance arguments. He urged the operator to keep trying, willed the phone to keep ringing, until Devon either took it off the hook or answered it, which meant she forgave him.

Devon paced, wondering what had happened to the fury she felt at Michel when she left Hanoi. She wondered why she was simultaneously feeling guilty and ignoring the phone.

Empathy? How absurd. Why in the hell should she feel sorry for Michel, who had cheated on her, who had fucked the British Barbie doll who talked like Julie Andrews. Why wasn't she feeling wounded? Where was her self-respect, her dignity? Where was her rage?

She paced from room to room, thinking of how they had made love. How they had sat reading Janet Flanner and the *Herald-Tribune*, in separate chairs with their feet up on the same stool. Michel in the tortoiseshell glasses he never wore in public, both of them sipping his favorite Petrus at $300 a bottle as if it were Coca-Cola.

She remembered the evening her friend Martine Toulon, a journalist from *Elle*, had called Michel's attitude about women prehistoric. He had flailed his arms and said to Devon, "You see how I love you, to put up with such disrespect from your friends?" Then he'd stormed into the bedroom only to appear ten minutes later, ready to take them both to dinner—naked, except for the mink stole wrapped around his waist, a pair of shabby socks and his black ankle boots.

In the salon, she thought of how she had found a pair of lace panties she had never seen before, stuffed between the sofa cushions. In the bedroom, she thought of the evening his friend Tonio had said that without Devon, *Amerique* would have been a soulless cartoon, and Michel had seduced Tonio's girl friend, on their bed, while Tonio and Devon played backgammon next door.

And in the kitchen, at the beautiful fruitwood table where she'd been arranging white peonies in a crystal bowl, she remembered him telling her, "I will never leave you, you know that, Devon. I cannot. I am the coward, who must always be the victim of women. I will drive you away and suffer. But I will never leave you."

She went into the bathroom, washed her face, and inspected the image staring back at her in the mirror. She had stood here, just like this, looking in the same mirror, the night King showed up.

"I guess I was wrong," King said, watching her from the bedroom door. "I thought the little bastard would make you miserable. But you look more radiant than ever. You must be happy."

She'd opened her mouth to reply. Would she really have confessed he hadn't been wrong? That now she understood what he'd tried to tell her about Michel? That now she believed he had been looking out for her?

Michel had appeared behind King and clapped his shoulder. "Let's go, babee. See if Paris remembers you, eh?"

And King had said, looking at Devon, "I came all the way to find out."

The telephone rang again. Devon went into the bedroom and answered it.

"Where have you been?" Michel shouted. "I have been calling for hours! You leave without a word. You don't even tell Adele you have returned."

"I saw May Fischoff this evening, Michel. She's in Paris. There's a movie she wants me to do. I'm going back to America."

"I will not discuss this. We cannot discuss this on a telephone."

"All right, then. When will you be back?"

"I must stay for a week here, then I go to Manila for two weeks."

"And after that?"

"I don't know! There are things I must do! I am making a film. I have people here, a crew, the press, people to whom I cannot just say, 'Goodbye, *mes amis,* I have a problem with a girl.' "

" 'Problem with a girl?' I've been your lover for the last seven years!"

"What is it you want? You want to destroy my work? You want me to drop everything and fly halfway across the world, to beg you to stay?"

"No. I need some time alone before I go home. This will work out fine."

"Ah, *merde!* You are impossible. You know that girl meant nothing to me. Nothing! You know I cannot be other than I am. What do you want?"

"To make peace with you and then leave."

"Marry me," he shouted. "There, I have said it. Okay, now you will stop this nonsense. You are making me crazy. How can I work like this? You must behave yourself now."

"I'm sorry, darling."

"Devon, you will wait for me? I will return as quickly as possible. I love you. I know what is happening to us. Another woman would have left. All I ask is that you wait until I return." His tone had changed, cautious instead of cocky and ranting.

"I will, Michel. I love you, too. Can we be friends, do you think? Will that be too difficult?"

"Ah, Devon, I am more your friend than you know. I will see you soon. I look forward to it—with fear and hope."

*   *   *

It was Michel who devised the solution for pacifying Inez. Early in 1977, he returned to Paris as he had promised, treating Devon with almost unbearable love and caring.

It was clear to him now that she was leaving. He'd given up trying to talk her out of it.

For a time, they'd crept about the apartment with their heads lowered and their eyes either teary or averted. The knowledge that their time together was nearly up had made the days they had left painfully precious.

The wine was bad, the flowers were dying. In the apartment where there had once been love and passion, they now endured lingering silences.

Then May called from Los Angeles to say she was going crazy.

"Avery has come up with a terrific idea for the screenplay, a cross between *Sunset Boulevard* and *The Barefoot Contessa*—a classic *film noir* of Hollywood. He's thinking of calling it *Cobras.* King loves the idea and thinks it'll work. Even Gilda likes it. Get this, Devon. She actually went out to dinner with Billy Buck last night."

"She's always loved Billy," Devon said. "What's so amazing about her having dinner with him?"

"Devon, the woman has dined on nothing but vodka and tranquilizers since Patrick shot his brains out. So everything was going along just fine," May said, "and then Hollis comes home a little while ago with a bloody nose and a cut over one eye. He was visiting Inez and she'd been drinking and drugging again. She'd thrown a raging tantrum and gone after Hollis with an andiron, all because Hollis tried to defend me."

"Defend you about what? What are you talking about?"

"She called me every name in the book," May continued, "from cradle-robbing cunt to poisonous traitor, because I was the one who asked Avery if he'd write the script. Never mind that it was Gilda's idea. It gets better, though. Not only did Hollis have to have five stitches over his left eye, she also tried to beat up her new boyfriend. I feel kind of responsible for that match made in hell. Mitch is a real hustler. I should know—he was entertaining me for a while until Hollis moved in. He's only three or four years older than Hollis and they used to do drugs together. I don't know whether he got Inez back on drugs or whether she's using him as a connection. Anyway, Inez tried to hit Mitch and he broke her arm."

"May, what are you going to do? This sounds awful!"

"I'm fresh out of inspiration. All I know is that if we don't find something productive and worthwhile for Inez to do, to write, or host, *Cobras* is history. And so is Gilda. Thanks for listening, Devon. I figured you were the only one I could trust with this horror story."

"What is it?" Michel asked.

Devon repeated May's story.

"But they are mad. Truly. Here is the true drama, more in the preparation and strife of the principals than in the script itself. This is the story I would want to tell. Compared to the truth, Avery's *Cobras* will be but the play within the play. You see, this is the story Inez should write!"

She called May back an hour later.

"A book about making the movie?"

"You said yourself it was a great story," Devon reminded her. "You said it would make a terrific book. Look at the ingredients, May. Gilda's first movie in how many years? Avery's first original screenplay. *Barracks Street Blues* and the other scripts he wrote in the past were all adaptations. That doesn't count. Except that this one reunited King and Avery, another first."

"And then, there's you," May said, warming to the notion. "Shit, Dev. Your return to America after seven years of self-exile. Your first movie with King. And with Gilda, who discovered you both."

"And then there's the movie itself—a Hollywood exposé Avery's thinking of calling *Cobras*. I can only think of a few thousand people who'd love to know where he got his dirt and who the characters really are—"

"Plus," said May, "if Inez writes it, I bet I can get some mileage out of that old clipping you mentioned. The one taken at my sweet sixteen. Ooh, Devon Barnes, this one I can sell, baby, like popsicles in the Mojave. This one cuts two ways—the book hypes the movie, the movie sells the book."

"May," Devon said cautiously, "what about Inez? Is she in shape to tackle a book?"

"It's now or never, isn't it? *If* I can get her a deal—and I'm sure

I can. Fee, fie, foe, fum, I smell six figures, and a step deal Astaire could dance to. She'll do it. She'll have to, or shut up about getting fucked out of fame and fortune by Gilda and me and the rest of the cruel, cruel world. This is for little Inez. Time to get off the pot—in more ways than one. And off the coke, pills, and booze, too."

"May, what if she really can't? What if, after all this time, she just doesn't have what it takes?"

"Who cares? As long as she says yes. As long as she'll give it a shot. Then, if she needs help, we'll get her a ghost. But first things first."

"I hate to be the voice of doom," Devon said, "but what if Gilda gets skittish about it? Decides she doesn't like the idea?"

May was silent for a moment. "We'll *make* her like it."

"How can you be so sure?"

"Am I building a twenty-room house in Topanga Canyon on a McDonald's franchise or because I'm the best fucking deal maker in the industry?"

"May, I'm a stubborn Texan and I don't know."

"Devon, I'm a fearless Jew and I don't care. Just get your butt back here where it belongs. I'll do the negotiating."

Over dinner at Ma Maison, May told King she *knew* Devon was going to do it, though she hadn't signed anything yet. She'd get Devon to phone Gilda from Paris, but she wanted King to go to The Pearls and lay the groundwork.

"She won't be easy, but give her a song and dance she can't refuse. You write the score and I'll get Devon to write the lyrics. You've got to make her think we've finally found a script worthy of her. And a package deal with box office written all over it."

The next day, King realized how right May had been. Gilda wasn't easy. He drove up to The Pearls for lunch, which she served under a canopied pavilion on the grounds, and found her adamantly opposed to the idea.

"Why should I?" Gilda asked over eggs benedict. "After what I've been through lately? And after what that imbecile did to me in the trades? Fifty? Christ! No fucking way. Screw 'em, as Patrick would have said. No, listen, baby, it was a sweet idea, but who needs it?"

"Gilda, I'm not saying you need it. But what have you got to lose?

The script will be a vehicle just for you. You'll have me, Devon, all of us around you. Talk about quality control."

Gilda shook her head, then took a healthy drink of her third bloody mary. "No. Absolutely not. Garbo had the right idea. She left the whole fucking lot of them at just the magic moment. Became a legend to be immortalized till Christ returns. Well, baby, perhaps I didn't see the magic moment in my own life at the right time, but that doesn't mean I don't see it now."

The next day, May went out to Topanga Canyon, where she was overseeing the construction of her first major real-estate purchase: a twenty-room adobe mansion on four acres of carpetlike grounds, with an enormous flagstone terrace, Olympic-size pool, and landscaping. It was costing her $3 million, plus another million for the interiors, but for her and Hollis it was worth it.

Pleased with the way things were going, she picked up the phone in her Rolls and dialed Devon in Paris as she headed back to the office.

It took Devon two weeks of transatlantic calls to The Pearls to finally persuade Gilda to do *Cobras.* On the last call, Devon had already heard every argument Gilda could make. Still, she persisted. Gilda's resistance was as worn as her patience.

"Baby, you know I love you," she said, "but there's no reason for me to make a comeback."

"Yes, there is!" Devon finally shouted in exasperation. "You're an actress!"

"Without a major movie in years."

"That's what Swanson said until *Sunset Boulevard!*"

Two weeks later, May called to give Devon and Michel an update. "I've got two hardcover houses drooling. I think we'll take it to auction, or maybe go for a combined hard and softcover deal."

"And Gilda liked the idea?"

"Well, I wouldn't go that far. Let's just say she won't make waves. She's got enough to worry about right now."

"She's so obsessive about privacy. I was sure she'd say no."

"She did, to the first suggestion I made—that Inez write *Portrait in Pearls: The True Story of Gilda Greenway.*"

"Oh, God," Devon said. "You didn't!"

"She didn't like the notion of Inez ghostwriting the autobiography of Gilda Greenway any better. I let her say no to three or four more brainstorms before I sprang *Cobras: The Making of a Movie* on her. Cut to the clinch—she'd used up her vetos. So, when are you coming back? Avery's flying in from London tomorrow. The first draft's done."

"I'm not ready yet."

"What're you going to do," May asked, "show up the day we start shooting?"

"Yes," Devon said.

Devon's fragile relationship with Michel grew hardy again in the months before she left. It was late summer of 1977 in Paris and they settled into a cease-fire of domestic coziness. They strolled through the chestnut trees with their low-slung branches like Courrèges pants, window-shopped on the rue de la Paix, listened to Blossom Dearie records, ate Alabama soul food at Chez Haines.

They were closer than ever, but never mentioned love.

One evening Devon sipped coffee and steamed milk, while Michel absentmindedly swirled the brandy in his snifter. A fire crackled in the hearth.

Michel glanced at her over the rim of his reading glasses. "How is the script?" he asked. "Has Avery created a masterpiece? A proper setting for such an illustrious cast?"

Devon looked up from the bound pages and smiled at him. "Well, it's classic Avery, anyway. Lust, greed, incest, homosexuality, betrayal, and puttin' on airs. And that sort of inbred 'family passion' stuff he does so well."

"And has he kept it as May said—you will play Gilda's sister?" She nodded. "Can you do that? Can you make that believable? You are . . . what? Eighteen years younger than she."

"Yes," Devon said. "The way Avery's written it, it's possible. And King's the stranger, the hustler Gilda falls in love with. It's sort of *Streetcar Named Desire Goes to Bel Air.* King's part steals the movie. Avery's written him in as irresistible again."

"He is in love with you," Michel said.

"Well, no. Not in love, exactly. No, it's all much steamier. Why are you smiling like that?"

Michel shrugged. "Go on, tell me."

"Well, he's not the type to fall in love—the way Avery's done it. Or admit it to himself, anyway. He just uses me to get at her. I mean, deep down, he probably does love me, but—"

"I was speaking of King," Michel said, fascinated suddenly by the amber brandy in his glass. "The *real* King and the real *you.* He is in love with you. Tell me, Devon, did you really not know this?"

She stared at him, waiting for him to smile again or give some evidence that he was teasing her. He looked up from the swirling brandy and saw her watching him, curious.

"You did not know?" he said. "I'm sorry. You look stricken. I thought you would be pleased."

"No."

"No, you are not pleased? No, you are not stricken? No, you think I have not told you the truth?"

"I think you're wrong. I think you're imagining it."

"Devon, I tell you why I am saying this aloud to you. Because I want what you have offered me. I want for us to be friends, to continue to love. I have thought about withholding this. But I love you. So I am giving to you now the most sincere gift of friendship I have to offer."

"Oh, Michel, I think you're mistaken."

"No, *he* told me this. He told me in Mexico that he was in love with you. And I didn't doubt him. I wished that you were with us there. King has found an extraordinary hiding place, near the Yucatán. It is a place much like him. It seems wild and dangerous, but not a breeze stirs that is not scented with peace. I said, 'Devon would adore this place.' And he told me his feelings about you. From the first moment he set eyes on you to the last moment, here, in this apartment. He believed you were content at last. He thought you were happy with me." Michel shrugged. Then he smiled again. "You were, weren't you, Devon? For a time? Everything changes. A woman cannot be happy in the dress she wore at her confirmation. We outgrow everything. This is life. And the most important thing in life is peace of mind. I hope you find yours."

TWENTY-TWO

AUTUMN 1977

"Welcome home, darling," May squealed, smothering Devon with a hug. "You're as good as your word, kiddo. They ———— started shooting last week. Your first scene is tomorrow."

Still holding Devon's hands, May stepped back and scrutinized her Ungaro suit admiringly. *"Très chic.* On you, even jet lag looks good. God, I can't believe you're really here. I thought you'd never make it."

The automatic doors of the Pan Am terminal building at LAX opened. A tall, tan young man with sun-bleached blond hair and a ruggedly boyish face stepped into the baggage-claim area. He was wearing faded jeans and motorcycle boots and a denim shirt buttoned to the throat. Devon's heart leapt. He looked so like King, especially the way he moved. He had broad shoulders, long, loping legs, and dark-rimmed eyes even bluer than King's. Eyes that searched the area, then lit with pleasure as he saw Devon looking at him. Embarrassed, she turned away.

"Devon!"

The tall, handsome boy walked over, hugged her, and planted an enthusiastic wet kiss on her mouth. He tasted like a Snicker's bar. "Wow! You look like a million bucks. Look at her. Doesn't she look hot, May?"

"Hollis!" Devon gasped.

May grinned and squeezed his arm affectionately. "Raised him from a seedling," she said.

A liveried chauffeur approached them. "Here, give me your claim check, Devon," Hollis said. "We'll get your stuff. Why don't you go on to the car. Mom's dying to see you."

"Inez? Inez is here?"

"Some surprise." May shook her head at Hollis.

"Go ahead," he said, "we're double-parked. If you have to move the car, just don't let Mitch drive, okay? He's whacked."

"I know you!" A man in a golf cap, orange slacks, and a short-sleeved blue shirt pointed at Devon, then snapped his fingers. "You're, you're, what's-her-name?"

"Anita Bryant," May said, taking Devon's arm and leading her away. "No autographs, puh-*leeze.*"

They hurried to the automatic doors.

"No, she ain't!" the man hollered after them. "She's the other one!"

Outside, a porter glanced at her, turned away, did a double-take. "Emma Blandish, right?" he said.

"No," said May, pulling Devon toward the curb. "She's the other one."

"Hey, Devon!" A bearded man in overalls raised two fingers in the air. "Peace, baby."

"Welcome home," May said, squeezing her arm again. "Are you crying?"

Devon tried to blink away the tears. "No," she said, fishing a handful of tissues from her purse and handing a couple to May, "but you are."

A black Cadillac limousine with smoked-glass windows was waiting at the curb. The rear door swung open.

"Get in here!" a deep and raspy voice commanded.

"Inez?" Devon ducked down and peered inside.

A dark-haired boy grinned up at her. "Mitch Misyak," he said, extending his hand. Abruptly, a pale claw clamped his shoulder and he tumbled back against the seat.

Huddled in the far corner of the velvet upholstered back seat, Inez Godwin was almost entirely hidden under a huge striped Gucci silk scarf and an immense pair of dark glasses. Her determined little chin poked out, white and delicate, above the dark mink collar of her jacket.

"Jesus H. Christ, get in already. Gimme a kiss, will ya?"

Devon stepped over the dark-haired boy's legs and into the limousine. "What a wonderful surprise," she said, embracing Inez.

"Look at you." Inez ran an icy hand along Devon's cheek. "Who says crime does not pay? I was expecting a wild-eyed radical in a quilted Mao jacket, instead I get a fashion plate from French *Vogue*. I'd sure like to see the portrait in your attic."

May joined them, taking up a considerable amount of room. "Doesn't she look great?"

"Clean living," Inez said. She took off her glasses. "Might as well get it over with." She sucked in her cheeks and fluttered her eyelids and mugged for Devon. "Go on. Lie. Like they all do. Say, 'Inez, you look mahvalous.' " Her hands were shaking.

"You've lost weight," said Devon, shocked at how gaunt Inez's face had become.

May turned to Inez and shrugged. "She fucked up. That's what she was supposed to say to *me.*"

"I'm drying out," Inez explained in her husky, cracked voice. "Haven't had a drink in nearly two weeks now. Haven't done a line of coke since—" She turned to Mitch. "When?"

"Couple of days."

"Oh, don't be a fool," Inez snapped. "Days, my ass. It must be a week, at least." She turned back to Devon. "I'm in training. Has May told you about the book I'm doing? Brilliant idea, if I do say so myself. You know I was supposed to write this fucking movie. It was all my idea to begin with. Then Gilda fucked me over but good, baby. We are talking of a royal screwing unparalleled since the Duke of Windsor slipped it to Wally Simpson."

"Who?" Mitch laughed.

"Forget it, Mitch," Inez said. "But Mitch knows. He was with me when I used to drive over there every morning, to The Pearls, and pry the bottle out of her hand. I bathed her, I washed her hair. Mrs. Denby couldn't get near her. She wouldn't let anyone near her but me. Am I telling the truth, May, or what?"

"It's true. She knows, Inez. I told her."

"It must have been awful for her. And for you."

"I'll tell you something, Devon. It was. She walked around all day in a filthy nightgown, never combed her hair, never washed. She was drunk from morning to night. Puked up on herself and didn't even notice it. And where were you, when Gilda needed you, huh? You and King and Avery? There wasn't one of you within shouting distance, baby, that's where."

"Inez," May cautioned.

Inez threw her a sidelong glance. "What?" she said. "Am I being rude? Impolite? What? I beat the bushes in this fucking town for friends and none of you crawled out."

"Mitch, why don't you see what happened to Hollis and Tommy, will you? See if you can give them a hand."

"Hey, May," Mitch said softly, grinning, "my days of playing fetch and roll over for you are finished, or haven't you noticed?"

"Darling, dogs are always dogs. They just find new fleas," said Inez. "Let's get out of here. I'm freezing my ass off."

"Thanks a heap, Inez," he said disgustedly, and left them.

"I'm sorry, Devon. It's just this business with Gilda. It's worn me down. I mean, it wasn't enough for her, screwing me out of writing the movie. The whole thing was my idea to begin with. But okay, I swallowed my pride. I came back to her with this absolutely brilliant goddamn book idea. I mean, ask May if five different publishers weren't dying to publish my book. And after all I'd done for Gilda, and after knifing me in the back about the movie. After all that, she put us through shit you wouldn't believe!"

"Inez," May said, rifling through her purse for a lemon drop, "you know how insecure she is, especially now."

"Now? Now, she's got every goddamn thing she could possibly ask for. May's been halfway around the world on a goddamn global scavenger hunt, for chrissake. Right, May? Off to London, to get Avery out of mothballs, or whatever balls he was into. Off to Paris, to bring back Tokyo Rose or the Voice of Radio Free Hanoi or whatever the hell they used to call you, Devon. Off to the mountains of Montana, Utah, wherever the hell it was you found King back in the saddle again."

She stopped abruptly and peered out the car window.

With Mitch trailing sullenly, Hollis and the chauffeur were returning to the car with Devon's luggage. Inez clutched Devon's wrist. "Don't say anything to Hollis."

She put her dark glasses back on and smiled at Mitch as he climbed into the car.

"Thanks, lover," she said, patting Mitch on the crotch.

They drove to the secluded house May had rented for Devon high in the Hollywood Hills, above Sunset. While Hollis and Mitch brought in the bags, May showed Devon through the cheerfully decorated rooms, all of which opened onto a handsomely planted redwood courtyard, with a sunken hot tub and a pool.

"*Voilà, mademoiselle.* You like? Had to fight off Sheena, Queen of the Jungle for this place."

"*Merci,* I love it." Devon hugged May and with an arm about her waist walked her to the front door.

"Sure you've got everything you need now?"

"Absolutely."

"I wish we could stay a while and help you settle in, but we've got to get Inez home."

"She looks awful, May. Do her hands shake like that all the time?"

"No, she's just weak right now. She's trying to kick booze and drugs all at once, and she looks like she's been left out on the Santa Monica Freeway overnight. But she'll be okay when she starts the book. She can't understand why she's not allowed on the set yet. That's all Gilda needs, Inez hanging around, all paranoid and palsied." May shook her head. "She's trying hard, Devon. Don't take her too seriously, will you?"

Inez was waiting in the back of the limo. "Thanks for coming to meet me," Devon said, reaching into the car and giving her a hug.

"I'm glad you're back. Sorry I didn't come in to see the place. I'm just exhausted. Next time, okay?"

"You have a standing invitation."

"Hollis," Inez yelled, "where's Mitch? We're waiting for him. Tell him he's holding us up. I want to get out of here."

"He went to the bathroom. He'll be right out."

"He's not in the bathroom," Inez confided to Devon. "He's doing coke. With a snort, he can't handle words with more than two syllables. Hollis," she shouted again. "Go get him, will you? Tell him I'm freezing out here. Tell him to— Oh, God, there he is. There you are, Mitch. Come on. We're all waiting for you. I'm dying here."

"Calm yourself, Inez," said May, getting into the limo. "We're leaving. You'll be fine. Mitch'll catch you some nice juicy spiders for dinner and we'll have you back in the crypt before nightfall."

Hollis kissed Devon goodbye and got into the car. Devon swung the back door shut, ducked down, and looked in at them.

"I'll call you later," May said. "Gilda'll probably phone you as soon as they wrap today's shooting. Get some rest."

"I will. Thanks again." She waved. "Say hi to King for me, Inez."

"I was just going to say the same thing to you," Inez shouted as the limo pulled away.

Gilda phoned at dusk. "Devon? Oh, baby, is it really you? I can't believe you're here at last."

"I was hoping you'd call."

"I won't believe it till I see you with my own eyes. Are you utterly exhausted or can you stop by tonight?"

"Give me five minutes to wash my face and find my shoes, and I'm on my way."

"You don't need shoes, baby. You're home now. Shall I send the car?"

"May's thought of everything, even a new Camaro. Seriously, what time do you want me?"

"Seriously? Right now."

Seven years—but the twenty-minute drive to Beverly Hills felt as familiar as if she'd done it yesterday. She turned on the radio and heard the hoarse, unfamiliar voice of a new rock singer passionately declare, "Baby, we were born to run."

How true, she thought, of me and King, Inez and May, too. But I'm back now.

She turned up the volume, electrified by the conviction in the singer's voice. Devon thought, And, oh, it feels so good to be home—and to be seeing my surrogate mama again.

She passed the Dean Martin sign, made the curve near Schwab's, smiled at the ridiculous ratty old palm trees that welcomed the tourists to Beverly Hills.

How could I have been gone this long? she wondered. What could have kept me away from this crazy city? From Gilda and my friends?

She thought about Michel. He would be finishing dinner right now, drinking Montrachet and being consoled by one of their friends, perhaps even by Sheila Farraday. She felt a momentary pang of *tristesse*, missing Paris, missing their life together. But then she heard the vibrant throb of the music—American rock 'n' roll, she thought, nothing like it!—and drove a little faster to cover the distance to The Pearls.

She could see Mrs. Denby through the window of the kitchen door. The housekeeper was wearing a large white apron over her black uniform and, on her hands, a pair of oversize oven mitts. The dour woman held a plump, wriggling creature by its tail.

"Mother o' God," Mrs. Denby grumbled as she opened the door, then rushed back to the utility table to fling the unhappy creature back into what appeared to be a cage full of mice.

"A rat?" Devon asked.

"No, one of the gerbils got out."

"I'm sorry I startled you," Devon said, reaching to embrace the housekeeper.

Mrs. Denby backed off stiffly, sidestepping the hug. "We was expecting you upstairs," she said, smoothing her skirt and trying, with the big mitts on, to tuck in a stray hair on her prim upsweep. "Gilda said you were back."

"I thought I'd come in the back way, like family," said Devon, feeling a little foolish.

"Well, you go ahead, now, we'll see you have everything you need in a minute. Just as soon as we've fed the creatures."

"Don't tell me she's added mice to the menagerie."

"No, them's the dinner. She's waiting for you, Devon."

"It's good to see you again, Mrs. Denby."

"Humph!"

Devon walked through the kitchen to the front of the mansion, smiling to herself at the implacable Mrs. Denby, who hadn't changed at all.

Barefoot, clad only in a plum-colored silk lounging robe, Gilda was curled up, asleep on the big white chaise in the living room. On the table beside her were a silver cocktail shaker and an empty martini glass. A bound script lay on its spine beneath her limp hand. A pair of reading glasses, which Devon had never known her to wear before, had inched down the bridge of her patrician nose. Her fiery auburn hair seemed artificially bright against the powdered paleness of her face.

In repose, her face seemed as beautiful as ever. But she woke with a start, gasped, and clutched her throat. And when she threw back her head and looked up, her mouth slack, her eyes squinting through the glasses, the ravages of time and sorrow were cruelly visible.

"Devon?"

Devon knelt beside the chaise. "Hello, darling," she whispered. "I'm home."

"Thank God." Gilda took Devon's face in her hands, touching her lips to Devon's forehead. "Oh, Devon, Patrick's gone. He left me, baby."

"I know, darling. I'm so sorry."

Gilda's mouth trembled. "I dream of him. I think I was dreaming about him just now."

"I'm sorry I startled you."

"No, no, it's all right. I'm so glad you're here. It's hard to wake up from a dream like that. It's always a shock to find out all over again, that he's . . . gone." She sighed and stroked Devon's cheek. "The big, dumb bastard. But you're here, aren't you, my baby girl? And so am I."

At that moment a brown-and-white cocker raced into the living room, barking and jumping at Gilda's feet.

"That's not—?"

"Tallulah," Gilda finished the sentence for her. "No, poor dear, she's gone, too. She got so old I practically had to carry her everywhere I went. Meet Tallulah Too." Gilda picked up the dog and cuddled her. "She's very sweet. She loves the other dogs and *hates* Mrs. Denby."

Gilda stood and pulled Devon to her feet. "You've put some meat on your bones. But you look like a flower, like a prize-winning petunia. What did they feed you over there?"

"Same fertilizer they fed the rest of the flowers."

"Look at you, you tower over me!"

Devon hugged her. "That's because you're barefoot, and I'm chugging around in these great spiked boots. But, Lord, I can feel your bones. You do feel fragile. You've lost weight."

"How much do they say the brain weighs?" Gilda asked. "Six or seven pounds? Chalk it up to that, baby. Or hadn't you heard that I'd lost my mind?" She winked and moved away.

"You must have been in terrible pain. Gilda, do you forgive me for not being here?"

"I think, for the first couple of months, I was too far gone to notice. Can I get you something to drink?"

"No, I'm fine."

Gilda lifted the cocktail shaker and shook the last drops into her glass. "Ask Inez. She'll tell you. She's told everyone else." She drank the residue. "I sound ungrateful, don't I? I'm not really. For all I know, she saved my life. Not that I'd actually have gone through with it, but I was feeling pretty melodramatic for a while. Wanna know what stopped me? It wasn't you, baby. Or May or King or Inez or Avery or even Mrs. Denby. It was the drunken revelation that if I did meet the old cowboy over there in never-never land, his wife would be there too. And we'd just wind up having to do the whole damn thing all over again."

Devon laughed.

"It seemed pretty sane to me, at the time. I decided I'd rather cry myself to sleep over a lost lover than a cheating ghost. I haven't been to his grave yet. He's buried beside her. But I've got to go soon, baby. I've got to forgive him and get on with it. Devon, will you go with me?"

"Of course I will," she said. And then she thought of another grave she hadn't yet visited, and she began to cry.

"It's all right, baby. You don't have to go with me. Avery'll do it. He absolutely flourishes in cemeteries, considering the number of people he's sent there."

"It's just that I've thought about my father a lot lately, too."

"I'd imagine so."

"What do you mean?"

"Well, you've turned out so much like him, haven't you?"

"Whatever do you mean?"

"Baby, you must have realized that by now. Even I've thought about it. I read the papers, read about you, all that Joan of the Blue Jeans business. And I burst with pride, baby. And then I'd think, Imagine how her poor dead father would feel. How proud he'd be to see the path she's chosen. After all, it's his path, isn't it, baby?"

"I never thought so. When I was young, I hated his causes because they kept him away from home so much. I thought I was running away from him. That I'd chosen this—acting, the movies, fame and fortune, you know—to be as different from him as I could be. Chosen everything he would have found empty and worthless."

"Know what May called you? 'Joan of the Barnes genes.'"

Devon laughed through her tears. "Did she really? Oh, Gilda, is it true? Do you think he'd have approved of me?"

"I do. Where is he buried? In Texas?"

"No. Right here in California. Somewhere near Bakersfield. I don't even know where."

"We'll find him, baby. Leave it to me. Will you look at the two of us?" Gilda said, beginning to laugh too. "They're going to take us away, fit us for matching straitjackets."

"Yeah, look at us," Devon said. "Nothing's changed, has it? Here you are taking care of me again when I ought to be comforting you."

"Don't worry about that," Gilda said. "You'll get your chance tomorrow. On the set. That's where I need all the help *I* can get."

"Scared?"

Gilda nodded. "Butterflies big as vampire bats."

"Me too. Me, too."

"Are you staying for dinner?" Mrs. Denby stood in the doorway, the expression on her face even less inviting than the tone of her invitation.

"Where's your gerbil?" Devon asked.

"That's dinner."

"Oh, stop!" Gilda said, rolling her eyes. "She *hates* all my animals. Now, baby, why don't you stay? You probably don't have a thing in your rented refrigerator."

"Another time, I promise," Devon said, yawning. "My jet lag is starting to get the better of me. Besides, I have to admit I've been thinking about a real American chiliburger ever since I landed. I think I'll hit Pink's and make it a very early night."

She turned to the housekeeper. "Thanks for the invitation, Mrs. Denby."

Giving Gilda a hug and a kiss on the cheek, she said, "See you in the morning. And thank you, too."

"For what?"

"For bringing me home, where I belong."

Devon arrived at the studio in Culver City at 7:00 A.M. The guard at the gate leaned out of his station and looked into the car.

"Harry." She smiled at him.

"Welcome back, Miss Barnes," he said. "Long time no see. What's it been, about six, seven years? I didn't know if you'd remember me."

"I know the feeling."

"Aw, you look great. What're you worried about?" He grinned at her. "We weren't expecting you for another hour yet. Mr. Ofant in publicity told me to call him when you got here, but he's not in yet. You're over on Three. You know where it is?"

"I think so. Unless they've moved the sound stages."

"Everything but. Straight on back and last building to the right. There'll be someone there to take your car. So, how's it feel to be back in the U.S. of A.?"

"Pretty good, so far."

"Like riding a bicycle, huh?"

She drove through the MGM lot, following familiar landmarks and new directional signs. The old stages had faded from pink to celery gray. A canteen truck was parked in front of the barnlike building in which *Cobras* was shooting. A small coven of grips and script assistants were standing outside the sound stage drinking coffee from styrofoam cups.

Devon got out of the car and walked toward the building.

"Good morning," she said to several people standing by the big old aluminum canteen truck, munching breakfast rolls. They seemed to be watching her from the corners of their eyes as she walked toward them. Her heart began to pound furiously.

"Shep," Devon said, recognizing the head carpenter.

"Howya doing, Miss Barnes?" He looked down at his feet.

She walked past them toward the sound stage. A man in a green bomber jacket said, "Remember me?"

"Noonan," she said. "John Noonan, right? The Whistler."

"He don't whistle no more," a heavyset man called to her. "Not since his boy got killed over in Nam, he don't."

"Killed by your pals," another man shouted.

"I'm so sorry, John," she said, reaching out to the man in the bomber jacket. "Not Johnny. I remember him. He was just a baby."

"Seventeen when he enlisted, seventeen when he died. Two days short of eighteen he was."

The man turned his back on her and walked away.

Two others followed him. "I hope you're happy with what you done," one of the other men yelled.

Devon walked to the door trying to contain her tears, feeling angry eyes on her back. Then she stopped suddenly and retraced her steps.

"Are you crazy?" she said not pausing to think. "Do you really think Johnny Noonan's death makes me happy? How could you say something like that to me? Who do you think you are? What do you think *I* am?"

The carpenter she'd said hello to first still couldn't look her in the eye.

"Shep," she said, trying to control her voice, "why can't you look at me? Are you ashamed? Are you afraid you'll remember me? Who I really am? I'm not a symbol. Not theirs or yours or anyone's. You know me and you're pretending that you don't. Shame on you!"

She turned away, trembling.

The motorcycle was parked against the side of the building. She hadn't noticed it before. King was holding the door to stage three open for her. "Hi," he said, putting his arm around her shoulder.

"Hi." She was shaking, her knees weak from the confrontation. And now here was King.

Their eyes met, and then she turned away abruptly. Not ready to find what Michel had told her was hers for the taking.

She entered the vast sound stage. "Were you here for that whole scene?"

He nodded.

"Why didn't you help me?" she asked. Why can't I ever meet his gaze? she thought.

"You didn't need any help," he said. "When you do, I'll be there. I'm not running away, Devon. Not anymore."

"Welcome back, darling."

Bud Dahlripple, the makeup man, came up to her. "Hello, beautiful." He hugged her, lifted a hank of her hair and shook his head. "What Paris?" he said. "Paris, Texas?"

One of the carpenters, a short, stout man in his sixties, waited shyly for Dahlripple to release her. "Manny Ohrenstein. I worked on *Two Can Do,*" he said, pressing her hand warmly. "It's good to see you again. God bless you." They came up to her then, each one of them, the ones who were glad she'd returned. They shook her hand and kissed her and said, "Welcome back, Miss Barnes." . . . "Welcome home, Devon." . . . "We're proud of you."

She held her smile as long as she could, even after she heard one of the grips say, "Ah, look at her, so glad to be back, she can't stop bawling."

Finally, she lost equilibrium and began to sob.

King was there, as he had promised. He put his arm around her again and hugged her. He said nothing, but there was strength and support in his silence. After a while, he walked her to the makeup trailer where Bud Dahlripple was waiting. "You going to be okay?"

She nodded, dabbing an eye. "Thanks."

"I just dropped by to say hello. I'm not in today's scene. But I'll stay if you want me to."

"I'll be fine."

"How about dinner?"

"I'm not ready. Tell Inez thanks, anyway. Did you know she and Hollis met me at the airport? Your son," she said, wanting to say something about Hollis, how tall he'd grown, how good and loving he seemed. Instead, she said, "Did you know about John Noonan's son?"

"Yes, and Bud's nephew."

"Let's not even talk about it," Bud said, handing Devon a smock.

"There's more than enough to be morbid about in this world. And on this set, too. It's your homecoming, darling. This is show biz. Slip into this smock and let me make you as gay and frivolous as Betty Boop. There's eighteen million bucks about to slide down the drain unless I can do something about those gorgeous red eyeballs."

"You're sure you're okay?" King said. He kissed her cheek and said, "All right. See you soon. Break a leg."

"Oooooh," Bud winced as King walked away. "How can he say that?"

"Tradition."

"I hope not. After what that little creep did to his wife."

"What? Oh, you're talking about Inez's arm. I heard."

"Who hasn't? They're *finis,* darling."

"The creep and Inez?"

"The King and Inez." Bud patted the seat of his famous leather barber chair. Others used folding chairs, director's chairs, high stools. Bud carted his venerable barber chair from set to set, a relic of the past, polished by the pants seats of Gable and Grable and Gardner and Greenway. In the old days, it was as much a fixture on the Metro lot as Leo the Lion.

"Seen La Greenway yet?" he asked, tucking a linen cloth around Devon's collar.

"Yesterday."

"I hope her private audiences are less demanding than her recent public appearances. It's been open season on balls around here. She's efficient as a surgeon. I love the lady, you know that. Have been balmy for her since *Night Anthem.* And, yes, dear, yes I know she's terrified, and terribly insecure, and that she's got lots riding on this extravaganza—"

"Be fair, Bud," Devon said, "she's just lost the one person she loved best in the world, depended on for years and years."

"Listen, Devon." Bud Dahlripple tilted her face into the light. "My sister, Alice, lost someone she loved, too. An eighteen-year-old kid they sent home in a doggie bag. It's been a rough season for survivors, darling. We could all do with a bit of kindness."

A production assistant poked her head into the room. "Hi, Bud. Seen Miss Greenway yet? OhmyGod, it's you," she said, looking at

Devon. "Er, excuse me. I didn't know you'd come in. I just got here myself."

"Annie, Devon Barnes. Annie's normally an articulate, competent girl," Bud said. "Today she decides to get star-struck."

The young woman blushed. "I'm awfully sorry to act like such a twerp, Miss Barnes. I'm a great admirer of yours. And I'm awfully glad you're here. I'll go tell Mr. Sperling. He's been waiting to see you." She backed out, then stuck her head in again. "You haven't seen Miss Greenway, have you?"

"What time is it?" Dahlripple asked impatiently.

The assistant looked at the stopwatch hanging around her neck. "Well, it's a little early, I guess. She was due half an hour ago. I just thought maybe."

"Devon, darling!" Nancy Brown, Marvin Ofant's assistant, burst into the makeup room as Bud put the finishing touches on Devon's Mondrian-shaped eyes. "When did you get here? Oscar wanted to see you in publicity before you set foot on the set. Darling, the newsmen have been storming the gates. Every rag with a stringer in town wants to do you. We wanted to brief you before we opened the floodgates. We've got the "Today" show, if you want it. ABC-News. "60 Minutes." Rona, Shirley Eder, Billy, Sidney Skolsky—"

A young man with a beard and fierce black eyes like hard raisins stuck his head into the room. "Good morning."

"Larry," Nancy said enthusiastically. "Did you see the lineup outside? Minicams and mikes. Marvin just wanted me to talk to Devon for a minute before we let them in."

"We haven't met," the young man said to Devon. "I'm your director, Lawrence Sperling. I've been looking forward to meeting you for weeks. Well, for years really. I want you to know how pleased I am that we'll be working together."

"Oh, my God," blurted Nancy. "The meeting of the year and not even a Polaroid in sight! I didn't know you two had never met! Devon, he's the best. You've heard of him, haven't you? Twenty-eight, he's had two nominations and one Oscar already."

"I saw *Prince Street* at Cannes," Devon said. "I've been looking forward to working with you, too."

"I hope you won't mind, then. I'm ordering a closed set today. I asked my assistant to send the press away."

Nancy gasped. "Larry, you can't do that! Marvin will murder me! This is the hottest movie we've got working. Everyone's dying to do a story on it."

"Tell Ofant to see me if there's a problem," Sperling said.

"A problem? Surely you jest! Five minutes after Marvin tells him you shut down the set, the old man'll be down here breathing fire!"

As Sperling firmly escorted the publicity assistant to the door, Inez Godwin swept past them, into the makeup room.

"If the set is closed, what is *she* doing here?" Nancy fumed.

"See my agent and kiss my ass," Inez said. "Ah, the divine Devon."

She kissed the air on either side of Devon's cheeks. Devon smelled alcohol and peppermint.

"You give good face, Bud. I should've seen you instead of Ralph Martin, the butcher of Beverly Hills."

"Mrs. Godwin, we weren't expecting you until next week," Sperling said.

"Me and Allan Funt," Inez said, winking at him. "When you least expect us."

"I'm telling Marvin," said the publicity assistant, dashing from the room so fast her spray net crackled.

Bud Dahlripple rolled his eyes and Devon burst out laughing.

Avery Calder walked into the room. "Well, I hope it was nothin' I *wrote!*" he shouted, throwing open his arms to Devon. "Gilda said you looked marvelous, but what does she know?"

The mischievous grin, the pink-tinted glasses, crisp white linen suit, silk ascot, the Panama hat—nothing could disguise how stunningly frail Avery had become. He smelled like formaldehyde.

"Oh, Lord," Devon said, hurrying into his arms. "Bud'll kill me for ruining my makeup, but, oh, Avery darling, it's good to see you."

"Is she crying again?" Dahlripple said, sniffling himself. "I'll kill her."

Avery squeezed her, then stepped back and held her hands. "Do you know what I was thinkin' this morning over my first screwdriver? I was rememberin' that night you read for me and Oscar McGrath in

New York. And then, I thought, it's nearly twenty years since the bitch has read a line of mine. Nearly twenty years, Devon! Can you believe it? It put me off my breakfast."

"Poor baby," said Inez, peering at him over the top of her dark glasses. "If I wasn't on the wagon, you could drink some of mine."

Avery stiffened, but maintained his cordial grin. "Sweetheart," he said to Inez, lowering his voice to a whisper, "what the fuck are you doin' here? La Gilda *est à qui,* baby. And you are not supposed to be. Or am I more terribly confused than usual?"

"How did you get in, Mrs. Godwin?" Sperling asked. "This is supposed to be a closed set. I left instructions."

Inez ignored him. "I'm fine, Avery. Just fine. You people worry so. I feel one hundred percent better today than I did yesterday. Look." She held out her hands. "Steady as a laser. No shakes. No pink elephants. I've got my tape recorder in here, somewhere," she said, rummaging through a Gucci duffle bag. "I'm raring to go."

Avery glanced nervously over his shoulder. "Sweetheart," he said, "I think that's a splendid idea. May's with Gilda now, tryin' to calm her down. I'll see if she can stall a bit. Just till we smuggle you out."

"What's wrong?" Devon asked.

"Aside from her everyday nerves, we ran into a horde of unhappy reporters on the steps of the Thalberg Buildin'. Someone had promised them you, my dear. And they were not movin' until they got you. It was everythin' we could do to get past them and into the studio."

"Let me see what I can do about getting them off the lot." Lawrence Sperling went to find Gilda.

"You'd think she'd be used to reporters by now." Inez was still rummaging frantically in her bag. "She's been dealing with the press since the invention of popcorn."

"It wasn't the press that got to her," Avery said, watching Sperling leave. "It was her beloved 'colleagues.' "

"What happened, Avery?" Devon asked as Dahlripple tried to repair her makeup.

"Well," he said, inserting a menthol cigarette into his jade-green Auntie Mame holder, "some of the men from her old crews were waiting outside. Stagehands, grips, poker pals from the old days. It was awful, really. They were all riled up."

"I know, I ran into them myself," she said between strokes of Dahlripple's blush brush.

"Well, they tried to prevent us from comin' in. They called Gilda names and—"

"Names? Because of me? What did they say?"

"Oh, you know, 'traitor,' 'pinko,' the usual red-white-and-blue rhetoric."

"And . . ."

"And, one of the old-timers said it was a disgrace to Patrick's memory for Gilda to act in the same movie as you. There you are. Sorry, darlin'. You'll see it on the six o'clock news."

"Wait a minute," Inez shouted, pulling the tape recorder out of her bag and waving it triumphantly. "Now just wait. I've *got* to get this on tape. Hold on, just till I hook up the mike."

"I'd better find Gilda," Devon said, getting out of the barber chair.

"No," Avery cautioned. "Give her a few minutes, darlin'. She's steamin'."

Gilda was pacing her elaborate dressing room, the one Greta Garbo had used so many years before, furiously chain-smoking and banging a pearl-handled hairbrush against her dressing room table so hard she sent telegrams and well-wisher notes on Tiffany cards flying to the floor. In all the excitement, Tallulah Too barked at everyone who entered.

"Goddamn it, how could they do this to me? I've known those people for years. Who the hell do they think they are? Calling me names like that?"

Then suddenly she stopped and said in a choked voice, "And Patrick . . . why did they have to say those things about Patrick? It's not true is it, May? Patrick was as proud to be an American as Duke Wayne, but he loved Devon. Loved her like a child. This isn't smearing his name, is it, baby?"

"Of course not." May went to her to give her a reassuring hug. "Those men, they're just angry because they've lost people themselves in a war they don't understand. That's what they're striking out at." She took a drag from her cigarette. "Come on, let's go. We've got a goddamn movie to make. Fuck every one of them."

Avery was still talking to Devon. "They were pretty rough on her."

May Fischoff blew into the room. "Rough? Pack of assassins. Is Inez here?"

She glanced and saw the emaciated Mrs. Godwin fumbling around with her purse. She looked like a fly in a silk pants suit.

"Here it is! The microphone." Inez tugged at the tangled length of cord snagged on the zipper of her Gucci bag. "Where's Mitch? I don't know how to set this damn thing up. Will someone go get him for me?" She jerked at the microphone cord, then turned the bag over and poured some of its contents out onto the dressing table. "Mitch!" she shouted over her shoulder. "Where the hell is he?" With a clatter, a little glass vial rolled off the table onto the floor. "Damn! Get that, will you?" Inez ordered Dahlripple.

May picked up the vial filled with white powder.

"Hello, agent." Inez grinned brightly and put a hand to her forehead in salute. "Brenda Starr reporting for duty. First day on the job, baby, and there's enough dirt for two books already. Where's Mitch? I don't know how to set up this goddamn tape recorder."

"I threw him out." She held up the little bottle. "What's this? Coke? Speed? Heroin? What?"

"You threw him out!" Inez's eyes widened with horror, then squinted with hatred. "How dare you!"

"You're not supposed to be here today, Inez. Let's go." May reached for her hand.

"I know why you threw him out, May."

"Inez," Devon said, "calm down, darling."

"And lower your voice, for God's sake, do you want this in Joyce Haber's column?" Avery whispered. "Where's Gilda?" he asked May.

"With Sperling, I hope. They're waiting for Sam Durand to come down to the set. Inez, listen, we have an agreement. You're not supposed to be here this week. Did you get confused?"

"You're just jealous," Inez shrieked, "because of Mitch. Because he won't fuck you anymore. It's true." She clawed at Devon's arm. "You know how she is. She was always jealous of me, wasn't she? She's very sick, Devon. She fucks little boys—"

The dressing room door flew open. Lawrence Sperling stalked in, looked around and shook his head. "May," he said, "I thought you were going to handle this for me."

Gilda stood behind him in the doorway, wearing a yellow velour terry cloth bathrobe with Max Factor stains on the collar. Her face was livid with rage. Her cat's eyes swept the room, settling on Inez.

"What the fuck is she doing here?"

"She's just leavin'," said Avery.

"She's confused," May offered. "She just got the dates screwed up."

"Bullshit." Inez tore free of Devon's restraining hand. "I came in because I'm reporting to work like everyone else. And Mitch is the only one who knows how to set up the tape recorder. And my dear friend May Fischoff threw him out. Now she's trying to get rid of me. And I know why. She's still got the hots for him. But Mitch won't fuck her anymore. He wants me. Eat your heart out, William Morris. Little Mitch is all grown up, and it's me he wants!"

"Inez," said Gilda coolly, "the last grown-up who had the hots for you was your father. And he had to be drunk to fuck you. Now beat it." She turned her back on them all. "Call me when the set is cleared," she said to Sperling, and walked out.

"Cobras!" Inez screamed as the guards dragged her off the set. "Avery's right! That's what you are. The whole rotten bunch of you! Especially you, Gilda."

A month later, a six-foot-long king cobra was delivered to The Pearls with a card that read, "Fangs for the memories. A Fan."

Inez denied having sent the snake. Along with everyone else, she urged Gilda to give it to the San Diego Zoo.

"But Gilda has had a pet fetish all her life," May told Billy Buck. "She even wrote a book about her pet chipmunk called *Chips and Me*. My father said that in the forties she used to take a mynah bird on publicity tours. Every dressing room she ever had was equipped with an aquarium. She once caught a rattlesnake on location in Durango and had one of the grips drive the damn thing back to L.A. in a fucking Jeep. At one point she had a donkey, a goat, and thirteen dogs until the neighbors complained about the smell and the fence and the goddamn barking. So now it's a cobra. What a sick joke."

But Gilda claimed that Mrs. Denby had fallen in love with the creature. Against all advice, she kept it.

TWENTY-THREE

AUTUMN 1977

"I'm talking to you," King said, spinning Devon around by the arm to face him. He took her hand roughly and placed it on his bare chest, forcing her fingers open, pressing her palm against his skin so she could feel his heart pounding.

She was wearing a satin slip. King was in tight cotton pajama bottoms, barefoot, and naked from the waist up.

Larry Sperling shook his head. "Let's try it again."

The boy with the clap-sticks chalked 81 and 12 on his board and jumped in front of the camera. "Scene eighty-one, take twelve," he called.

It was late afternoon. Gilda had left the studio in a foul mood after sitting around most of the day, waiting for King and Devon to complete their scene. Inez, who was now officially permitted on the set, had only been showing up for an hour a day after lunch. May had hired a methodical young film student to take notes for Inez, whose only complaints about the arrangement were that the boy was too serious, too short, and had red hair. "All redheads smell like peanut butter."

King reached for Devon again. She turned, this time before he even touched her. His hand grazed her shoulder. "Sorry," he said.

"No, it was my fault."

"Keep it running," Sperling told the cameraman. "Again, King. Grab her arm. Devon, just wait. Go limp until he touches you, okay? Just keep going."

"I'm talking to you," King said, prying open her hand and pressing it against his chest.

"What's that move, Devon?" Sperling asked. "What's going on?"

She shielded her eyes and said, "What move?"

"You pulled away from him. You're supposed to get closer, not back off."

"I didn't pull away, did I?"

Exasperated, King nodded. Devon burst into tears.

"Right. Cut," Sperling said, thrusting his hands into the pockets of his chinos and hunching his shoulders. "Let's take a break, okay?"

King began to walk away. A dresser ran up to Devon and threw a robe over her bare shoulders. Dahlripple's assistant rushed to repair her hair. "Please," Devon said, waving him away. "King, wait."

Sperling clapped his hands. "Okay, everybody off the set, unless you have something to do in this scene. Let's try it without an audience."

Devon hurried after King. "I'd ask you to be patient, but I know you have been. I'm sorry. I don't know why I keep screwing up."

"Neither do I," he said, "especially since this isn't the first love scene we've shot. If you were going to freak out on me, I figured it would've been last week, when we were rolling around in bed together."

"It's strange, isn't it? I was completely in character for that one. It wasn't you and me, it was Rollins and Carrie."

"Avery says he thought Sperling was going to douse us with a pail of water instead of calling cut."

"Today, it keeps being me and you," she said, miserably.

"So much for charisma."

"I don't know. I think maybe I'm afraid to get into it again. After that scene last week, I was so tired, and so goddamn blue. It was all I could do to get home and crawl under the covers."

"Annie, what time is it?" King called to Sperling's assistant.

"Four forty-nine."

"Devon," he said softly, taking her shoulders, "let's get it on the next take, and Avery and I will take you to the Palm and buy you a magnum of champagne and a big juicy prime rib."

She thought about it and sighed.

"Hey, I'm not the type to kiss and run," he continued in his slow, seductive drawl. "We'll do the scene, scrub our faces, and bomb out of here for some grub. Don't worry, darling. We'll get it. Sooner or later, I'll grab your hand and press it against me, like this." He took her hand, gently, and held it to his heart. "And then I'll see in your eyes that you're feeling my heart beating, you know, like you're supposed to. Yeah, just like that. Well, look at you, Devon Barnes. That's how you're supposed to look in Technicolor."

She looked at him with a lazy smile, slowly swaying her hips in character. "The name's Carrie," she whispered.

He slipped his arms around her waist and gave her his deep and dangerous blue-eyed look. "Girl, I've been making love to you by other names for twenty years."

She rested her cheek on his bare chest. "How thick did you say that steak's gonna be?"

"Larry," King hollered, without letting go of her. "We're ready to try it again. We're going to go all the way this time. Aren't we, girl?"

They wandered back to the set arm in arm. She kept her arms around his waist while Bud's assistant repaired her hair. She held King and turned her head, so the makeup girl could clean the smudges under her eyes and apply fresh base and mascara.

Only when the boy with the clap-stick called "Scene eighty-one, take thirteen" did Devon relinquish him. She stared, as she was supposed to, out the make-believe window, at the painted landscape. She hugged herself, as she was supposed to, and felt as if her flesh had memory, where his fingers had been on her arms, his chest against her cheek, his heart in the palm of her hand.

"Lucky thirteen," Sperling shouted, five minutes later. "That's it. Cut! Thank you and good night. It was worth the wait. Sleep tight, you guys. You get to sleep late tomorrow. The call isn't until—" He turned to Annie.

"Eight-fifteen," she said. "A.M."

* * *

King refilled Devon's glass, emptying the second bottle of champagne. He stuck the bottle upside down in the bucket and raised his hand to signal the waiter.

"Oh, Lord, give us a break, King," Devon said.

"Yes, do," Avery concurred. "You've been pourin' with a mighty free hand this evenin'. I, for one, am stewed."

"I, for two," said Devon. "And what about you? How come you can still move your lips? I can't even find mine."

King tilted Devon's face and kissed her.

"Oh, God," said Avery, "where is Vincente Minnelli now that we need someone to call 'Cut'?"

"So that's where they were," said Devon, touching her lips.

King leaned back against the banquette.

"Cigarette?" Avery offered. "I believe it's traditional."

"Are you guys going to finish those steaks?" King asked. "Look at you, ripped to the gills and haven't eaten two bites of those beautiful babies."

Avery glanced at the thick steak, cold now, sitting in its congealed fat. He pushed the plate toward King. "Here, Paul Bunyan," he said, taking King's champagne glass. "Call it even."

The waiter appeared with the bottle of Perrier Jouet and was about to remove the cork.

"Don't bother," King said. "I'll take care of it when we're ready."

"King, know what this reminds me of?" Devon smiled. "Sitting here, surrounded by friends. May's birthday party. Her sweet sixteen, at '21.'"

"May Fischoff's sweet sixteen? Oh, my," said Avery. "What a keen memory you have, my old dear. And me sittin' here with early senility settin' in."

"I was in love with King," Devon confided.

"That's not memory, that's fantasy," King said. "She's a little confused, our old dear. I was in love with *her*. Madly. Didn't know what hit me. I sat next to her, planning our life together, swear to God."

Avery raised an eyebrow at them. "Well, what would Gertie Lawrence sing at a time like this?"

"You're really a pain in the ass, King. Here I reveal the shameful secret of my youth. And you make fun of me. Give me your hand. That's my heart fluttering. That's how nervous I am. King, darling, I *really* was in love with you."

"Take your hand off that child's bosom, before we all wind up in the supermarket," Avery scolded.

"I'm still in love with you, Devon."

"Wind up in the supermarket?" Devon said.

"Yes, on the cover of one of those checkout-counter rags. They print the most unflattering photos in torrid color. Everyone looks like a strawberry sundae."

"Excuse me," King said, "I think you stepped on my line."

"Oh, I beg your pardon." Avery peered down his nose, through the wire rims of his pink-tinted glasses. "You were sayin'?"

"I said, I'm still in love with you, Devon."

"Oh," she said. "What are we going to do about it? Are you going to kiss me?"

He did.

Avery drummed his fingers on the table.

"The *Star* uses color. But personally, I prefer the stark black-and-white forties look of the *Enquirer*. Of course, now there's Time-Life's new glossy to consider. What's it called, *People?* Oh, do take a breath, darlin's."

"You knew," King said.

"Does it matter?"

"No. I know why you were able to do the scene today, after we talked."

"Why, darling?" Devon asked.

Avery signaled for the check.

"Because I promised to buy you dinner after."

"But, look, I haven't eaten it."

"No, it's not that. It's because you knew we'd be together after the scene. That we wouldn't just get all worked up and have Larry holler, 'Okay, it's a take,' and then walk away from each other again."

"Excuse me," Avery said, looking over Devon's shoulder at King. "Have you got a nice, crisp hundred?" He held up the check.

"Do you take plastic?" King asked.

"If it's in pill form, I probably have. Oh, listen, why don't I just sign for it? Life's short. Go on, dears, I didn't mean to interrupt. Just think of it as a commercial break."

"So you think I'm a pushover? That's what you were saying, wasn't it? Promise me dinner, and I'll fuck like a bunny, is that it?"

"Will you?" he asked, sliding his hand under her skirt, and up along her thigh.

She closed her eyes. "Right here, if you want."

"Is it only that you're drunk?"

"Is it only why you wanted me drunk?"

"Children," said Avery, "I think it's time to go home to Beatrix Potter."

"Oh, no," said Devon. "We were just going to fuck like bunnies. Right here, Avery."

"Oh, don't." He saw King's hand moving under her skirt, and swatted it with the back of a spoon. "Let's skip dessert, what do you say? I don't think they serve carrot cake here. Miss Barnes, think you could give me a lift home, before you and Peter Cottontail hit the hutch?"

"Hold on," King said, lifting himself from the seat and sliding his hand into his pants pocket.

"Good Lord," Avery said, "you're not going to ask me to rub it for luck, are you?"

King grabbed the unopened champagne bottle, then pulled out his keys, disengaged the BMW key from the ring, and slapped it down in front of Avery. "Take my bike."

"Not unless it's got a sidecar. Excuse me," he said to the waiter. "Would you mind callin' a cab for me?"

"Of course, Mr. Calder," the waiter said. "Where are you going?"

"Chateau Marmont."

"I live just above Sunset," the waiter said. "If you don't mind waiting a bit, I'd be happy to give you a lift."

"Well, aren't you sweet," said Avery. "Thanks anyway but I'm in my pristine Gertrude Lawrence phase." He turned to the lovebirds. "Now I know what Gertie would sing about here." He hummed a bar of "I'll See You Again." "I suppose you want to be an actor."

"No strings," the waiter said. "I'm a playwright."

Avery sighed. "Oh, my," he said, whistling. "The woods are full of bunnies tonight."

* * *

They were groping and kissing like horny kids even before they got inside Devon's house.

"Wait," Devon said hoarsely, fumbling for the light switch and laughing with excitement and anticipation.

"Do you have champagne glasses?" he asked, uncorking the bottle of Perrier Jouet from the Palm.

She grabbed two Venetian crystals and led him into her bedroom.

"This is ridiculous, King, but I suddenly feel like a nervous kid. My heart is beating so hard I can't breathe."

"Devon . . ." He stroked her cheek and ears and lips with the back of his hand. Then he caressed her neck and rubbed circles with his fingers over the exposed skin just above her breasts.

She was melting under this touch. She couldn't think. She was alive only to King's presence and her desire for him.

"Devon, Devon," he whispered.

"Why did we wait so long?"

He bent down and kissed her. She couldn't bear the tension— could no longer prolong the moment when she would feel him against her.

She moved away and impatiently shrugged off her silk shirt. She stepped out of her pants and boots.

He put a glass to her lips and she drank the champagne, while he quickly pulled off his clothes.

Then they were clinging to each other, their bodies aflame with the desire that had been building for so many years. They tumbled on to her bed, their arms and legs entangled.

Their mouths and bellies pressed hard against each other. They stroked each other hungrily. Devon pulled King to her, her body begging him to enter her.

King thrust deep, withdrew, thrust again as Devon pushed her hips up to meet him and tightened her muscles around him. Then all she knew was that King was there with her and that she was flowing around him in waves and ripples that had her crying out as she soared with him into the moment of absolute, perfect ecstasy.

"Hello, Devon," he said, after they'd stopped panting and gasping for breath.

"Hello, King." She stretched out on top of him, crossing her arms on his chest and resting her chin on them.

" 'When I die I'm going to heaven 'cause I've done my time in hell.' What's that from?"

"Deau's jacket," she said. "It was embroidered on the back of one of Deauville's jackets."

"Deauville. Oh, Lord, yes. It's getting crowded in here all of a sudden."

"We've taken a lot of detours to get here, haven't we, King? Bound to be excess luggage. Claim checks from all over the world."

"Gay Paree."

"Rome."

He chuckled. "First-class baggage."

"Mexico," Devon said.

"If Michel told you the truth about Mexico, then you know I wasn't there with him." He put his arms around Devon's waist and hugged her tight against him. He felt her hip bones and the taut curve of her belly.

"I was there with you," he said, feeling her thighs, warm and damp, pressing into his. He could part them with just a gentle movement. He knew she would open for him again.

Devon ran her fingers through his coarse blond hair. Her velvety breasts brushed against his skin as her hands explored his face.

"Love of my life," he sighed.

She explored his stomach and the forest of hair between his legs. She watched as he grew hard again.

"Can't get enough of me, can you?" she laughed.

"More champagne?" King reached over and picked up the bottle on her bed table.

Devon shook her head, but he was already pouring some into her glass.

"Lie back," he said.

She gasped as King trickled champagne over her breasts and onto her stomach. He dipped his fingers into the glass and rubbed her nipples between his thumb and index finger.

"My champagne woman," he said, ignoring her weak protests as she squirmed beneath his touch.

Devon's laugh became an unending series of breathless moans as he splashed the clear, bubbling champagne down the length of her body until her breasts and stomach and the vee between her thighs were tingling from the champagne bath.

"King, King."

She couldn't stop saying his name, just as she couldn't help herself from arching upward to find his mouth and hands.

But he found her first. He pinned her hands above her head and licked every inch of her sticky skin. His lips sucked and drank her.

Devon was dimly aware of a voice—her voice—begging King never to stop.

Never.

Ever.

And then she was aware of nothing but her desperate need for him.

And then, nothing.

"I love you, King," she said much later.

With his hands, he traced the curve of her back, her waist and hips, the rise of her buttocks.

"Devon," he said, filling his hands with her and rolling over so that they lay side by side, facing each other.

"You have such marvelous eyes," she said, smiling.

"You always looked away. What were you—"

"I was afraid. There was always a party going on in your eyes and I wasn't invited. Maybe I was afraid I'd look in your eyes and find out there was nobody home. I don't know."

He pulled her close to him. They lay locked together, Devon's cheek nestled in the damp pocket between his collarbone and neck.

"I've always been so in love with you," Devon said. "I think I was afraid to see your love. Even now it frightens me. But it's all I've ever wanted."

"Then what frightens you?"

"That I don't deserve you. That you'll leave me."

"Why?"

"What if I hurt you? What if I get scared? Look what happened with Deau. With Michel. I left them. I always run away."

"Well, we have that in common. Devon," he said after a moment, "maybe you were just running *to* something. Someone."

"Oh, King, I don't care what happens. Maybe *you* will leave *me*.

Maybe I'll get so scared and worried that I'll run away first. I know from my own experience that nothing lasts forever. But right now I have what I want."

"I know," he said. "Me, too."

"King . . ."

"What, honey?"

"I know I've scarred your life with all this running away. And maybe the scar tissue doesn't show, but it's there, inside. If it takes me the rest of my life, I want to make that up to you. I'm not a totally restructured person since I've come back from France, God knows. I'm still neurotic as hell. But I can cope. I don't understand complacency, but I don't understand the grubby things you have to do to feed the hungry or heal the sick, either. I wanted to change things, but I didn't have the money or the technology. All I had was compassion. I think I made a contribution. But I grew frustrated. I came home. And now I want to start over again, this time with you."

"Devon . . ."

"No, let me finish. What I'm trying to say is I know all of us have suffered emotional violence. You can't immunize yourself against that. All you can do is get your priorities straight and give as much affection as you get. I'd give anything to undo the past, but since I can't do that, I'd give anything for another chance. I promise to give it my best shot."

He held her so close she could feel his heart, feel the pulse throbbing in his throat with the tip of her tongue. "I promise to let you try," he said.

"It feels like Christmas morning, being with you," Devon said.

"Kind of warm for Christmas," he whispered into her hair.

"Tell me about Mexico. The place you found. Michel made it sound like paradise."

"It's down near the Yucatán. Puerto Cruz. Practically a sandbar. Eight, maybe ten miles of good beach wedged between the Gulf and the jungle. The water is as blue as a coral reef in the Caribbean and above it the town rises like an arrow, straight up from the cliffs. There's nothing to do there but think. The big action of the day is an occasional marlin splashing out of the water to interrupt your thoughts, but then the fish goes back to the ocean floor and you go back to the peace deep inside your mind. You sit in the sand with nothing on and you feel the heat and the trade winds and you throw away all the clocks and nothing matters anymore. It's the cleanest air in the world in the day, and at night, when the humidity comes in, it gets sultry. Like a Sydney Greenstreet movie."

She laughed. "What a strange word for you to use."

"Sultry?" He rolled her onto her back again, and propped himself up on one elbow. His fingers brushed over the curve of her belly and gently parted the damp, dark hair between her legs.

"This is what I meant," he said. "Damp and salty, like you. I thought about making love with you in the sand, on a bed of ferns. The soft furry ferns and vines that come creeping out of the jungle onto the beach. If I'd kissed you there you'd have gotten pregnant." He brushed his lips against her swollen nipples. "I dreamed about your breasts, bursting with sweet milk."

"Take me there, King," she whispered, her soft, strong arms enfolding him.

"I will," he murmured. "I will."

He left her, spent and asleep, at three in the morning, and came back at six-thirty, with a sack of fresh rolls, a thermos of *café au lait*, and a bouquet of furry ferns.

"It wasn't just a dream," Devon said, opening her eyes and smiling as he tiptoed into her bedroom.

"I picked up some food. You didn't have much dinner last night." He sat down next to her on the bed and kissed her hand.

She pulled him down to her and kissed him. "I had the kind of feast I wanted."

"Good. How about tonight?"

"Let's skip the steak."

"I know a terrific seafood joint up the coast."

Her face clouded over. "King," she began.

He put a finger to her lips. "You like swordfish steak or scampi?" He took her finger away and kissed her. "It's the only decision you need to make today, Devon. Give me a little time."

Six weeks into production Gilda was still edgy. She had yet to see a single frame of film they'd shot. Finally, late one afternoon, Avery talked her into viewing the rushes.

"Who is that cow?" she said. Sunk low in her chair, a hand over her eyes, she looked at the screen through occasionally parted fingers. "It can't be me, baby. I'd borrow Pat's rifle tomorrow, if I thought I really looked like that."

"Well," she told Devon and King that evening over dinner at Ma Maison, "at least it ain't art. If they gave Oscars for brass balls, I'd be the year's big winner." She emptied her glass of white wine. "Although you two are running a close second."

King had moved out of his Holmby Hills estate and into May's empty Malibu cottage a week after he spent the night with Devon. Devon at first felt guilty every time she looked at Inez. But after several days she was far too involved with *Cobras* by day and King by night to be conscious of much else.

She was running on adrenaline and love. Except for occasional dinners with Gilda and Avery, she and King spent most of their off-camera moments together, talking, laughing, making love. They were celebrating the fact that they had finally stood still long enough after all these years to find each other.

They had invited Gilda to dinner that evening, figuring she might want some moral support if she didn't like the rushes. They had seen some several days earlier and couldn't decide whether the film was going to be brilliant or a total disaster. The electricity between the two of them was obvious and exciting. But Devon thought Gilda looked edgy, often bone-weary. She knew Gilda had reservations from the start, and in the dailies, the nervousness sometimes showed.

"I sure as hell hope I wasn't wrong to let you all talk me into doing this movie." Gilda had barely touched her shrimp diablo. She knew what *Cobras* meant to her career. She also worried about the alternatives. *If you're over forty in this town, you're left for a grease spot on the side of the road.* She didn't want to place a want ad in the trades, like Bette Davis. She didn't want to sit around waiting to play mother superiors, like Loretta Young. She didn't want to crawl into a bottle and die, like so many other aging legends had done—and were doing now. She didn't want to let it all hang out in some tell-all scandal book, then remind the slumbering public she was still alive on Merv Griffin.

No, the big screen was still her first love, the place where she could really shine. If only she wasn't so bloody terrified. "I feel like I'm really putting myself on the line this time. If it turns out to be a fiasco . . ." She grimaced, then changed the subject. "Have you two stopped making goo-goo eyes at each other long enough to think about the future? Sometimes I feel like I got Inez and the two of you into this—though I had the best intentions—so now it's up to me to clean up the mess."

"I'm planning to talk to Inez about the divorce as soon as the picture wraps," King said. "That was our agreement all along."

"And I suppose that means you're here to stay, baby." Gilda smiled at Devon. "My God, don't tell me you're blushing. It's not as if you're kids with lots of time to spare. Why not get married as soon as possible and make me a grandma?"

"That's exactly what I've been telling this stubborn woman," King said.

Devon reached across the table to give Gilda's hand a loving squeeze.

"It's not time yet," she said. "I want to wait until King is really free and clear. Besides, right now we're having so much fun that it's hard to make long-term plans."

"I just don't want to see you making the same mistake I did—wasting a lifetime, waiting for the moment that passes so quickly it's gone before you've grabbed it. You walk, you fall, you get up again. You're all grown up before you know it. And then you hear that distant drum and you wonder where the hell the time went. While your back was turned, it just slipped away."

Gilda's beautiful gray-green eyes filled with tears.

"What do I have? You kids. You're all I have. And if you ever let me down . . ."

She blinked away the tears and forced a smile onto her face. "Shit, look at me getting all sentimental. Why is my glass empty? King, you can't even keep me in wine. How are you going to take care of Devon?" She rolled her eyes upward. "Patrick, you poor dear bastard," she said. "Watch out for these two idiots." Then she laughed. "I want to make the toast at your wedding brunch, kids—so don't you dare disappear before I do. I have a lot of well-chosen words for both of you."

Inez claimed she was working too hard to care about King's departure.

"Besides," she announced to May and Billy Buck during lunch at the Polo Lounge, "Mitch is every bit as big as King—and years younger." She held out her trembling hands. "Look at me," she said. "This is what this writing business does to you. No wonder Fitzgerald hit the bottle. And he didn't even have a house and family to take care of."

She missed the look of amused exasperation that passed between May and Billy.

May had always said Inez was the only person she knew, even in Beverly Hills, who had a black belt in shopping. Today, she had discovered op-art fashion and was wearing plastic jewelry—dominoes, a clock watch, a sundial bracelet, big square glass earrings with ball bearings rolling around inside glass barometers.

"Graphic fashion, darling," she explained. "I'm out to startle people, have fun. Everything in this town depends on how amusing you are."

Or, thought Billy, how desperate.

"Which reminds me, May," Inez went on. "I ran into Hollis last week and I was not amused. His hair looks like shit. Can't you take him to a barber? He looks like a member of the Manson gang." She pushed away her untouched dessert and got up from the table. "Excuse me. I'll be right back."

"Must be hell on the kidneys," May said. "You've only gone to the powder room five times since we got here."

"Powder room. Did you hear that, Billy? We call that a Fischoffism—a double entendre delivered with the subtlety of a sledgehammer. Powder, get it? May," she hissed, "I'm getting sick of your snide remarks and insinuations."

"Oh, come on, Inez. That's what it's called," said Billy.

"Pardonnez moi," said May, "but while you're in the crapper, then, you might want to check the mirror. Or have you forgotten that was its original use? You have white dust all over your nostrils."

Inez rubbed her nose and licked her fingertips. "Powdered sugar, definitely."

"From what? You ordered a Cobb salad and a lemon mousse. Although I can't imagine why. You haven't touched anything you've ordered so far, except the three vodkas."

"But who's counting?" said Billy.

"Fuck you both. And order me a cognac, will you, Billy? I'm going to the ladies' lounge to snort up a fucking blizzard of flake."

Six weeks later Devon sat in the back of a limousine. A Hermès shoulder bag was on the seat next to her, and in the trunk were two more large suitcases. As the driver angled into the winding road that led to The Pearls, Devon remembered what Gilda had said the night she'd had dinner with her and King at Ma Maison.

"If you ever let me down . . ."

Was she really making the right decision? Devon wondered. There was Gilda, alone and consumed with self-doubts that she was no more than a dusty strip of celluloid, a used-up movie star whose best performances were growing mold in a studio vault. Admittedly, this was a terrible time to leave.

There was plenty of trouble on the set—and off. The Directors Guild had shut them down for a week because the producers had hired non-Guild people. Then the electricians and best boys had pulled a wildcat strike, which took two weeks of negotiating with the Teamsters to settle.

They were already $2 million over budget. The studio execs were screaming for Gilda's head—and everybody else's.

To top it all off, Avery was drinking heavily again. After he was evicted from the Chateau Marmont for setting fire to his suite, the script supervisor had arrived at his rented house on Maple Drive one day at noon to go over some revisions, only to find Avery spread-eagled on a shower curtain on the living room floor, hosting a Crisco party for five young actors who were all butt naked.

Larry Sperling was doing his best to keep the project from falling apart. He'd been curious when Devon informed him she was leaving town and pressed him to wrap up her remaining scenes early. But his hands were too full with other problems to do anything more than pacify her.

"Yeah, sure, we're almost done with you, anyway. Tell Joe it's okay to work out a quick schedule for you." He lit up another cigarette and brushed away her pleas that he not mention their conversation. Devon knew her secret was safe with him.

But how was she going to tell Gilda?

And King . . .

Leaving them behind was one of the hardest things she'd ever done, but in her heart, she knew she'd made the right choice.

"I'll be out in twenty minutes," she told the limo driver as he opened the door for her.

"You should call first," said Mrs. Denby, unfriendly as ever. "Well, don't just stand there, come in. I'll tell her you're here."

Devon stood in the living room thinking, Dear God, please don't let her hate me for this.

"Baby, what a nice surprise," said Gilda, sweeping into the room. Although it was midafternoon, Gilda was still dressed in her green velvet robe. "But you should have given me some warning. *Us* magazine was supposed to interview me today, but the idiot reporter canceled. Bad enough that *People* never even called—but to have *Us* change its mind . . ." She waved her hand, ridding the air of the unpleasant thought. "So I cold-creamed my face and decided to spend the afternoon in bed. I have to be at the set at seven-thirty tomorrow morning. Some fun, huh? How about a drink or something."

"No, thanks, Gilda. I just have a few minutes—"

"Wait! Let me guess—you came by to tell me that you and King have set a date for the wedding. Oh, baby—"

"I'm leaving, Gilda," Devon said quietly.

Gilda stood motionless. "Leaving?"

"I'm on my way to the airport. I have a limo waiting for me outside." Devon's control broke and she walked over to Gilda and took her hands. They were cold as ice packs.

"*What* are you talking about? The picture's not even finished yet. Where the hell are you going?" Gilda's voice was shrill with pain and anger. "How dare you run out on me like this!"

"I can't tell you anything more right now, but I swear, I'm not running out on you—"

"The hell you're not! What do you mean, 'You can't tell me'? This is Gilda you're talking to, baby, not George Christy from the *Hollywood Reporter.*"

"Gilda, please! I can't talk about it now. I just have to work this out on my own."

"Work *what* out on your own? How *dare* you not include me. After everything we've been through!"

Gilda paced the room, her bare feet slapping angrily on the white marble floor. She walked over to the antique marble-topped armoire, grabbed a menthol cigarette from the silver case and lit it, her hand shaking.

"It's because this movie's a disaster, isn't it? You know it as well as I do!"

"No, Gilda—"

"It is. They're going to crucify us for *Cobras.*"

Devon's protests broke off as Mrs. Denby appeared in the doorway.

"What do *you* want?" Gilda shrieked. "Goddamn it, why do you creep around here, eavesdropping on me?"

"I heard you shouting. I thought you might need me." The housekeeper's pale, pinched face was flushed with shame and resentment as she glanced at Devon. "Why are you getting her so upset?"

"Get out of here!" Gilda raged.

Tallulah Too, the carbon copy of the dog Gilda had raised during her early Hollywood days, barked and went flying out of the room.

"It's you people who're going to drive her to an early grave," Mrs. Denby spat at Devon as she stalked out of the living room. "All you Hollywood hotshots."

"Please, darling," Devon pleaded. "I don't have much time."

Gilda whirled to face her. "Sit down!" she commanded. She poured herself a shot of whiskey from the liquor cabinet, then said, "I know it has to do with this movie." Suddenly she began to scream. "Damn you! Damn you all! What a mess I've made of it all—Patrick, and now you. All my children."

She began counting on her fingertips.

"A drug addict. A fool who's fallen in love with a boy she can't hope to hold. An irresponsible womanizer who's squandered his talent for years. And you! You, who I loved best of all—a rootless, ungrateful bitch."

Devon cried, "I need you. Don't you understand? *I need you!*"

For the first time in all the years since she'd met Gilda, Devon saw the older woman sneer with a face distorted with what looked very much like hate.

"Don't give me this little girl bullshit routine. You think I'm going to buy that after you've traipsed all over the world? You—the darling of the liberal press, shacking up all over Europe and Asia with a Frenchman who smells out pussy like a cat smells out a fish market? And where was I all that time? You didn't need me so badly you couldn't stay away for seven years. Well, baby, I need *you* to understand. Look at me," she shouted, "at what I am now. A leftover from another era who can't even *give away* interviews, who's lucky to do a 'Love Boat' or a goddamn soap that gets a three percent market share. And now you—you and King—how convenient, two little lovebirds, like you're Liz and Dick, running away and leaving *me* to pick up the pieces of this sinking *Titanic* . . ."

She collapsed on the chaise longue, utterly exhausted by her outburst.

There was silence in the room. Finally Devon said, "I'm going without King."

Gilda looked up. "Something's really wrong, isn't it?" she asked. "You're in trouble, Devon. What is it? That business about your politics? Please, you *must* tell me."

Devon crossed the room to sit beside her. "You have to trust me. I promise I'll write you in a couple of weeks, as soon as I get myself settled."

"Does King know where you're going?"

"He doesn't even know I'm leaving. I had to tell Larry Sperling, of course, and I spent most of last week dubbing. My looping is finished. Most of the picture is interiors, so Larry says we won't need any wild tracks. Post-production will be a snap. It's not *Star Wars*, where the actors wrap and the real work begins in the editing lab. And, darling, everyone says in spite of all the problems it's going to be a wonderful movie. And you're going to be wonderful in it."

She hesitated, biting the inside of her lower lip, then added, "I know this is hard for you to understand, but I'd rather you not tell King anything. He needs some time alone, too. I'll be in touch with him myself when I'm ready."

Gilda spoke so quietly that Devon could hardly hear her. "You're a fool, Devon Barnes. You're throwing away the best thing in the world —and you won't even let me help you out of whatever this mess is you've gotten yourself into. Well, I'm damn tired, and if that's—"

"Your driver says it's time to go!" Mrs. Denby suddenly reappeared, livid. "He's out there blasting that horn so loud he's got the creatures all in an uproar. The whole aviary's screeching. The gardener will be cleaning feathers off the lawn for a week."

"Give me a kiss, if not your blessings," Devon said.

"I suppose you want me to see you to the door as well," Gilda said frigidly. "Favors—that seems to be all you want of me, Devon. 'Find me my father's grave,' you said. 'Kiss me nicely while I run out on you.' Well, I'll kiss you goodbye and wish you luck. But if you ever come waltzing through my door again and decide to give me an explanation, Devon Barnes, it better be a damned good one."

After Devon's departure, international curiosity centered like a laser on the return to films of Gilda Greenway. During the weeks that followed, she was interviewed by the *Hollywood Reporter, Ladies' Home Journal, Redbook,* the wire services, the *New York Times, Harper's Bazaar,* the *Chicago Tribune,* the *Washington Post,* and *Cosmopolitan.* But it was Billy Buck who got the real story. *Esquire* paid him handsomely for a profile they called "Gilda's Back—Let 'Em Eat Pearls," and Billy got to know his subject as well as his elbow.

Whenever Gilda had a few margaritas under her Gucci belt, she'd start reminiscing about her childhood in an accent thick as blackstrap. "It wasn't no Rodgers and Hammerstein musical, honey, let me tell you." Her eyes would mist when she recalled the twilight suppers on her uncle Freddy's screen porch, swatting flies while she licked the dasher on a freezer of peach ice cream. Or catching lightning bugs in a Mason jar.

Gilda Rae Quinn was a simple girl whose only crime was to be born beautiful. It was Orval and her sister Vy who had all the dreams. "If you think I'm somethin' you shoulda seen Vy. She was plain as a churn but she had enough energy for both of us. 'Sister, if I can't be nothin' in this world, at least *you* can,' she'd say. It was Vy who forced me to try out for the school play. *Rain* by Somerset Maugham. The folks in Hilltop never knew what hit them and neither did Vy. She thought it was a disgrace. I didn't have much talent, but everyone thought I was *sincere*. And I was already pretty stacked even as a scruffy little dirty-necked teenager."

The fan magazines had told part of the story—about her husbands and her love affairs, her madcap life in Rome dancing on tabletops with Spanish bullfighters, her passion for chocolate—but they never captured the essence of this uncaged bird in bare feet.

"When I got to Hollywood, Vy came with me for a short while. It was Vy who told Louis B. Mayer to go fuck himself. For all I know, he did, too. He was fucking everything else that walked through the front gate at MGM. All I can tell you is by the 1950s I had worked my way up to $4,000 a week when everybody else was getting three. Mayer always hated me, and Lana and Ava, too. We weren't ladies, see, and we knew all the wrong people. Mayer liked hats and gloves. He had the hots for Greer Garson. But the old asshole understood one thing —box office. When I made a picture, the cash registers played a tune that made the Hit Parade. Hell, I don't know what I had, but I must've been doing something right. I did twelve pictures in a row and they kept coming back for more. Some of them were stinkers."

Billy knew. He'd read about how she'd dug in her heels. Mayer would threaten to put her on suspension like Bette Davis over at Warner's, but her ace in the hole was Ida Koverman, Mayer's right hand at Metro.

"If Ida liked you, you had it made," Gilda explained to Billy. "Every time the old man threatened me, I'd call Ida and she'd say, 'I'll square it with L.B.' You didn't just walk into Mayer's office, no matter who you were. You called Ida Koverman first. Then he'd sit you down under the American flag and say, 'There are no bad pictures, Gilda. There are only bad actresses. Listen to me as though I'm your father, and you'll never be one.' That's how you got along with all of the monsters who ran this town. In their presence, you played the game. Then when you were off the lot, you did whatever the hell you wanted to do and tried to keep them from finding out about it. That phony father-daughter pretense was used on all the girls at Metro.

"Then when the old man started losing control in the late forties, he saw the handwriting on the wall. I was at Metro from 1940 to 1952. One by one, the contract players walked through the door marked

'Exit' and you were on your own from that day on. When the studios lost their movie theaters in the antitrust fiasco, they also lost their stable of indentured servants. The golden era was dead and the kids took over. Then it didn't matter who you were—Gable or Garland—it was every man for himself.

"What the hell! I made twenty-five or thirty pictures under my contract—I've lost count—and when it was over, I had just about had it. I made a few free-lance deals after that, but most of them were lousy. The films I'll be remembered for, if any, were all made in the good old days."

Billy had seen them all. From countless balcony seats he had fallen for the "Pearls Girl" along with the rest of America's youth. He had watched her spike Van Johnson's milk shakes, dance with Fred Astaire, and swoon in the arms of Robert Taylor. At midnight shows in Greenwich Village, he had chuckled when the limp-wristed film buffs mouthed the lines to one of Gilda's classics, *The Lady Waited:* "I never knew you were a woman of steel," said Clark Gable, scooping up a handful of Gilda's angora sweater as they embraced. "I'm not, darling," echoed the audience, "I'm a woman of tin foil."

In *The Bridge* she played a nun. In the filth, degradation, and hunger of Sumatra under the Japanese, after tramping through the jungle for six days, she held a dying child in her arms and prayed for rain. In *Ebb Tide,* she nursed a blind pianist back to health and inspired his greatest concerto—all from her death bed in a tuberculosis sanitorium. In *Jinxed Lady,* she was a lady mobster who turned the tables on the Mafia to avenge the murder of the cop she loved.

Billy had cheered them all, and couldn't believe the woman he worshiped in .35-millimeter over so many Reese's peanut butter cups and Hershey bars had now chosen him as her confidant.

She knew how to play the game, how to pose for pictures, how to tell a raunchy anecdote on the set to make the visiting ink-stained wretches lick their chops. "Gilda Greenway gives great interview!" wrote a gay reporter from the *Village Voice.* But they didn't fool her. And she saved her best after-hours stories for Billy.

"I've always distrusted the press. But I've always gotten along with those conniving bastards. Why did Hedda Hopper protect me at the height of her reign of terror? Because when nobody else in Hollywood would have anything to do with her son Bill, he was living rent-free in my guest house. It was a reporter from the *Denver Post* who gave me the clap for the first time. I didn't know what it was and I'd never heard of penicillin. I got blood poisoning and damn near died. Took me six months to recover from that one. And all I got out of it was a full-page feature in the Sunday supplement called 'A Night to Remember with a Hollywood Glamourpuss!' The motherfucker sent it to me with a note scrawled across the top of the page saying, 'Baby, you were swell!' After that, I kept fucking but I stopped reading."

Her mind was a Ping-Pong game and her body paid dearly for it. One day was "Open Sesame" and everybody got a present, from the Mexican gardener to the exercise instructor who dropped around in his Jesus van to rub her back with avocado oil. The next day was the Black Hole of Calcutta and she'd sink into what she called "the mean reds," drinking Jack Daniel's and apple juice until she was numb, cursing everyone on the TV screen, locking herself in a dark room and smoking until she didn't even feel the sting.

"How that woman still wears the same size six she wore twenty years ago is a bigger Hollywood mystery than the death of Jean Harlow," said May. "It's called self-protection."

"How do you mean?" Billy was walking the agent from the projection room where they had just seen the latest batch of dailies.

"When you've been pushed around in this business long enough, you stop believing in people and all you've got left is your looks. If you basically have a loving, giving nature yet reach a certain pinnacle of success at the same time, you get used. Who can you trust? The public is fickle. The fans make you and break you. Your private life is suspect, too. The only thing left for the old broads is the mirror. When all else fails, Gilda makes sure the camera still loves her."

Billy's interview grew into something more. He became Gilda's chum, her escort, her playback. He ran her through her lines. Sometimes he slept over at The Pearls to get her through the ordeal of another restless night alone. Her luxurious, untidy bedroom at The Pearls, smelling of oranges, chrysanthemums, and the fading scent of White Shoulders, flickering with firelight, was always tacitly chosen as a meeting place. Here she spent sleepless hours of the night pacing, the only sound in her quiet house the sound of the blender. Here he watched her lonely silhouette, lit only by the light of the open refrigerator door in her bedroom mini-bar, making pitchers of margaritas.

Often he'd find the strangest cross-references in her leather-bound address book, organized the same unique way her mind worked. Once he was having trouble finding Jimmy Stewart's phone number.

"Look under B," she shouted from the bathtub.

There it was—under "Bridge Players."

Another time he discovered a once-prominent Hollywood star who was now down on her luck listed under *U*—for understudies.

One night they went to Dominick's and ran into Barbara Stanwyck. "Howya doin'?" Gilda asked, pausing at her table.

"Hanging in there," said Stanwyck in her scratchy, subterranean voice.

They slid into their own booth. "That dame has hated me ever since Robert Taylor put the make on me in 1949. Memory of a bull elephant."

Billy never knew whether to believe her or not. She had told so many stories that she was beginning to believe her own press clippings.

"Believe her," said King, in the commissary. "Chances are she's telling the truth. That woman has done just about everything twice. One night in the forties, she's at this big dinner party at Romanoff's, see. And Samuel Goldwyn has just let loose with one of his legendary goofs, with all the words in the wrong places. So Gilda up and says, 'According to *Time* magazine, one out of three Americans will be illiterate by the year 2000. Mr. Goldwyn, you've got a sixty-year head start.' It made Louella Parsons's column."

They laughed and sipped beer. "Did you ever hear the story behind her feud with Bruce Gerber?" King asked Billy. "You know he's the biggest closet queen in town. He's been the head honcho at just about every studio in town and every time the red-headed little fag moves he thinks he's saving the industry. Well, he and Gilda hate each other. Mention his name in her presence and she says, 'He makes spider sperm,' and leaves the room.

"It started at the Cannes Film Festival. Gilda and Avery run into Bruce, who is cruising the beach looking for a boy and pretending he's looking for a new star. Avery invites them all to dinner one night at a Moroccan restaurant behind the Carlton and Avery brings along a little French boy—real blond and cute, like Brigitte Bardot with side-burns. Brucie gets horny as hell and takes the kid back to the hotel. It's love at first sight and Hollywood's sleaziest mogul discovers the joys of Vaseline.

"Next thing you know the kid has moved to California and is shacked up in Laurel Canyon at Brucie's house. It's bliss for the town's most eligible bachelor for a while, but hell on his social status. He can't invite anyone over because he'll have to explain his house guest and he can't exactly take the kid to Betsy Bloomingdale's for a sit-down. So Gerber calls Gilda and asks her to take the kid off his hands. Gilda leaves with the kid, the kid pulls a big scene, threatens to remove what's left of Brucie's red hair with a butcher knife, and Bruce blames Gilda for getting him into this pain in the first place. Tells her he'll fix it so she'll never work in the picture business as long as she lives—well, that blew the top off the teapot.

"About a year later the kid is back in town. Gilda invites Bruce to The Pearls, begging him to forgive her, declaring undying love, and making a peace offering. His already bloated ego is flattered, so he accepts. Gilda calls Inez and tells her to get ready for a new chapter in Hollywood history and we go to The Pearls for the big reunion. Meanwhile, Gilda calls out the troops and puts on the dog. Every major studio head in town is present for this one. And when dinner arrives, it's Moroccan food. Bruce turns the color of a Concord grape and Gilda says, 'Fellas, I'd like to introduce my newest discovery—fresh from France. Or have you already discovered him first, dear?' And the beady-eyed little closet queen starts choking on his cous-cous. Out of nowhere comes this kid, stark naked, with his schlong hanging down to his knees, and he walks right up and sits down on Bruce Gerber's big fat lap and says, 'I'll always thank Mr. Gerber here for discovering me first. Miss Greenway gets the commission, but my heart belongs to Daddy!' Brucie shit a brick. Then in the chaos Gilda leans across the table and says, 'You aren't enjoying your cous-cous, dear, and you were so wild about it in Cannes!' And she pours a bottle of Chianti into his soup! Joyce Haber ran the whole story as a blind item in the *Times*. It ruined his reputation in this town. The guy still thinks he's in the closet, but now it's the only closet in town with klieg lights."

Billy was beginning to get the picture. It was a hell of a story, but most of it was unprintable. Gilda was a woman of enormous appetites, great compassion, and heartrending sensitivity. But she was also a complex creature of extreme mood shifts and terrifying self-doubts. To her fellow actors, she could be stubborn and unyielding. To her crew, she was a comrade in arms. Despite their early misgivings about her appearance in the same film with Devon Barnes, they adored her and they let her know it. Many of the technicians on *Cobras* were old-timers who had worked on her former films, hand-picked because they understood her neuroses and made her feel comfortable. They knew she had found them work at a time when jobs were scarce, and they showed their appreciation in a thousand little ways between set-ups. They poured her coffee and brought home-baked cookies. They told her raunchy jokes and let her look through their viewfinders. They positioned forbidden mirrors at opportune places on the set so she could check her hair and lip gloss even in the middle of a take. On the set she was the queen and they were her loyal serfs.

At home, it was different. There were stains on the wall of her bedroom where she had thrown food trays at Mrs. Denby, and occasional smells in the carpet where her bladder had given up on her way to the toilet. "If only Patrick was here," she'd moan. Or, "I'm too told old to get it up anymore." She'd given up on love and she knew she'd never have any security unless she bought it herself. The "bottom line," as Billy saw it, was her overwhelming inner fear of being exposed as a humongous star with a very tiny talent. But there was something admirable about her drive—her determination to make one last stab at movie greatness before she went down for the count.

On the day after a drunken binge she'd bloat up like a bullfrog and they couldn't photograph her. More than once during *Cobras,* they had to shoot the back of her head. Sometimes she'd phone in sick and they'd shoot around her. Two days later she'd arrive at 7:00 A.M., radiant as a dahlia, trailed by lhasa apsos wearing diamond collars, talking smooth and pinching the light man on the behind. "Harry, do something special today with the pink gel like you used to do with Kim Novak," she'd wink. And the rushes were glorious.

Cobras crawled out of the editing labs at the end of the winter, went tottering into spring, and collapsed of box-office anemia. "Bright,

358 / REX REED

beautiful, and vapid," hissed *Time* magazine. "The kind of moth-chewed Southern Gothic that smells like rotten magnolias," screeched Pauline Kael, who went on to barbecue Avery Calder's screenplay. "Too much star-studded weight to carry its pale little plot," groused the *New York Times.*

Everyone praised the performances by King Godwin and Devon Barnes, and the important critics over the age of twenty-five were in general agreement that anything with Gilda Greenway was worth the price of admission. Gilda was flattered, but a small vein in her left temple danced a feverish rhumba when she read one particularly bovine female critic's stern advice to "play her own age next time—if there is a next time."

Billy Buck's review was kind, saving his reprimands for Larry Sperling's languid direction and the cinematographer for shooting Gilda "with so many filter lenses this still rhapsodically beautiful icon looks like she's been photographed through the bottom of a mayonnaise jar." Gilda shrieked when she read that one. "Well, baby, how else would you photograph an old ham?"

Devon read the *Variety* reports about the film's reviews in a seedy taverna in Mexico, almost choking on her spicy sangrita. Scathing was an understatement. In the end, *Cobras* came in $8 million over budget. It had to be rescored three times because the director sued the studio over the use of a soundtrack he hadn't approved. *Cobras* bankrupted the two independent producers May had strong-armed into financing it, and it was five years before Sperling worked again.

In the final analysis, *Cobras* went down in the books as the most titanic all-star turkey since *The Misfits.*

King went into a French-Israeli co-production about an American espionage unit trapped by the Palestinians, filmed on location in Almeria, Spain. Avery Calder, stricken by the devastating beating his script received, threw in the towel and moved to London.

Gilda retreated to the sanctuary of The Pearls and made peace. They had tried to make a movie about real people, but the industry had changed. It was now a time of *Star Wars* and *Close Encounters* of the Steven Spielberg kind. May called with pep talks and rumors of new scripts, but Gilda knew her silent phone told the real story. She had given it all she had to give, and the old Tabasco was sapped. "The only roles left for women over fifty in this town are ax murderesses and ailing mothers. Roz Russell once told me, 'Stay away from the mothers, dear —the audience always cares more about the daughters.' I'll wait for a good script about Alzheimer's."

Her voice had always come from somewhere in the basement. Now it came from the fallout shelter. The old *oomph* was still there. But the will was gone. Little did she know that *Cobras* would turn out to be her swan song. Devon's, too.

TWENTY-FOUR

DECEMBER 26, 1979

S tuck behind three Winnebago campers at a traffic light on Vermont Avenue, Billy Buck drummed his fingers on the dashboard.

Devon had been silent for most of the ride back to town. Billy was a professional journalist—but even as a professional, he knew there were times when it was better *not* to ask questions. Besides, after his three Margarita lunch, he needed his reserve energy to focus on the road.

They were in a seedy section of Los Angeles the movies never showed. Billy had been here only once before, when the MGM librarian had driven him to the old Metro vaults on Vermont Avenue where the nitrate film cans were stored before the nitrate films were transferred to safety film. Because of several fires on the back lot, the flammable reels of early nitrate stock had been moved from Culver City to an air-conditioned warehouse in a run-down neighborhood where few people from Beverly Hills had ever been.

Billy had been trying to track down old deleted numbers from MGM musicals. He remembered the irony he felt that day, rummaging with a flashlight through storage bins in search of Fred Astaire dance numbers, Judy Garland songs, and Marx Brothers routines—discarded and forgotten as the weeds growing through the cracks in the ugly sidewalks outside.

Once a neighborhood where blue-collar workers lived in neat, respectable shingle houses, the *barrio* between Figuero and Vermont was now inhabited by Cubans and Mexicans. Drug raids were prominent and knifings were so frequent the newspapers didn't even bother to report them.

It was a neighborhood of body shops and vacant lots, where the air smelled of motor oil and cooking grease. Billy couldn't imagine what Devon Barnes was doing here.

"Turn right up ahead," Devon said. "We're almost there."

"Devon . . ." Billy felt silly. This is what Gilda must have been going through, he thought. "You won't tell me where you've been, but will you at least tell me whether you're here to stay? I'd hate to say hello and goodbye to you the same day."

"No more running, Billy, I promise. Right now my future's a little up in the air, but I do know there won't be any more disappearing acts."

"Are you going to be all right?" Billy asked anxiously.

"All right? Oh, because of the police. . . . I'm seeing Detective Biggs at five this afternoon. Billy, you do believe that I have nothing to hide, don't you?"

"You know me, honey. I believe anything."

"In a pig's eye, as we used to say down in Mullin, Texas." She laughed. "Lord, I haven't used that expression in years. It was one of my daddy's favorites. Pretty ironic. He was one of the most trusting men ever to walk this earth."

"I guess Gilda never found your father's grave, did she?"

He turned on Mariposa, where Devon told him to, and found himself driving down a shabby street lined with fading pastel-colored bungalows, their paint peeling, their shutters broken. Several small children waved and smiled as he drove past their hopscotch game.

"She did, actually. As angry and hurt as she was after I left, she had the records traced. He was buried in a little Mexican cemetery up in the San Joaquin Valley."

"What a woman she was," Billy said. "So you'll be able to visit his grave."

"I already did, Billy. Christmas Eve."

"But when did you talk to Gilda?"

Devon sighed.

"Why all this cloak-and-dagger secrecy?" He shook his head, then winced from the pain of a developing headache. "Did you bump into anyone while you were up there?" he asked, trying to sound casual.

"You mean, do I have any witnesses? Billy, my love, you make a better journalist than police investigator. Why don't you leave that to Biggs?"

"Okay, but tell me this—those pearls you were wearing . . . I keep thinking how much they looked like Gilda's."

"They were Gilda's," Devon said. Then she pointed to a dusty stucco house a few yards ahead, half hidden by a banana tree turning brown in the heat. "Right there."

"Here?" Billy asked dubiously.

"I have friends here. They took me in on Christmas Eve, when I ran away from The Pearls." She reached for the car door handle.

"Ran away? With Gilda's pearls?"

He reached over and grabbed her arm as she was getting out of the car.

"Please, Billy, I shouldn't have let that slip out. And I'm late." She leaned over to kiss his cheek. "I have to see King before I say anything else. There are some things I need to tell him."

"Like who's hiding in there, for instance?" He looked at the house. The screen door had opened. A plump brown woman with a red scarf around her head stepped out onto the porch, carrying a small child in her arms.

"I have to go. Thanks, Billy. For everything." She jumped out and ran up the walk.

"Devon, wait," he called.

But she didn't. The brown woman held the screen door open for her. When the door slammed shut behind them, a scrawny chicken scurried out from under the porch in a frenzy of feathers and dust.

TWENTY-FIVE

DECEMBER 26, 1979

H ollis Godwin drove his red Thunderbird convertible into the driveway of his mother's Holmby Hills estate.

"You sure you don't mind?" he asked May. "She looked so lousy today. I just want to check on her. Then I'll take you home."

As soon as they walked out of the funeral chapel, pushing through the autograph hounds and Gilda's weeping fans, Hollis had torn off his jacket, rolled it into a ball, and stuffed it into a seat well between them like the impatient school kid he still sometimes was. Now he tugged off his tie and unbuttoned his shirt collar, running a freckled hand through his hair. He always reminded May of King when he did that. He's twenty-one, May marveled, almost the same age King had been when Hollis was born.

"No," she sighed, touching Hollis's cheek and running a fingertip over the little hairline scar that parted his left eyebrow. "I don't mind. I'll wait here."

"You okay?"

"About par for the course."

"I won't be long," he promised.

May watched him as he sprinted across the lawn at the side of the house, heading toward the tennis courts and pool. He turned just as he was rounding the corner and waved.

Where did you come from? May asked silently. She regularly asked him that, and Hollis would always grin that goofy jack o'lantern grin, just as he was doing now. She loved him so much. Even now when every nerve in her body was tensing into a first-class spasm.

His deeply tanned face was framed by blond, sun-streaked hair, a shade darker than his father's, and his eyes were even more brilliantly blue than King's. This was a true child of the sunny West Coast, with a disposition, now that he and May had grown comfortable in their relationship, to match.

When he was thirteen, he had begged May to adopt him. At fourteen, he had run away from home and "hidden" at her beach house for two weeks. That was when Hollis had decided that May needed someone to look after her, and he'd elected himself her guardian and gadfly.

"How can you live like this?" he'd say, his arms full of soiled blouses, or empty Weight Watcher containers he'd collected from her floor, or the misplaced books and scripts she'd been looking for. "Why don't you lose some weight? You're a looker, May, but you're fat as a hedgehog," he'd say.

"You're my godmother," he'd bitch at her. "You're supposed to set a good example. I don't think you ought to be sleeping around, you know? Especially with such losers."

Finally, she forced herself to sit him down and fight back. "Enough," she'd shouted. "Enough! This is it, buster. What you see is what you get. Too sloppy, too promiscuous. This is what fat looks like. And it's too damn bad. I am also your godmother. Take it or leave it."

She looked at him, fighting back the tears, a big kid with blond hair streaked by sun and salt air, broad, brown shoulders slumped forward, hands hooked in the belt loops of his bleached tight-fitting Levi's. Hollis Godwin looked back and said, "You can't do this to me, May. I love you."

That was the first time he said it. Overwhelmed by his fierce sincerity, she was rendered speechless. Then she'd taken a deep breath and said, "Where did you come from?"

"Looking good, May."

She shielded her eyes and looked up. Mitch Misyak was ambling toward the car, rolling up his shirt sleeves. "Where's the kid?"

"He went around back to see Inez. Is she okay? She looked awful this morning."

"Her feelings run deep," Mitch said. "Why don't you come in? She could use a friend today. So could I. My God, you're looking super, Buttercup."

"A cup of butter is more like it, melting in this heat."

He leaned against the Thunderbird. May had to squint into the hazy sunlight to see his face, half hidden behind his brown-lens Foster Grants. His hip rested on the edge of the windshield, his crotch nearly level with her face. "I'd have never left if I'd known you were going to shake down to such a hot handful, Buttercup. Mama, you do look good."

"There's something hanging from your nose, Mitch," May said. "Coke or snot, I can't tell at this distance. Here." She pulled a handkerchief out of her purse, spit on it, and offered it to Inez's lover. "Wipe off the evidence."

Mitch touched his nostrils, and tasted his finger. "It isn't coke. Come on, May." He shifted his hips and tugged at his jeans as if his jock strap was too tight. "You remember how good it was. I miss you, mama."

Poor Inez, May thought. She shook her head. "Mitch, let me be honest, okay? I'll spell it out for you. Go fuck yourself."

"Getting all you need, right?"

"And then some."

"Oh, nice, sweetheart. You always were a class act."

"Your arms look good. Nice tan. You can hardly see the tracks."

"Up yours, May," he said, rolling down his sleeves.

"Seriously," she said, smiling. "You need to take better care of Inez. If anything happens to her, you're back on the street, where you aren't going to fetch the big bucks you're used to, understand? No house, no Jag, no clothes, *rien*, baby. Zipsky. So if you plan to keep stuffing her nose full of shit, you're cutting your own throat, Mitch. You're supposed to be keeping her clean. She was stoned out of her mind at the chapel this morning."

"Yeah," he said. "It was a sad day for us all."

Hollis came up suddenly behind Mitch, put an arm on his shoulder, and spun him around. "Goddamn it, Mitch. She's all fucked up again."

"Hey, Hollis, my man. Howya doing? Hey, babe, this one ain't my fault. She picked up a stash, I don't even know where, and she was blowing all morning. She filled the Vicks inhaler, you know, and she must've snorted up a gram before I even noticed. She was wired before we got to Forest Lawn. It's Gilda, you know? She's taking it hard. What can I do? I'll ride it out with her. She'll be clean in a day or two. It's just Gilda, you know?"

Up at the top of Topanga Canyon Road, a row of cypress trees swayed against the sky. From halfway up the mountain, May could see the young, sturdy trees and, just to the right of them, the soaring silhouette of her home. The sight always brought her pleasure, always took her by surprise, since it was the first thing in her life she had ever created from her own imagination. It was all hers, and it was perfect.

She had ordered seventy-five trees from the south of France and worked diligently with the landscapers to determine exactly where and how they should be planted, spaced six feet apart, like sentinels guarding a spaceship. She had toiled for months with the architect to design the house, standing now like a huge chunk of adobe sculpture in striking contrast to the constantly stirring trees. She, May "Fuck-up" Fischoff, had chosen right for a change, and created beauty instead of chaos.

Everyone expected the worst. It was just like May, they joked, to spend $3 million on a house and fill it with Woolworth *tchotchkies.* But she fooled them. From her childhood in her family's dark apartment on West End Avenue, she had developed an almost puritanical dislike for clutter. No doilies here. No stuffy Victorian needlepoint or mahogany armoires, either.

Eschewing anything chic or trendy, she opted for an open, earthy pueblo style, like the sun-bleached Santa Fe landscapes in paintings by Georgia O'Keeffe. The exterior was a terrestrial sphere, but the interior was intentionally devoid of straight edges; everything was soft and round, like May herself used to be. The burnished tile floors and sanded stucco walls of the entrance hall led to rooms with textured walls faded to a pale, cool Mediterranean blue, accented by aged wooden ceiling beams. The furniture, mostly natural pine and vintage wicker, had also faded to a soft vanilla. The floors were pickled and bleached, then glossed to a mirrored sheen with seven coats of polyurethane.

Textured walls, giant cactus plants, and Indian artifacts maintained the New Mexico mood, offering "the peace and tranquility I need after a day in the ratfuck of Hollywood," May said. There were Navajo rugs in front of the open stone fireplaces, primitive pillows made from Indian rug fragments on the white cotton sofas, and lamp bases that were once fishing baskets. Steer horns hung on a wall above a worn leather couch and blue ceramic vases and shredded lace curtains invited a spacious feeling of timeless relaxation.

Her house, high on this hill behind the cypress orchard, was the best present she'd ever given herself, next to Hollis.

No matter what Gilda had said.

As Hollis guided the Thunderbird up the winding road, May gazed from the window and felt a shudder, remembering the fights she and Gilda had recently staged. About Hollis, about the television deal May had been negotiating for Gilda for the past year. "A role," May had promised, "that will make Joan Collins look like a whore on food stamps."

There had been so many flare-ups in the past few months, and the arguments were always the same. Especially about Hollis.

After all the years of hoping that Gilda had been right, that someday fat little May would have it all, the last piece had finally fallen into place.

Hollis's beauty and youth had stunned her. She was no longer the fat, jolly May who eagerly fucked cute young hustlers, then kicked them out of the house so she could gorge on ice cream and dietetic cashew butter. She loved Hollis and she resented him for loving her— for loving her now, when he would leave her someday. Gilda had been right, it was inevitable.

Five years ago, on her thirty-fourth birthday, May had gone to visit the set where King was filming *The Last Soldier.* He and Gilda had cooked up some reason why she *had* to be there that day—she couldn't remember what they'd said—then surprised her with cake and champagne. When she'd muttered about how she loathed public celebrations of her birthday, Gilda had said, "But, May, it's practically a tradition. Remember your sixteenth birthday lunch at '21'?"

May was sitting in the canvas chair with King's name stitched across the back when a boy, clad only in a tiny, fig-leaf bikini, appeared before her, bumping and grinding, and singing, "Happy birthday to you."

May had laughed good-naturedly, saluting her friends' appreciation of her taste for hunks.

The boy finished his performance, then plunked himself down on her lap and gave her a juicy birthday kiss. And everyone laughed again.

The noise of the canvas seat ripping in half was as loud and crude as a fart. Everyone laughed even harder. Everyone but May and sixteen-year-old Hollis Godwin, who'd dropped by the set with Mitch Misyak, one of May's regulars that year.

As flashbulbs exploded in her face, and the bikini boy, sprawled across her belly, mugged for the cameras, Hollis shoved his way through the crowd of grips, actors, and technicians. He hauled the bikini boy off May's lap, helped her to her feet, put a protective arm around her, and led her off the sound stage.

She liked to tell people that she'd never looked back. It had been about a year since she'd seen him and he'd grown a lot. He was much taller than she, and his hair was shorter. The arm around her waist was man-size and powerful.

May shook her head at him. "Jesus, Hollis," she said, "you're gorgeous."

"Yeah, I was hoping you'd notice," he grinned. "May, what am I going to do with you?" He lit a joint, pulled a couple of tokes, and offered it to her.

"Still dancing on the lip of the volcano?" she said, as she exhaled.

"I hear you're hot for junkies."

"An equal opportunity employer."

"Your taste in guys still stinks. Mitch is, like, a friend, but he's a scumbag, May, with a big mouth."

"His mouth ain't all that's big," she said.

"Aw, shit, May, shut up, will ya?" Hollis was driving a Harley motorcycle in those days. He handed her a helmet.

She said, "Are you nuts? If I climb on the back of this thing, you'll have a flat tire all the way to Malibu, baby."

"Goddamn it, May," he said.

He drove her down to the beach, came in for a beer, and never left.

They talked until the sun disappeared into the Pacific like a yellow watermelon, and she'd lit some Rigaud candles. They talked about Hollis's problems with drugs and May's problems with men. She said she thought she'd been making up for all the boys she'd never fucked when she was young. He said he thought drugs were his tit, the only things Inez hadn't given him.

They agreed that what they both needed was love. And that what they both wanted was to give it. The problem was, who could you trust in this town? Who was worthy, who wouldn't hold out on you, wouldn't advertise it up and down the Strip?

They were stoned on grass and wine, when the phone rang. May said, "No, Mitch, I don't want you to come by. I've got company. *Hollis,* yeah, little Hollis. Is he moving in? Hang on, Mitch, I'll ask him. Hollis," she said, "I'm tired of all this crap. You want to move in again? Like when you were fourteen? You want to live with me and pick up my dirty laundry and feed me diet Pepsi?"

"Fuckin' A," Hollis said. "Give me that phone. Hey, Mitch, don't call here anymore, okay? You want to talk to me, use my number at my mom's house. Leave a message. Don't bother this lady anymore. Yeah, lady, that's what I said." Hollis winked at May. "My lady. Meal ticket? You bet—breakfast, lunch, and dinner. Only, man, I don't need a meal ticket with May. We're going to live on love and mung bean sprouts."

May stood up and deliberately picked up a Baggie full of pot on the table between them. Holding it between two fingers, she slid open the glass door to the sundeck, walked over to the edge, and dumped the pot into the sand.

Hollis smiled.

"What else do you have?" she asked.

He stood up and emptied his pockets. He had four more joints, a gram bottle of coke, a couple of 'ludes, and four ecstasies in a Tylenol bottle. Together they fed the drugs to the trash compactor. "How soon can you move in?" she asked.

"I'm in," he said.

"Beauty, brains, success," Gilda had promised, "and love."

Well, she'd always had brains.

She had worked her ass off for success.

And she'd lost the goddamn weight—eighty-six pounds.

Gilda had been so proud of her.

Until May told her the denouement in the third act.

"I'm in love with Hollis," she'd said.

"But he's just a child," Gilda had said more than once. "Do you honestly think that Hollis is going to stay with you until you're old and gray? Oh, come on, grow up."

"You can't stand the idea because you see yourself getting old. Having Hollis around makes you feel all the more so. It has nothing to do with me."

"Oh, horseshit!" Gilda's retort was a nasty cackle. "Christ! Patrick was older than me, so was Big Ted. I'm not afraid of age. But what about you? Right now the age difference doesn't matter so much, but what about when you're sixty and he's forty-two? When you're seventy and he's fifty-two? He's gonna stay around then? Shit!"

"You bitch," May had said coldly. "I'll deal with it then."

Of course, she'd thought, gazing out the window, we would have worked it out. . . . I could never stay angry long with Gilda.

Until the other day when she phoned me about the Aaron Spelling deal.

I'd still kill her for that.

"Something bothering you?" Hollis asked as he shifted the Thunderbird's gears, coming out of the hairpin turn halfway up the mountain.

"Sometimes you're so perceptive," she said.

"I'm trying to help. Obviously you don't want it."

"Want or need?" she asked irritably.

He stared at her. Then turned his eyes back to the road. "May, I'm your lover. Your best friend. Don't forget that."

She didn't say a word. She turned away from him and continued to stare out her window.

It's only a matter of time before they question me, she thought. King certainly didn't do it. She almost laughed to herself. If the fucking police knew anything at all, they'd know he wasn't capable of it. No motive. He loved Gilda too much. Well, I loved her, but I've got a motive.

A damn good one.

May shivered.

From her window, from this angle of the winding road, the roof of her house was obscured by the untamed forest. The tangled vines, thick, prickly shrubs, and half-dead overhanging limbs of the trees seemed suddenly oppressive to her, chaotic and ugly compared to the orderly cypresses at the top of the mountain. She thought of Gilda, and the absence of Gilda.

She suddenly felt lost.

And scared.

"Earth to May. Come in, May."

"Don't mind me, Hollis. I'm just tired. Another chapter ended today."

When they pulled into the semicircular drive of the house, they were both overwhelmed—as they always were—by just how *big* the place was. A monument to money, May thought. No, that wasn't really what it was, more like a reward for eighteen-hour days and a constantly nagging hiatal hernia. Money was but a means to buy it.

Hollis parked the Thunderbird at the entrance. May unlocked the front door and took off her hat as they walked into the house through the inner courtyard. The morning papers—which they hadn't had time to read before the funeral—were on the hall table. She grabbed them as she walked into the study, tossing her black coat toward the fireside chair. The coat landed on the Navajo rug. She knew Hollis would heckle her if she didn't pick it up, but it didn't matter.

Not today.

She knelt in front of the fireplace, stacking papers and kindling on the grate. Hollis brought in a tray of fresh coffee and two mugs, and set it down behind her on the rug. He knelt beside her as he leafed through the newspaper until he found Billy Buck's column.

"How old was Gilda when this picture was taken?" he asked, smoothing the paper flat before him.

May looked over his shoulder. "Oh, my God, that picture. . . . Well, she was born in 1922, so she must have been thirty-four. Lord, Gilda, you were fabulous. And, oh, will you look at me? Sweet sixteen, and what an unhappy blimp. Your mother looks gorgeous though, doesn't she? In Harriet Brinkley's cashmere. Oh, and look at King—and Devon."

"I wish I'd gotten to know Gilda better," Hollis said. "She was really beautiful, wasn't she?"

"I wish she knew you better, too," May said.

Hollis looked up. "What's wrong, May?"

"Nothing. I'm edgy, is all." She stared at the picture of Gilda smiling, surrounded by her admirers, secure in their love. Not even the grainy newspaper reproduction could obscure her elegance and beauty. It was a portrait of a woman who had everything she wanted.

"Of course, I thought she was beautiful," she said, hearing the trace of bitterness in her voice. "I mean, I'd heard about that face all my life. But I stopped seeing it for myself. I don't remember her being quite so . . . exquisite. She was my gorgeous godmother, my dear friend and adviser, my famous client, and then my own personal Gethsemane. When I was a kid, I worshiped her. I never thought she could be cruel."

"Cruel?"

"Do you love me, Hollis?" May asked, staring into the fire.

"Ah, shit, May. What's going on?" He put a hand on her shoulder. "Come on," he said, "you've been acting flaky since they called about Gilda. Before that, even. Something's up. You have to tell me."

"I don't want to talk about it."

"I hate it when you do that. I tell you everything. Everything I think and feel and know. And you're always holding out on me, acting superior, being my goddamned patronizing mama. You're not my mama, May. And you're not my godmother, anymore, you know? I'm the guy you live with. The one you sleep with. Shit, May, what are you doing—you gonna let me into your bed and lock me out of the rest of it? No way."

"It's something Gilda said, that's all."

"About what? About me?"

"No," she lied. "Of course not. Leave me alone, Hollis, please," she begged, bringing her hand up to touch his. "Pay no attention to me. I'm angry and grieving. I'm pissed off that she's gone, and there's so much I still want to say to her."

He pulled his hand from under hers and stood abruptly.

"Where are you going?" she asked.

He was halfway to the door. "Out," he called without breaking stride. "I've got to get out of here for a while." The door slammed behind him.

TWENTY-SIX

DECEMBER 26, 1979

K ing had been trying to read the script for the past hour, with little success. It was based on an Elmore Leonard novel. The lead was an angry jaded cop who waits to catch a comely killer with cold-blooded ethics. A cop. The thought sent an ice pick through his gut.

May had sent it to him two weeks ago.

Two weeks, King thought. A lot had happened in two weeks.

He took his feet off the rattan coffee table and swiveled in his chair so he could look through the louvered doors past the wooden deck to the beach. His clothes were still on the floor where he'd thrown them after the funeral, changing quickly into faded jeans and a white cable-knit boat-neck sweater for a walk along the shore. Sand still clung to his toes; he had tracked it onto the white cotton rug.

He'd been renting May's Malibu house for two years now, ever since he'd moved out of his Holmby Hills place when Devon had come back into his life.

Devon.

What a shock to see her at the funeral this morning. And where was she now? He'd left messages on Billy Buck's machine and with his own answering service. He'd told May to call him the minute she knew anything. And here he was, with sand in his shoes, sand in his bed, sand blowing through his life again. What a time for the only woman he'd ever loved to reappear, just when he was almost resigned to living with his loneliness.

King stared through the glass doors at the Pacific. The noise of the sea was subdued; he could see the baskets of red and white impatiens hanging from the deck railing, swaying with the wind. He never knew what they were called until Devon told him.

"I love your impatiens," she said the first day he had brought her here.

"Gee," he answered dumbly, hypnotized by her beauty. "And I thought I was particularly calm today."

She had hooted that wild, melodic Texas laugh. "Silly, that's the name of the flowers."

She had grilled some swordfish that night with new potatoes and steamed corn on the cob, and they had made love in front of the fire on May's nautical-blue floor pillows, listening to Stan Getz records. King rubbed his eyes to erase the memories, but no relief was possible for the ache he felt inside. Without Devon, he was an empty shell, like the conch on May's fireplace mantel.

He glanced around at the comfortable room, navy and white, with floppy sailcloth-upholstered rattan chairs augmenting the nautical design theme May had chosen when she bought the place. King felt as old—and as temporary—as the hunk of driftwood, dry and bleached as a cow horn, he used for a doorstop. He'd taken it for granted, never realizing until now what a sanctuary the beach house had been for him after Devon walked out of his life, without a word, without a note.

He surveyed the once-neat living room, cluttered with unread scripts, empty yogurt containers, coffee mugs, and piles of jockey shorts and jogging shoes, and thought of the debris that cluttered his life. Now, unable to concentrate, he tossed the screenplay onto the table and picked up a newspaper, which was opened to Billy Buck's column and the "Four Fans" picture. Three grinning girls and one clumsy jock, trying to look cool. And Gilda, smiling her dazzling smile.

"Put your tongue behind your teeth," she'd told them.

He'd practiced that smile later, at his apartment on West Forty-sixth Street, while he was putting on the waiter's uniform Deauville Tolin loaned him to wear to the theater that night.

"You won't believe who I'm going with, man. Never in a million years."

Of course, Deau hadn't believe him. She was a movie star, one of the most famous and beautiful women of her day. He looked at the grainy newspaper photograph. They all paled beside her, even Devon.

Gilda. Her lush, perfect smile. The high cheekbones and pale cat's eyes. Her fiery hair cascading over one shoulder. Her hand in a kid leather glove wrapped around the stem of a champagne class.

That same hand, soft and bare, had straightened his tie that long-ago night. He'd waited in his shiny waiter's suit, pacing beneath the brightly lit marquee, until a white Cadillac pulled up in front of the theater.

Gilda emerged, graciously acknowledging the cries of her admirers. Avery was right behind her, already two sheets to the wind.

She took off her long white gloves, straightened his tie, and brushed back his hair.

"What do you think, Avery? Do we have movie star material here, or just lovely-to-look-at?"

Avery gave King the once-over. "Oh, definitely material," he said. "Velvet and ermine, my dear, and enough left over for a second pair of pants."

Gilda was so kind and loving then. Through the years, he'd always counted on her support. He knew Devon was number one with her, but he'd thought of himself as her next-in-line heir.

So when Devon disappeared—when she seemed to have vanished without a trace—he'd naturally gone first to Gilda.

But she wouldn't tell him what had happened, except to say, "She's gone, King." They were on the *Cobras* set. Gilda was retouching her makeup between setups in her portable dressing-room trailer near the honey wagon.

"Gone? Gone where?" he asked.

"I haven't the faintest idea," Gilda said coldly. "And I'm not sure I care all that much."

King could feel beads of sweat on his forehead. He'd waited almost twenty years for Devon Barnes. Now, inexplicably, she'd walked right out of his life.

And Gilda, the woman he'd escorted so proudly to the opening performance of *The Way Back Home,* stood before him, hard lines chiseled into the skin around her eyes and mouth.

"I know it had something to do with you," Gilda said. "First, you destroyed Inez—"

"You know Inez had her finger on the self-destruct button long before I married her," King interrupted. He sagged down into the deck chair in Gilda's trailer, breathing heavily.

"Well, why has she left?"

"Gilda, dammit, if I knew that, I assure you I wouldn't be asking you."

He gulped and brushed his hand across his eyes, wanting to cry for the first time since he was a kid and had seen his daddy blown sky high.

"This is rich," Gilda said. "The *Hollywood Reporter* would love to see Mr. Macho with the biggest tallywhacker in the business sitting here with tears in his eyes because another girl just left town."

King felt a sharp pain tightening around his chest. He could feel the blood drain from his face.

"Gilda, what's happening?" he whispered.

Gilda looked momentarily shaken. "I'm beginning to feel for the first time as if life is passing me by," she said with uncharacteristic weakness. "I wake up these mornings and look in the mirror and I see myself dying."

She brushed a tear away from the corner of her eye.

King pulled himself up wearily and walked out of the trailer.

"Take care," he said

"Don't I always?" she replied.

But he hadn't taken his own advice. The weeks and months that followed had been a nightmare. Gilda became increasingly difficult and remote, especially after *Cobras* was released and clobbered by the critics. And Avery had fled to London, leaving King without a friend or confidant.

He'd finally thrown himself into his work—his usual cure-all for the solitude in his heart that had haunted him for years. Despite the failure of *Cobras,* he was still a bankable star with box-office magic. But he was lonely, and sometimes missed the early days in Hollywood when he and Avery kept the gossip columnists in business.

Then, five months ago, Avery had phoned him from London. He was so weak that his voice was barely audible over the transatlantic line. He was eager to leave for his villa in St. Paul de Vence, he said, but was forced to stay on in London—just until his fanatical doctors administered one last battery of punishing tests.

"Then, my boy, I'm off to sunnier climes." He said he'd been daydreaming of the long, lazy afternoons at the Colombe d'Or, arguing politics with James Baldwin and Simone Signoret over the noise of the old men playing *boule* in the square. "The most peaceful of all places, baby. You look out over the olive trees below the walled city while the white doves eat yo' rolls and the sky turns purple with twilight and they still haven't cleared away yo' lunch. Nobody cares if the critics don't like ya. They're too busy reviewin' the critics themselves. I love it there. I don't want no more clocks in my life, baby. No more clocks."

There was still a trace of the old paprika. "At night, I can cruise the casinos in Monte Carlo," Avery said, chuckling mischievously. That reminded him of something he'd been meaning to tell King for some time.

"What was the name of that Felliniesque whore you and Michel Weiss-France brought from Vegas years ago?" he wheezed.

"Margie," King said.

"Yes, that's it. King, darlin' nephew, she was awfully indiscreet and I'm afraid Gilda and I were, too. We took her to The Pearls that evening. She was pretty well fried. We all were. Anyway, what began as a lark ended with your Margie mailin' Gilda a rather extraordinary set of films. Have you any idea what I'm talkin' about?"

Oh, shit, King thought, trying to remember what he must have looked like, all horny adolescent excitement and awkwardness. He remembered the mattress on the floor, Margie with her giant tits, and a dog, a goddamn *dog.*

"It was a stupid prank," Avery went on in his wheezy voice. "She needed money, and she said she had somethin' to sell. We thought the films were safer in our hands, you see. And, yes, we also thought they'd be amusin'. They weren't *Camille,* baby, but they *were* amusin'."

They'd dressed him up in studded vests, cod pieces, and leather straps. He was just a kid from the boonies, green as new corn, he'd just bought the motorcycle, and he'd been so proud of the second hand engineer's boots he'd bought to go with it. Stompin' boots. Black leather, thick and broken, seasoned boots. And he'd worn them in at least two of the fuck films. Oh man, what an asshole he'd been.

"We even talked of invitin' you to the screening, but, of course, we didn't—"

All I need, King thought, his apprehension turning to anger as Avery's voice became fainter and more plaintive.

"Forgive me," Avery said. "You know I'd never do anythin' to hurt you. I just wanted to—"

"What did you do with them?" King cut him off. "After you got your rocks off, I mean?"

"Oh," Avery said, stricken. "Please." And he began to cough. King waited in stony silence.

"Gilda still has them, I imagine. Will you ever forgive me?"

"What a fucking pain in the ass you are, Avery. You and Gilda sitting around watching fuck films I made when I was a kid."

Avery was coughing again. "You really piss me off," King said. "Have a nice holiday."

Then he hung up.

The next day, drinking coffee on the deck of May's beach house, he thought about how generous and loyal Avery had always been.

Avery—his friend and mentor.

It was Avery who had given him his start, held his hand and washed his face when he was sick, introduced him to cunts and kings, demonstrated friendship and devotion on a thousand occasions in his troubled life, stood up to the lions of Broadway like a feisty pit terrier to get an unknown actor the lead in *Barracks Street Blues*. He truly loved the man, so frail and old now, sapped of his old ginger.

He called London, but there was no answer in Avery's flat. Then he tried the villa at St. Paul de Vence, until late into the night. Finally, Gilda phoned him for the first time since the nightmarish failure of *Cobras*.

"King," she said, her voice hoarse, "I wanted to tell you before you read it in the papers. Avery died last night."

It wasn't possible. He had to apologize to Avery. He had to tell him he loved him, that he didn't give a flying fuck about the porno films. Even now, King wanted to speak to him.

Especially now.

Poor Avery. His once-great talent had lost ground to newer and more prolific writers. His work was no longer trendy. In the past few years he found himself savaged by the same critics who had once anointed him with adulation. Between the aesthetic pretensions and the public exhibitionism, Avery's balance had crumbled badly. With a lump in his throat, King pictured him at the end—a lonely boulevardier in a soiled ascot, dying alone of emphysema and God knows what other maladies, coughing up blood on his white linen plantation suit.

King could no longer sit still. He got up and began pacing the length of the living room, stopping to stare blindly at the red-and-yellow Roy Lichtenstein on the wall, then turning back in the direction of the glass doors.

The tension was unbearable. He glanced at his watch. 3:30. Too early for the news. Maybe there was something on the radio. He switched on May's stereo and turned the dial until he found an all-news station.

King paced, nervously chain-smoking, through several minutes of a report on a beached whale in San Diego. Then he heard the announcer say, "Still no real leads into the investigation of the Gilda Greenway murder, which took place Christmas Eve at her lavish Beverly Hills estate, The Pearls. Miss Greenway, one of the most famous Hollywood stars of the forties, was a close friend and one-time co-star of Kingston Godwin, who was questioned and released by Los Angeles police after he was found at the murder scene. Police are still seeking a motive, since nothing was apparently taken from The Pearls, nor was there any sign of a forced entry."

Damn. He wondered whether Biggs had believed his story. He picked up the telephone and dialed Billy Buck's number for the sixth time that day.

Then he heard a car pull into the driveway. The adrenaline rushed through him like a caffeine high.

Devon, he thought.

Taking a deep breath, he tried to slow his racing pulse.

Through the frosted glass of the front door, he watched the figure approaching the house.

Too tall. Too big to be Devon.

"Hey, Dad," Hollis said, when he opened the door. "Jesus, you look like I feel."

"That good, huh?" King said. "Where's May?"

The boy's face darkened. "She's home. She's driving me crazy. I had to get away for a while."

"Want a beer?"

"Got a joint?" Hollis asked.

King looked at him.

"I said a joint. I didn't ask for a syringe."

"I thought you were Pat Boone these days. Everything but the saddle oxfords. May says you've got your act together, doing great at the agency. She said you brought in two new clients."

Hollis shrugged. "A couple of kids I went to school with. They put together a group. They're good."

"Kids you went to school with?"

"Okay, kids I *cut* school with. Is that better? You satisfied? Jesus, give me a break. Everybody's busting my chops today."

"Sorry," King said, clapping Hollis's shoulder, leading him out to the deck. "There's grass here, somewhere. If you can find it, you can smoke it."

"Look at this pigpen. It's worse than when May lived here alone."

"Hey, I just straightened it up. Give me a break, too, okay?"

"She didn't call, did she?"

"Who, May?"

"Devon."

King shook his head.

"I hate to hit you with this now," Hollis said, perched nervously on the edge of the deck railing. "I know you've had a rough couple of days. But I need to talk to somebody. I'm going nuts. May is acting so damn weird. Something's bugging her and she won't tell me what it is. Mitch was coming on to her at Mom's Christmas party, but I trust May enough to know that nothing happened between them. All I know is she's had a bug up her ass ever since Christmas Eve. Since I stayed at the party, instead of leaving early with her."

"Why *did* she leave so early?" King asked. "I didn't even get a chance to talk to her."

Hollis ran his fingers through his blond hair, unconsciously imitating the exact gesture King used when he was troubled or tired. He took a long time answering.

"She said she didn't want to run into Gilda. She was pissed off at her. I think it had something to do with the Aaron Spelling TV deal May's been slaving over. I wish to hell I'd taken her home myself."

He looked at his father, silently pleading with him to say, Don't worry. It's not what you think. May didn't kill Gilda.

"Why didn't you take May home?" King asked, looking away from his son's gaze.

"What do you mean, why didn't I?"

"You think I was going to walk out on Mom, on Christmas Eve, with you there? I mean, I'm glad you came. It was a noble gesture. Very "Father Knows Best." What a guy. But did you happen to notice that she was pretty fucked up?"

"I noticed."

"Yeah, right. But it didn't occur to you to do anything about it, right? I'm the one who had to stay with her."

"You didn't have to, Hollis," King said softly.

"I didn't stay that long, only a couple of hours after May left. I couldn't leave her. She was fucked up because you were there."

"You know that's not true."

"You and Gilda, then. If Gilda had showed up, it would have been different."

"Yeah," King said, "and maybe we wouldn't have spent the morning at Forest Lawn."

"What's *that* supposed to mean?"

"I don't know," King said, staring out at the surf. "Like you said, it's been a rough couple of days."

"I'm worried about Mom," Hollis continued. "She dragged me upstairs and tried to bribe me with coke. Pulled out a Z from under her bed, like one of those bag ladies, honest to God. She's got stuff stashed everywhere. She was ranting about Gilda. You know, how it was the last straw, the final insult, Gilda not showing up at the Christmas party."

A lazy gull circled aimlessly, a noisy gray intruder in the peaceful cobalt sky. The two men watched in silence, lost in their thoughts. Then Hollis continued. "She made me stand guard at the bedroom door, Dad, while she was in the bathroom. I thought she was just pulling some paranoid crap. But she was shooting up. She doesn't know I saw her."

"And you didn't stop her?"

Hollis whirled around angrily. "What was I supposed to do? Call the cops? She's my mother. At least I stayed with her. At least I didn't run out on her the way you did."

"Hollis," King protested.

"Shit!" the boy spat. "That's what you would have done! Hey, Inez, you got a little drug problem? See ya. Hop into the old T-bird and fly away, right? Just like my old man. Take off, just like that seagull. There's a problem here? Run!"

The words hit King with the impact of an explosion, knocked him back, breathless. He sat down, suddenly realizing the running had to stop. It was an old feeling, as old as the smell of smoke on a Louisiana highway that came back to him at times like this. Once, he'd seen his world blow up before his eyes. Instinct had commanded him to run and never look back. He'd been running ever since.

"Hollis, I'm sorry," King said. He got up and walked over to where the boy was standing.

"Aw, shit! Look at me," Hollis cried. "I *am* like you. I want to do the same thing to May that you've been doing to me all my life. She's in trouble. And I feel like saying, Screw this, I'm taking off. She's acting as if she's done something terrible. And she won't tell me what it is. May's hurting. Mom's in the worst shape I've ever seen her. And you're sitting here looking like Boris Karloff." He turned away again, and looked back out at the sea.

How long, King wondered, had it been since he'd talked to his son? Told him anything that really mattered. Staring at Hollis's broad shoulders, the sun-streaked blond hair curling over his collar, King suddenly hoped it wasn't too late.

"Hollis," he said, touching him tentatively on the shoulder, "let's take a walk on the beach and talk."

"Are you sure you want to?" Hollis said.

"Damn sure."

It had been years since King had even thought about his child-hood. They walked along the water's edge as Hollis listened, fascinated. King talked about his first days in New York, about the marine recruiting station where he'd been rejected, and about Alvin Beamer, the recruit from Louisiana. He described the three-room railroad flat on West Forty-sixth Street.

Finally, he said, "I was poor and hungry, so I did something stupid. I made some porn films."

"No shit," Hollis said, impressed.

"Yeah," King said. He took a breath. "Before he died, Avery told me Gilda had them. She'd promised to give them to me as a Christmas present. They're probably still under her tree—gift-wrapped, with my name on the card."

Hollis whistled.

"That's why I was at The Pearls the night Gilda was murdered. She'd said she was going to bring them with her to your mother's party. When she didn't show up, I decided to stop by and see what happened to her. And I didn't want those damn reels floating around town."

"Then someone saw you going in and called the cops?"

King shook his head. "The cops were called *before* I set foot in The Pearls."

Hollis shuddered. "It was the killer. It had to be. Whoever called the cops killed her, right?"

A light, cool breeze blew in off the ocean.

"Let's go back," King said. "It's getting chilly."

"Who called?"

"A woman."

Hollis stopped abruptly. "Dad," he said, "May won't tell me where she went that night after she left the party. It's one of the things that's driving a wedge between us now."

He picked up a small shell and hurled it into the waves.

"I love May. I don't want to leave her. If she's in trouble, I want to help her. Whatever it is, I don't want to run."

"I can't see it," King said. "I can't imagine May hurting Gilda.

She loved her. Gilda practically raised May. Whatever it is, she'll tell you about it eventually."

"You think so?"

"You're not a runner, Hollis. You're a lover."

"Oh, Dad." Hollis punched his father's arm. "If I'm such a great lover, maybe you could get me into one of your next porn flicks," he said with a laugh.

Then he sprinted down the beach in the direction of the house.

King slowly followed Hollis's footprints in the sand, marveling at the strength and compassion he saw in the young man. He and Inez were more fortunate than they deserved to have raised such a son. Although, to be honest, he had to admit that Hollis had raised himself.

What a mess King had made of his life. Inez. Hollis. Gilda. Devon.

No wonder she'd run from him.

His steps quickened. Perhaps Billy Buck had returned his calls. Billy could tell him where Devon was, how he could find her.

He felt unaccountably optimistic as he hosed sand from his feet and climbed the deck stairs two at a time toward the open doors of the living room.

He froze.

He could hardly believe what he saw.

Raven black hair tumbling down past the shoulders.

Violet eyes glinting with the reflection of the setting sun.

Tall, slim figure accentuated by the faded man's shirt and dungarees.

The full bottom lip trembling even as the smile said, I'm scared. But I still love you.

In her arms she held a small, curly-headed child, her hair the identical shade of black. The child gazed at him serenely, sucking happily on her left thumb.

"Hello, King," she said.

"Devon," he smiled.

"Quinn, honey, say hello to your daddy," Devon said to the little girl.

The child hid her head in Devon's shoulder.

"I don't understand," said King.

Devon's smile widened.

"She's our daughter, King."

King gently touched the child's back. She turned her tiny face toward him and took her thumb out of her mouth.

"Dada?"

"She's beautiful, Devon. She looks just like you."

"But she has your stubbornness and charm. And your eyes."

The little girl stared at him with eyes blue as periwinkles, framed by thick black curly eyelashes. He put his arms out and she allowed him to take her from Devon without protest.

He kissed her soft baby cheek and said, "Hello, Quinn." He wanted to say much more but the lump in his throat blocked the words, so he hugged her instead. He wanted to cry.

He sat down on the couch and settled her on his lap. Devon sat next to him. Only now with her arm touching his, her leg brushing against his, did he believe it was really true—she was here, in this room, beside him.

"Uh, Dad," said Hollis, poking his head through the doorway of the kitchen. "I just phoned May from the wall phone."

King had forgotten his son was still in the house.

"I think this is my cue to exit stage left," Hollis said. "Thanks for the advice. May says to come over if and when you three have had your fill of one another. We're looking forward to getting to know Miss Quinn." He blew a kiss toward them. "Bye, Devon—and try to stick around this time, okay?"

Quinn had discovered the script that King had earlier discarded on the couch. She was happily banging on the brown cardboard cover and trying to open it up.

"Story, Mama?" she asked.

"Soon, baby, we'll read you a story," Devon assured her. The child babbled happily as she climbed off King's lap to get closer to the bound volume.

"I know I have a lot of explaining to do, King," Devon said, taking his hand and twining his fingers in his. "I know how hurt and angry you must have been. But I had to leave. When I found out I was pregnant, there was no question but that I was going to have this baby.

That was what I wanted more than anything in the world—except you. But you were still married, and I knew how long it could take before Inez would be willing to let you go."

"But, Devon, why didn't you tell me?" He heard the anger in his voice and took a breath to calm himself. "We could have been together, lived together . . ."

"Please, King, hear me out." She brought his hand to her lips and kissed it tenderly.

"You married Inez because you *had* to, were forced to. Because there was a baby on the way. I didn't want to do that to you again. And I thought you might need some time for yourself, on your own, without anyone making demands on your emotions. I needed you to love our baby because you wanted to, not because you had to. Besides," she continued, her voice faltering for the first time, "we are talking about Hollywood, 1977. I was having nightmares imagining the headlines: 'DEVON BARNES BEARS STUD KING GODWIN'S LOVECHILD!' "

Quinn pulled at Devon's leg. "Mama, Mama, *agua.* " She pointed toward the ocean. *"Mi arena."*

"Our bilingual baby," Devon laughed. "Yes, honey," she said, scooping her up, "let's go play in your sand."

They walked hand in hand along the beach, watching Quinn as she ran and jumped through the wet sand. "She loves the beach," said Devon. "It's the asphalt and concrete that bothers her. And wearing shoes. She hates shoes. Like Gilda."

"Why does she know Spanish?" King asked.

Devon told him how she'd fled to Puerto Cruz, to that special place he'd so lovingly described to her the first night they spent together. She'd thought he might turn up one day—after all, it *was* his paradise—so they could enjoy its lush simplicity together.

He shook his head. "No, I couldn't be there without dreaming about you, thinking of you constantly. And I missed you so much I could hardly stand it."

He hugged her so fiercely she was momentarily breathless.

"But why did you decide to come back now? For Gilda's funeral?"

"I knew this would be the first Christmas Quinn might remember, and I thought about those Christmases I spent in Texas at Maybelle's ranch after my daddy died and my mother sometimes forgot to drop by. I wanted her to be with her family—with you and Gilda."

She looked at King with stricken eyes, turning moist with tears. "Oh, King, King," she wept, "how could this have happened?"

"Mama cry?" Quinn said, her mouth turning down as if she, too, might begin to cry in imitation.

"No, angel, everything's all right," Devon said, bending down to kiss Quinn reassuringly, fighting back her tears.

"Tell Daddy why I named you Quinn," Devon said.

The little girl reached her short, tanned arms toward him, signaling that she wanted to be picked up.

"Grandma," she said, bouncing happily in his grasp like a Raggedy Ann doll. "Grandma Gilda."

King looked at Devon questioningly.

"Gilda's family name. Before Ted Kearny made her change it to Greenway."

"Did Gilda ever know about Quinn?"

"Not until the other day when we got to The Pearls."

Devon didn't know how Gilda would react to seeing her again. She'd written to Gilda every couple of months but had not received even one postcard in response during the two years she'd been gone. She worried about Gilda's state of mind, especially after she read George Christy's column: "GILDA GREENWAY: GOING GARBO'S WAY."

> Now that *Cobras* has earned its niche in cinema legend as the most spectacular, talent-laden failure in the history of Hollywood, Gilda Greenway, the one-time great star, has become a virtual recluse—and with good reason. All she has to do is walk into any restaurant in town, and a hush descends upon the room as if she were filming an E. F. Hutton commercial. Who can blame her for staying home? This is a town where venom drips from the mouths of Hollywood wives who delight in picking her reputation clean like desert vultures polishing off the carcass of a dead cow.

Devon could only imagine what Gilda must have thought when she read that column. She had to see her. She had to give Gilda and

Quinn the chance to meet each other. So Devon had decided to make the journey north from the jungle and beach of Puerto Cruz to Los Angeles, another kind of jungle.

They'd arrived in the late afternoon. After the long drive beneath the relentless Mexican sun, the exhausting plane trip, and the harrowing freeway traffic, the atmosphere inside the familiar iron gates seemed especially quiet. The early twilight air was cool, and Devon could hear the birds cawing and singing in the aviary. Quinn was so enchanted by the ducks that honked at them from the lawn that she even took her thumb out of her mouth to bang the car window.

Mrs. Denby opened the door. Her face registered shock and outrage.

"Hello, Mrs. Denby, is Gilda home?" Devon said as pleasantly as she could.

"Where else do you think she could be?" the housekeeper snapped.

"Good. I'm looking forward to seeing her."

"Indeed! What makes you think you have any right to come here unannounced—or that she wants to see *you?*" Mrs. Denby was fairly spitting with anger. "Haven't you people done enough damage? She's the laughingstock of this town. You dragged her into the *Cobras* mess, then stamped *her* name all over the disaster. And now you have the *gall* to show up, thinking there's still a place for you in her life."

She set her mouth grimly, glared at Devon for an instant, then started to slam the door in Devon's face.

But Devon was quicker. With Quinn crying in her arms, she pushed her way inside, past Mrs. Denby, and said, "I'm sorry, Mrs. Denby, but this is one time you're overruled."

"I'll call the police," the woman hissed.

"Do whatever you like, Mrs. Denby. You always have."

Devon peered into the empty living room, thought for a moment. Then she swept up the long, winding staircase.

She walked down the long hallway, past the screening room where she and King had groped sadly for each other on his wedding day. She walked past the guest rooms . . .

So many memories . . .

So long ago . . .

Through Gilda's bedroom door she could hear the sound of the television.

She knocked on the door, but there was no response. She quietly pushed it open.

In the sitting room, just beyond Gilda's enormous canopied bed, huddled a solitary figure, wrapped in a green velvet robe. She held a cigarette in one hand, a drink in the other.

Devon didn't say a word. Her heart was beating wildly. Even Quinn was absolutely silent, as if sensing the weight of emotion in the hushed room.

Gilda was watching the three o'clock "Dialing for Dollars" feature. They were showing *Night Anthem,* the movie in which, nearly forty years earlier, Gilda had thrown a strand of pearls over her shoulder and pronounced her most famous line: "He's got *me.*"

"Gilda," Devon said, almost meekly.

"Gilda," she said again, louder this time.

Gilda put down her drink and switched off the television set with the remote-control device. She stood up, turned around, and brushed a wisp of uncombed hair off the glorious face, void of all makeup. She stared at Devon, holding the child in her arms. "How the hell did you get in here?" she said.

"Gilda, I had to see you. It's almost Christmas . . ." *God, how she loved this woman!* She felt the sting of tears. "I love you. Can't you forgive me so we can put all the bitterness behind us?"

Gilda drank in Devon's beloved face, her tremulous smile, her wild tangle of long black hair. She'd missed her so much. Her long-lost daughter had finally come home. She was torn between emotions, polarized by indecision.

Cautiously, she asked, "Whose kid is that?"

Devon knelt down. Her eyes were level with Quinn's.

"Baby, this is your grandma Gilda."

"My God, I hate that word," Gilda said throatily.

Devon looked up at her. "But I thought you always wanted a granddaughter."

"Why? So she can abandon me the way my children have?"

Quinn toddled over to Gilda, gurgling her baby noises.

Gilda sucked nervously on her cigarette. "What's her name?" she asked.

"Quinn."

Gilda clutched her robe. The blood drained from her face. "Christ! Why on earth would you name a child Quinn?"

"To honor you. You know that as far as I'm concerned you are my mother. And Quinn is your name."

"Honor me? This seems to be the season for honoring me. First the Academy of Motion Picture Arts and Sciences—and now you."

"What are you talking about?"

"Well, baby, after the disaster with *Cobras* and me practically being laughed out of town, Hollywood has all of a sudden had a typical change of heart. They're giving me a special Oscar. They call it a Lifetime Achievement Award or something. I guess that's the shovel they give you when they think you've got one foot in the grave already."

"Gilda, that's wonderful," Devon said, stepping forward to hug her. But Gilda stood stiff and unyielding.

"What brought you back?" she asked finally.

"You and King. I wanted the three people I love most in the world to be together."

"Well, I do declare. If it's not Rebecca of Sunnybrook Farm."

Tears brimmed in Devon's eyes. "Gilda, please don't play the ice queen with me. I know how angry you were when I left, and I know how angry you must be with all of us. But, Gilda, it wasn't our fault. Didn't you read my letters? Or did you just toss them in the garbage? Why do you think I kept writing you for the past two years?"

"Who's the father?" Gilda asked coolly, turning to mash out her cigarette with quick, stabbing gestures.

"Isn't it obvious? Look at her eyes."

"Does King know?"

"Not yet. I wanted to see you first and talk to you."

"I'm hungry, Mama. Hungry."

Gilda's chill suddenly melted. "Oh, baby, are you hungry?" she cooed. "Should we go downstairs and get you some dinner? Devon," she snapped, "can't you take care of this poor dear child? Just because *you're* utterly irresponsible doesn't mean this little one has to suffer."

She took Quinn's hand and led her out of the room, telling her all the way about her dogs and birds and all the pretty things she would show her.

Devon knew that no matter what other angry words Gilda might conjure, in her heart she had already forgiven her.

Exhausted from the difficult trip and the emotional confrontation with Gilda, Devon decided that all her questions and the rest of the story could wait until the next day. Quinn fell asleep over supper with gingerbread all over her chin. Devon followed her to bed just a little while later.

She awoke the next morning with a vague recollection of Quinn wriggling beside her and whispering, "Go to Grandma, Mama."

The child was gone.

Devon threw on a robe and hurried down the stairs, calling, "Gilda? Quinn?"

She found the two of them on Gilda's sun-bathed terrace off the breakfast room, where Quinn was sipping milk from a glass of St. Lambert crystal and Gilda was cutting up French toast for her.

"Gilda," Devon laughed. "You're asking for trouble giving her that priceless crystal."

"Oh, baby, who the hell cares?" Gilda said airily. "For my money, she can break anything she wants. At least I know there's some life around here again. How about coffee?"

She rang the bell beside her plate, and Mrs. Denby appeared.

"Devon will have coffee, orange juice, and buttered toast. And please don't burn it."

Mrs. Denby seemed to be on the verge of speaking, but stopped herself and merely muttered, "Very well," before she shuffled off to the kitchen.

"The old bat can't stand the competition," Gilda said. "Well, you still have a lot of explaining to do, Devon Barnes, but this little dumpling is worth her weight in gold."

In the morning light, Gilda looked ten years younger than she had the day before. She was smiling now, and the tense, hard lines around her mouth were softer. Devon reached over and hugged her tightly.

"It's good to be home," she said.

They lingered over breakfast as Quinn made friends with Tallulah Too and drew pictures on the marble floor of the sundeck. Devon made belated explanations to Gilda—why she'd left so suddenly and mysteriously, how she felt she'd made the right decision, why she'd chosen to come home now.

"But I still want to find my father's grave," she said. "I need to tell him I understand why he left me and my mother."

Gilda blushed, as if she had been caught doing something naughty.

"Don't think I *ever* for *one* minute forgave you for walking out on me," she said with a trace of anger, "but I did manage to find out where your father is buried. Lord knows why I even bothered to—"

Devon's cry of joy was so sudden and sharp that Quinn looked up in alarm.

"I don't deserve you, truly I don't," Devon said.

Gilda's protests were interrupted by the ringing of the telephone.

"Get that, will you?" she shouted to Mrs. Denby.

A moment later the housekeeper came out. "May Fischoff *insists* on speaking with you."

"Fine. Bring me the phone."

Mrs. Denby did, and Gilda picked up the receiver.

"Hello, May. . . . Yes, I know I didn't return your call yesterday but I was busy with something . . . Don't bug me, May . . . Yes, *of course* I realize how hard you've worked on this. It's about time you did something for me . . . No, I can't now. I'm entertaining out-of-town guests." She looked at Devon and gave her a broad wink.

"Well, I don't know. . . . I may be having second thoughts. . . . You heard me . . . Look, I can't discuss it with you now. I'll call you back in a while."

She hung up without saying goodbye to May.

"What was that all about?" Devon asked.

Gilda shrugged impatiently. "May has some notion about getting me to do a television series. I suppose it's tempting, the money's great, but look at me—"

She posed dramatically, her head thrown back, her hands on her hips.

"Do you really think the camera will still love this face and body? And I'm not sure I'm ready to kill myself working five days a week for a show that probably won't last beyond the first season. I let her talk me into it because I've been so bored, but now that you're back, and I have this little precious doll here, what's the point?"

"How is May?"

"Doing well for herself, I must say. Though I always knew she would. She's lost all that baby fat."

Devon grinned to herself. Trust Gilda to call May's layers of extra poundage, the result of years of binging, "baby fat."

"Is she still living with Hollis?"

Gilda sighed angrily. "She is, the damn fool. She won't listen to me, that poor misguided goddaughter of mine. I've told her time and again that she's not facing reality. That when the day comes and Hollis decided he wants children, he'll walk out on her just the way Ted Kearny walked out on me. Men are like that. But she can't admit that she's wrong and I'm right."

She lit a cigarette and inhaled deeply. "Devon, I just had the most marvelous idea. Inez is giving a Christmas Eve wake tonight. It'll probably be gruesome, but everyone will be there—May, Hollis, King, Billy, and about 150 other so-called friends of Inez. Why don't you come with me? Think what fun the two of us will have making a dramatic entrance together—like Bette Davis and Miriam Hopkins in *Old Acquaintance.*"

Devon stretched and stood up. "It's tempting, Gilda. It *would* be a hoot. But I have to see King alone, before I see anyone else. And even before that, I'd like to make my peace with my father."

"Sure, baby, just leave me to walk into that party to face the crows all by my lonesome," Gilda said. But when she saw the remorse on Devon's face, she said, "Don't pay any attention to a bitter old lady. I've managed without you for two years, I can make it for another night. And I do understand about your father. I'll go find the directions to the cemetery—it's just a bit north of Bakersfield, as I recall—and you can go whenever you're ready."

Devon hadn't expected Gilda to forgive her so easily. She mentally held her breath, waiting for the older woman to lash out again, to reproach her for the pain she'd inflicted by her absence. But Gilda was too preoccupied with entertaining Quinn. She gave her a tour of the menagerie ("Haven't been back there in months," Gilda told Devon); splashed with her in the shallow end of the pool; read Quinn's favorite storybook, *The Runaway Bunny,* twice before putting her down for her nap; and insisted on personally preparing a late lunch for her when the child woke up at one o'clock.

"Don't worry about us," she said breezily. Quinn was breathless from giggling at Gilda's funny faces. "You go take a shower or whatever. The child takes after her grandmother—does just fine without you."

Gilda and Quinn were still giggling together when Devon came downstairs and into the kitchen, ready to begin her long drive to Bakersfield.

"Let me wash your face, baby." She held Quinn up to the sink.

"You can still change your mind about spending Christmas Eve with me," Gilda said, trying to sound as if she didn't really care.

"You know I would, but . . ." Devon rubbed the back of her neck. "Gilda, I didn't even bring you a Christmas present."

"You know, Quinn," Gilda said mischievously, "your mother is a very silly lady. She doesn't know that you are the very best Christmas present I've received since Patrick Wainwright handed me a pearl necklace."

Quinn laughed, not understanding the joke, but knowing that Gilda was a very amusing person.

Gilda turned back to Devon.

"But, baby," she continued, "I don't have a present for *you.*" She momentarily narrowed her eyes, then smiled.

"Oh, yes, I do. Come, Quinn, let's go get your silly mama's Christmas present."

Devon shook her head, amused by Gilda's performance. She was about to pour herself a cup of coffee when Mrs. Denby walked slowly into the room.

"Some coffee, Mrs. Denby?" she asked.

"In case you need reminding, missy, I *am* the housekeeper at The Pearls, and this *is* my home. I don't need a stranger to be offering me a cup of my own coffee."

"Oh, for heaven's sake . . ." Why bother, Devon thought. The woman had never liked her—hadn't liked any of Gilda's adopted "family," as far as she knew. She sat down at the antique pine baker's table and sipped her coffee, thinking about the long drive ahead, and all the words she'd never said to her father while he was alive.

"Mama, Mama." Quinn skipped into the room, with Gilda a few steps behind her.

Gilda's hands were behind her back. On her face was a sly, triumphant grin. Without so much as acknowledging that Mrs. Denby was present, she walked over to the kitchen table. "Stand up and close your eyes," she ordered Devon. "And wait until I tell you to open them."

Devon obediently did so.

The room was very quiet, except for the sound of Quinn babbling with her child's excitement about "pretty, pretty," and the noises of the dogs and birds carried by the breeze from the menagerie.

Something light and cool brushed against the back of Devon's neck.

There was a loud crash.

Devon's eyes flew open and an anguished gasp broke the silence.

Mrs. Denby's tormented eyes were fixed on Devon, her gnarled, arthritic fingers clenched in a fist.

At Mrs. Denby's feet were the shards and slivers of the Spode bone-china cup from which she'd been drinking.

Devon looked down. She was wearing a long, magnificent strand of perfect pearls—*Gilda's legendary necklace.*

"Oh, no . . ." she began.

But she was cut off by Mrs. Denby.

"Gilda, how *dare* you give the pearls to her!" the housekeeper screamed. Her face was white with rage.

Frightened by the commotion, Quinn began to cry loudly. Why was the ugly old lady ruining her grandma's pretty surprise?

"Mrs. Denby." Gilda pronounced each word very slowly and carefully. "How *dare* you speak to me like that! You seem to have forgotten who you are here," she said, as Devon comforted her sobbing daughter.

Mrs. Denby glared at Gilda.

"Your behavior is intolerable," Gilda continued. "Since you cannot treat my guests with respect, you can get out of my home. And I don't want you back until they're gone."

"Gilda—" Devon began.

"Devon, this doesn't concern you," Gilda said sharply.

Mrs. Denby hadn't moved. She was scarcely breathing.

"Do you understand what I'm saying?"

Gilda jabbed her red-painted fingernail in the housekeeper's direction.

"Get out of my home and don't come back until you hear from me."

"You must be joking," Mrs. Denby gasped.

"You know I don't joke with you. You heard me—take the week off."

Gilda turned to Devon and Quinn.

"There, my precious. The bad lady is going away. Why don't you and your mama come help me to find Tallulah Too?"

With the still whimpering Quinn sandwiched between them, Gilda and Devon walked out of the room.

Mrs. Denby pushed her shoulders back, smoothed down her apron, and straightened the collar of her uniform. Then she quietly opened the kitchen door and headed down the flagstone path in the direction of the menagerie.

The gardener was pruning the pink and crimson azalea shrubs.

"Morning, Mrs. Denby," he said as she passed.

He got no response.

She marched slowly past the pool where Dennis, the pool boy, was scooping leaves off the top of the water.

He looked up, waiting for her to say, as she usually did, "Get that pool *clean*. Don't you waste Miss Greenway's time and money."

She didn't even glance at him.

She walked through the grove of eucalyptus and turned off the path into the cool, semidark building that housed Gilda Greenway's once famous collection of exotic pets.

Gilda's three Colombian capuchin monkeys chattered in their cage, waiting to be fed. Jorge, the most daring and greedy of the three, scampered to the front of the cage and stuck his tiny black paw through the bars, baring his teeth and begging for an apple.

Mrs. Denby watched him for a moment.

Then she grabbed his paw and smashed it back and forth against the bars until his squeals and howls filled every corner of the animal house and echoed across the grounds.

"You little bastard," she snarled.

The toucans screeched in their cage, frightened by by the monkey's piercing cries.

"Bastards, all of you—bastards!" Mrs. Denby shouted above the din.

She seized the bird cage and rattled it until the screams of the toucans joined the cacophony of the monkeys.

Mrs. Denby's bellows of pain were indistinguishable from those of the animals. Her cries of anguish echoed into the ceiling and beyond . . .

Outside, the pool boy walked halfway down the path, wondering whether he should investigate the uproar. He called questioningly to the gardener.

"Forget it," the gardener called back. "That old woman's plumb crazy."

Soaking in a Caswell-Massey bubble bath and singing along with Peggy Lee on her stereo, Gilda heard nothing. She'd put Mrs. Denby out of her thoughts and had made her mind up about what she wanted to say to May Fischoff.

She stepped out of the circular, sunken, Italian white-marble bathtub and dried herself with her oversize hand-monogrammed Pratesi towel. Slipping on her robe, she went into her sitting room and dialed May's unlisted home number.

"May," she said, without so much as a hello.

"Hello, Gilda."

May was sitting at her Spanish colonial desk, now covered with notes about the television deal she'd been working on for Gilda. The relaxed, southwestern desert decor of her home office was a sharp contrast to the sleek glass and Saporiti chrome in the offices she maintained on Beverly Boulevard.

Here, in the private sanctuary where she was spending more and more time away from the office, she allowed herself expensive antiques, colorful flowered fabrics, and Chesterfield sofas. The portrait of Norma Fischoff by Augustus Johns hung on the chili-pepper red wall behind her desk.

The cost of the antique desk did not prevent May from propping her bare feet on its surface as she leaned back on the cowhide chair to take the phone. ("Give me lots of expensive antiques," she'd told her Group A decorator, Larry Mako, "but I want a chair I can bounce on.")

"We're that close to finishing this deal," she said happily into the phone, "and I just wanted to go over a couple of small things with you."

"I've changed my mind," Gilda said. "I'm not doing the series."

"What!"

"You heard me. Forget the deal. I'm not interested."

May swung her feet off the desk and stood up.

"Gilda, what the hell are you talking about?"

"I've got better things to do with my life. I've had it with making love to the camera and then reading snide comments about how I'm aging gracefully."

"Goddamn it, Gilda," May said, slicing her carefully manicured hand through the air, "I've spent the last twelve months negotiating the sweetest deal in television history. I got Aaron Spelling to agree to a $2,250,000-a-year contract with a $1.5 million penalty clause—and you're telling me you have better things to do?"

May was pacing back and forth across the Navajo rug. What had gotten into Gilda? Was she nuts?

"Stuff it, May. It's probably just another two-bit crapola soap opera."

"Bullshit. Spelling's building the show around you. Word is this show will have a three-year run and blow *Dallas* off the air. *Please,* you're throwing everything away. Do you know how hard I fought for you to get this part? To convince them that you had it all over Lana Turner and Jane Wyman? How can you do this to me?"

Gilda had the remote control on mute as she switched the channels looking for an old movie.

"May, give it a rest. You always were a selfish bitch. Never thinking of anyone but yourself—"

"I'm a selfish bitch!" she screamed. "After everything I've done for you—you who needed the fucking money when your goddamn cowboy kicked the bucket and left you high and dry? You who never managed a goddamn penny you earned? And now you're turning down over $2 million for a role so easy you could phone it in from the corner bar?"

May's hands were trembling so badly she could hardly hold the phone.

"You got it, baby. *Sayonara.*"

May picked up a priceless eighteenth-century English enamel box and hurled it against the oak-framed Remington on the opposite wall.

"You cunt! You goddamn cunt! Whore! I'll ruin you. I'll make sure you never work in this town again!"

It was unclear whether she or Gilda was the first to slam down the phone.

Devon looked at her watch. "We should be getting back," she said. "I told Lieutenant Biggs I'd see him at five. Come, Quinn, we have to go now."

"Daddy?" Quinn asked anxiously. She had already fallen madly in love with this man who smelled like candy, who hugged her and made her laugh.

"Yes," King said, brushing the sand off her cheek. "Daddy's coming, too. It'll be a long time before I let the two of you out of my sight." His eyes were on Quinn, but Devon knew his words were for her.

"Well, from now on, just try to get rid of me." She seemed radiant.

The three of them strolled back to the house, stopping every few feet as Quinn spotted yet another pretty shell to add to the collection she was storing in her father's pants pockets.

"King," said Devon, "I was at The Pearls the night Gilda died."

"Dev, why didn't you come to me?" asked King.

"It was the middle of the night when I ran out of the house. I hadn't seen you for two years. A hell of a way for me to come back into your life—'Hi, darling, I'm back, something terrible has happened, and by the way, meet your daughter, Quinn.' I needed time to think."

"*Casa, casa,*" cried Quinn.

"Yes, baby, we're almost at the house," Devon smiled. "We've been staying with some people in the *barrio.* Our housekeeper in Puerto Cruz has family there. I bought a bunch of Christmas presents for them. Wonderful people. They didn't say a word when I showed up after midnight. They've been very good to Quinn and me."

"We must have just missed each other that night at The Pearls," King said. "I was there, too. The story of our lives."

"Well, it's high time we rewrote the script."

He put his strong arms around her. "I lost you a long time ago, and I spent the rest of my life picking up the pieces—pieces of you. One night I slept with your hair, the next one-nighter had your nose. Once I even reached over in my sleep and touched some broad's thigh and I guess I spoke your name. She threw me out."

"Good for her." Devon poked him in the ribs and playfully kicked sand at his knees.

"I'm not going to let go of you again. From now on, it's the three of us, all in it together." He kissed her tenderly. "I don't know what we're going to live on, though. After this scandal, I probably can't get arrested in this town."

As soon as he said it, they laughed, as if on cue.

"You wanna take that back?" Devon laughed.

"Come here, you gorgeous hussy." He grabbed her again, laughing, while Quinn clapped her chubby hands with glee.

TWENTY-SEVEN

DECEMBER 26, 1979

B illy Buck stepped gracefully into the air-conditioned cool-
ness of his secluded Bel Air hacienda and gathered up the
pile of mail the postman had earlier pushed through the slot
in his door. There were the usual fan letters and mash notes, invitations
to movie screenings of all the leftover flotsam that hadn't been released
in time for Christmas, two bills, a letter from his sister in Atlanta, and
a catalogue from Williams-Sonoma.

He had a monster-size headache. Too much heat, alcohol, grief,
tension, and too many unanswered questions. He thought about a bath,
but rejected the idea. The way things had been going the last couple
of days, he wouldn't be surprised to find Janet Leigh in the shower.

He went to the armoire in his Spanish country-style living room,
switched on the sound system hidden behind its polished doors, and
the house filled with the debonair sound of Bobby Short playing Gersh-
win. As exhausted as he was, he still appreciated the serene beauty of
his home. Visitors often expressed surprise that he hadn't decorated

with early French and English antiques. His standard response to such comments was, "But this *is* Los Angeles, not Scarsdale."

The leaf-pattern linen sofas, the floral-pattern easy chair with its matching ottoman, the one-of-a-kind eighteenth-century white, blue, and gold floor tiles, all suited him perfectly.

Billy went into the kitchen, squeezed a lime into a glass of Perrier, and popped two Alka-Seltzers. Unbuttoning his white button-down oxford shirt from Carroll & Co., he walked into his study and paused by the stunning Karsh portrait of Gilda.

His sly-eyed white angora cat, a present from Doris Day three Christmases ago, was stretched out on top of his answering machine. The long hairs that clung to the machine were evidence that this was Voyager's favorite resting spot. The message light blinked nonstop. His phone must have been ringing off the hook all day. He pushed the "playback" button, then stretched out on the tartan-plaid sofa, sipped the Perrier, and listened to his messages.

"Billy, this is Margaret Gardner. I'm in Athens with Melina. Isn't it awful about Gilda? I know how close you were. We just wanted you to know we're thinking of you. Hope you're okay. Melina sends her love."

"Billy, this is King. Tell Devon to call me right away."

"Hi, sweetie, it's Liza. What's new in Hollywood? I've been working night and day 'cause I'm opening at the Sands on New Year's Eve. Can you make it?"

"Mitch Misyak here. Inez wants to talk to you. Drop by anytime."

"Billy, baby. It's Byron Kerr. Aren't you the sly dog? But you could have told a fellow news hound that you and Devon were planning to ride off into the sunset together."

"King again. If you're home, please pick up the phone. . . . Okay. Tell Devon I gotta talk to her."

"Hi, Billy, it's May. Call me as soon as you can."

"Darling, this is Gloria. I was devastated to hear about Gilda. You must be a wreck. I'll be on the West Coast next Tuesday for a Murjani jeans promotion. Give me a call at the Beverly Wilshire. We must have dinner."

"Goddamn it, Billy. Where the hell is Devon? I'm at the beach house. Could you *please*—"

Billy leaned over and pressed the off button. Poor King. Well, if

Devon wasn't there yet, she'd be arriving any minute. No point in ruining her surprise.

His unlisted private line rang. *Devon?*

"Hello," he said.

"Billy? This is Mitch."

"Mitch who?"

"Inez's friend. Mitch Misyak."

"How the hell did you get this number?"

"What difference does it make? Hey, don't you check your messages?"

"I'm about to do so now. Then I'm calling the phone company to change this number."

"Inez wants to see you. She's got an exclusive for you."

"Yeah," said Billy, "well, I've got an exclusive for her. Tell Inez she—"

"Suit yourself," Mitch said brusquely. "By the way, she says she knows who shot Gilda."

"What were you pulling before?" Mitch said, opening the door even before Billy rang the bell. "You know me, man. I used to go with May Fischoff. I've been living with Inez for over two years now, ever since her old man split. I've seen you a hundred times."

"Were we ever introduced?" Billy asked. Of course, he recognized the kid. His hair was shorter than it had been in the days he'd hung around with Hollis. Billy wondered if he was still dealing. I must be slipping, he thought. Living with Inez is like being in dealer heaven. The hostess with the mostest cash and stash in Holmby Hills.

"Not formally," Mitch Misyak said.

"Well, there you are," said Billy. "I'm a stickler for etiquette. Where's you boss?"

"Out by the pool. . . . Mr. Buck?"

Billy turned. "Yes, Mr. Misyak?"

"She's been snorting coke since eight o'clock this morning. You gotta take what she says with a grain of salt, if you know what I mean."

"I think she's beyond salt, son, but thanks for the advice."

"*De nada.* Snappy exit you pulled off this morning with Devon Barnes. Inez shit a brick when Devon showed up at the chapel. Where's she been hiding all this time?"

"Read all about it in my column." Billy smiled graciously.

"I like your column. I'd like to do something to get into your column. Maybe I already have. Who knows?" He leered. "I get around."

"Get as far as The Pearls, did you?"

"Not me, baby. No, I just hang out on the fringes. Better view. You know, you can't see the big picture too close up."

Billy was tired. He lowered his sunglasses and let his eyes sweep deliberately over Mitch, from his sockless Gucci loafers to his three-sock crotch, all the way up to his hustler grin. "From where I'm standing," Billy said, pushing his glasses back up his nose, "there's nothing big about the picture."

Inez was bundled like a first-cabin passenger on the *QE2*, riding out a storm in mid-Atlantic. She was almost completely covered in white terry cloth, except for her face, barely visible under a white turban. Her eyes were hidden behind huge reflecting sunglasses.

"Hello, Inez," Billy said. My hat's off to you, he thought. For sheer capacity, she belonged in the *Guinness Book of Records.* On the glass table next to her lounge chair a forlorn half-empty bottle of Stolichnaya tilted sideways in a silver bucket of melting ice. Next to the bucket was a Steuben ashtray full of cigarette butts. And a nasal inhalator, a gram bottle of white powder, a tiny silver spoon, a rolled up fifty-dollar bill, a straight-edge razor blade, and myriad rainbow-colored pills.

"Having a light lunch?"

"Help yourself," said Inez. "You want anything? Mitch'll get you whatever you need."

Billy shook his head. "How're you doing, honey?" he asked softly, pulling up a white lacquered beach chair.

"How do I look like I'm doing? Like I went to a funeral this morning?" She laughed joylessly. "I think they cremated the wrong body. They could've taken mine, all the use I've been getting out of it. Right, Mitch?"

"Doing the laundry again? I got a couple of sweaty jocks upstairs you can air if you run short."

"Take a personality suppressant, Mitch," Billy said, shifting in the chair with his back to the boy.

"He's a bastard," Inez said. "But then, most of my friends are.

Right, Mitchie? How's she feel, big May? Like a fucking bag of dog biscuits now, right? I thought she'd be too skinny for you. You like a little meat on the bone, don't you? Baby, you could use a little meat on *your* bone. You're grinding it down to a pencil nub, Mitchie."

"Coke," Mitch said to Billy. "I keep telling her to lay off if she can't handle it. What're you going to do? She's, like, self-destructive beyond belief. Didn't I tell you, Inez? Come on, have I been trying to keep you clean, or what?"

"I saw you, Mitch—grinding away on May like La Machine. Now that Devon's back, King'll have something to poke, too. These are my friends, we're talking about, Billy, my best friends."

"I told you I didn't ball her, Inez. All I did was see her to her car. You told me to be polite to your friends."

"If Hollis finds out about how polite you were to his woman, your face is going to look a lot worse than mine."

Billy winced.

"When did you start subscribing to *Soldier of Fortune,* Inez?"

"Honey, Mitch is no Boy Scout."

She whipped off her sunglasses. One eye was sealed shut from a shiner so big no sirloin could fix it. Her right cheekbone was bruised and red.

Mitch had to be a southpaw, Billy reasoned. He glanced at the boy. Sure enough, there was a brand new Band-Aid covering the knuckles of the kid's left hand.

"She may seem in control now," Mitch explained, "but she was freaking out thoroughly when we got home from Forest Lawn. Then Hollis and May came by to check her out. After they left, she started in on me about May again. Next thing I know, she's going for the spike, you know?"

Billy looked baffled. "The spike?"

"Spike. Needles. Syringe. She was wired to the max and she was going to speedball. First off, I promised Hollis I'd get her to slow down. Second, speedball is all I need for her to do. Croak city. She is not in the best physical shape in the world. Or mental either—but that's your problem. Mine was I wanted that fucking spike out of her arm. She started smacking me around, so I decked her. I'd rather deck her than sit around and watch her shooting up, and next thing I know, this place turns into a fucking precinct, you know."

"Inez," Billy said, "one of my dearest friends in the world was murdered two days ago. I'm not in the mood to referee a domestic quarrel. I came over because you said you had a story for me. You said you know who shot Gilda."

"I do."

She unscrewed the top of the glass bottle, dipped the silver spoon into the finely cut cocaine, and raised it to her right nostril, blocking the left nostril with her index finger

"Key," she said appreciatively. "Billy, you may be in mourning, but I'm not singing a funeral march. As far as I'm concerned, there is one less bitch in the world today."

She inhaled a second spoonful in her left nostril.

"Billy, you're a writer. I've got a gold mine here. I just need a little help shaping it. I want you to do the book. With me, of course. By Inez Hollister-Godwin, as told to Billy Buck."

Billy had no idea what she was rambling about. "Inez, get to the point. Who killed Gilda?"

She straightened the terry cloth turban on her head, lowered her sunglasses, and peered at him through one eye. "Who do you think, you silly goose?"

The sun was beginning to set by the time Inez finished her story. "If you don't believe me, look in the toilet tank in my room." She's mad, thought Billy. But she may be telling the truth.

Inez was huddled under her afghan, bare feet exposed. She'd lit another cigarette. Smoke curled from her lips as she stared catatonically into the swimming pool. The last of the December sunlight mottled the waters pink and red.

Mitch walked Billy up the hill to the house.

"She really loved Gilda," Mitch said. "Like a mother."

To the right of the pool was the grape arbor where King had tried to warn Devon about Michel Weiss-France. Beyond the arbor were the tennis courts where, at yet another party, Billy had walked with Devon and listened to her fantastic tale. "Are you going to call the police and tell them you're being followed by boring men?" he'd teased her.

Here on the terrace, Gilda and Avery had laughed, gossiped, and entertained the peroxide blonde King had brought back from Las Vegas. And Hollis had been a full head shorter than Billy the night he'd rushed past—his long sun-bleached hair streaming behind him—in search of his beloved May.

"So what are you going to do?" Mitch asked.

"I'm going to the bathroom," said Billy. "Do you mind?"

"Come on, man. I mean, about Inez."

Upstairs, Billy crossed the master bedroom to the luxurious brass-and-marble bathroom. He lifted the toilet tank lid. Through the blue-tinted water freshener he saw it. *Well, maybe she was telling the truth.* Then he turned to the wall phone and dialed Detective Lionel Biggs's direct line.

TWENTY-EIGHT

4:58 P.M., DECEMBER 26, 1979

B iggs had a sour stomach. Besides finding out that Gilda Greenway had *not* died of a gunshot wound, but was dead before she was shot; besides discovering that Inez Godwin had wrecked her car at The Pearls at about the same time Gilda had died—he'd received yet another telephone tirade from his supervisor, ball-less Harry Monahan.

Which was why he now needed two Maalox.

Washing down the emulsifier with a glass of milk, he saw King Godwin and Devon Barnes through the glass window. King was holding a small child.

"Well, well. You're good for your word, Miss Barnes. Come on in." *And how about confessing to this murder?* he thought.

Devon sat down. King and Quinn took a seat outside. Biggs shut the door. He smiled wearily. He was nearing the end of his rope. They exchanged mild pleasantries, then Biggs blurted, "Now, why don't you tell me all about your stay at Gilda Greenway's?"

Devon brushed her hair off her forehead. Biggs couldn't help but think how much more beautiful she was than her photographs. Cameras didn't do her justice. Stunning, really.

"Well, first I think I'd better tell you I was the person who called 911 anonymously on Christmas Eve."

Biggs raised an eyebrow.

"So you reported the murder. But why didn't you tell the emergency operator who you were?"

Devon sighed. "There were a lot of reasons. I wasn't thinking. I was . . . frightened. My God, I'd just seen . . . I guess I was shell-shocked. And I had my daughter with me."

"Your daughter?"

"Yes. That's another reason I didn't want to identify myself." She caught the choke in her voice and controlled it, then continued. "You've got to remember, I'd just seen Gilda—I thought of her as my mother. Then she was dead—murdered."

He nodded.

"And," she added, "I also didn't think the operator would take me seriously. I mean, can you imagine someone calling up, saying, 'This is Devon Barnes, I'd like to report a murder.' Who'd believe it? They'd say, 'Sure, lady, and Santa's in bed with you, too, right?' "

Biggs said, "I see your point, Miss Barnes. But tell me more about what happened at The Pearls."

He opened a drawer and quietly pressed the "record" button of his cassette recorder.

"I'd gone up just north of Bakersfield to visit my father's grave. Gilda had located it for me, after years of searching. I came in the day before from Mexico, where I've been living for the past two years. I stayed with Gilda the first night, went up to Bakersfield in the early afternoon on Christmas Eve, and came back that same night. It was rather late . . ."

Devon remembered it all too clearly.

She had just turned her Avis-rented Cutlass off Coldwater Canyon and onto the side street leading to The Pearls. She had been thinking all the way from the cemetery how glad she was that she'd decided to come back to the States. Back to Gilda and King and all that she'd left behind. Finding her father's grave, after thinking about it for so long, finally provided the peace she needed to make her life complete. She had made peace with Gilda, her surrogate mother, and now with her poor, deceased father. The father she never really knew, but for whom she'd felt such lasting adoration.

She would always be grateful to Gilda for finding the cemetery for her.

She glanced at her daughter, asleep in the car seat, and turned toward the steep driveway toward The Pearls.

As she approached the gates that guarded the driveway, they swung open automatically.

She rounded the curve to the front of the house and slowed. Something was wrong. The front door of the mansion stood open.

An eerie light blinked from the front hall.

She parked the Cutlass and got out, leaving Quinn still sleeping in her seat.

Her senses were alert.

She could *feel* the anxiety tightening in her muscles.

For an instant she thought about jumping back in the car and leaving. Why was she so reluctant to go into the house? The night was silent. As though there weren't a living thing around for miles. She walked up to The Pearls, one slow step at a time, and went inside.

The eerie light was from the Christmas tree in the living room. It was the only light on the first floor.

She wanted to call out to Gilda.

But she was afraid.

Devon turned the corner and went into the living room.

There was Gilda.

Relief flooded through her. She let out a loud sigh, almost laughing. Thank God Gilda was here.

"Oh, Gilda! I saw the light on and the door open and was nearly scared to death."

Devon walked toward Gilda, the heels of her boots clacking on the marble floor.

"Darling, I've had the most wonderful day. I found my father's grave and made my peace, thanks to you."

"Merry Christmas." She leaned over to kiss Gilda.

Then she took a closer look. She saw the gunshot wound.

The scream would not come.

She backed away, gasping for breath, feeling her knees buckle. *I have to stay calm,* she told herself. *I have to stay calm. This isn't happening. It's just a bad dream. It'll all be over when I wake up.* She dropped to her hands and knees, swallowing big gulps of air. *This isn't real, this isn't happening.*

But she looked up and saw the blood.

"Gilda!" she cried at the corpse, whose eyes were staring straight at her.

There was no reply.

Pushing herself up from the floor, she backed away, wondering if the killer was still there. She wanted to turn around, but the circulation in her hands and feet seemed to stop. She felt numb, paralyzed with shock and terror. The only motor reflexes still working were in her brain.

What if he's still here, hiding in the house? Behind me now? Quinn!

What if he's outside? Saw the car? Saw Quinn!

She turned and ran.

As she frantically jerked open the car door, she heard the loud hum of the entrance gates.

A car was approaching.

Oh, God, no! He's coming back!

She was shaking so badly she couldn't fit the key in the ignition.

She heard the car engine getting closer.

The key! The key wouldn't fit!

She glimpsed the sweep of headlights.

She could hear the car accelerating.

Calm, I have to be calm.

She jammed the key into the ignition and slammed her foot to the gas pedal.

She engine turned over and flooded.

"Shit!" she screamed.

The car's headlights flashed across the front of the house.

Finally, the engine caught.

Devon threw the car into drive and roared toward the exit gates. In her rearview mirror she saw a car pull up in front of the mansion.

"And what time was this?" Biggs asked, sitting right up at his desk, arms folded in front of him.

"About eleven-thirty," Devon replied.

"That must have been King. He says he got there at eleven-thirty."

"I know that now. But I was petrified. I called 911 from the first phone booth I could find."

Detective O'Brien knocked on Biggs's door. "Sorry to interrupt, Lionel, but I thought you'd want to see this right away. It just came from Mission Street."

Mission Street.

The Los Angeles County Forensic Science Center.

O'Brien handed over the folder with Biggs's name on it. It was a manila envelope marked CONFIDENTIAL.

He tore it open as O'Brien shut the door.

"Excuse me a minute," Biggs said to Devon.

It was the final autopsy report, including the toxicology report, on Gilda Greenway. He read the freshly typed pages, scanning much of the same material he'd seen earlier that afternoon. Then he came to the toxicology report, and the coroner's concluding comments, under "Cause of Death."

He read it.

Then he reread it.

He slumped in his chair, forgetting all about the suspect in front of him.

"I don't believe it. This is getting weirder than a goddamn Lon Chaney picture."

He flipped through the report, backward and forward, and looked at a copy of the spectrometer graph toxicology had enclosed.

There it was.

The cause of death.

Jesus. His entire case was going down the crapper. His one shot —gone. Goodbye to all the publicity. Goodbye to his promotion. His book. His television series. *Shit!* All his work for this?

His head throbbed. He couldn't think straight.

The phone in his office shrilled. After the third ring he picked it up. "Biggs. What is it?" he asked wearily.

"Lionel, this is Billy Buck."

"Yeah, Billy. Listen, thanks for calling but I'm gonna have to call you back."

"Biggs, I think I've got your murderer."

Biggs straightened up in his chair. "Oh, yeah? Tell me about it."

"I'm over at Inez Godwin's place, in Holmby Hills. I want to ask you something. Did you ever find the gun the murderer used?"

Biggs watched Devon pick at one of her fingernails. Through the glass window of his door he could see King Godwin and the little girl waiting patiently. Officers walked by, as curious as anybody else to see a real-life movie star. Big deal. This was getting to be a very large pain in the ass.

"No, we never found it. You got something?"

"The gun, maybe."

"What make?"

"Thirty-eight special."

"Really?" Biggs asked, his interest growing.

"Yeah. There's one sitting here at the bottom of a toilet tank. Inez says she used it to kill Gilda."

"Oh. Well, I know she wrecked her car in front of The Pearls that night."

Devon was trying to pretend she wasn't listening, but Biggs could tell she was.

"In fact," Biggs went on, "it might as well have been a Christmas open house. Inez, Devon, and King were all there. Only one missing was May Fischoff. Too bad the hostess couldn't serve egg nog."

Devon blanched. Then she began to weep quietly.

"Well, as far as May's concerned," Billy Buck said, "you know how agents are: they make the deal, take the money, but never stick around for the applause. You don't seem overly excited about the gun, Biggs."

"Listen, is King's wife there now?"

"Ex-wife, and yes, she is. In body, Detective, if not in mind. She's been coking and drinking all day."

"Real party girl."

"She claims she drove over to The Pearls Christmas Eve, ran her car up over the curb and hit a palm tree. She says she walked up the hill, found the front door open, and went in."

"She say what she was doing there? Making house calls on Christmas Eve is for Santa Claus."

"Yeah," Billy Buck said. "You remember I told you yesterday morning Gilda was invited to a Christmas Eve party at Inez's house? Well, Gilda had reluctantly said yes, then she went to dinner at Chasen's with me instead. Inez is famous for getting people to her parties who would otherwise never speak to her. This time Gilda was the bait. She promised everyone in town they'd see Gilda Greenway's first big social appearance in two years. When Gilda didn't show, Inez took it as a personal affront *and* a public slap in the face. A deliberate attempt to ruin her already shaky social standing. She was so freaked out on coke that she went berserk—berserk enough to drive over to The Pearls."

"She say where Gilda was?"

"In the living room. She could see her by the lights from the Christmas tree. Remember, though, Inez was full of drugs that night so you have to take it for what it's worth. In fact, she could use some help now."

"I'll send a car to pick her up. How far gone is she? Do we need Emergency Medical?"

"You might."

"Hang on." Biggs punched an inside line and relayed an order for a car to be dispatched to the Godwin house in Holmby Hills.

"Okay," the detective said, returning to the line with Billy. "There's a team on the way."

"Anyway, she said she saw Gilda and said, 'Thanks for making an appearance at my party, bitch!' and then started firing. She says she only meant to shake her up. She went nuts when she saw the blood, and ran. Since her car was wrecked, she went out on Coldwater Canyon and flagged someone down. This guy drove her back here around eleven-fifteen, her boyfriend says. Then he went to get the car with a friend, but it had already been towed. And at that point, there were squad cars all over the place."

"Well," Biggs sighed, "this is interesting, but it doesn't solve the case."

"What do you mean?"

"I mean," he said looking straight at Devon, "that a bullet is *not* what killed her."

"What are you talking about?" Devon asked, echoing Billy Buck almost verbatim.

"You heard me. I got this goddamn report from the coroner's office that says without a doubt the gunshot did not kill her. Inez shot Gilda after she was *already dead!*"

Devon rushed from the office. Biggs could see her talking animatedly to King.

"Are you serious?" Billy asked. "Then what killed her?"

"A cobra. Gilda Greenway died of cobra venom poisoning. She was bitten by a snake shortly before she was shot. It's the weirdest fucking case I've been on in a long time—where the hell would someone get a cobra?"

Billy sat down heavily on the edge of Inez's bathtub.

"One of her fans sent her a cobra when she was filming that movie —*Cobras*. We begged her to get rid of it, but she refused. She liked the idea of having it as a pet. She kept it out back in her menagerie. But how did it get to her living room?"

"I've been wondering that myself. I don't now. Maybe it got out of its cage somehow. . . . That still doesn't tell us who called her at Chasen's. Or why she was holding that 'Four Fans' picture."

"So if Gilda was already dead, Inez really isn't guilty of murder, is she?"

"No, I mean, we could book her on attempted murder, but it would probably get thrown out."

Billy looked down from the bathroom window. Mitch Misyak was sitting on the pool lounge chair, holding the blanket under which Inez had huddled. A police officer, one foot resting on the chaise cushion, was standing in front of him, talking, nodding, jotting notes on a little pad hidden in his hand.

The cop surprised Billy. He hadn't heard any sirens. He'd wanted to say goodbye to Inez before they took her away.

He watched her now, walking toward the front of the house, a policeman and a man dressed in whites, a paramedic probably, on either side of her. She was hugging herself, still barefoot in the oversize terry cloth robe, crying and laughing at the same time.

"They're here," he told Biggs. "Poor Inez."

"Poor Inez?" Lionel Biggs asked. "Who're you kidding?"

"Sorry, Biggs, I'm exhausted. You know where you can find me."

He looked around the pink bathroom and said, "What a zoo this town is."

He looked at himself in the mirror and grimaced. "Hell of a column this would make," he told his reflection. "Ah, Gilda, how you would love to sit and recycle this dirt. Here's looking at you, kid."

TWENTY-NINE

AUGUST 27, 1984

I t was not a good day. In addition to the usual Monday blahs, Billy Buck's secretary, Patsy Lustig, had sprained her wrist playing tennis and wouldn't go near the typewriter. He would have to ask for an extension on the Clint Eastwood piece. He had a 9:00 A.M. breakfast with the West Coast editor of *People* at the Beverly Wilshire and a 10:30 appointment with Dr. Solomon, "dermatologist to the stars," to get a mole removed on his left shoulder blade.

The Labor Day weekend was fast approaching and he didn't have a single invitation to leave town. He phoned the office after breakfast to see if anything had turned up in the mail. At this point he'd settle for a trip to Vegas for a complimentary Mai Tai at Caesar's.

"Bills. A screening notice from MGM-UA."

"Are they still in business?" The old studio where Gilda Greenway had become a legend now looked like a tomb. The back lot had long been sold to real-estate developers; the costumes, props, and even the orchestrations from the MGM musicals disposed of at auction. Outtakes from the great classics of movie history were lost, missing, or pilfered by former employees.

Cavernous sound stages where Astaire danced and Atlanta burned had been razed. The Tarzan jungle was now a parking lot, the Esther Williams swimming pool lay buried beneath a row of ugly, low-income condos. Like every other studio in town, the Oz that once defined the style, the elegance, and the dreams of American moviegoers at Metro had been reduced to dust by a mason's hammer, its remaining space requisitioned by independent television crews for sitcoms and cop shows. Somewhere, Billy felt certain, Louis B. Mayer was groaning in his grave.

"Oh, and there's something from Barney Ufland that is sort of curious."

"Barney who?"

"You know. The guy in Santa Barbara who arranged the Mitchum interview that time when he was being sued for knocking out some dame in New York with a basketball."

How could he forget? Mitchum was off the sauce that day and mean as a rabid terrier. "What's he got?" His time was running out and he didn't have another quarter.

"He sent a clip from the paper up there. Some old lady got hit by a motorcycle and—"

"It can wait. I'll be back by noon if Solomon doesn't take my goddamn back off."

He almost did. By the time he got home and kicked off his loafers, his left side was burning like he'd been blow-torched. The vodka mist didn't help much, but the thought that he could now afford the Baccarat goblet it was in was momentarily reassuring.

Patsy had left the Clint Eastwood notes on top of his typewriter with the mail. He sipped with one hand and rifled through the junk on his desk with the other. The brief note from Barney Ufland— "Thought the enclosed might interest you"—was stapled to a newspaper clipping from the *Santa Barbara News-Press*.

Under the headline "LOCAL WOMAN INJURED IN ACCIDENT" was a photograph of a gray-haired woman wearing a ski sweater from L. L.

Bean and an expression that was almost as stern as her jawline. The copy read:

> Mrs. Viola Scribner, 73, was injured yesterday in the driveway of her home by a motorcycle that skidded out of control on a gravel incline. The motorcyclist, identified as Ray Cooney, 25, of Montecito, was unharmed. The elderly woman is listed in stable condition at St. Francis Hospital after suffering lacerations of the hands and face and a broken collarbone. Mrs. Scribner, who lives at 33 Pine Road, is the sister of the late Hollywood film star, Gilda Greenway.

The Baccarat crystal smashed like a pretzel. Billy was too stunned to pick up the shards of glass. He looked at the photo again. It meant nothing. Had anybody ever actually *seen* a picture of Vy? Gilda had said she had been dead since their early arrival in Hollywood, back in the forties.

His photographic memory hadn't made him the crown prince of show-biz journalism for nothing. He remembered Gilda's exact words: "Poor Vy went back to Oklahoma to clear out all of our memories there and she and Orval died in a fire. It still brings tears to my eyes to talk about it. Let's change the subject, sugar." But if Vy had been around all these years, why had Gilda lied? And why was she omitted from any mention in the will? Gilda had left everything to various animal foundations and neuter-spay clinics. Wouldn't she at least have bequeathed an earring to the only living relative she had left in the world?

He pushed Voyager away from the telephone and dialed May Fischoff's private line.

"This is May Fischoff's secretary," answered a young man with a southern drawl. "Who may I say is calling?"

"Billy Buck."

"One moment, Mr. Buck."

An efficient-sounding young woman got on the line next.

"Anything I can do for you, Mr. Buck? She's working at home today and doesn't want to be disturbed."

"Tell May if she doesn't get on the phone this instant, I'll send Mitch Misyak over in half an hour."

"Mitch Misyak?" The young woman sounded puzzled, but she put him on hold. May picked up an instant later.

"Billy? It's me. I'm on the home extension. You think I'm sitting around watching "General Hospital"? I'm hysterical with work. This better be good."

"May, I must see you."

"Hollis is in New York. I've got three deals that were supposed to be signed and delivered yesterday. It better be important."

Billy drove out to her house in Topanga Canyon. He knew a Monday lunch with May was like an audience with the pope on Easter Sunday, but he was an old friend who didn't make casual dates without reason. "I'm a WASP columnist, and I've got some information about Gilda."

"Well, I'm a Jewish agent, and I don't care. Listen, Billy, Gilda is a closed book. Nobody else cares, either."

"Then look at this." He produced the newspaper clipping.

May read it. "Holy shit! The famous Vy is still alive. Or almost."

She looked at the photo. Her eyes grew big as campaign buttons. "Holy fucking mother of—Billy, don't you know who this is? It's Mrs. Danvers from Horror Hotel! You know, the old Denby broad who scared the living daylights out of everyone of us for years. Gilda's housekeeper was her own goddamn sister!"

Devon was pouring salt on the slugs in her vegetable garden with a Morton's box when she heard the telephone ringing in the kitchen. It had been an idyllic Connecticut summer. In the almost five years since she and King had bought the house in Roxbury, she had made peace with her soul, her life, and herself. Now all three seemed connected, as though by some beautific force that watched her, smiling, from behind the clouds on the hill above the maple trees.

Arthur Miller lived on the next road, in the farmhouse he bought for Marilyn Monroe during one of her escapes from the punishing business of make-believe. Marilyn had taken long walks in short-shorts and gingham shirts, her gilded hair tied in a dirty rag, past the very house where Devon and King now lived. She had picked wild daisies and learned to make her own spaghetti and given interviews at the time about retiring and living like a real person, close to nature. Marilyn hadn't made it. But Devon had.

After Gilda's death, they had been cleared of all charges officially, but the suspicions remained. King's career had been affected by the negative publicity, and he knew it. Three picture deals had died on the negotiating table, and a detective series May had sweated over for months barely made it beyond the pilot. "It's just the times, that's all —nobody's working in the picture business unless they're from 'Saturday Night Live,' " May said soothingly, but the writing was on the wall and King didn't need contact lenses to see it.

So they got Devon's country furniture out of storage, packed up Quinn, and moved back east, where it all began. Into a white colonial house with green shutters and thirty-eight acres of freedom. Lionel Biggs had presented King with the porno films he found under Gilda Greenway's Christmas tree as a going away present. King got a running lead on an NBC soap and Devon learned how to test the soil for its acid content, grow beefsteak tomatoes big as ostrich eggs, and cook like Julia Child.

In the summer, she grew enough produce to feed half of Litchfield County. In the autumn, she and King raked their own leaves, made jack o'lanterns for Quinn from their own pumpkins, and spent long evenings lingering in front of one of their five fireplaces sipping applejack brandy Devon made from their own orchard. During the long, frosty New England winters, when everything looked like a Grandma Moses holiday card, they read books and made ice cream from fresh snow and feasted on nourishing soups made from the summer yield Devon had painstakingly canned, frozen, and pickled on long September afternoons while Quinn was in school. Spring was a rhapsody of flowers. Devon lay in her navy blue bedroom with an early fire in the grate to warm the chill and watched the French lilacs grow outside her homemade organdy curtains. There were peonies big as cabbages, roses, and sweet williams.

And now, on summer days yawning into early frost, there were zinnias and asters and dahlias to gather, as well as pesto sauce to store with the last of the basil from the herb garden. It was on days like this, while King was in the city and Quinn was playing at the neighbor's pool, feeling the final warm rush of summer slip away, that Devon most savored her life. And resented the sound of ringing phones.

"For God's sake, what took you so long?"

"Hi, May. I was chasing the slugs out of the garden. I've still got one final tomato crop before the first frost hits the vines."

"Darling, you've been hanging out with brussels sprouts so long I live in mortal terror you're soon gonna turn into one yourself. Why don't you get your ass out here? I can get you a 'Love Boat' in a second."

"Do it, and I'll never speak to you again. Besides, who would an old broad like me play with? Chevy Chase? You know there's nothing going on for a housewife over forty. King and I are very content just being the Paul Newman and Joanne Woodward of Cactus Gulch."

"I want a peach pie from the peach trees Hollis and I gave you guys last spring. We're coming for Christmas, so get the eggnog ready. I'm sure you'll lay the eggs yourself."

"King is having dinner with Hollis tonight. He's staying over to do two tapings tomorrow. I asked Hollis to drive out to Connecticut, but he says he's flying back to the Coast in the morning."

"He can't stay away from me that long, you know that. He's not a kid anymore, but he still gets an erection every time I squeeze his ear. We must be doing something right."

"When are you two going to get married and make me your mother-in-law?"

"You bitch. We're very happy the way we are and, my God, Dev, the kid's a genius in business. So why take chances? In the immortal words of Mr. Elvis Presley, why buy the cow when you can get milk through the fence? How's King?"

"He's such a country squire that he even won a prize this summer at the Litchfield County Fair for the biggest zucchini."

"I've heard about his zucchini, dear, though I must admit I never took a bite of it myself. Listen, darling, enough of this update from the *Farmer's Almanac*. There's somebody sitting here growing zits from anxiety. Don't tell him anything you don't want to read. Kiss ass, he writes." She handed the receiver to Billy. "Here. It's Ma Kettle on the line."

Billy Buck took the phone in May's kitchen. "Devon, it's Billy."

"I feel like it's my birthday. Both of you at once. What a treat. How are things in Glocca Morra, anyway?"

"The leprechauns are dead, I'm afraid. Haven't you heard? The picture business is dead, too. It's all science-fiction movies and Steven Spielberg's masturbatory fantasies in the nursery. Oh, God, Devon, where did we all go wrong? They now give Academy Awards to people like Sylvester Stallone! The man cannot say a single word with more than three syllables in it. Everyone on the screen is from the Nautilus school of dramatic art. I never thought I'd live to say it, but all the real people are on television."

Devon laughed. "I wouldn't know. The last film I saw was *Jaws*. King brought home a cassette of it. I've had bigger scares from my fishbowl. I'm living a different life now. I'm just another one of those boring housewives who reads *McCall's*."

"Suzanne Somers is boring. You, never."

"Suzanne Somers is working. Me, never."

"Devon, don't you miss it?"

"Billy, I've got a child nearly seven years old who's reading *The Catcher in the Rye*. I am never bored. Yesterday she asked King, 'Daddy, what's a lesbian?' "

"Tell her some of Daddy's best friends are."

"Tell me about it. But I don't really miss the business. I work with retarded children three days a week. I can knit a sweater, cane a chair, and make the best pot of chicken and dumplings this side of the Mississippi before you can remember the plot of the last James Bond Movie you saw."

"I don't even remember the name of the last James Bond movie I saw. I don't even remember the last movie I saw, and I saw it three days ago."

"May still sends us scripts. God, the drivel they're writing now. King gets a few good parts thrown his way. I think he's going to do a play next season in New York. It's pretty good, Billy. It's about child abuse. It made me think of Inez. How is she, Billy?"

It was a sad story. Inez had been in a private sanitarium in Santa Monica for almost three years. The doctors had lost hope of her ever regaining her sanity.

"I saw her last month. You wouldn't recognize her, Devon. She thinks she's the long-lost daughter of Zelda Fitzgerald. She watches King on television and talks to him. When I saw her she said she asked King for a divorce and he never even answered her. She said he just went right on talking to somebody else on the soap like she wasn't even there. She lives in a world of dolls and illusions. Hollis and May take very good care of her. She lacks nothing, wants nothing, remembers nothing. Seems perfectly rational, yet the attendants won't even leave her alone with a fork in her room. She's tried to commit suicide so many times the scars look like bracelets."

"Gilda would die all over again if she knew."

"Devon, that's why we called. We've uncovered some new facts that could open up a whole new line of questioning about Gilda's death."

The warmth corroded. All the way from Connecticut, he could hear Devon's syrupy voice turn lemony cold. "Facts?"

He told her about the newspaper clipping, and discovery. After a long silence, she spoke. "Billy, give it a rest. Lionel Biggs sealed the files. Gilda rests in peace. Let the rest of us do the same."

"Will you tell King?"

"I'll tell him. But I don't think he cares."

She phoned King at NBC, but he'd left for the day. He was somewhere having a drink before dinner with his son. The sun was melting into the foothills above the split-rail fences across the dusty road. Devon returned to her tomato plants, humming. From the radio in the kitchen window she heard the Beatles singing "With a Little Help from My Friends." Even the Beatles were golden oldies now. She laughed aloud, leaned her head against the garden fence near the yellow tea roses, and ate a salted tomato. The only camera around to record the moment was the clocklike face of the early rising end-of-summer moon, and it was smiling, too.

"Listen, baby, Hollis is in New York, the cook is off, and you are looking at a broad who was twenty years old before she found out hard-boiled eggs didn't get laid by hard-boiled chickens. I'd offer you a late lunch, but I wouldn't know what to do with a tuna salad if it didn't get sent over by Nate and Al's. I'm too worked up to eat. I'm going to have a banana yogurt and get back to work."

Billy's brain was turning cartwheels. He kept rubbing the newspaper clipping between his thumb and forefinger until the face of Edna Denby, or Viola Scribner, was almost obliterated.

May watched glumly, sipping herbal tea, while he nervously put a call through to the hospital in Santa Barbara. The day nurse transferred him to a resident doctor who told him the patient had been released in a neck brace three days ago. She left no forwarding address. Santa Barbara Information had no listing for anyone with the name Viola Scribner.

"Calm down, Billy, you'll get a hernia," said May. "That clipping's probably a week old."

He called Barney Ufland. "That clipping has opened up a can of worms. See if you can find out what happened to that old lady. She couldn't have disappeared into thin air." Ufland promised to call him back Tuesday. "No, tonight, damn it. This is a murder case we're talking about, not a Disney picture."

"Now listen, Brenda Starr, there isn't gonna be a sequel." May had just about reached the limit of her patience. The perimeters were already frayed. "There is no murder case. I'm just as shocked as you to learn this old trout's still alive. But I don't give a ratfuck, do you hear me? I never told you this, Billy, but I was there that night, too. Nobody saw me. I didn't even get past the gate. The first thing I saw was Inez, reeling like a crazy down the street outside The Pearls on foot. Her car was smashed up. I circled around, trying to decide what to do. Then I saw Devon wheeling out with a baby in her car. I didn't even know she *had* a baby! Then King shows up and I got out of there like a bat out of hell. I guess the cops showed up a minute later. Who knew Gilda was already dead when we all got there?"

Billy followed May to the living room. They sat by the big stone fireplace while she continued. "Then I heard the story about the snake. A goddamn fucking snake, for chrissake. If you wrote it all out in a script, I swear to God not even I could sell it.

"So now, on Christmas Eve, she goes to dinner with you and somebody calls her at Chasen's and she leaves in a nervous sweat. Who called? Nobody knows. Then she goes home and dies of a fucking cobra bite. Who let it out of the cage? Mrs. Denby wasn't home. Was it Quinn? Devon doesn't know. I went over the whole thing with Lionel Biggs five years ago and he didn't know, either. The suspects were eliminated for lack of evidence. Mrs. Denby disappeared, but she was never a suspect in the first place. The body was cremated before the coroner ever got around to telling Biggs about the snake. It was Christmas, for chrissake; all you got in this whole fucking town that day was answering machines. He didn't find out about the snake until the day of the funeral. They almost fired the coroner for that one. It was a royal fuckup all the way around.

"Now you want to drag it all out again, only let me tell you something once and for all. Nobody cares. Lionel Biggs may still care. I haven't talked to him in five years. But nobody else does. They don't even know who Gilda Greenway was in this town."

She poured Billy a diet Pepsi from the bar. "We've had other scandals since then. Natalie Wood was washed up in Catalina and they still don't know what happened to her. Grace Kelly choked to death on a highway in France and they never revealed the facts about that case, either. Then we had poor John Belushi freaking out on drugs like something that just crawled out of a roach motel. Bill Holden put his head through a wall. Cancer, heart attacks, or something else natural but just as horrifying took Ingrid Bergman, Henry Fonda, Gloria Swanson. To the people who go to fucking Matt Dillon movies, Gilda Greenway is just a question in Trivial Pursuit."

Billy felt like a dead skunk was rotting in his gut. He couldn't believe what he was hearing. May Fischoff, a woman Gilda had raised like her own since the days before Pampers, soiling her memory like this.

"Didn't you love her? Didn't you care?"

"Listen. I loved her. With all my heart. We all did. But Gilda left us with her own personal effects. She gave us all the truth. She taught us it's okay to change. She gave us her own personal vision of courage. And she gave at least three of us the balls to find our own peace. Where are the Four Fans now? One's in the cracker factory, two are hiding out in the heartland auditioning for Norman Rockwell and waiting for the return of the *Saturday Evening Post*. And the fourth? Look inside me, Billy—inside the skinny chick in the lacquered hair and the Bob Mackie gowns with Hollywood at her feet—and you'll still find a fat little Jewish girl trying to get out. But Gilda left us with the courage to be ourselves, to find our own peace, and not be ashamed of how we found it. The industry may laugh at King and Devon and their cellar full of apple butter, but they're living through the first and only happy years they've ever known. Listen, nobody can be that corny and not be sincere. People call me a hard cunt, laugh about my business partnership with a live-in partner young enough to be my own son, and they won't show up at my funeral until they find out who else is going to be there. But what they don't know is that for the first time in my own life I feel safe, secure, fulfilled with Hollis. Sure, I'm scared shitless that one of these days he'll find someone his own age and head for Fort Lauderdale. But it hasn't happened yet, and even if it does, I know it's better to have had it all than never to have been there.

"You know what Gilda left under the tree the Christmas she died? She couldn't draw the side of a barn with a magic marker, but she needlepointed me a pillow. It's crooked, the stitches don't match, and the colors look like the wallpaper in a Tijuana whorehouse, but it's the treasure of my life. Biggs gave it to me after they closed the investigation. It's a pillow with the letters FTA on it. There was a note inside: 'To May from Mama—fuck them all!' I will take it to my grave. It's the talisman I live by. That's the way I made my my peace. Same way she made hers."

May walked Billy to his car, leaned in the window while he found his keys, and pinched him on the ear. "Remember, Billy. She clawed her way to the top of a business where every day is like swallowing razor blades, but when she bled nobody saw her because she did all her bleeding inside. And when it was over, she knew it. Fate robbed her of her exit line, but it would probably have gone something like this: 'Do it your own way, but do it. When it's all over you'll know you at least made one person happy.'

"She was one helluva pearl, Billy, in a business full of Woolworth rhinestones. Don't take that final dignity away from her now. We all found our own peace in her image. What happened five years ago on Christmas Eve we'll never know. Leave us alone now. Everything must change. Nobody cares."

Billy Buck cared. It mustn't end like this. He had to tell the story. Let the hacks write their own *Mommie Dearest.* Billy would write the truth. "There are no more stories in this naked city," May had said. But she was wrong. Rita Hayworth had Alzheimer's, Lana Turner found God, Elizabeth Taylor found the Betty Ford clinic. Gilda's story was even better, even if it had no ending. What would he title it? He thought of *A Cobra with Class,* but he knew the critics would call that tasteless. Gilda herself would probably throw back her head and roar, "Where is Maria Montez now that we need her?" The perfect title, of course, was *The Snake Has All the Lines,* but Jean Kerr had beat him to it.

Finally it came to him, behind the wheel of his XKE, on the Pacific Coast Highway, driving home from May's. The book would be called *Personal Effects.* He already had most of the notes. He thought of it as performing a service, doing his part to keep the glamor of Hollywood alive. He would never win a Pulitzer, but he was making a contribution.

There was only one piece of the puzzle still missing. He had to find Vy—or Mrs. Denby. When he checked the answering machine, there were the usual messages from his friends, would-be friends, studio PR people, and sources. There was also a message from Barney Ufland. "No trace of the party requested on this end. The house at 33 Pine Road was sold two days ago to a couple named Peterson through a realtor named Carstairs. The deal was made, sealed, and closed within twenty-four hours and the agent's fee paid with a cashier's check. He says the old lady left with no forwarding address."

Billy turned to the *B*'s in his personal Rolodex and dialed Lionel Biggs. A woman's voice on the other end sounded sleepy and cautious. "This is Billy Buck and I must speak to Mr. Biggs. Is he in?"

There was air on the line. Then the woman said, slowly, "Is this some kind of a joke, Mr. Buck?"

"I apologize for the inconvenient hour, but I have some information about the Gilda Greenway case that I know will interest him."

"Gilda Green—— What are you talking about? Mr. Buck, my husband died three years ago. He was mowing the grass when his heart gave out. No warning, nothing. Twenty-five years on the force and all they gave me was the equivalent of Social Security. My husband was so tired and overworked, Mr. Buck, I doubt if he even remembered Gilda Greenway himself at that point. I doubt if anybody does."

THIRTY

DECEMBER 24, 1984

O n the fifth anniversary of Gilda's death, three people showed up at Forest Lawn—a visiting doorknob manufacturer from Altoona, Pennsylvania, his wife, and their seven-year-old daughter, who kept whining, "I want to go to Disneyland." On the same day, Billy Buck ran a special Christmas Eve column. Instead of his annual fantasy Christmas wishes for Hollywood stars, he devoted the entire column to the memory of a Hollywood legend and her Four Fans. He wrote about King and Devon, about the unhappy fate of Inez, and the survival power of May, who was carrying on in the film industry as Gilda would have wanted. And then he wrapped it up.

> In a business where everyone has the attention span of green-head flies, Gilda Greenway is the one they'll remember with awe. The business today is run by baby moguls who were only yesterday parking cars at Chasen's or working in May Fischoff's mail room.

Gilda would have been an old swan in their new Hollywood duck pond, but boy do they need her style and quality now. She died in 1979, a still-young 57, in a business that didn't even remember who Greta Garbo was.

But in *Cobras,* her last film, she proved again what the charisma of a real star was all about. If only Gilda herself could have seen what the camera saw. But she didn't. She was driven by a gnawing, sickening inner fear of insecurity no detective could unravel. Clever writers who profiled her for pretentious magazines described her as "haunted by demons, private and permanently housed—squatters who moved into her soul and grew roots." But none of them knew the secret.

The secret was her terror that someone might discover that she really wasn't very good. She had no training, no tools, no acting technique. She never answered her fan mail. She avoided talk shows, hated seminars, turned down all offers to appear in person at cinematheques, film festivals, and retrospectives of her films at UCLA or the Museum of Modern Art. She really didn't think much of herself and she was afraid her low opinion might rub off, like germs.

She was right, of course—and wrong. She knew nothing about acting. She didn't know art from arthritis. But on the set, she knew where the key light was and how to stay in it. She had that magic quality, rare as a blue giraffe, only the camera can define. Gable had it, Garbo and Garland, Cooper and Crawford, Tracy and Hepburn. And Marilyn, too. It's an intangible quality nobody can decribe but millions of moviegoers will always feel— the star quality that separates the legends from the losers.

Gilda's gone, but her legacy lives on, through the miracle of film. Years from now, I'll forget today's films about hopped-up horny teenagers, violent aggression, and diabolical slashers in Santa Claus suits. But I'll never forget the films of Gilda Greenway.

Everyone who wasn't in Palm Springs for Christmas phoned in their praise. But the call Billy wanted most didn't come until late that evening.

KTLA in Los Angeles played *The Bridge* at 11:00 P.M. Billy counted twenty-three commercial interruptions, and the big rape scene that won Gilda her first Oscar nomination in 1947 was missing completely. Depressed and disgusted, he drained one last swig of brandy and reached for the lamp switch to turn out the light when the phone startled him. From deep within, galvanized by instinct, he knew it was the call he had been waiting for.

Billy paused for a moment before he stepped into the small, institutionally furnished room on the second floor of the Rose of Sharon Nursing Home in Half Moon Bay. The name on the door read "Mrs. Viola Scribner." A nurse hovered over an elderly woman lying in a narrow, single bed. She held the woman's wrist in her hand and was counting seconds on her watch. Billy waited until the nurse had removed the thermometer from her patient's mouth.

"Mrs. Denby?" Billy said.

The old woman gripped the thin green blanket with her gnarled hands as she raised her head to peer at him.

"Mr. Buck, I was wondering when you'd show up," she said finally.

"Bella will leave us alone." She motioned with a shaking finger to the nurse. "You're a witch, aren't you, Bella?"

The nurse, her face as wrinkled and liver-spotted as a bloodhound's, winked at Billy as she left the room, making circles with her index finger at her temple. *"Meshugenah,"* Bella said. "Says she's Gilda Greenway's sister."

"Thank you for the flowers," Mrs. Denby said after the nurse had closed the door. "If you'd taken any more time getting here, you could've brought them to my grave."

"You look as though you'll be with us for a while," he said, permitting himself a smile. He couldn't bring himself to lie and tell her she looked well. Her face was thin and waxy, like a horse's skull, the skin so taut that he noticed for the first time the dominant severity of her cheekbones. "I came as soon as I could get away, Mrs. Denby. Your phone call was quite a surprise. How are you?"

"Five years. If I hadn't read your column, I'd hardly believe it myself. They carry it up here, in the *Chronicle*. It was a touching tribute, Mr. Buck. My sister always liked you."

"Your sister, Mrs. Denby?" Billy asked mildly.

"I told you Gilda was my sister. Didn't I tell you that when I phoned?"

"Well, yes—"

"But you don't believe me, do you?" Mrs. Denby cackled suddenly. "Neither does Bella. That's the funniest part, you see. If I waltzed into the sheriff's office right now and said, 'I'm Gilda Greenway's sister and I know who murdered her,' what do you suppose they'd do? Laugh, I expect. It's because no one cares about her anymore, except you and me, Mr. Buck. We have that in common."

The old lady groaned as she struggled to sit up.

"You're right, Mrs. Denby. We have that in common. I do still care about Gilda. I think of her often."

"So do I, Mr. Buck, as I have every hour of my life since the day she was born. I reared her, you see. I was more a mother to her than a sister. Fifteen years between me and Gilda, and five brothers in between. Me, being the eldest, it was my job to help Mama the most."

Gilda's big sister. Billy remembered brief moments of conversation. *My big sister, Vy.*

Viola.

How had she concealed it so long?

"And nobody fussed over her more than me," Mrs. Denby continued. "Oh, I loved that child, strong-willed and trouble as she was from the first. If not for me, she'd have had nothing, never even have left Hilltop, Okalhoma, Mr. Buck." She studied him. "I see what you're thinking. Crazy old lady putting on airs."

"I'm sure you loved her, Mrs. Denby."

"You cannot imagine how much. You'd have to have seen her and also seen the way we lived back then. Everything was gray where we lived, Mr. Buck." She closed her eyes as if the past was a picture painted on the inside of her eyelids.

"Our old weathered house out in the middle of nowhere, the dirt road leading up to it, even the laundry on the clothesline was yellow-gray. We lived in a world of gray and yellow dust. And then *she* came along."

Mrs. Denby's voice grew stronger. "A blazing flower in the desert, as different from my brothers and me as day from night. Her temper was fiery as the color of her hair. Her smile was sassy. She'd look at you with that grin, with those cat's eyes of hers, and you lost the heart to scold her."

She opened her eyes, and sighed. "I knew she was special from the very beginning. And I told her so. Oh, before she could even understand a word I was saying, I'd rock her in my arms and tell her where we'd go when she grew up and about the beautiful clothes she'd have and handsome beaux and furs and cars.

"The Lord had another plan for her, but I interfered with it. Knowing, one day, I'd pay for my sin of pride, I saved her life. I'm not sorry for it. If I hadn't, she'd have died too young and I'd never have gotten free of that awful gray place."

Billy knew that Vy had traveled with Gilda from Tulsa to New York City in 1938. He'd heard that she instantly loathed the big city. Gilda said Vy called it "Sodom and Gomorrah with runty men and buildings big as donkey dicks. You can't look up and you can't look down—'cause there's crap in the air and crap on the ground."

She'd come to New York as Gilda's chaperone, after which, Billy had always assumed, she'd returned to her Oklahoma husband and lived happily, or unhappily, ever after.

"When did you save her life, Mrs. Denby?" Billy asked.

"She was four and I must have been nineteen. Orval was courting me. We were out on the front porch. I never much cared for all that pawing and smooching, but he was my steady beau and he was always telling me what everybody was up to and what was only natural we should be doing. So there he was, trying to kiss me again, when I pushed him away and sprung up to my feet. I said, 'Where's the baby? Where's Gilda Rae?' Mr. Buck, I'm telling you, I knew that girl was in trouble. So I looked down by the side of the house and there she was, crawling around in the dirt. And just as I'm coming over to her, don't I see a rattler coiled up under the sideboard of Orval's truck, shaking his butt and hissing just about right in her face. Well, I fell down onto my knees right there in the dust and started praying with all my might. I said, 'Sweet Jesus, this child is special to me. I'll do anything, if you save her. I'll dedicate her life to you. And mine to her. I'll watch over her always and see she lives a righteous life.' A righteous life, I promised Him. Well, you know what her life was like."

"The snake," Billy prompted. "What happened?"

"The Lord answered me." Mrs. Denby turned her face toward the window, which looked out at the curve of Half Moon Bay. "He told me, 'No, this child is a demon, as drawn to the serpent as Eve herself.' That was when I made my fateful decision."

She turned back to Billy. "I snatched Gilda up quick as could be and it was me the serpent struck instead, his forked tongue in my ankle. I screamed for Daddy and Orval, and they cut open my foot and Daddy sucked out the venom and they dragged me over to the doctor.

"I always knew Gilda would be someone special. I used to take her with me to the picture show. I was seeing a boy who worked there weekends. Gilda Rae was so little she could sit in my lap. Later on, when she got bigger, we'd sneak in the alley door because we didn't have the nickel for the tickets.

"It was my husband, Orval, took the pictures of her that Larry Malnish saw. I talked Mr. Flynn, whose shop it was, into putting the portrait of Gilda in his window. And when Larry wanted to take Gilda with him to New York City, the only way she'd go was if I went with her. Orval said, 'I need you here, Vy. Who's going to cook my supper and wash my clothes?' I said, 'Orval, you're my husband, but Gilda is my blood.' I went with her and never saw that man again. If he is alive, he is still my husband because divorce is a sin, but I never cared much for him, and if the truth be known, Mr. Buck, I don't think I missed him or Hilltop, Oklahoma, a day in my life."

"But what happened?" Billy said. "I thought you'd gone back to Oklahoma years ago. You went to New York to be Gilda's chaperone. How did you become her housekeeper?"

"Well, you know how it was in those days. Seems silly now, when nothing can shock you about any of these movie stars, the things they do and say. But then it was different. Everything mattered—what your name was, where you came from, what you wore and ate and who you went dancing with. I was just a country gal. I never even finished school. Larry Malnish was teaching Gilda how to talk and walk and wear gloves and shoes, though he never succeeded there," Mrs. Denby laughed.

"I stayed at the hotel while Larry took Gilda to the nightclubs and shows. I ironed her clothes and did her hair and it was fine with me. I was still her sister then. But when that big Ted Kearny came along,

everything changed. I loathed that Kearny man. I warned Gilda, but
she fell in love with him at first sight and wouldn't hear a word against
him. That was when Larry Malnish asked me to pretend I was Gilda's
'companion' instead of her sister. Kearny didn't mind sleeping with a
child of seventeen, of course. But Larry said it wouldn't do for Gilda
to have a big old Okie who talked with a twang for a sister. I said to
her, 'Is this what you want? To become the concubine of this man?
To renounce your family and your religion?' And she started to cry, you
know. Oh, she could wrap me round her little finger. Always. 'Please,
please, Vy,' she begged. 'I can't live without him. Don't make me
choose between you. Stay with me. Do what Larry wants for now.' So
I did, for a little while. But after what happened, her murdering the
child, you know—"

Mrs. Denby paused and squinted at Billy.

"Yes, I know. Gilda had an abortion."

"Then I thought, this is what God meant that day he sent the
serpent into the yard. He knew this devil's spawn would kill the child
in her womb one day. After the abortion, it grew bad between us.
Finally, after we had moved out West, Gilda asked me to go. Only for
a while, she said. She gave me a little house up in Santa Barbara. Kearny
owned it, I think."

"Is that where you've been living these past five years?"

"Yes. I just now sold it after this accident. I was getting too old
to keep it up myself anyway. And some people had been pestering me
for a year now about buying it. That house was all my sister ever did
for me. At least she didn't give that to Devon Barnes and her bastard
child."

"Mrs. Denby, Devon wasn't Gilda's heir. Most of her estate went
to various animal protection funds."

"I know that, Mr. Buck. But those pearls she gave Devon Barnes
—those pearls were mine." The old woman's pale face suddenly blazed
red with anger.

"You came back to her after Kearny married?" Billy said.

"I did. Oh, she needed me then. Larry Malnish begged me to
come back. He was the only one who knew the truth about Gilda and
me, and he took the secret with him to hell. I loved being with Gilda
at The Pearls. Just the two of us again, sharing secrets and dreams as

we used to. I was so happy for her when she fell in love with dear Patrick."

"It didn't bother you that he was a married man?"

"Oh, no," Mrs. Denby said. "He was a Catholic, you see. It wasn't his fault. I understood him. I admired him. And then, of course, he was a movie star. A true movie star, Mr. Buck, not the mumbling, slouching, scratching kind we're treated to nowadays."

"King Godwin?" Billy guessed aloud.

"Yes." Mrs. Denby squared her shoulders, but they were no longer formidable. "Godwin and his kind. Actors. The world is full of actors, Mr. Buck. Most of them poor, and only a few as lucky and rich as Mr. Godwin. But movie stars—it takes more than money and fame to be a true star."

"How do you feel about May Fischoff?" Billy asked on a hunch.

"I thought she was a slovenly whore. Gilda never understood Frank Fischoff's attitude toward his daughter, but I understood it perfectly. She was an embarrassment. He sent her away, hoping she'd change, but I think it was associating with the others that ruined her. That school they sent her to—Gilda thought it was one of the best in the country. Well, you see the trash she met at that fine academy. Inez Godwin! Oh, and let's not forget Miss Barnes."

Billy said, "You never cared much for the Four Fans, did you?"

"I loathed those sniveling brats. I was looking after her just as I had in the old days. Suddenly Gilda wanted children. Wasn't I family enough? She went to New York to visit Patrick and found her little ready-made family. All so needy and greedy. And just when we'd made a perfect life for ourselves. We were so happy, Gilda, Patrick, and me.

"I told her they'd leave her. I was right about Ted Kearny, but she'd forgotten that, of course. And, of course, they did leave her. When Patrick died, God rest his soul, there was only me, really. Do you remember those days, Mr. Buck? Oh, I do. I was there. I never ran away."

"I never realized you felt that way about the Four Fans," Billy said, thinking Clint Eastwood couldn't have delivered the line with tighter understatement.

"They robbed me of the only person I had in the world. All of them—rich, with friends and lovers and fans of their own. She'd nourished them for years. But it was me that nourished *her.* Then every time one of those ingrates needed her, I got pushed aside. We were all right after a while. Gilda had enough of films. We might have gone off somewhere and rested a spell. But Inez and May talked her into going back to work. Then, home came the prodigals, King and Devon. I liked Mr. Calder. I asked him about his film, whatever made him call it *Cobras.* He said it had a number of meanings. It was about the venomous nature of Hollywood relationships and also about the snake as seducer, the snake in the garden of Eden. And then, it came clear to me, Mr. Buck. Do you see?"

"I'm not quite sure I do, Mrs. Denby."

"I sent her that cobra, Mr. Buck, two years before she died. I wanted to remind her of our blood ties. I wanted to remind her that I'd saved her life once. That I'd challenged God Himself to spare her. I sent her the snake. She was so wrapped up in her movie and her precious children again, she never even connected it with me.

"For a time she hated them. The movie was no good. They all ran out on her again and she hated them for it. At last I was happy. Then, Mr. Buck, she sent me away. It was Christmas week. I said, 'This is family time, Gilda. This is no time for me to hide up in Santa Barbara all alone. And what will you do?' You see, I cared, Mr. Buck. I begged her to tell me what was wrong. She said only that she wanted to be alone. So I left. And when I returned to look in on her, Devon Barnes and her bastard child had taken my place. It was them Gilda wanted to share her Christmas with! And when she gave away my pearls— That necklace, you see, that was to be mine. Patrick's necklace. My own beloved Patrick, who wanted me to have those glorious pearls. Well, I took it as a sign from God, Mr. Buck—the sign I'd waited for all those years. I knew one day God would make me pay for my stupidity and pride in keeping alive the one He'd marked for death. I knew He would make me kill my sister."

Billy could picture the scene as the old woman talked. It had everything but the camera angles.

Christmas Eve.

And Gilda had sent her away.

"Get out of my home and don't come back until you hear from me," Gilda had told her. But it was her home, too.

She'd done as Gilda had ordered, and she'd left The Pearls.

Then she had decided it was time to do the Lord's work.

She had let herself into the house through the service entrance. She knew every inch of every room so well that she didn't even have to turn on the lights. She soundlessly made her way into the living room, bitterly noting the pile of gaily wrapped gifts under the Christmas tree. Not one was for her.

And the note on the mantle over the fireplace:

Devon, my love—Changed my mind about Inez's party. Sweet Billy is taking me to Chasen's for dinner. Come join us if you're in the mood—and bring my precious baby.

Mama

Mrs. Denby crumpled the note and shoved it deep into the pocket of her dress. Then she shuffled into the library—Patrick's library— where the large, morocco-bound scrapbooks lined the bottom three shelves of the bookcases with the other relics of Gilda's past. She had appointed herself the keeper of the photographs and clippings, arranging everything chronologically, from the first train trip she and Gilda had taken to New York City, straight through to the souvenir program for the premiere of *Cobras*.

She removed the volume labeled 1955–1960 in gold leaf on the spine. She turned the page to the *Variety* announcement of Avery Calder's play, starring Patrick Wainwright. And there, opposite the *Playbill* and the matches from Sardi's, was the wretched photograph in its paper souvenir frame from "21." There they were, grinning sheepishly at her—always smiles to her face, laughter and disrespect behind her back. The Four Fans were a new breed of catfish—hungry and graceless. When Mrs. Denby looked into their wickedly smiling faces, she saw vampires.

She had been close to fifty when they had pushed their way into Gilda's life. Could they guess the price she'd paid for the star's success? Could they understand that, selflessly, she had led a life of anonymity in the shadow of her sister? No, to them she was merely a sinister yet comical servant, an interfering busybody lurking in the shadows who tried to shield Gilda from their selfish demands.

How could they understand the grand dreams of her own she'd handed down to Gilda, along with her outgrown homemade feed-sack dresses? Back in Hilltop, long ago, Hollywood had seemed to her an oasis of palm trees and blue waters in a world of parched earth and poverty. The movies were where she discovered a life beyond despair, where everything sparkled—cars, marble staircases, men's shoes, women's eyes; a world without a speck of dust, brimming with clever people and laughter and happiness and love. A place where life was lived in Technicolor and all hopes were possible. These children had robbed her of the pleasure of sharing the dream with Gilda. They had turned everything to ugliness.

Here, in Patrick's library, alone on Christmas Eve, she gazed at the photograph of her tormentors, and at the wicked child she'd saved against God's will from death. Viola tore the picture out of the scrapbook, and returned the book to the shelf.

She hurried through the dark to the outdoor menagerie where the cobra slept in its cage. She put on her feeding gloves, carefully removed the creature, and slipped it into the gift box. The serpent coiled itself comfortably into the nest of straw. Mrs. Denby closed the box. Then, as an afterthought, she gently laid a bit of tissue paper over the placid snake and placed the photograph on top of the tissue paper. The snake didn't stir.

All she needed now was to wrap the box in Christmas tinsel and watch as her sister opened it, as Gilda reached in and woke the sleeping serpent. For how many years had he slept and waited? More than fifty years since she'd snatched Gilda Rae from the snake's fangs.

Viola set the box down on the table in the entrance hall. She dialed the number of Chasen's and said it was an emergency, she must speak with Gilda Greenway at once.

"Yes?" Gilda answered. "Devon, is it you? Are you back?"

"It's Vy," Mrs. Denby said.

"Vy? What the hell do you want? Where are you?"

"At The Pearls, Gilda. I just stopped by to give you your Christmas gift. I thought you'd be home by now."

"I told you, you miserable bitch, to get out of my house. Have you gone senile? I don't need you to tuck me in and read *The Night Before Christmas.*"

Ever since the time she broke down during one of Gilda's drunken, vicious tantrums, and Gilda had threatened to send her away forever, Mrs. Denby had trained herself not to react to Gilda's outbursts. But now, suddenly, she began to cry, all her anger and hurt and resentment pouring out in sobs she could not suppress. It no longer mattered. If Gilda wanted her out of the house and out of her life, so be it. But she would have her moment, first.

"Gilda," Mrs. Denby said, her plea more real than sham, "won't you please come home so we can be together this Christmas Eve?"

"My Lord, you're a damn pain in the ass, you know that, don't you? Well, now that you've gone and ruined whatever chance I had of enjoying my Christmas dinner, yes, I'll come on home. But, honey," she said, before slamming down the phone, "this present better be damn good."

Mrs. Denby put the gift-wrapped box under the tree with the other presents and waited. She sat quietly on the oak bench in the front hallway, watching the grandfather clock, her hands folded in her lap, savoring the fullness of this moment. She dozed off for several minutes but was awakened by the sound of Gilda fumbling with her keys.

And then Gilda opened the door and walked into the darkened house.

"I've had it with you, Vy. I've made up my mind. I want you out of here, for good. You've stuck around way too many years."

"Gilda, it's Christmas. Can't this wait until after the holidays?"

She ignored Gilda's hateful words and urged her into the living room. Gilda sat down on the chaise, kicked off her shoes, and wriggled her toes, as if she were a child again, back in the Oklahoma dust.

Mrs. Denby went over to the Christmas tree and gently lifted the wrapped package.

"Merry Christmas, Gilda Rae," she said, handing her sister the box.

"Vy, you know I loathe that name. Why must you torture me?"

She lifted off the top of the box.

"What's this?" she asked, removing the photograph.

"A nest of vipers . . ." Mrs. Denby whispered.

But Gilda wasn't listening. She reached into the box.

"I am no longer your servant, Gilda Rae. From this moment on, I am a servant of the Lord!" cried Vy, her pupils dilating.

The hooded cobra rose from the box and struck.

Its fangs ripped into the soft, satiny flesh just above Gilda's right wrist. She fell back on the chaise and screamed. The photograph was still in her hand.

She screamed again, her horrified, pleading eyes locked with Vy's mad stare.

Then she clutched at her breasts, gasping for breath. Her gray-green eyes twitched violently until the old woman thought they might explode, like shards of kaleidoscopic glass.

Vy stood beside the Christmas tree and waited patiently for the convulsions to end. When her sister's shaking and twitching stopped, she put the feeding gloves on again, picked up the snake, which had curled among the Christmas gifts, and dropped it back into the box, slamming the lid fast before it could rise again.

"Goodbye, Gilda Rae," she said, and left the room as quietly as she had entered, carrying the box under her arm.

A macabre mask of ossified horror, reflected in the blinking tree lights, was all that remained of the fabled beauty that was once Gilda Greenway's.

"You just stood there?" Billy Buck said, transfixed.

"Just like Mrs. Danvers in *Rebecca.*"

"Like who?"

"That's who they used to call me, behind my back."

Billy stared at the old woman. She seemed to have gained strength from her recital. Her gray-green eyes, accentuated by the prominent cheekbones, sparkled as she shared with him the occasion of her ultimate triumph. Color flushed her anemic cheeks.

"But I'm a journalist, not a priest, Mrs. Denby," he said at last. "Why are you telling me all this?"

"It's not a priest I need, Mr. Buck. I was only doing what the Lord wanted. But I read your column. 'Gilda Greenway is the one they'll remember,' you said. Now you must write about me. Let them remember me as well. Because without me, there would never have been any Gilda Greenway."

There was a knock on the door. A nurse's aid poked her head in the room. "Some juice or water for the movie star's sister?" she asked with a grin and a wink.

"If you don't mind, I'd like some water," Billy said. *And a double shot of bourbon on the side, please.*

"They humor me," Mrs. Denby said. "But nobody believes I'm really Gilda's sister."

"Why now? Why are you finally letting out the truth?"

"Because, Mr. Buck, I'm an old woman, and it's time I had my moment of glory. I would have told them, those police who came crawling around. Frankly, I was disappointed that not one of them questioned me properly. I even met that stupid detective, that Biggs, at The Pearls, but he didn't so much as ask me if I had an alibi that night. So I decided it was God's will that the police have mashed potatoes for brains. Not that they could have tracked me down. My little house in Santa Barbara was in my real name. So were all of my official papers. Edna Denby never existed except as the name of a bit character in one of Gilda's earliest films. That was always our little joke. And now yours, as well."

Billy stood up to go.

"Mrs. Denby, was it you who called Detective Biggs after the funeral to tell him that Devon Barnes had been at The Pearls on Christmas Eve?"

Mrs. Denby's face lit up.

"Mr. Buck, you are such a smart man. That's just why I want you to write my story."

She lifted her head and leaned toward him with sudden intensity.

"I want the world to know who I really was, who I am. A far better actress than my sister, Mr. Buck. I played my role for years. But I lived in the shadow. Now I want to die in the light. Tell my story, Mr. Buck. Let them know. Make me famous."

"I have to go, Mrs. Denby."

"But you will tell the truth, won't you? You're a journalist. You have an obligation to tell the truth."

Billy worried that her heart was too frail to withstand the strain of her agitation.

He patted her hands and said soothingly, "I'll do my best, Mrs. Denby." Then he walked out of the room and down the ugly battleship-gray corridor of the nursing home.

A drink, he thought to himself. A stiff drink, and I'll be okay. Then I'll think about the long drive back to L.A. He remembered a time, long ago, when he had first arrived in Hollywood. He'd innocently written a story about Gilda, and mentioned Big Ted Kearny, not realizing the subject was taboo. The studio PR man exploded. His friends thought he was crazy. But he was committed to telling the truth.

He avoided Gilda for a while, afraid she'd tear him apart, or freeze him dead. But then, of course, Hollywood being Hollywood, he ran into her at a party. She took his arm, led him into an empty room, and sat him down next to her on the couch.

She listened to his stammered, awkward apology, then interrupted at last with a patient smile.

"Billy Buck," she said, "I think you'll learn our ways quickly enough. But, baby, let me help you out with an important lesson." She touched her strand of pearls, like the dial on a Ouija board. "Baby," Gilda had said, "why tell the truth when you can create the legend?"

Billy Buck disconnected the phones, closed the cocoa-brown shutters in his wood-paneled study, and poured himself a double shot of Chivas. Then he filled the silver Cole Porter cigarette box he had purchased at Sotheby's with fresh Marlboros and set beside it the white porcelain Tiffany ashtray with the Hirschfeld drawing of Carol Channing signed "Carol loves Billy" in her daffy third-grade scrawl. He adjusted the student lamp, turned on the word processor, and cracked his knuckles. Twice he touched the keyboard, then withdrew, thinking misty, faraway thoughts. Then he started to write:

PERSONAL EFFECTS
PROLOGUE
December 26, 1979

Gilda would have hated it . . .